## Praise for *Earth Afire*

"Thirty-five years after he introduced Ender to
the world, it's great to see that [Card] is still making
magic in this imaginative world."

—*New York Journal of Books*

"Highly intelligent, self-reliant children—
Card's trademark—are as excellent as ever. . . .
What we're witnessing is how and why Ender's
child armies came to be."

—*Kirkus Reviews*

# THE SWARM

## Volume One of
## THE SECOND FORMIC WAR

# Orson Scott Card
## and Aaron Johnston

TOR®

A TOM DOHERTY ASSOCIATES BOOK | NEW YORK

This is a work of fiction. All of the characters, organizations, and events portrayed in this novel are either products of the authors' imaginations or are used fictitiously.

THE SWARM

Copyright © 2016 by Orson Scott Card and Aaron Johnston

All rights reserved.

A Tor Book
Published by Tom Doherty Associates
175 Fifth Avenue
New York, NY 10010

www.tor-forge.com

Tor® is a registered trademark of Macmillan Publishing Group, LLC.

ISBN 978-0-7653-7563-6

Our books may be purchased in bulk for promotional, educational, or business use. Please contact your local bookseller or the Macmillan Corporate and Premium Sales Department at 1-800-221-7945, extension 5442, or by e-mail at MacmillanSpecialMarkets@macmillan.com.

First Edition: August 2016
First Mass Market Edition: February 2018

Printed in the United States of America

0 9 8 7 6 5

*To Lynn Hendee,*
*who has the mind of Ender,*
*the mettle of Mazer,*
*and the heart of Valentine*

I divide officers into four classes—the clever, the lazy, the stupid, and the industrious. The man who is clever and lazy is fit for the very highest commands. He has the temperament and the requisite nerves to deal with all situations. Those who are clever and industrious are fitted for the high staff appointments. Use can be made of those who are stupid and lazy. But whoever is stupid and industrious must be removed immediately.

—General Baron Kurt von Hammerstein-Equord, German Chief of Army Command (1930–33)

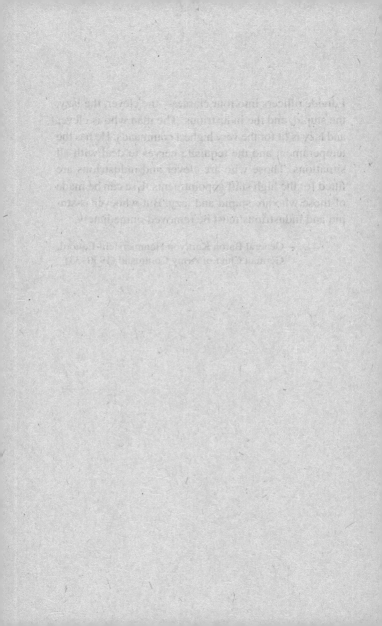

# CONTENTS

# THE SWARM

# CHAPTER 1

## Copernicus

The First Formic War was a close-fought thing. The Formic invaders had the capacity to destroy all life that was based on our particular array of amino acids, which, being indigestible to them, was not worth preserving. The Hive Queen did not view her actions as an attack, but rather as a leisurely beginning to the formification of Earth.

We eked out our victory against an enemy whose commander—whose mind—was millions of kilometers away. Later we would learn that the Hive Queen commanded her workers through philotic connections that seemed not to attenuate or slow down with distance; signals from the human brain take longer to reach our fingers than it took the Hive Queen to receive sensory information from her workers, learn that the pesky native life-form was resisting the advance ship's ministrations, and repurpose those workers as soldiers.

Then the humans blew out the interior of the advance ship and killed every last one of her workers. Not only would she arrive at this new planet without the native biota already having been replaced by compatible life-forms, but she would also be forced to approach it with an effective military strategy. She immediately conferred with her sisters on all the other populated planets, showing them how the humans had behaved, the structure of their bodies, the weapons they had used.

Colonization of new worlds always brought challenges that required improvisation, but now for the first time a Formic colony was encountering friction that was intelligent, organized, and effective. However, if there was one thing the Hive Queens were experts at, it was war.

She had come in search of a place to spawn another iteration of the Formic civilization, a peaceful, domestic mission, or so she supposed. Now, she and her sisters could reach back into their not-so-very-ancient memory of brutal wars between Hive Queens, which had spawned a sophisticated military technology.

With the approval of her sisters, she dismantled almost the entire apparatus of colonization and converted the materials of the vast mothership into the requisite number of invasion craft. She had intended to wield only her delicate, sacred ovipositor, but finding the way blocked, she drew her sword.

—Demosthenes, *A History of the Formic Wars,* Vol. 3

Mazer Rackham drifted away from the space station, sealed inside a capsule no bigger than a coffin, his weapons and gear pressed tight against him. The capsule tumbled end over end, spinning in three dimensions through zero gravity. Mazer's equilibrium was gone in an instant. Up and down no longer had meaning. All he could do now was close his eyes, concentrate, and try to find the pattern in his rotations.

The speed and spin of the capsule changed with every test flight, and so Mazer never knew how fast or in what manner the capsule was going to rotate until the sling mechanism inside the space station's launch bay had tossed him out into the blackness of space.

This spin wasn't bad, he realized. He had done plenty of test flights far worse than this one, with the rotations so fast and uneven that it was all he could do to keep from vomiting. This, by comparison, was a Sunday stroll. A lazy spin, at a negligible speed. Like a discarded piece of space debris casually drifting through the Black—which of course was the intent.

The capsule was a tactical trick. A work of camouflage made to resemble a twisted hunk of ship debris, charred and jagged at the edges as if it had been torn from a ship in a violent explosion. A whole team of artists from the International Fleet had worked on its design for weeks, meticulously painting and bending every square inch of the metal exterior until it looked like space junk. Barely worth anyone's notice except as a possible collision threat. The Formics would see it, dismiss it as harmless, and the marine concealed inside could float right up to the Formic ship and cut his way inside.

A nice idea. But Mazer had his doubts. Doubts he had expressed in every test-flight report. Whether anyone actually read the reports and paid him any attention he couldn't tell.

He cleared his mind and focused on the task at hand: finding the pattern in the capsule's spin.

Mazer let his body go limp, feeling the centripetal forces pulling at him from multiple directions.

The spin was a sequence repeating itself again and again. An object in motion remained in motion. If Mazer could identify that sequence, if he could anticipate how the capsule would spin next, he could prepare himself properly to exit the capsule when he reached his target.

Our brains weren't programmed for this, he thought. A lifetime of living in a gravitational environment has trained us to process trajectories completely differently.

He wondered if he would ever get used to zero G. Even

after years of training in space he still felt like an awkward novice, not because his movements were clumsy but because he was nowhere near as agile out here as he had once been on Earth.

If I had started out here as a child, he thought, or if I had begun training as a tween, this would all be second nature by now.

He envied the free-miner recruits for this very reason. Most of them were born in space on asteroid-mining vessels throughout the Kuiper or Asteroid belts. Zero G was their home. Flight came easily. Spinning, launching, mapping a trajectory. They didn't have to think about it; they just moved.

Of course the bureaucracy at the IF kept free miners from reaching any legitimate position of influence within the Fleet. Those positions were held by experienced soldiers from Earth, the career officers who had clawed their way to the top and weren't about to let blue-collar rock diggers give them any orders. That left free miners with the remedial jobs within the Fleet: mechanics, load operators, shipbuilders, cooks. Critical entities, to be sure. But why not train them for combat? They had more experience with the environment. Teaching them to handle a weapon seemed easier than teaching Earth-grown soldiers to think in zero G.

Or why not pair free miners with soldiers? Mazer had made the suggestion to a dozen different commanders. Have the free miner teach the marine how to fly and have the marine teach the free miner the essentials of combat. Unify the cultures. Share information and expertise. Break down the barriers and integrate the personnel to produce soldiers more capable in every way.

Oh, how Mazer's commanding officers had laughed at that. Silly, silly Mazer. Don't you get it? Don't you understand your place? There are soldiers and there are worker bees, and the uneducated rock diggers will always be the bees.

Free miners saved us, Mazer had countered. If not for their help we would've lost the war.

But he had quickly learned that saying so only invited isolation and dismissal. Do your job, Mazer, they said. Either you're one of us or you're one of them. If you're one of us, you won't keep trying to drag outsiders into IF command.

Nobody seemed to care that Mazer had actually fought the Formic invaders, on Earth and in space. All that mattered was his official record—in which his elite training was pretty much trumped by charges of insubordination. The elite training was from New Zealand, after all—not one of the great powers, so treating him well wouldn't give the bureaucrat any career advantage.

And there was no point in explaining that his "insubordination" consisted of him fighting the Formics in China when every other nation was obeying China's demand that they stay out. That insubordination had led to the nuclear destruction of one of the Formics' earthside bases and then later to the gutting of the Formic mothership. But none of that was in his file.

No, not a mothership, Mazer reminded himself. A scout ship. We thought we were facing an invasion army, but the Formics that landed on Earth were merely the advance party, the terraformers, the workers sent ahead to prepare Earth soil for Formic vegetation. Farmers, basically. And the gases they had sprayed across southeast China that had killed forty million people were not military weapons, but terraforming tools. Weed killer. They were simply clearing the land and running off the rodents so that new occupants could move in.

Mazer had helped put an end to it, but since the operation had been deemed classified, his file made no mention of his involvement. And his commanding officers went by what was in his file.

It didn't help that the International Fleet was hopelessly

broken. Infighting, bureaucracy, dogmatic command, rivalries, conflicting agendas, careerists. In the three years since joining up, Mazer had seen it all.

He had known this would happen. You couldn't combine the militaries of the world into a single army and suddenly expect everyone to play nice. Rivalries would persist. Cultures would clash. Centuries of mistrust between enemies would linger. Plus there was the added challenge of coming to a unified consensus on discipline, structure, hierarchy, process—the most basic models of operation. And since no two militaries were alike, and since everyone dismissed every other nation's military philosophies as misguided, watching the IF try to function as a single organization was like tossing a slab of meat to wolves.

Still, Mazer had remained patient. No, optimistic, believing that the threat to the human race would eventually take precedence over all other considerations. Yet now, stationed at an IF outpost at L4—gravitationally balanced between Earth and Luna—Mazer's hope in the IF was fading.

He didn't let them stop him, however. He had his missions and he would fulfill them. The International Fleet might rot from the inside out, but Mazer would do his duty as best as he knew how.

After several minutes of concentration, he finally found the pattern in the capsule's spin.

Mazer blinked a command to initiate the gyroscope to see if he was right. A holographic model of the capsule appeared on his heads-up display—HUD—inside his helmet. He had been correct. There was the pattern of his spin. A constant through space, giving order to a seemingly random tumble.

He blinked a second command and the holo disappeared, replaced with an image of his target: an old derelict supply ship directly ahead of him. The ship had been pulled from a scrapyard somewhere and painted and modified to resemble a miniaturized version of the Formic scout ship.

A familiar voice sounded over the radio. "Four hundred meters to target."

It was Rimas, one of the three marines in Mazer's breach team. They were each inside their own capsule tumbling through space behind Mazer, heading toward the same derelict ship.

The tactic had worked once in the last war, but the capsules in that instance had approached their target from multiple angles. The IF wouldn't always have that luxury in combat, so the IF had devised these smaller capsules with advanced avionics. Could a team of four marines approach a target from the same direction and carry out a complex, coordinated strike without colliding with one another or raising alarms?

"Three hundred meters," said Rimas. "Get ready, my fellow guinea pigs. Prepare for exit and launch."

Shambhani spoke next. He was the youngest of the bunch. A Pakistani from Karachi. "We're not guinea pigs, Rimas. We're lab rats. Running through mazes. Pushing buttons. Getting shocks. But no prize at the end."

Kaufman, the fourth member of the team and a former commando in GSG9, the special ops unit of the German Federal Police, laughed over the radio. "We can't be lab rats, Shambhani. No rat would be stupid enough to crawl inside these cans."

Mazer smiled. Lab rats. It was a fair comparison. As marines in the International Fleet's Weapons and Materials Research Division—WAMRED—it was Mazer and his team's responsibility to test the latest experimental tech being considered for combat. Everything from biometric-enabled socks to shielded landing crafts. Some of it worked. Some of it didn't. Some of it was so stupid in its design that it was more likely to get a marine killed than save him from the enemy. The stupid designs were easy to dismiss, but tech like the capsules was harder to evaluate. Could they work? Yes. Would they work? Probably not. And it was in this gray area of ambiguity where the bureaucrats and defense contractors did their worst, with everyone fighting to protect their own proposed tech and projects. It meant a lot of bad tech was getting the rubber stamp of approval, and there was little Mazer could do about it.

"Two hundred meters," said Rimas. "Here we go, Captain. The radio is yours."

"All right, gentlemen," said Mazer. "Now that we're all dizzy and discombobulated, let's get to work. Know your rotation. Exit smart. If you miss the target, you'll drift off into oblivion and be no help to any of us. We land, we set the charges, and we clear the area. Rimas you have point."

"Yes, sir."

They had practiced the maneuver dozens of times, but they knew better than to treat this as routine. They would go in as if their lives depended on it because one day that might be the case. Precise movements, complete coordination. Anything less was failure.

A chime sounded in Mazer's earpiece. A proximity warning. "Approaching the drop," he said. "Here we go."

When his capsule got to its nearest approach to the ship's surface, Mazer opened the door, pulled himself out of the cockpit, and fired propulsion from the back of his spacesuit, pushing himself, untethered, toward the target ship.

The maneuver would be impossible if he didn't first understand how the capsule was spinning. And even then it was incredibly difficult to pull off, not only because of the capsule's rotations but also because the capsule was approaching the target not on a direct course, but at a diagonal vector that merely passed by the ship at a safe but short distance. A collision course would alert the Formics' collision-avoidance system; they would fire on the capsule to protect their hull. But a nonthreatening flyby would likely go ignored. The trick was getting close enough to make the leap and yet staying far enough away so as not to draw attention. All without altering the original course of the capsule—for any sudden shift in trajectory might raise Formic alarms.

Mazer tapped his propulsion twice more, then brought up his feet and landed on the hull. The soles of his boots were made of Nan-Ooze, a thick gel composed of thousands of nanobots that attached to every scratch or irregularity on the surface of the ship. Mazer ordered the Nan-Ooze to go rigid, and it solidified inside the scratches, locking his feet in place and anchoring him to the ship.

He drew his slaser—short for self-aiming laser—and advanced toward the breach site, walking as quickly as his goo boots allowed. He scanned right and left along the surface of the ship, keeping an eye out for any computer-generated Formics that might appear on his HUD.

Ahead of him, Rimas landed on the breach site, a large circle on the side of the ship. Rimas then knelt in the center of the circle and anchored the guidebox to the hull. The guidebox emitted four low-powered lasers, pointing north, south, east, and west, indicating where along the edge of the circle Mazer and his team should place the four cubes of the breach weapon.

Gungsu Industries, the Korean contractors who had built the weapon, called it a gravity disruptor—GD. It used four tidal forces to tear an opening in the ship large enough for the marines to crawl through. It did so with four separate cubes placed on the surface of the ship in a square pattern. The four corners of the square created four overlapping triangles that could tear apart any surface. Yet to work, the cubes had to be placed exactly right, meaning far enough apart that the curvature of the hull would put the surface in the straight lines between them. Placed wrong, the cubes could create shrapnel clouds or fail to tear a large enough hole.

Rimas left the guidebox in place and went to one of the four points where a cube should be set. He pulled his cube from his pouch, twisted it to activate it, and set it Nan-Ooze side down. "Rimas here. The baby is delivered."

"Roger that," said Mazer. "We're right behind you."

Mazer and the others reached the circle as Rimas stood up and drew his slaser, covering them.

Mazer moved to his assigned position and removed his own cube from his pouch. He twisted the mechanism to activate it, noting once again that the action felt far too cumbersome with his bulky gloved fingers.

There's too much assembly here, he thought. Too many possibilities for human error. We need to simplify this before we move to live tests. He made a mental note to inform the engineers.

"We've got bugs," said Rimas.

Mazer lifted his head and saw, projected on his HUD, five virtual Formics in spacesuits scuttling on all six appendages across the surface of the ship toward them, each of them armed with a glowing jar weapon and moving fast. The augmented reality simulation melded so well with the real environment that Mazer instinctively reached for his weapon. Then he calmed and focused his attention back on his cube, leaving the Formics to Rimas, his point man.

Rimas took out four Formics with four quick shots, and the creatures exploded into pixels before disappearing from everyone's HUD.

"Cube Two is set," said Kaufman. Then he was up on one knee, aiming his slaser and picking off Formics with deadly accuracy. For every two Formics vaporized, four more appeared in their place, closing in from multiple sides and firing their jar guns as they came.

Shambhani swore.

Mazer turned and saw that an image of a doily was now projected onto Shambhani's chest along with the words KILLED IN ACTION. "You're hit, Sham," said Mazer. "You're out."

Doilies were small, flat, bioluminescent organisms fired from the Formic jar guns. In any other circumstance they would be beautiful to look upon. Weblike in structure, they resembled a magnified snowflake, with its many symmetrical crystals and stellar dendrites—or an intricately crocheted doily lying atop an antique piece of furniture. Here, however, encircled about in a clear gel as thick and sticky as tar, doilies were weapons of death. The gel acted as an adhesive when the doily struck its target. Then, upon impact, the doily released a peroxide polymer that reacted violently with the adhesive gel. The polymer was a natural injury response, chemicals released to cope with internal bruising. Formics had obviously engineered the doilies to overexpress the polymer, in much the same way that bacteria are tricked into overexpressing proteins. The result was a contained and highly directional explosion, tearing apart the human's spacesuit and all the bone, skin, muscle, and organs inside it. Mazer had seen it happen, and they were memories best forgotten.

"I can finish it," said Sham. "I'm almost done." He was still trying to open and set his cube.

"You're dead," said Mazer. "Stop. Nothing you do from now on will count in our results. Leave it for me."

Mazer locked down his own cube. "Cube Three is set." Then he launched himself at Sham, whose boot tips and knees were still anchored to the hull. Mazer collided with him, grabbing Sham around the upper body to keep himself from ricocheting off into space. Then Mazer swung his legs down, took Sham's cube, gave it a final twist to activate it, and anchored it to the hull.

"Cube Four is set," Mazer said. "Clear the square." He moved a safe distance away from the square and said, "Launch!"

He winked a command, and the Nan-Ooze sole of his boots released their grip on the surface save for a small square of Nan-Ooze in the center of his foot. Mazer leaped upward away from the ship, with the Nan-Ooze forming into a long thin polymer line, growing thinner and thinner as it extended, tethering him to the small square of Nan-Ooze still rooted to the ship.

Mazer was firing the whole time. He took out three virtual Formics. Then a fourth. Rimas and Kaufman fired also, soaring up beside him. Then Kaufman was hit, and his Nan-Ooze ceased extending.

Mazer soared another ten meters. Then his skinnywire snapped taut, stopping his ascent thirty meters above the ship.

"Fire," he said.

Had the gravity disruptor been live, and not merely practice cubes, the cubes would have unleashed their tidal forces and ripped a hole in the hull, throwing the torn debris inward.

Mazer and Rimas took out the last few virtual Formics, and then all was still.

Mazer shut down his slaser and said, "Reel in." The Nan-Ooze pulled him downward, the polymer nanotech line getting thicker and thicker until it formed back into the sole of his boot when he reached the surface.

At that point, the exercise was over.

Mazer got on the radio with the space station and called for an extraction. Then he turned to see that his teammates were all deep in thought, heads down, mentally retracing their steps. He had trained them to do this, to dedicate the time immediately following an operation to silently consider what they had just done. Where were they weak? What had they failed to consider? How could they improve?

They remained in silence for the duration of the flight back to WAMRED. It wasn't until they had changed out of their gear and gathered in the debriefing room, feet anchored to the floor, that Mazer spoke again. He started his recording device to ensure that he captured everything they discussed.

"Mission succeeded but we lost two men," he said. "Fifty percent wastage. Not acceptable. Thoughts?"

Rimas spoke first. "We had a whole Formic army coming at us from every side. We weren't ready for that."

"There were a lot," Mazer agreed. "But that might be exactly the battle conditions marines face."

"It wasn't just the numbers," said Rimas. "They were all staying really close to the hull this time. Combat-crawling. That made it hard to get a bead on them without standing up and further exposing myself. If I had had better cover from a standing position, I could've inflicted a lot more damage instead of worrying about getting shot."

"There is no cover," said Shambhani. "There's nothing on the surface of the ship we could have used."

"What if marines were to bring cover with them?" said Rimas.

"How?" Kaufman asked. "In the capsules? There's no room for anything else. And if you make the cockpit any bigger to accommodate more cargo, you risk drawing unwanted attention to the thing. It starts looking less like debris and more like a ship."

"What about shields?" asked Sham. "Like riot police carry. We could use them as covers for the cockpits. That way, the shield wouldn't take up any more room inside the capsule."

"No riot shield is going to stop a doily," said Kaufman.

"Not a traditional riot shield," Sham said. "It wouldn't be made of fiberglass. You'd need something sturdier. Steel maybe."

Kaufman shook his head. "Wouldn't work. Your feet are locked to the surface by Nan-Ooze. The force of the blast would slam you back against the hull of the ship. Your legs would break. Think ugly, compound fractures."

"That's easy to fix," said Rimas. "We program the Nan-Ooze to release all but one heel or all but one toe of the boot."

"Fair enough," said Kaufman, "but you're still going to get your ass slammed against the ship like a rag doll. You might not break your legs, but you're bound to break something. And anyway there are other problems. Steel would add a lot of mass. It would be hard to maneuver. Plus it would occupy one of your hands. Now you're one-handed."

"Beats getting a doily to the chest," said Sham.

"What if the front of the shield were covered in a layer of Nan-Ooze?" Mazer said. "It could surround and smother the doily on impact, before it exploded."

"I've never seen Nan-Ooze move that fast," said Rimas. "The doily would detonate before the Nan-Ooze surrounded it."

"Maybe the Nan-Ooze doesn't have to move at all," said Mazer. "It's nanotech in a weightless environment. We can make it as thick as necessary, say, fifteen centimeters to give the projectile a deep enough surface to embed itself. And we control the consistency of the Nan-Ooze as well, soft enough so that the doily punches into it and yet not so soft that the Nan-Ooze splatters."

"Like lard," said Rimas.

"The doily gets completely submerged before it detonates," said Mazer. "It would dampen the explosion, take the brunt of the blast. It might even be enough to keep you on your feet."

"And even if the Nan-Ooze disperses violently," said Sham, "it can self-propel and return to the shield."

"I still can't shake the problem that now I'm one-handed," said Kaufman. "I've got this unwieldy thing strapped to me, impeding my movements."

Mazer shrugged. "So maybe the Nan-Ooze doesn't cover a shield. Or maybe it's not even Nan-Ooze. But the idea of nanotech remains. So we get a semipermeable cloud of nanobots that loosely form a shield. Marines can see through it like thin haze. But as a doily approaches, the haze forms into a shield to enfold the doily and encase it, to make it nothing but a harmless thud against their bodies."

"So the shield's not strapped to me?" Kaufman asked.

"No," said Mazer. "It's a hovering cloud of nanobots. They only have to be flight-capable in zero atmosphere and zero G. They could hold themselves in place relative to each other by magnetics."

He flipped on the holotable, and began drawing up what he had in mind. It was a crude sketch—Mazer was no artist—but his team understood the basic design. They discussed it for several hours, tweaking the design as they went along until they had a concept that felt practical and addressed all their concerns. By then Shambhani had replaced Mazer's original sketch with a detailed model.

"You know, this actually might work," said Shambhani.

"I have no idea how to build it," said Rimas. "I'm no nano-engineer. But the idea seems solid. If nothing else, it gives the development guys a starting place. This could save a lot of lives."

"Agreed," said Mazer. "Good work. I'll post the design on the forum and see what everyone thinks."

The forum was an online community Mazer had created on the IF's intranet. Junior officers from all over the solar system gathered there to share tactics, tech ideas, and new intel on the enemy, including academic papers and whatever the scientific community was publishing about the Formics.

When the forum launched two years ago, Mazer had assumed he would get a few dozen participants at most. Now the site had over two thousand daily users.

Mazer waited until he was in the barracks that night and zipped up in his sleep sack before logging in to the forum with his tablet. He browsed for a few minutes, checking the sub forums for any new posts. A researcher out of Caltech was studying a small organelle harvested from one of the Formic cadavers. A Chinese chemical company was developing genetically altered rice seed that was supposedly resistant to Formic bioweapons. A lieutenant overseeing a team of laser-line operators at a relay station near Jupiter had tweaked their transmitter's operating system and increased transmission speeds by 14 percent. His post included instructions on how others could do the same.

Mazer skimmed through these posts and others, soaking up whatever he thought significant. He read through some of the comments and was pleased to see that they were polite and well-considered. New insight was shared, feedback was given, modifications were proposed.

It baffled Mazer that most senior commanders didn't think this way. They hated sharing intel. The idea of a forum would make their eyes twitch. Intel was something to keep hidden and use only for personal gain.

Mazer didn't understand it, and he knew it was a waste of time to even try. Nothing he did would ever change their thinking. All he could do was share his own.

He generated a new post and uploaded the model of the nanoshield, describing it in detail and inviting criticism. Is this feasible? Worth pursuing? What are the possible drawbacks, defects, dangers, consequences? Then he published the post, signed off, and waited for feedback.

His inbox was next. He smiled when he saw the e-mail from Kim. Were all wives this faithful in their correspondence, he wondered. Kim wrote every day, no exceptions. Even when she was working double shifts at Imbrium Memorial on Luna, she still found time between patients to tap out a quick message.

The hospital was being inundated with refugees, her e-mail said. A virus was spreading through the camps. Nothing life-threatening, but the hospital was keeping infants and the elderly and the worst cases for observation. Beds were scarce. Mazer could almost hear the frustration in Kim's words.

The refugees were mostly free miners from the Belt who had sold their ships to the IF to support the war effort and escape the trade. The miners had used the funds to reach Luna and now had nowhere to go. Few had enough money to carry their families to Earth, and even those who could afford passage were now uncertain if they wanted a life in Earth's gravity. Decades in zero G had left some of them so weak-boned and unambulatory that life on Earth would mean confinement to a wheelchair.

"The news reports don't do these people justice," wrote Kim. "They're afraid. The adults as much as the children. The war ended three years ago, but for them it's an ongoing fight. If I spoke Farsi and Vietnamese and all the languages of sub-Saharan Africa, I could maybe comfort some of them and put their minds at ease. But for many, I can only smile and give their hands a squeeze. It would break your heart to see some of these parents clinging to their sick children."

She ended the way she always did: "Tell me you're safe. Remember I love you. Believe we can win."

Mazer read the e-mail again. She was there in the words. Everything he loved about her was on display. And yet it pained him to read it because she was a world away, living a life he was no longer a part of.

He closed his inbox and opened the vid he kept on his desktop. The sound was muted, but Mazer had watched the vid so many times, he could practically hear every word. On-screen Kim waved at the camera from the kitchen of their apartment on Luna as she chopped vegetables for a soup she was making. Mazer had recorded the vid on their second week of marriage. Him, stationed on Luna. Her, new to the hospital. They both worked impossible hours, but at least they could sleep in each other's arms at night—even if it meant one of them was getting to bed long after the other had already turned in.

Such a brief window of time, he thought. They had known

then that the Formics were returning, but there were days when they had allowed themselves to forget for a few hours how uncertain their future was. It was what a marriage should be. Now it seemed unlikely that they would ever have days together again.

As always, Kim's final sentence left him off balance: Believe we can win. Have faith in the IF, she was saying, faith in yourself. He couldn't tell her how impossible that was, first to believe and then to achieve. News flash: The unrelenting human spirit was not going to be enough. All of us exerting our best effort, tech, tactics, and strategies would still leave us on the losing side. Last time we were lucky; this time we have no chance.

He pushed the thought away, closed the vid, and returned to the forum, hoping to find a few responses to the nanoshield, anything to take his mind off the life he should be living on Luna.

To his surprise, the forum was exploding with new posts. COPERNICUS DESTROYED read the title of one. HEGEMON HOLDING PRESS CONFERENCE NOW read another.

Mazer quickly climbed out of his sleep sack and launched across the barracks toward the holotable. Copernicus. One of the eight Parallax telescopes placed in orbit out beyond the solar system. Before the war, scientists had used the scopes for exoplanet research or to track potential collision threats coming into system. Once we realized the Formic fleet was coming and only a few years away, the Hegemony had seized control of the telescopes to track the Formic fleet's approach. Copernicus was the most important of the bunch, for it was positioned out beyond the system between us and the Formic fleet, giving us our best view of the enemy.

Now it was gone.

Mazer flipped on the holofield and dug through the transmissions that trickled in constantly from Luna, not caring how much noise he was making.

Shambhani appeared at Mazer's side, shielding his eyes from the light and still fighting sleep. "What's going on, Mazer?"

"The forum," said Mazer. "We're getting reports that Copernicus has been destroyed."

Shambhani was awake in an instant. "Destroyed? By what? Please tell me it was a collision."

Mazer was hoping the same. A collision would be a natural phenomenon, perhaps from a comet or asteroid or dense cosmic dust. Or perhaps even from another man-made object, though all of those possibilities seemed highly unlikely. Copernicus was a tiny speck in a massive stretch of empty space. The chances of it getting struck by anything were incredibly small. Plus, the satellite had a collision-avoidance system that would push it out of the path of any approaching threat.

Mazer found the file a moment later. It had come in on the news feeds on the last transmission cycle, broadcast an hour ago. He selected it, and the flat vid began to play in the holofield. Ukko Jukes, the Hegemon of Earth, stood at a podium. He had aged since Mazer had seen him last, and he looked weary. Behind him hung the seal of the Hegemony, and to his left stood various admirals of the Fleet.

"Approximately ten days ago," said Ukko, "Copernicus, one of the eight Parallax satellites, was destroyed by a single Formic fighter."

The words were like a blow to Mazer's chest.

"How is that possible?" said Shambhani. "The Formics aren't even here yet."

"Quiet," said Rimas. Others in the barracks were gathering now.

"Let me emphasize," said Ukko, "this Formic fighter was alone. The Formic fleet is still a great distance away from our system. I don't want anyone to get the impression that the Formics are upon us, ready to engage our outposts and ships in the Kuiper Belt. That is not the case. While we should all be alarmed, this should not incite a panic. That said, Copernicus is a significant loss. Of all the Parallax telescopes, it was the most valuable militarily, giving us the best view of the Formics."

The word "view" was used loosely here, Mazer knew. We could not "see" the Formic fleet in the traditional sense. Copernicus was a computer. It merely spat out data. Analysts then extrapolated likely ship positions, distances, and speeds, filling in the gaps with guesswork and probabilities. Earth still didn't know how many ships were coming, for example. But the data from Copernicus, incomplete as it was, was invaluable.

Ukko continued. "Two IF fighters tracked the Formic fighter to a small asteroid in the Kuiper Belt sixteen hours ago and terminated the threat."

"They blew it up?" said Rimas. "How stupid can you get!"

Mazer agreed. We should have captured it. There were a hundred questions that would never be answered now. If the ship was that small, had it come alone? It was clearly not big enough to be an interstellar ship. It must have come from one of the warships. But how?

There were other questions as well. Did the Formics understand Copernicus's military significance? Could they read its data? Was this a deliberate dismantling of our intelligence infrastructure in preparation for an invasion? Or were they merely targeting all artificial satellites, and they simply hit the closest one first?

Surely Ukko understood how strategically misguided it was to destroy the fighter. Was he losing his influence over the Strategos and the Polemarch? Or was this a misjudgment by them all?

Kim, if we're led by fools, how can we possibly believe that we can win?

The Hegemon continued, rattling off specific details about

the attack. Time, place, the kind of IF fighters used. He even showed a brief vid taken from the IF fighters as they attacked the lone Formic ship.

Mazer kept waiting for Ukko to explain the backup system the IF would employ to track the Formics now that Copernicus was destroyed. But no such information was offered. Ukko eventually gave the podium to one of the rear admirals to take questions, perhaps knowing that the questions would be brutal.

The rear admiral gave the usual nonanswers, trying his best to demonstrate that the IF still had matters under control. It was a weak performance, and by the time the transmission ended and the holo winked out, Mazer felt even more uneasy.

"Why didn't they capture that fighter?" asked Rimas.

"Maybe they couldn't," said Shambhani. "Maybe destroying it was the only option."

"Or maybe they could have," said Mazer, "but they felt like they had to destroy it to put everyone's mind at ease. Make a show of force, reassure the world that we still have a fighting chance. Terminate the threat and win the PR game. Remember, the IF can't hide the loss of Copernicus. The press regularly receives reports from the IF on the data Copernicus gathers. If that source of intel suddenly ran dry, the press would eventually figure out why. Better for the IF to destroy the fighter and make a vid of them doing so than to let this single Formic fighter go unchallenged and seem smarter and faster than the entire International Fleet."

"So they blew up the fighter to save face?" asked Shambhani.

"Maybe," said Mazer. "But I'm more concerned about the loss of Copernicus than I am about how the IF plays the press. We're essentially blind now. The one slight observational advantage we had is severely limited. The seven other Parallax satellites are so far away from the position of Copernicus that they won't be much help in making up for what Copernicus no longer reports to us. We're going to have to be smarter and faster and flawless now. No casualties, no slip-ups."

"People aren't stupid," said Kaufman. "The IF can't spin this one. Taking out the assassin doesn't change the fact that the king is still dead. And in terms of technology, that satellite was our king."

"So we're pretty much screwed," said Shambhani.

"Ukko Jukes and the big brass don't seem to think so," said Rimas. "Everybody in that press conference acted like we had scored a major victory."

" 'Act' is the appropriate word here," said Mazer. "That press conference was a performance. Ukko and the admirals understand the situation. They're just trying to paper over how badly screwed we are."

# CHAPTER 2

## Bingwen

To: ukko.jukes%hegemon@heg.gov
From: robinov%strategos@ifcom.gov/centcom
Subject: Sanction the Chinese

Dear Ukko,

The public needs a show of strength. With Copernicus down, the IF's detractors are out in force. I have politicians from every country in the Crescent—Israel, Egypt, Lebanon, Syria, Jordan—calling for my resignation and threatening to ignore Hegemony taxation if I am not removed. Never mind that losing Copernicus was the Polemarch's fault and not my own. Swift action must be taken to calm the panic and silence the naysayers. I implore you to approve and fund new weapons, give us more troops, and demonstrate the Hegemony's commitment to a strong defense.

You know as well as I do where those troops can come from. Nearly every military on Earth has committed soldiers to the IF except the Chinese. I recognize that their military feels thin after its devastating losses, but who better understands the need for a space-based defense than the very nation that suffered the most during the war? Now is the time for you to use your incomparable negotiating skills to bring Beijing around. To give you credible leverage, some level of economic sanctions would surely get international support, especially from the other nations of the Warsaw Pact. My contacts in Russia assure me that their ambassadors would endorse the move. If raising public alarm would help you, I could inform the media that we cannot defend our military assets or our citizens if the Chinese leave us woefully understaffed. You and I are taking heat we do not deserve. Wound the Chinese with words, and hit them in their purses, and they will have no choice but to concede.

Respectfully,
Yulian
Strategos

—Office of the Hegemony Sealed Archives, Imbrium, Luna, May 12, 2118

Bingwen went alone to the Formic tunnels that night, wearing his black battle suit and a climbing harness. He left the officers' barracks at midnight and mounted his skim cycle under the cover of darkness. No guards were on duty. All was quiet. He slid on his helmet, switched on its night vision, and flew west, soaring across a shallow valley in the northeast corner of Guangxi province.

Three years ago, before all of southeast China burned, the valley here had been green with rice. Families from nearby villages had worked the fields, with their straw hats and sun-bleached clothes, while laughing children played and sang and worked alongside their parents. Then the Formics had gassed everything and peeled back the landscape, leaving the valley black and smoking and littered with corpses. It gladdened Bingwen to see the grasses returning now, creating a sea of green just visible in the moonlight, like a biological show of defiance, a refusal to be defeated. Burn us out, you furry bastards, and we will only grow back again.

No villagers would ever see this land again, however. The military owned it now. It was one of the many new bases that had sprung up since the war. Here soldiers trained and learned how to defend China should the Formics ever reach this soil again.

Bingwen flew with all of his lights off, pushing the skim cycle as fast as it would take him, the valley floor a blur beneath him. It felt like an escape, as if he were actually doing it this time, as if he were really running, putting the military behind him and heading southwest toward Vietnam. Toward freedom.

But of course he would never make it. The tracking chip inside him would alert Captain Li and the others the instant he stepped off base. They would track him down and collect him easily. And even if he somehow *did* elude them and removed the chip, what would he do? The International Fleet would not take him. He was far too young. And if he found employment and waited until he was eighteen, the war would be long over. Or, more likely, he would be dead, the Earth would belong to the enemy, and he would have done nothing to help stop it. At least here, hell that it was, he was doing something, accomplishing something. At least he was a soldier.

The checkpoint came into view ahead of him, and Bingwen began to slow.

During daylight hours the Formic tunnels were filled with soldiers running training exercises. But at night, after the temperature dropped and the lights were extinguished, the tunnels were dark and still and deserted, just as Bingwen wanted them. For it was in this setting, with all evidence of the human world gone, that Bingwen could focus his mind completely on the enemy.

He parked his skim cycle near the checkpoint. A pair of guards were posted outside the gatehouse. They came to attention and saluted when Bingwen approached. He spoke a greeting in Chinese and returned the salute, moving around their barrier and continuing toward the giant hole in the ground. The first dozen times he had come here, the guards had dutifully checked his credentials before letting him pass, but now his presence was routine, if not expected.

It still felt odd to have grown men salute him, even now, a year after making lieutenant. It went against the natural order of things. Particularly in China, where respect was reserved for your elders and those with experience. Twelve-year-old boys were to be deferential, submissive, silent, and low. Everyone was your senior. Everyone deserved your respect. You were nothing. To give a boy command was an offense not only to the individual obligated to obey those commands, but also to China, to its heritage, its families, its very soul. And yet here Bingwen was, commanding a squadron of fifty grown men in the Chinese army, all of whom hated having a boy as their commander.

But of course that was the point. Captain Li had handpicked the men for Bingwen's squadron because their psychological profiles suggested that they would vehemently resist Bingwen's authority and maybe even take steps to remove him. They were thugs, hardliners, traditionalists—men who could not abide the idea of a child giving them any orders. Bingwen knew they wouldn't dare attack him publicly or defy him openly. For there was a higher power that could inflict harsh punishments for any show of insubordination. But they could despise him in their hearts and find less obvious ways to resist him.

Usually, after a period of working with Bingwen, the men

would soften somewhat. A few even grew to respect him. He was not as incompetent and weak as they had assumed. Some even began to defend him when others spoke ill of him or called him "the Child."

Of course that was always when Captain Li would yank those men out of the squad and replace them with men who took great offense at having to serve under a child. It meant Bingwen was commanding a different group of men every two months or so, with Captain Li finding soldiers even more unyielding and malicious than the ones before. The most recent replacements, a group of four men, had come from a military prison along the coast. Bingwen couldn't access their records, but they seemed like the kind of men who were in prison for good reason.

But that was Captain Li, molding Bingwen through the school of pain.

Bingwen reached the hole in the ground, a perfectly cylindrical crater dug straight into the earth, measuring seventy meters deep and nine hundred meters across. It was just as the Formics had left it three years ago when one of their landers had lifted off from this spot and headed back into space to fight Mazer and the Mobile Operations Police, or MOPs, at the scout ship. The crater was visible from space. It stood out like a bullet wound to Earth, a reminder of how unstoppable the enemy had been, how technologically superior.

Bingwen moved along the safety fence, making his way toward the scaffolding staircase that led down to the crater floor. In the moonlight he could make out hundreds of tunnel entrances at the bottom of the hole, as if an army of monster groundhogs had had a field day here.

Bingwen smiled. Groundhogs. If only.

He reached the staircase and clattered down to the bottom. The soil at the floor of the crater was hard-packed clay, dried in the sun. Bingwen flipped on his helmet light and saw hundreds of tunnel entrances on the ground ahead of him, as if he were standing on a giant sieve. The Chinese had built complex surface-drainage systems around the site to funnel rainwater away from the crater, as well as another drainage system on the floor of the crater between all the tunnel entrances, using narrower pipe. The result was a piping system that branched out in every direction in front of him and worked surprisingly well. Some water did get down into the tunnels, but pumps sucked the water away and discouraged erosion and flooding.

Bingwen's tunnel was in the center of the crater. He reached it by walking atop the drainage pipes, turning one way and then another like a well-trained mouse in an elaborate maze. A tall pyramidal iron structure stood over the top of the tunnel entrance. A winch was secured to the bottom of the structure, allowing soldiers to hook in and descend down into the darkness. Bingwen snapped the winch's D-ring onto his climbing harness and lowered himself into the hole.

The shaft wasn't much wider than the span of his arms, but if Bingwen kept his limbs close to his body he could easily avoid the narrow ledges and rocks that jutted out from the wall every few meters or so. Bingwen imagined the Formics using these ledges to descend, dropping from one ledge to the next like monkeys swinging down to the lower branches of a tree with a fluid, swift grace.

The Formics had likely come up the shafts the same way, leaping from one ledge to the next, their strong forelimbs pulling them upward with that same easy grace. Bingwen knew the Formics had the strength for it. As a tagalong and then an adopted member of the Mobile Operations Police, he had witnessed dozens of engagements with the enemy in China. He had seen the Formics' clenched fists pound on soldiers in the heat of battle, exuding a brutality and strength far greater than their diminutive size suggested.

His feet touched bottom, and he unhooked the D-ring. To his right, installed on the tunnel wall, was a thin projection tube that extended into the tunnel and disappeared from sight. Bingwen took the cable from the winch and hooked it to the small transmission device mounted at the base of the projection tube, nearly hidden from view.

Then he turned and faced the tunnel leading away from the shaft. It was only a meter tall, so Bingwen got down on all fours and crawled forward. Most adults could crawl through these taller tunnels, but there were some places that required them to get on their bellies and squirm. Bingwen had a much easier time. There were even places where he could stand and crouch slightly and continue on foot.

He reached the spot where the tunnel forked into four different passageways. He took the one on the far right, a slightly descending tunnel full of twists and dips and intersections, the light from his helmet cutting through the darkness. Without mapping equipment, one could easily get lost down here. The special ops teams knew that fact well. One of their favorite training exercises was to lead a man deep into the tunnels and then leave him there, giving him nothing but a few cans of supplemental oxygen, with instructions to find his way out in the dark. It was near impossible to do, but that was mostly the point. It was a test of mental endurance more than anything.

Bingwen twisted and turned and moved randomly, not thinking about where he was going. His wrist pad was tracking his movements, but he tried not to look at it. Occasionally he reached a dug-out space as big as a room that even adults could stand up in. Perhaps the Formics had congregated in these chambers for some reason. Why, Bingwen could only guess. To breed? To eat? To sleep? There was nothing here to give any hint of its purpose.

He stopped in one of the larger rooms and punched in the code to initiate the simulation. Four thin projection tubes running along the tunnel walls above and to either side of him turned on, filling the room with a faint holofield. The projection tubes continued uninterrupted throughout the tunnel system, so that now a single holofield filled every passageway. Since Bingwen was standing in the field, the sim knew exactly where he was located.

Bingwen crouched down in the center of the tunnel's chamber and waited, keeping the various tunnel entrances in his peripheral vision so he could see the attack before it came.

The first Formic appeared a moment later, bounding down the tunnel directly in front of him, its six limbs launching it forward with the power of a jungle cat springing on its prey.

Bingwen's slaser was on the forearm of his battle suit, but he didn't raise his arm to fire. He wanted to witness the creature's every movement, even up to the moment when it delivered the death stroke. Bingwen noted every placement of its arms, forelegs, and hind legs; the way it dipped and bobbed its head to maintain its balance as it scurried forward; the way it had banked up the side wall when the tunnel had turned sharply; the way it breathed, accelerated, fixed its empty eyes upon him; the way it leaped at the last moment, to grab the head and snap the neck.

The creature struck him and exploded into a shower of pixels.

This was Bingwen's custom: to let the first one get him, to face death and welcome it, to show the enemy that he would not cower. And with that done, he dropped to his knees and scurried away, taking note of how the creatures chased him, caught him, worked in pairs or small groups to cut off his exit or guide him into a dead end. He used his slaser to kill the ones he could. Others reached him and exploded when they touched him.

All of the creatures' movements were based on actual vids taken from soldiers in the war. Some had even come from soldiers brave enough to enter these tunnels, though those vids were all recovered after the fact, once the Chinese had cleared the tunnels and found their corpses.

After half an hour, Bingwen's knees were sore and he was sweating profusely. He turned off the sim and sank to the tunnel floor, catching his breath. If it comes to tunnel warfare, we lose, he thought. We would never win here. The enemy would have every advantage.

Bingwen removed his helmet momentarily to drink from his canteen, then he put his helmet back on and took his writing tablet out of his pack. He ran a cable from the tablet to the projection tube and turned on the tube. It had taken him a few weeks to figure out how to get on the nets. His access on base was restricted to sites that Captain Li and the military approved of, which were mostly the military's intranet. He could get the news and world events, but always through the military's filter, which would have the reader believe that China was the most advanced nation on Earth and the envy of everyone. Bingwen knew better. To get unrestricted access he had to use the few resources at his disposal, namely the tunnels and their equipment. The winch tower outside served as a crude transmitter and receiver after Bingwen had installed a few discreet pieces of hardware there. The projection tubes provided the needed power, and the winch cable connected the two.

In moments, he had a sat link. His frequent exercises here at night were a good cover for his real purpose for coming. Captain Li no doubt knew about Bingwen's trips to the hole, and he no doubt checked the sim database to ensure that Bingwen had indeed come to train. And so Bingwen did train, using the last few minutes of his visit to sign in to Mazer's forum.

For his username he had chosen the number and surname of a current Uruguayan soccer star, and whenever Bingwen posted, he dropped in the occasional Spanish slang or colloquialism to remove any suspicion that he might be Chinese. Even Mazer didn't know who he was in the forum.

He reviewed Mazer's most recent submission and sketches

for the nanoshield. Bingwen was no engineer, but he recognized a promising idea when he saw one. The design could work well in tunnel combat in space, as the shield could move to the front or rear of the soldier as needed, depending on the direction of attack. And since the shield could fluctuate in size and shape, it could accommodate the ever-changing widths and heights of the tunnels. It could even allow the soldier to pierce the shield with the barrel of a slaser and fire at the enemy without any fear of exposure.

Bingwen expressed all of this in his post, adding who he thought might be the best manufacturer for such a tool. Juke Limited was obvious, but there were others as well. Gungsu Industries had shown promise in nanotech, as had Micronix—

The screen went blank, his sat link severed. Why? Interference? The projection tube on the wall was still operative. As was his tablet. Which meant the problem was with the cable or the winch. Bingwen didn't take any chances. He stored his gear and hustled for the exit. As he approached, he began to feel uneasy. He stopped, crouched, and turned up his helmet's exterior mike to maximum so that he might pick up even the softest of sounds ahead. A whirring noise flooded his ears, and he recognized the sound of the winch cable unspooling as someone made a quick decent. It was not the same sound the winch made when *Bingwen* used it, however; this was a lower frequency, as if the cable was strained and carrying a heavier weight. An adult.

Bingwen stayed where he was and listened. Feet touched the ground. A D-clip snapped and released. The winch screamed as it hauled up the line. There was a moment of silence, and then the whine of the winch returned: slow, strained, and steady—a second adult coming down.

It was one in the morning. Whoever was coming was coming for him. He listened for voices but heard nothing, which meant they were either well trained or wearing full helmets that covered their faces and sealed to their suits. Bingwen ran through every possible frequency—including the encrypted ones—until he found the one they were using. Two voices. Men. Speaking Mandarin.

"—dark as death down here."

"You go first."

"That hole's not big enough for a dog to crawl through. You go first."

"Soldiers go in all the time. Move."

"Why don't we wait for him outside? He's got to come out sooner or later. We tag him when he pokes his head out."

"Then it won't look like an accident. We've got our orders. If we leave the body deep enough they won't find it for weeks."

"They'll smell it for weeks, though."

"Just move."

Bingwen retreated back into the tunnel. He recognized those voices. They belonged to two of the recent transfers into the squadron, two of the thugs Captain Li had brought in. Typical. Captain Li had probably given them the order himself. The men had no idea they were being used.

Bingwen picked up his pace and hustled farther into the tunnel.

All of the projection tubes on the walls came to life, and the holofield once again filled the tunnel. A large three-dimensional arrow appeared in the air in front of Bingwen, pointing at his chest. Then another arrow appeared behind it, and another, extending all the way down the tunnel in front of him. Similar arrows from side tunnels hovered to his right and left, pointing at him.

"He'll know we're here now."

"Doesn't matter. He's not going anywhere."

They would follow the arrows right to him. It was the same system rescuers used to find lost soldiers after the exercises. Or the arrows could be used to guide the soldier toward the exit. The holofield was working against him, he realized, and since it filled the tunnel, he couldn't escape it or hide.

Bingwen paused to think. He had two advantages. One, the men clearly had no experience with the tunnels. And two, Bingwen's size—he could move much faster than they could through the narrow passages. It bothered him that he didn't know what he was up against, however.

What weapons were these men carrying? If they needed his death to look like an accident, it would be handwork, most likely. Choking or smothering or a broken neck. Hard to make a laser wound through the heart look like an accident. Yet weapons would still come in handy. They needed to subdue him, catch him, force him to comply. A knife would be useful, as would a slaser.

Then there was their equipment. Harnesses, helmets with radios—not standard-issue gear. Someone had equipped them. Li, most likely, or someone operating under his orders. Which meant Bingwen would be wise to assume they had every piece of field hardware at their disposal.

He decided to test that theory.

He tapped his wrist pad and turned on the simulation. The Formic holos were so lifelike and fierce and terrifying that at least one new recruit cracked each week, dropping to the tunnel floor and crying for rescue like an abandoned child. The holos would be especially unnerving to someone who had never experienced them before and who might not even know they were part of the training.

The soldiers' screams a moment later confirmed that fact. Bingwen heard the soft, high-pitched whine of their lasers. And then one man shouted for the other to calm down. "They're not real. It's a sim."

"Well turn it off."

"I don't know how. Ignore them."

"I can't ignore them. They're charging us."

Bingwen of course had Formics coming for him as well, but he paid them no mind, and they shattered into pixels when they reached him. He moved to the nearest holo projector, and wired in his tablet. He could not turn off the arrows with his wrist pad, for it was not a command he had initiated. But he could change their target. He did so and the arrows flipped, pointing at one of the men in the tunnels.

Bingwen took a side tunnel then and made his way east, connecting with another tunnel system that had a separate exit to the surface accessible via a gradual slope and a few switchbacks. It took Bingwen ten minutes to reach the surface, but when he did, all was quiet. He came out with his lights off and scanned the area with his night vision. The winch tower was two hundred meters to his right. Bingwen zoomed in with his optics and was relieved to see that the winch cable was still extended down into the tunnel, meaning the men had not yet found their way out. Not surprising. Even if they had known the way, they would not have had time to crawl through all the narrow places Bingwen had ensured would be between them and their exit.

He sprinted to the winch tower and reeled in the cable, tying it off at the top. Then he removed the pieces of transmitter hardware he had installed on the tower months ago. Finally he tapped at his wrist pad again to increase the number of Formics in the simulation below from a dozen at any given time to a thousand. The holofield would be filled with so many holos of charging Formics, that they would look like a river of light, rushing forward, arms outstretched to kill. The bombardment of holos would be so constant and disruptive and relentless, that the men's senses would be too overwhelmed to make sense of anything. It would be nightmarish. Bingwen almost felt sorry for them.

He hustled to his skim cycle and rocketed back to base. He changed into his sleep suit and then woke every man in his squadron, ordering them outside to stand in formation. The men obeyed, shivering in the cold, barefoot and dressed in their undergarments.

Bingwen faced them. "I have just been awakened by reports that men from this squadron sneaked out and left these barracks after hours. I laughed at such an accusation. 'This squadron?' I told the accuser. 'The 301? No, sir, you must be mistaken. These men, these excellent soldiers, would never allow two of their own to be so foolish. They would stop men from such flagrant insubordination. For ours is a squadron of discipline, unity, and absolute respect for the military code of conduct. No, sir. Not this squadron. Because we understand that the offense of one is the offense of all. There is no finer group of soldiers in all the world,' I said. Sergeant, prove me right. Roll call."

The two missing culprits were soon identified. Their names were called out, but there was no reply.

Bingwen feigned shock. He shook his head, deflated. Then he squared his shoulders and faced his men. "Clearly I have failed you," he said. "I have failed to teach the importance of respecting our elders who established this code of conduct. I have failed to instill a sense of brotherhood, a sense of mutual responsibility. I have failed to teach you that foolish decisions endanger us all. In war, discipline is paramount to survival. And yes, we are now at war. Copernicus is destroyed. The enemy returns. Yet what example do we give our mothers and fathers who look to us to protect their homes and fields and children? Disobedience? Delinquency? Rebelliousness?" He shook his head. "No, we must right this wrong immediately. We must take our punishment and start anew. Sergeant, order your men to follow me to the brig, where we will serve a two-day sentence."

The sergeant shouted the orders. Bingwen led them in a jog to the brig, which was located on the other side of the base, two kilometers away. Bingwen ordered the jailer on duty to open the available cells. The men were filed inside, ten to a cell.

Bingwen then stood in front of all the cells and removed his shirt. "Jailer, I have failed these men. Take this cane and deliver three strikes across my back."

Bingwen handed the man the cane and turned his back to him, bringing his arms forward to expose his full back and take his strikes.

The jailer, a mere private, hesitated. He looked around him at the others, confused. Then he turned back to Bingwen. "Sir, I cannot possibly strike an officer."

"I order you, Private."

The men were all crowding the front of the cells to watch.

"But, sir, the military does not inflict corporal punishment."

Bingwen faced the man and seized the cane. "Very well." He turned to his men in the cells and chose the biggest and strongest among them. "Corporal Mayzu, come deliver three strikes. That is an order."

The jailer let Mayzu out. The man took the cane. He was broad-shouldered and thick. He seemed uncertain. He hesitated. "Sir, I do not feel comfortable striking an officer."

"Do it," Bingwen said.

The first blow knocked Bingwen to his knees, pain exploding across his entire upper body. He thought for a moment that he might pass out, but he gathered himself and got back to his feet. He stumbled forward to the nearest cell and grabbed the bars to steady himself.

"Two more, Mayzu."

There was silence. "But, sir, you are . . ."

Bingwen turned and faced him. "What, Mayzu? A boy? A child?"

Mayzu didn't respond.

Bingwen faced his men, his back screaming in pain. "Is that what I am to you all? A child?"

The men were silent.

"The Formics slaughtered my parents, burned my village, assaulted my homeland. There is no greater privilege than to give my life to defend China again, whether I am twelve or two hundred. We will be the finest squadron in this army, and we will not allow a stupid act of insubordination to weaken us and threaten our ability to defend our people."

Bingwen turned back to the bars and gripped them once again. "Mayzu, two more. And if I lose consciousness, you will drag me into a cell."

There was a long silence.

Then the second blow came, hard across the already tender flesh.

Bingwen did not remember the third strike. When he awoke, he was on his stomach in the medical wing, with wet bandages draped across his bare back.

Captain Li was sitting in the chair beside the bed. "I will say this, Bingwen, you always surprise me. Just when I think I know how you will respond, you do something like this."

Bingwen said nothing. Captain Li had been with him ever since the Chinese military took Bingwen away from Mazer. Li had been only a lieutenant then.

"Your back will take weeks to heal," Li said. "And for what? To earn the respect of your men, to show them that your heart is given completely to China? To paint yourself a worthy commander? I wish I could have heard your speech. The jailer was near tears when he recounted it. I thought he might start singing the national anthem."

Bingwen didn't respond.

"I let your men out of the brig after six hours. I told them that was punishment enough. Oh, and we found the men in the tunnels, curled up into balls, crying like children, forgive the expression. They had both soiled themselves. And who can blame them? So many Formics. I fear both men may be scarred psychologically. Question is, what to do with them?

I can't return them to your squadron. There are already whispers among your men to maim them both on sight. Was that the point of your theatrics? To turn your squadron against these delinquents, to have your men inflict the justice you are too cowardly to inflict yourself?"

Captain Li crossed one leg over the other and leaned back in his chair. "Honestly, Bingwen. You would rather take a cane across the back than shoot men guilty of attempted murder?"

"Is that what I was supposed to do?" Bingwen asked. "Shoot them? They were following orders. Though I cannot imagine who would give them such a command."

Captain Li grinned. "Yes, it is troubling. But when the Formics return, you will thank me for making you a soldier, Bingwen. You may not like my methods, but you will never be the weapon we need you to be if you live by a morality other than the correct one."

"And what morality is that, sir? Yours?"

Captain Li stood and buttoned up the jacket of his uniform. "We also checked your tablet. How strange that you would take one down into the tunnels. When we opened your files, all we found were your journal entries, all of which were surprisingly complimentary of me. Needless to say, I was amused. I could threaten to have you caned to find out what you were actually doing down there, but of course caning is not permitted and right now I need you well. I have been ordered to assemble a unique group of soldiers for training in the Belt. China, it seems, has finally agreed to give troops to the International Fleet. You will be happy to know that you will be among them, although because of your age your involvement will not be public knowledge. You'll be an experiment of sorts. The school is called Variable Gravity Acclimatization School, or VGAS, but everyone calls it Gravity Camp, or GravCamp for short. The IF has been training soldiers there for years. So get well. You leave in a week."

He moved for the exit, but Bingwen stopped him with a question.

"And you, sir? What is to become of you?"

Li smiled. "I'm coming with you, of course. To be your commanding officer and take a position at the school. As I informed our superiors, you would not want it any other way."

Li smiled wider and exited, leaving Bingwen alone with his bandages.

# CHAPTER 3

# Vaganov

As with all armed conflicts, the Second Formic War took its toll on our most fundamental social unit: the family. What made this war unique, however, was that it not only enlisted our sons and daughters into combat, but it also dictated how and when the free citizens of Earth could produce sons and daughters in the first place.

Because it was considered essential that all human activities be centered on the production of war materiel to fight the Formics in space, as far from Earth as possible, the Hegemony Council determined that Earth's economic resources must not be dissipated by trying to meet the needs of a growing population. Food production, housing, transportation, and medical facilities needed to be maintained at fixed levels so that all new production could be directed toward the construction of an effective war fleet during the brief time before the main Formic invasion force would arrive.

Countries like Iran, India, Uzbekistan, and the United States had long practiced passive, voluntary population control, mostly consisting of free access to birth control and the natural tendency of prosperous people to have fewer children; or somewhat more aggressive laws that disallowed men and women with multiple children to run for public office or receive certain benefits. But it was China's one-child policy that served as the ultimate model for the population laws instituted by the Hegemony prior to the Second Formic War. The child limit was set at two per family, doubling the Chinese quota, but failure to comply with this more generous policy resulted in fines, loss of property, and, in some tightly policed countries, incarceration.

Resistance to the laws was heaviest in those nations with a large Catholic population, such as Poland, which initially won an exemption of conscience for its Catholic citizens. That exemption was later swept aside once the Hegemony's political control was firmly set. Nations where Muslims historically had larger families and a tradition of resistance to outside interference in cultural matters, such as Bangladesh and Pakistan, also resisted.

The people most affected by the population laws, however, were the children born in defiance of the laws, or, rarely, those whose parents had been granted a Hegemony exemption. These third children—and in rare cases fourth and fifth children—were scorned, isolated, or taunted as Formic sympathizers. Their persecution—which included violent attacks from their peers, and in some cases from adults—is an often overlooked and shameful result of the population restrictions.

—Demosthenes, *A History of the Formic Wars,* Vol. 3

Mazer received a message on his wrist pad at breakfast to report to Colonel Vaganov's office immediately.

The summons surprised Mazer. He had never met the colonel. Vaganov had come to WAMRED only a month ago to assume command, and so far he had taken a hands-off approach with the breach teams. What Mazer knew about Vaganov was impressive, however. Before joining the IF, Vaganov had served as a battle cruiser commander in the Russian navy and then with the Admiralty in Saint Petersburg. His most recent post as the director of the International Fleet's Department of Acquisitions at CentCom on Luna was a high-profile position that had him rubbing shoulders with both the Hegemony and the private sector. His rise through the ranks meant real ability, either as a commander or as an upsucking bureaucrat. Mazer was hoping he could figure out which before Vaganov led them into combat.

The flight from the cafeteria to the colonel's office was a series of twists and turns through the labyrinth of the space station. WAMRED was actually five space stations cobbled together, each one donated from a different country when the International Fleet first formed. Linked together, with sturdy docking tubes between them, the stations formed an asymmetrical, odd-shaped structure, like something a child would assemble with a stack of random pipes.

Mazer initiated his boot magnets as he approached the colonel's office, and the door slid open automatically.

Colonel Vaganov was anchored to the floor behind his holotable. He was young for his rank, and unlike the other Russian officers Mazer had known—who always maintained a rather austere disposition—Vaganov actually smiled when Mazer entered.

"Captain Mazer Rackham," he said. "Come in, come in. I was just reviewing your record here."

It was then that Mazer noticed the military file hovering in the air above Vaganov's holotable.

Here it comes, thought Mazer. He'll see the complaints of insubordination and peg me as a troublemaker.

But Vaganov's mood didn't change after reviewing the file in silence for a moment. "I see here that you've been in the IF since it formed," said Vaganov.

"Yes, sir," said Mazer. "I spent one year at CentCom, and two years here."

Vaganov nodded. "Our paths didn't cross at CentCom, but that doesn't surprise me. That place is practically a city. Your wife is still on Luna, I take it?"

"Yes, sir," Mazer said. "She's an ER doctor at Imbrium Memorial."

Vaganov smiled. "A doctor? Well, someone has to earn the bread for the family. We certainly don't get it in the IF."

Mazer was impressed with Vaganov's command of Common. There was only the slightest hint of a Russian accent.

"Do you communicate with your wife at least weekly, Mazer? E-mails perhaps? Holos? Whatever?"

The question struck Mazer as odd. What business was it of the colonel's how often he spoke with Kim?

As if registering his thoughts, Vaganov smiled. "I ask, Mazer, not to pry but because I believe you are a husband first and a soldier second. I suspect I'd get a wrist slap from Cent-Com for saying so. They couldn't care less about your personal life. In their minds you are a blunt object to be thrown at the enemy and nothing more. But I disagree. I have little patience for a man who doesn't keep his commitments to his wife and family. It is a sign of weak character and usually indicative of how he will keep his commitments to his fellow soldiers in the field. That's not the type of officer I want in command of my troops."

In all his years of service, Mazer had never heard any commander express that opinion. Most seemed to believe the opposite. You were a soldier and only a soldier, subject to the commander and only the commander. Family obligations were an inconvenient distraction.

Mazer's surprise must have registered on his face, because Vaganov laughed.

"My opinions unsettle you, I see," Vaganov said.

"No, sir," said Mazer. "On the contrary. I agree with you. I've just never heard a commanding officer hold that opinion."

Vaganov laughed again. "I am a rare bird. Some people hear a melody. Most people hear squawking."

It was a strange metaphor, but it amused Vaganov. Mazer doubted it was true. You didn't become the director of acquisitions or of WAMRED by squawking your way to the top.

"To answer your original question," said Mazer. "Yes, my wife and I communicate often."

Vaganov nodded. "I'm glad to hear it. I've noticed however that you have not been attending the officer socials."

Is that what this was about? thought Mazer. Copernicus is destroyed, the IF is unstable, and Vaganov is concerned about attendance at his silly parties?

The socials were weekly get-togethers held in the officers' lounge. Vaganov had organized the events shortly after taking command. Mazer had attended the first one out of obligation, but he had left as soon as it became apparent that the event was nothing more than an informal brown-nosing affair, wherein junior officers fawned over Vaganov and his senior aides in the hope of getting in their good graces.

"I'm not one for socials, sir," said Mazer. "I hope you'll forgive my absence."

"Of course," said Vaganov. He glanced back at Mazer's record. "It says here that you fought the Formics in China, but there's very little information or specifics. All I see are complaints of insubordination."

He looked back at Mazer as if expecting an explanation.

"Some of my senior officers in the NZSAS and our counterparts in the Chinese army were not pleased with my decision to engage the enemy and offer assistance to wounded civilians," said Mazer.

Vaganov nodded as if he expected this. "Yes. The NZSAS. That's the New Zealand Special Air Service?"

"That's correct, sir."

"Special Forces."

"Yes, sir."

Vaganov frowned. "So you're in China, you rescue civilians, you give the Formics hell, and all you get for it in return are strikes on your record." He shook his head. "That sounds about right. If I didn't know any better I'd say I was back in Russia."

Vaganov waved a hand through the files and made them disappear. "Do you know why we're going to lose this war, Mazer? Do you know the biggest weakness in the Fleet? The largest chink in our armor? It's not our weapons. It's not our inferior tech, or our numbers, or our lack of combat experience in space. It's *skomorokhi*. That's a Russian word. Do you know it?"

"No, sir."

"It means 'buffoons.' Idiots, Mazer. That's why we will lose. Incompetent leadership. There are far too many men with stripes on their shoulders who care more about getting additional stripes or protecting the ones they have than they care about the twelve billion people of Earth. I know that sounds ludicrous, but it is a fact. A fact you know all too well, I suspect, because when I see those notes of insubordination on your record, I know precisely the type of man who put them there. I know because I've served under men like that myself, men who have tried similar tactics to discredit me. They tear down junior officers they consider a threat, they fear thinking they don't understand, they blame everyone around them for their own mistakes. And because these are charismatic men, and semi-intelligent men, they can fool those above them into thinking them tactical geniuses surrounded by fools."

Vaganov stood erect and clasped his hands behind his back. "I know what type of soldier you are, Mazer. I've seen records like this time and again. And they always belong to soldiers who give a damn, soldiers who do what's right." He raised a finger. "Don't mistake me. I'm not advocating insubordination. Disobey a lawful order from me, and there will be serious consequences."

He smiled. "And I know why you don't come to the socials, Mazer. You skip them because you can't stand a kiss-up. The sight of all that fawning and pandering makes you sick to the stomach." His smile widened. "But you see, that's just it. That's why I hold these socials whenever I receive a new post. I am looking for soldiers like you, Mazer, soldiers who are so repulsed by those games and turned off by the bureaucracy that they would risk offending their CO by not showing up." He laughed. "The only thing I hate more than an idiot commander is a brown-nosing junior officer. Oh sure, I act entertained. I'll take their praise and compliments all day, but I'll hate them for it." He smiled. "That surprises you, doesn't it?"

"It's not what I expected, sir," said Mazer.

"I trust you'll keep this little secret between us," said Vaganov. "If the kiss-ups knew how self-defeating their behavior really was, they'd change. That's why I consider them so unreliable. They shift with the wind." He shook his head. "No, there is only one way to gain my favor, Mazer. By being the best damn soldier you can be. By dedicating yourself completely to whatever missions you're assigned. Is that clear?"

"Yes, sir."

"I think you're one of those soldiers, Mazer. In fact, I'd bet my life on it."

Mazer wasn't sure how to respond. "Thank you, sir."

"That lofty opinion of you is not mine alone," said Vaganov. "I asked my advisers to tell me which of our breach teams was the best, and they all, independent of each other, picked yours."

"Thank you, sir. My men are very competent. I think I got the best in the IF."

"Or you made them that way, more likely," said Vaganov. "An army is only as strong as its commander, including an army of only four men. In any case, I see that you and your men are one of the teams testing the gravity disruptor."

"Yes, sir."

Vaganov nodded. "And what do you think of the device?"

Mazer hesitated. "Permission to speak candidly, sir."

Vaganov motioned for Mazer to proceed. "Please."

"Sir, the gravity disruptor is a do-or-die weapon," Mazer said. "If it fails, marines die. They cannot retreat. Nor can they be rescued. Any craft that attempted to do so would be incinerated instantly. We either penetrate that hull and take the ship, or we lose good marines. And based on our tests, I think it highly likely that the GD will fail."

Colonel Vaganov reached into the holofield and brought up a report. "If that's your assessment, Mazer, then why do you run so many tests? It says here that you and your men have tested the GD nearly twice as many times as the other teams. Far more times than is recommended."

"The IF may adopt this tech, sir," Mazer said, "whether I agree with that decision or not. Should that occur, we must know the best operational tactics to minimize casualties and maximize success. That means taking every aspect of this operation into consideration and holding it up to intense scrutiny. Not just the tech itself, but how we deliver the tech, how we work as a team to set and activate the cubes. The op seems rather straightforward, I know, but my team has discovered many potential improvements. Everything from specific choreography to new tech marines might find useful."

"New tech?" asked Vaganov. "Like what exactly?"

"A few days ago we developed a rudimentary design for a

nanobot shield that would catch and dampen explosive Formic doily rounds." Mazer explained the premise behind the shields. Then, with Colonel Vaganov's permission, he reached into the holofield and dug through the station's files until he brought up the model Shambhani had created.

"I see," said Vaganov. "Interesting. Have you told anyone outside your team about this design?"

Mazer hesitated. The IF didn't explicitly forbid private forums like the one Mazer had created, but Mazer had never met a commander who liked the idea. If he divulged the forum to Vaganov, there was the risk that Vaganov would order him to shut it down. Mazer could probably argue whether that was a lawful order or not, but he didn't want to risk it. So he answered honestly without mentioning the forum.

"I've shared it with a few junior officers, yes."

Vaganov shook his head. "Next time, don't. If you share ideas with junior officers, they'll only run it up the chain as if it were their own. What's worse, their simpleminded commanders will dismiss the tech outright because they won't understand it. Then these same commanders will fight against the tech's approval should it resurface elsewhere, lest they look like the fool for not approving it initially. That's how these people think, Mazer. They'll do anything to protect their own image. I saw it all the time at Acquisitions. It's senseless and stupid, but that's the IF. Share your ideas with others outside your circle, and you're throwing pearls before swine."

Mazer considered that. On one hand, he agreed. He had seen commanders act in the very way Vaganov described. Yet guarding ideas wasn't the solution either.

"If you have ideas," said Vaganov, "anything that requires development, bring them to me. Let me employ our engineers and get some momentum behind it before some dimwit commander puts a bullet in it. While at Acquisitions I developed relationships with people who can make things happen. They trust me. If I connect you with them, they'll listen to you."

Mazer didn't like the arrangement. If he took Vaganov's orders to the letter, he would never post to the forum again, he would bring everything directly and only to the colonel. That would defeat the very purpose of the forum and hinder the proliferation of ideas.

And yet . . . if Vaganov was sincere, if he had the connections he claimed, he might break down all the barriers Mazer and others had encountered as they tried moving intel and ideas up the chain.

"Are we clear?" said Vaganov.

"Understood," said Mazer.

Vaganov nodded, the matter settled. "Good. Now, back to the gravity disruptor. You think the device will fail. Why?"

"Several reasons," said Mazer. "One, Formics communicate instantaneously across great distances without tech. As soon as one Formic figures out we're using camouflaged capsules, every Formic on every ship will know. They won't take chances after that. They'll obliterate every scrap of debris approaching their ships. Big or small."

Vaganov nodded. "Go on."

"Problem two," said Mazer. "It's unlikely that the GD can penetrate the hull of a Formic ship. We have their scout ship from the previous war in our possession . . . well, technically Juke Limited has it, but it doesn't matter anyway because the engineers at Juke can't even scratch its surface. Nothing damages that hull. It's an indestructible alien alloy that remains a total mystery. Ukko Jukes believed gravity manipulation could damage it, but he was wrong. The GD is built upon the same principle. It will likely prove ineffective as well."

"The hull of the Formic scout ship is not the only material the Formics use to construct their ships," said Vaganov. "The Juke gravity weapon ripped Formic fighters to shreds."

Mazer nodded. "Fighters, yes. But those were small vessels not intended for interstellar flight and built with a different alloy. The ships *we* need to breach are the big interstellar ships en route to our solar system. They will likely have indestructible hulls much like the scout ship."

"Probably," Vaganov agreed. "Anything else?"

"The GD's delivery system," said Mazer. "The pieces must be hand-delivered and set. Which means if the capsules don't deliver the marines, the mission fails. In our test runs, we use a dummy Formic ship that's adrift. In battle, Formic ships will be active and mobile, capable of altering their speed and trajectory at any moment. If they do while the capsules are en route, which is highly likely, the marines will miss the target altogether and float off into space."

"The GD is by no means a perfect system," said Vaganov. "Unfortunately, it's the best we have at the moment, and time is running short. The loss of Copernicus has the world in an uproar. Confidence in the IF is at an all-time low. This is a delicate situation, Mazer. If we appear weak and inept, we could lose support from superpowers like the US and China, whose taxes fund the Hegemony and the IF. That would only leave us weaker than we already are."

Mazer nodded. He understood the state of things.

"That's where you come in," said Vaganov. "The Hegemon wants to announce new tech in our arsenal to put people's minds at ease, something that shows we're prepared for the fight ahead."

"The gravity disruptor," said Mazer.

Vaganov nodded. "The Hegemon wants to unveil it to the press. The capsules and the GD will illustrate that we can strike the Formics to the heart."

"That's premature," said Mazer. "And misleading. We don't know that the GD will work. In all likelihood it won't."

"That's not the point," said Vaganov. "The point is to provide the *perception* of strength. Whether the GD sees combat or not is irrelevant. The Hegemon wants to give the press a dog and pony show, and that's precisely what we will give them."

"How?" said Mazer. "The engineers haven't even begun testing live charges. We're still practicing with dummy cubes."

"No more," said Vaganov. "Tomorrow morning you will begin testing with live charges."

Mazer couldn't hide his surprise. "Sir, every computer simulation thus far has shown that the hull's integrity responds in unpredictable ways. Cracks form outside the detonation zone. Shrapnel is heavy. The engineers are still calibrating the device. They'll tell you it's not ready."

"I have spoken with the engineers," said Vaganov. "And I have given them my instructions. They'll be ready."

"They *assure* you they'll be ready or you have *ordered* them to be ready?"

Vaganov's pleasant expression fell. "Careful, Mazer. You overstep your bounds the moment you question my orders."

"Sir," said Mazer, "with all due respect, testing the GD on human ships teaches us little about how the Formic hull material will react. We'd be testing on watermelons and making conclusions about bowling balls."

"That fact is not lost on me, Captain. But we don't have Formic ships to practice on. The scout ship is property of Juke Limited, and they won't grant us access."

"If any piece of the GD malfunctions," said Mazer, "it would alter the direction of the tidal forces at play. The results could be disastrous. Shards of hull material could burst outward and cut through my team like paper."

"I am aware of the danger," said Vaganov. "As well as the challenges of the task. That is why I'm employing my best team. You'll begin tomorrow at 0700. My aides will forward you the particulars." Vaganov turned back to his desk.

It was a dismissal.

Well there you have it, Mazer thought. Vaganov was no

ally, after all. In fact, he might even be more dangerous than the bureaucrats, for he was willing to needlessly endanger soldiers to please his superiors.

"Permission to submit a formal objection," said Mazer.

Colonel Vaganov didn't look at him. "If you feel the need to cover your ass, Mazer, by all means do so."

It was all Mazer *could* do. He straightened, saluted, and was out the door without another word.

Mazer's team set out the following morning on schedule, with Mazer leading them in his capsule. Their destination this time was a C-class harvester—an early vessel in the space-mining industry designed to latch on to small, near-Earth asteroids and pull them to a harvesting station where miners would pick them clean of iron ore and precious metals.

"Just like we practiced," Mazer said. "The cubes may be live, but nothing we do changes."

At the appropriate time, he launched from his capsule and touched down on the surface, locking his Nan-Ooze boots into place. Three small vid screens on the left side of his HUD showed him the helmet cams of his teammates, who touched down nearby.

The team moved swiftly, covering each other as they anchored their cubes to the hull. There would be no augmented-reality battle this time. This was get in and detonate.

Mazer felt tense as he withdrew from the detonation zone and launched upward with the others. Four lines of Nan-Ooze stretched as the team shot away from the ship. Then the skinnywires snapped taut as they reached the maximum height.

"Cubes align," Mazer said, giving the order for the activated cubes to recognize each other, the last step before deploying the weapon.

To Mazer's horror, however, only three of the four cubes emitted a green go light.

"Cubes align," Mazer repeated.

Nothing changed. One cube was nonresponsive.

Mazer opened a radio frequency. "Control, this is Captain Rackham. We have a faulty cube here. Request permission to abort test, over."

The technician's voice crackled back over the radio. "Captain, this is Control. Your request is denied. Proceed to contingency Beta. Over."

Mazer frowned, furious, then he pushed his frustration aside and refocused himself.

There was a chance that one of the four team members would be killed in action or lost in transit, or that a cube would somehow prove defective, so a contingency had been created in the mission plan. The three remaining cubes would form a single triangle instead of four overlapping triangles. The tidal forces wouldn't be as strong, and the resultant breach may not be as large, but the hope was that the team could still penetrate the hull and fulfill the mission.

Mazer glanced at the others. "Cubes, engage contingency Beta. Authorization Captain Rackham."

The visual on his HUD told him the three cubes had realigned and were ready.

"Deploy," said Mazer.

A force punched through the steel-reinforced hull as if it were thin aluminum, ripping jagged sections of the hull inward and sending cracks in every direction, as if the entire ship were about to crumble. A half second later the ship rocked to one side as the center of the breach widened unevenly, consuming one cube of the GD and then another, ripping, tearing, caving inward. Mazer spun, yanked to the right by his tether, slamming into someone, he didn't know who.

A scream of pain in his earpiece. Shrapnel flew around him, whizzing by his visor. He spun, disoriented, twisted in his tether line or maybe someone else's, then he slammed into the side of the ship and bounced off, arms flailing, pain shooting up his shoulder, the ship vibrating for an instant beneath him.

And then the vibrating stopped.

As quickly as it had begun, the violence on the ship's surface ceased. Cracks froze in place, no longer extending, and the hole in the side ceased bending inward.

Mazer, however, didn't stop. He was still in motion, spinning to his left, his tether further tangling with someone else's.

He reached down, trying to orient himself, and grabbed the tether at his ankle, his body in a ball. Then he struck the side of the ship again and grabbed at a crevice in the hull. The act was instinctual, and for a terrifying instant he thought the jagged edge might rip his suit. But no, the material held.

"I'm hit," Shambhani said, his voice heavy with pain. "Reel in."

Mazer saw him to his left. Sham was crumpled in a ball as his tether reeled him in. Mazer got his own feet under him and stood, his equilibrium still unsteady, the ship drifting slowly to one side beneath him, causing the canvas of stars around him to shift disorientingly to one side.

Mazer reached Sham just as Sham reached the surface. A piece of shrapnel had sliced through Sham's calf, leaving a gaping hole in his suit. The wound was open and purpling but spilling no blood. The suit's self-sealing mechanism had saved Sham's life by abandoning his leg from the knee down. Kaufman and Rimas gathered around him as Mazer shouted orders over the radio for an emergency EVAC crew.

By the time the medic ship arrived and pulled them all inside, Sham's leg had turned black, and his breathing was shallow. The medics cut his suit free and began working on him at once, but Mazer knew that there was little chance of saving the leg. They docked at the space station, and Mazer followed the stretcher to the medical wing. Nurses turned him away at the operating room and told him he was not allowed to wait here. They would contact him once there was news.

Mazer hovered there in the corridor for a moment until he realized he was still in his suit. He looked a mess.

He left and showered. By the time he was back in uniform a message on his wrist pad informed him that Shambhani had lost his leg and was now in recovery. He was not allowed any visitors.

Mazer went straight to Colonel Vaganov's office. The room was empty, but he saw Vaganov in the adjacent conference room through the large glass windows. Vaganov was facing an Asian woman Mazer didn't recognize. A civilian, by the look of her. Business suit, formal demeanor.

Mazer couldn't hear their conversation, but the woman seemed to be the one directing affairs. After several minutes Vaganov nodded and then turned on the holotable and made a call. In moments the head of Ukko Jukes, the Hegemon of Earth, materialized in the holofield. A brief conversation followed. At one point Vaganov played a series of vids in the holofield for Ukko. Each one showed a different breach team conducting a test with the GD on a different target. The cubes were all live and successfully ripped holes in the hulls. Mazer noticed that in every test, all four cubes were lit and operative.

The last vid was of Mazer's team. Vaganov paused the vid on a close-up shot of the four cubes in place, with only three lit and ready to fire. Then he played the rest of the vid, which was edited. It cut back and forth between various cameras in a way that minimized the violence of the explosion. The concluding shot was of the hole in the side of the ship. Shambhani never made an appearance. No emergency EVAC. No rescue. No wounded leg.

The Hegemon nodded his approval, spoke briefly, and then ended the call.

Mazer watched as Vaganov and the woman shared a celebratory handshake. Then Vaganov escorted her out. They found Mazer in the corridor and Vaganov looked surprised. "Captain Rackham, the man of the moment. I present to you—"

"Hea Woo Han," said the woman, offering her hand. "You did excellent work today, Captain. Thank you."

"Ms. Woo Han is the director of research and development at Gungsu Industries," Vaganov said.

Mazer understood. Gungsu was the Korean defense contractor that had designed the gravity disruptor. In the past few years they had gone from being a relative unknown in the weapons industry to a major player in the market.

"Colonel Vaganov also shared with me your design for the nanoshield," said Woo Han. "We're intrigued. My engineers will want to discuss the project with you. A collaborative exploration of the tech is in order, I think, with you assisting our team as a WAMRED liaison. Colonel Vaganov can share with you our proposal."

Vaganov nodded. "Gladly." He turned to Mazer. "Wait in my office, Captain Rackham. After I escort Ms. Woo Han back to her ship, we'll discuss the matter in detail."

Everything was clear now. Vaganov was being deferential to a defense contractor instead of the other way around. Gungsu had him in their pocket. It made sense. Gungsu was a company of engineers. They didn't know how to navigate the military bureaucracy. They needed commanders with influence who could put tech on the fast track to approval, who could help them penetrate the red tape and beat out competitors.

Vaganov had come from Acquisitions. Had he begun his relationship with Gungsu then? That might explain Gungsu's rapid ascent in the industry. The very man writing the checks was an ally.

What had they promised Vaganov? Mazer wondered. Not direct payments, of course. That would be too risky, too easy to uncover.

No, it would be some other method of compensation. A promised position on the Gungsu board when the war was over, perhaps, with a generous salary and a role as a consultant. It wasn't an uncommon practice. Retired brass often took up positions at the big players. Maybe Vaganov had simply been given the offer in advance.

"The presentation went very well," Vaganov said upon returning. "The Hegemony was grateful. I expressed your concerns about the GD to Gungsu, and they found all of your complaints legitimate. They want to address every issue and make the system as safe as possible. Woo Han's offer to you to work as a liaison is a real one, by the way. It has my approval. You can assist with the GD and the development of the nanoshield."

"The idea for the nanoshield wasn't mine," said Mazer. "It was Corporal Shambhani's."

"Yes yes, he'll get full credit in the report, I'm sure," said Vaganov.

"Corporal Shambhani is the one who lost his leg because of shrapnel today, sir."

"I haven't seen the medical report," said Vaganov, "but I'll take your word for it. If his idea works, then his contribution will continue even after he's given his medical discharge. Unless he opts to stay in. We need men with ideas."

Colonel Vaganov put a hand on Mazer's shoulder. "Don't be too hard on yourself, Captain. You know as well as I do that training accidents are par for the course. We do our best to avoid them, but we are in the business of handling weapons of war. Accidents will happen."

Yes, thought Mazer. How deft of you to deflect blame from yourself by passing it to me.

What was the GD contract worth, Mazer wondered? Four billion credits? Five? Buying a colonel in Acquisitions and then helping place him in command of WAMRED would cost far less.

"Gungsu must be grateful for your guidance," Mazer said.

Colonel Vaganov dismissed the thought with a flick of his wrist. "We're talking about you now, Captain. Opportunities like this don't come often in the IF. You won't see any bump in pay, but it will pay off in the long run."

I'm sure it will, thought Mazer.

"There are other perks as well," said Vaganov. "You'll have to frequent Gungsu's base of operations on Luna, which would allow you to visit your wife occasionally. That would make her happy, I bet."

"It would," said Mazer.

"Good. I'll have someone prepare the paperwork."

He started for the door.

"The defective cube," said Mazer.

Vaganov stopped, turned back.

"It was deliberate," said Mazer.

He should have realized it before now. The Hegemony would demand that all potential applications be tested, which meant the colonel had to test the single-triangle formation. Yet he also needed that test to succeed. So he had given working cubes to the other teams and the faulty cube to the one team most likely to succeed despite the setback.

"It was data the Hegemony required," said Vaganov. "If they were going to go with the GD, we needed to prove it versatile and combat ready."

"If?" Mazer said. "Meaning it wasn't tech the Hegemony asked for. They asked for something to put the world's mind at ease, and you gave them a recommendation on what that tech should be?"

"I fail to see your point," said Vaganov.

"You gave them the gravity disruptor," said Mazer. "Out of all the proposed tech, you gave them the one that wasn't ready to showcase."

Vaganov's expression darkened. "Are you questioning my judgment?"

"I'm questioning the motivation," said Mazer. "There are dozens of projects in development here from other defense contractors. Why Gungsu? Why the GD?"

"My motivations?" said Vaganov. "Perhaps you've forgotten, Captain, but there is a fleet of Formics heading this way with more firepower than we've cooked up in our worst nightmares. How many marines and pilots will we lose if we fail to take out just one of those warships? A thousand? Ten thousand? A man's leg is an acceptable attrition rate. You may not like that math, but such is the arithmetic of war. Be grateful one leg is all we lost."

It was a baseless argument. The GDs wouldn't work against the warships. Vaganov had even agreed to that fact. The man was clearly abandoning logic in pursuit of another agenda. He simply wanted to shut Mazer up.

Don't push him too far, Mazer thought, not before you've confirmed your suspicions.

"You'll forgive me," said Mazer, bowing his head slightly. "My emotions are raw, sir, and I forgot my place. Shambhani is a dear friend, and I'm taking his loss too personally. I apologize for speaking out of turn."

Vaganov visibly relaxed. "I understand. It is an unfortunate loss."

"I don't think it's wise to take the nanoshield to Gungsu, though," said Mazer. "Their track record in nanotech is not nearly as good as others. The nanoshield would be better off in the hands of Juke Limited or Galaxy Defense, I think."

Vaganov looked amused, as if he had just heard the mindless prattle of a child. "Leave that to me, Mazer. I was in Acquisitions. I have a good sense of a company's capabilities."

"I don't doubt it, sir," said Mazer, "but Shambhani, when he filed for the patent, explicitly stated that he wouldn't want Gungsu developing this. I think he'll object."

Vaganov's face fell. "Well, Shambhani has no say in the matter, whether he filed for a patent or not. He is an employee of the IF, and therefore we hold all intellectual property rights. He's a fool to think otherwise. Gungsu has the project, and with Gungsu it will remain."

It was all the confirmation Mazer needed.

"You will forgive me, sir," he said, "but I cannot accept a liaison position with Gungsu."

Vaganov's anger returned. "This isn't open for discussion, Mazer. I'm not making an offer for your consideration. Gungsu insists on this."

"With all due respect," said Mazer. "I am not beholden to a corporation, sir. No soldier is."

The subtext was obvious, and for a moment, neither man spoke. In the silence Mazer could see the wheels in Vaganov's mind spinning, wheels that seemed to say, "He knows."

Vaganov brushed an invisible speck of dust off his sleeve, his demeanor suddenly relaxed. "You surprise me, Captain. I thought someone as smart as you would know how the military works."

Vaganov pressed a button on his wrist pad, and one of his lieutenants entered the room.

"Sir?" the lieutenant said.

"Call two MPs to take Captain Rackham here into custody on charges of failure to obey a lawful order and gross negligence in the line of duty, resulting in a member of his team to be needlessly wounded."

"Yes, sir," said the lieutenant and exited.

"I submitted a formal objection," said Mazer. Which was to say: I won't be the one who bears responsibility.

Vaganov looked perplexed. "Objection? I received no such document."

The implication was clear. Any record of Mazer's objection no longer existed.

"We have vids of the operation, though," said Vaganov. "I'm sure you'll be exonerated. Eventually."

It didn't matter, Mazer knew. Even if he was acquitted, a

court-martial would taint him. He'd end up on a supply ship in the Belt with a mop in his hand. He had pushed Vaganov too far. He had dug around the root to uncover the truth and dug himself a hole in the process.

*I should have left it alone,* he thought.

But no. Shambhani deserved better. The marines who would die in the capsules once the war began deserved better. Kim and every free citizen of Earth who believed the IF would protect them deserved better.

The MPs arrived and were civil, almost apologetic. Mazer knew them both. They were good soldiers. Once they were certain Mazer had no weapons, they confiscated his wrist pad and then confined him to private quarters where he was to remain until being transported to Luna for his court-martial. He would never see his team again.

*We're going to lose,* Mazer thought. *If men like Vaganov lead us, Earth will fall and Kim will die.*

*I can't let that happen. There has to be another way, despite the corruption and the blind incompetence. The IF may be a lost cause, but the war doesn't have to be.*

# CHAPTER 4

# Victor

To: vico.delgado@freebeltmail.net
From: notoccamsrazor@stayanonymous.net
Subject: Tunnel cart

Victor,

I received your 3D model for the tunnel carts. A simple but useful device. I'm surprised we haven't seen more tech designed to help marines move quickly through a Formic ship. I realize now that so much emphasis has been placed on getting us to the ships and breaching their hulls, that too little consideration has been given to how we'll proceed once we're inside.

I have a few concerns, mostly centered on how the marines will get into and out of your tunnel cart. I scribbled a few notes on the model (see attachment). Basically, the shoulder and crotch straps seem secure, but is there another system that would allow the marine to detach himself faster? What you have works, but in a combat situation, it could prove to be a death trap. A marine may need to abandon the cart in a hurry to assume a defensive position or to maneuver through a difficult opening. A quick-release latch perhaps. Something to allow instant mobility outside the ordinary Formic interior tunnel system.

Or another thought: Could your cart be changed to a kind of harness a marine could wear that would maintain his position in the middle of the tunnel and allow low-friction movement, as your cart does? Perhaps using extensions that reach above and below him? I foresee difficulties in maintaining balance, but you're the only human engineer with real experience, both in zero G and in moving around inside a Formic ship. Give it some thought, anyway. If the tunnel cart really is the only possible design, so be it.

My CO has ordered me not to publish any more designs even on the secure IF nets, so for now I am unable to share this with others. Also I will likely be leaving WAMRED to face a court-martial. Long story. Suffice it to say, problems persist.

But fret not. Once you're finished, we'll find another way to get this into the hands of marines. Even if I'm no longer with the International Fleet. We both know there are back channels that can get an essential design past the red tape and into production.

Old Soldier

—*Mazer Rackham: Selected Correspondence,* International Fleet Archives, CentCom, Luna

Victor opened the hatch to the ship's engine room, and black smoke billowed out into his face, stinging his eyes and filling his nostrils with hot acrid fumes. He coughed into the crook of his arm and pulled a bandana from his pocket to shield his mouth and nose. The flashing alert on his wrist pad informed him that the fire inside the engine room had been extinguished. The foam pellets he had installed last year had done their duty well, inflating and popping and smothering the flames with white, sticky extinguishing foam.

Victor felt some relief at that news, but he was hardly at ease now. How far were they from the nearest depot? Four months? Five? If the fire or smoke had damaged life support, the family could be in serious trouble.

Magoosa flew up beside him and caught a handhold to stop himself, his eyes wide with panic. "Fire?"

Victor kept his voice calm. Magoosa was a good apprentice, but to frighten the Somali boy might lead to mistakes. "The fire is out, Goos. But we need to act quickly to ventilate the engine room. Fly around to the other side and open the far hatch to let the smoke out."

"But smoke will get in the corridor."

"Better here than in the engine room where the smoke will gum up the systems. Now go."

Magoosa nodded then launched down the side corridor, coughing as he went.

Victor lowered his goggles over his eyes, called up the ship's main computer on his HUD, and blinked a few commands to turn on the ventilators inside the engine room. Then he sealed off this corridor before the smoke dissipated throughout the ship. Smoke, he knew, was a slow assassin. It would snake its way into circuits and components and leave a black tacky residue that collected dust and gunk over time. Eventually that would cause the processors to overheat, which would lead to all kinds of breakdowns.

Victor took a deep breath and pulled his body up through the hatch and into the smoke.

The engine room was centrally located on the ship, with

two main corridors wrapping around it on either side. All of the ship's life-support systems were housed here: oxygen generation, HVAC, water purification—all of it stacked on top of each other with narrow gaps between each large piece of hardware. Moving from one end of the room to the other required a bit of acrobatic maneuvering, twisting and bending the body through zero G, like a snake wiggling its way through a three-dimensional maze.

Bad design, as far as Victor was concerned. Positioning all the life-support systems in the center of the ship protected them from collision threats, but putting them all together had dangerous drawbacks as well. If one caught fire they could all go up. And out here in the Kuiper Belt, where free-miner families were so far apart that rescue was rarely an option, even a small fire could be catastrophic.

I should have rearranged all this when I had the chance, Victor thought.

When he had joined the crew two years ago, he had brought with him all the tools and equipment necessary to convert the Gagak from a salvage ship into an asteroid mining vessel. Drills, suits, saws, quickships. All new tech, all top grade. The conversion hadn't been easy. A salvage ship was basically a thin-hulled box with a propulsion system—light and fast and easily maneuverable. A mining ship was the opposite: thick and indestructible so it could withstand the torque and abuse the heavy equipment would inflict when the ship anchored to an asteroid and dug out a mine.

For the Gagak, that meant reinforcing existing beams, building new ones, adding new trusses, welding more shield plates to the hull—doing everything possible to strengthen the ship's structural integrity. Essentially rebuilding the vessel from the inside out. Victor had wanted to rearrange the life-support systems at that time and spread them around the ship. But Arjuna—the Somali captain and Magoosa's father—

had resisted the idea, not wanting to risk damaging equipment by moving it.

Victor hadn't pushed the issue. He was the newcomer at the time, the outsider. He was already changing the family's livelihood by converting their ship and pushing them out into the Kuiper Belt. How much more demanding could he be? It was Arjuna's ship, not Victor's. So he had remained cooperative and compromising and dropped the issue. That had been a mistake.

Victor grabbed a pipe and pulled himself forward, relieved that the pipe was not hot to the touch. That was a good sign. The heat from the fire hadn't reached this far. That gave him a flicker of hope.

That hope faded as soon as he reached the center of the room where the fire had obviously started. It was the oxygen extractor. The metal casing around it was hot and streaked with scorch marks, its paint charred and bubbly at the edges.

Victor removed the anchor screws and pulled the casing free, exposing the oxygen extractor's inner components. The harsh scent of burned plastic and fried components almost made him gag.

"Can you fix it?" Magoosa asked. He had arrived to Victor's left, covering his mouth with an emergency oxygen mask.

"The main processor is melted," said Victor. "So is all the wiring. It's fried." He touched one of the boards with the tip of his screwdriver, and the piece folded inward, the plastic now gooey and pliable. "Besides, everything's covered in foam. There's no salvaging this."

"But you can fix it, right?" said Magoosa. "That's the oxygen extractor. If we don't have that, we don't breathe."

"We have several months of reserve oxygen in the tanks," Victor said. "We'll rely on that for now while we scrounge up some replacement parts."

"Replacements from where?" said Magoosa. "We're months away from the nearest depot."

"We'll make the parts," said Victor.

Shipbuilders knew that crews would have breakdowns, so the engineers had standardized a lot of the original parts. The processor from the washing machine might be similar or even identical to the processor here. Victor would simply have to remove it from the washing machine, make a mold, and print a duplicate.

"So we *can* fix it," Magoosa said.

"Probably," said Victor. "Maybe. Right now our priority is to get rid of the smoke. Let's pull the air purifiers from the workshop and set them up in the corridor. Then we'll come back in here with the vacs and clean out the air vents."

They left the engine room and found a crowd of people gathered in the corridor, where the smoke had thinned into a thin murky haze. Everyone coughed and shouted questions at once.

"Quiet!" a voice said over the din. "Give the man some room."

The crowd turned and saw that Arjuna, the captain, had arrived from the helm and was hovering at the other end of the corridor. Arjuna was a physically imposing sight. Most of the Somali crewmen were thin and waiflike, but Arjuna was wide in the chest and arms, with a voice that demanded obedience. "This corridor needs to be ventilated. Get the children out of here."

Several children were watching from behind the bulkheads. Some were from Victor's Venezuelan family, but most were children of the Somali crew.

The crowd moved away, shooing the children toward the far hatch. Magoosa left to fetch the air purifiers, and eventually Victor and Arjuna were alone.

"What happened?" asked Arjuna.

Victor told him about the fire. "I may be able to fix the OE if I can find and make the right parts. I'm not sure yet."

"You need to be sure, Vico. Because there are only two options here. We either stay the course toward the asteroid and count on you to fix this, or we change course now, make for a depot, and pray that our oxygen reserves get us there."

"I haven't done the calculations," said Victor, "but if we have enough surplus oxygen in the reserve tanks to give us a little leeway, I'd ask that you let me try to fix this before we decide. We'd use a lot fuel decelerating and changing course, which means once we reached the depot, we'd have to *buy* fuel to replace what we've used. That could be as much as a quarter of our yearly income. But if we can reach the asteroid, we can extract the fuel from the ice for free once we separate the hydrogen and oxygen."

"I'm aware of the economics, Vico. My concern is the safety of this crew. There are nearly one hundred people on this ship, forty-three of whom are children. If we all asphyxiate for lack of oxygen, it won't matter how much money we've saved or earned. Likewise, if we reach the asteroid with a broken oxygen extractor, it won't matter how much ice we harvest since we won't be able to use it."

"I'll fix the OE," said Victor.

"You're sure?"

"Seventy percent sure. I won't know for certain until I get in there and try to rebuild it. Give me forty-eight hours. If I can't fix everything by then, we head for the depot."

Arjuna glanced toward the engine room. "I should have let you spread the life-support systems around the ship." He shook his head and sighed. "First Copernicus. Now this."

Victor shrugged. "This is an old ship. Pieces break down."

"We should have stayed in the Asteroid Belt and stuck with salvage," said Arjuna. "We were fine working salvage. I understood salvage. We had contacts, buyers, a system that worked. Now we're out here in a frozen wasteland, chipping away at ice and rock and getting ourselves killed."

"Let Magoosa and me fix this," said Victor. "I'll text you hourly updates."

Arjuna nodded then launched back down the corridor toward the helm.

Magoosa soon returned with the air purifiers, and Victor helped him set them up in the corridors. Then they cleaned the engine room with the minivacs.

"You think the Formics ever have problems like this?" Magoosa asked. "Fires and breakdowns and crazy repairs?"

"Probably," said Victor. "But much of their tech is mechanical. There's less electrical work, so less chance of fire."

"You think a Formic fighter would ever come after us?"

"Doubt it," said Victor. "There's no reason for Formics to come to this sector. There aren't any military targets out here. It's just a bunch of icy rocks. This is probably one of the safest places in the system. That's why your dad agreed to come out here. We're nowhere near the Formic fleet's current trajectory. If they come straight into system like the Formic scout ship did in the first war, they'll be far away from here and pass us by. The IF will confront them in the Asteroid Belt and annihilate them."

"Do you believe that?" Magoosa asked. "That we'll win?"

"We won last time," Victor said. If you can call forty million people dead and all of southeast China burned to a crisp a victory, he thought.

"This time will be different," said Magoosa. "We took on a single ship in the first war. This time we'll be taking on ten or more."

"It's going to be a challenge," Victor agreed. "But we have to believe in the IF or life gets rather hopeless."

"Are you going to enlist?" Magoosa asked.

"I'm not a soldier, Goos. I'm a mechanic."

"The IF needs mechanics. They need everyone. There's a

list on the nets of hundreds of jobs they hope to fill. Thousands maybe."

"They also need free miners to supply them with harvested iron and precious metals. We're doing our part right where we are."

Magoosa furrowed his brow. "But you fought in the first war. You practically *won* the first war. How can you turn your back on the IF now?"

"I'm not turning my back on anyone. I was never *in* the IF, Goos. I was just thrown in with a group of soldiers. Imala and I happened to be where we were needed, and we helped as best as we could. There was nothing more to it than that."

"It was more than that. Imala has told me stories. You helped create some of the tech that won us the war."

"Calling it tech is a little generous. We were throwing stuff together, doing the best we could with what we had available. No different than what you and I are doing right now."

"I see you sketching on your wrist pad sometimes. I see you drawing up ideas for tech. That's for the IF, right?"

"They're sketches, Goos. That's it. The IF has real engineers for that sort of thing. I'm just tinkering around."

"I bet you've designed all kinds of cool weapons."

"Actually, my sketches aren't weapons. That's not my area of expertise. I design tools that help marines do their jobs."

"Have you sent any ideas to the IF?"

Victor smiled. "The IF doesn't exactly have a suggestion box, Goos. But I do send my sketches to a friend. A marine Imala and I met during the war. He gives good feedback."

Magoosa nearly dropped his vacuum. "You know a marine?"

Victor chuckled. "His name's Mazer Rackham. You'd like him."

"What's he like? Big guy? Strong?"

"Actually he's on the short side. But he's Maori, so he was

born from a warrior culture. Smart, levelheaded, strategic. What I suspect the IF wants from every soldier."

"First chance I get I'm enlisting. You tell your marine friend to watch out for the Goos. I'm going to take down every bug myself."

"War is horrific, Goos. Whatever romantic idea you may have of fighting Formics is wrong. Believe me. War is no place you want to be."

"It's exactly where I want to be. We have an obligation to defend our planet and our species. Each of us has a duty."

"That sounds like the propaganda vids talking."

"You don't believe the vids? You don't think we have a duty?"

"We have a duty to defend ourselves, yes," Victor said, "but I also believe that soldiering should be left to trained soldiers."

"I *will* be a trained soldier. I can wield a weapon as well as anyone, I bet."

"You're fourteen, Goos. You won't get that chance for another four years."

"There are boys out there not much older than me who have lied about their age and gotten in fine. I've read about it in the forums. I could pass for eighteen soon. I'm tall enough."

"Chances of your father letting you go are nonexistent. Besides, we're months away from any recruiting station. You're stuck with us for the time being."

Magoosa frowned. "For the time being."

When they finished vacuuming, Victor called up the ship's schematics on his wrist pad, pausing at the various machines to dive inside them and analyze their components. The washing machine didn't have the right processor, but the oven had one that was similar.

The women working in the kitchen were not pleased by the news.

"You want to take the oven apart?" Ubax said. She was

Arjuna's second oldest wife and Magoosa's mother. She ran the kitchen with three other members of the crew, and they looked to be in the middle of baking something. Her English was better than most, but she had a thick Somali accent. She folded her arms and glared at Victor. "How am I supposed to cook without an oven, Vico?"

"I'll only need the processor for a few hours," Victor said. "So I can make a copy of it. Then I'll bring it back and reinstall it."

"And if you break the processor?" Ubax asked.

"Then we'll eat cold oatmeal for the next six months. How bad could that be?" He gave her his best smile, but she was not amused.

"We'll be careful," he said.

He and Magoosa removed the processor and carried it back to the workshop. They placed it in the scanning vat and began identifying which components they could print and which they'd have to find elsewhere.

They made good progress for several hours, and then Edimar entered the workshop and asked to speak to Victor in private. Victor could tell at once that something troubled his cousin. As the family spotter, Edimar was always the first person on board to know when danger was ahead. She worked alone in the ship's crow's nest deciphering data from the Eye—the ship's scanning computer that watched for possible collision threats. So if Edimar was uneasy, she had good reason.

Victor took her aside. "What is it, Mar?"

Edimar bit her lip and hesitated. She was eighteen now, a woman grown, but sometimes she seemed much younger.

Over the past few years, she had become a celebrity of sorts, for it was Edimar who had first spotted the Formic scout ship on its approach to Earth prior to the First Formic War when she was only fourteen. And then, after the war, while everyone on Earth was still celebrating mankind's victory, Edimar had detected the approaching Formic fleet and alerted the world of the coming second war. Now people who had really good eyesight were said to have "Edimar Eyes." Or if something was uncovered that had long been in plain sight and yet ignored, it was called the "Edimar Effect."

Edimar had shrugged off the attention, always turning down interview requests when they had come.

"You look worried," said Victor.

"More like confused," Edimar said. "It's about 2030CT."

Asteroid 2030CT was the ship's current destination. It was a water-ice asteroid with a likely composition of iron, nickel, and precious metals. It wasn't a particularly interesting rock. Just under two kilometers long. Slightly atypical orbit. No different than billions of others.

"What about it?" said Victor.

"Well, it's not reflecting light properly anymore. It's dark. Darker than it's ever been on the cameras. And it happened within the last few weeks. The filters are fine. I checked them all. The rock is simply dimmer. Any idea why that might happen?"

Victor considered for a moment. "Your guess is as good as mine. Something obstructing our view, maybe? Space dust?"

"Maybe," she said. "But the dimness has persisted. If it were small particles, you would think they would have dissipated by now."

"Okay, well, we're in the Kuiper Belt," Victor said. "So this rock is probably covered in a layer of ice and frozen ammonia. Maybe it collided with something, and ice broke off. So more of the rock is exposed and less light is reflected."

"I thought of that. But I would have seen another object, and a collision that strong would have knocked it off its orbit."

"Maybe it's a snowball," said Victor.

Snowballs were frozen wads of gravel held together by ice. Unlike traditional asteroids, which were one solid hunk of rock, snowballs shattered into pieces the instant you started digging.

"Are you sure the asteroid is unoccupied?" said Victor. "Maybe there's a family there digging at it and breaking it up. If it's smaller, it would certainly reflect less light."

"No one's there. I've watched it for two months. There haven't been any cinders in or out."

A cinder was a heat signature, usually from a ship's propulsion system. They were typically visible in the infrared spectrum, even from a considerable distance, especially out here where there was so much open space. Cinders were like big flashing signs that alerted everyone remotely close that you were in the neighborhood.

Victor shrugged. "I'm stumped, Mar. Have you talked to Arjuna?"

"I wanted to talk to you first, in case I'm missing something obvious."

"You know the equipment, Mar. I don't. If you trust it, if you checked the filters and everything seems to be working, I'd talk to Arjuna."

She hesitated. "He won't like that."

"He needs to know. Arjuna may want to send a probe ahead or reconsider our approach as a precaution."

She nodded. "Right. I'll talk to him."

She left. Victor returned to work, but the idea of an asteroid growing dimmer stuck with him. It didn't make sense. Was the International Fleet testing a new weapon? Something powerful enough to chip away at an asteroid piece by piece? That seemed plausible. A lot of corporates tested new tech in the Kuiper Belt, far from the prying eyes of competitors. Perhaps the IF was doing the same.

When the scanner was done, Victor returned the processor to the oven.

He and Magoosa worked in the engine room well into their sleep shift. There were more boards to print and more components to borrow from elsewhere on the ship—and they had to alter the design of the OE slightly to fit what they had available—but finally, after nearly twenty hours, Victor finished soldering and turned the OE back on. It hummed quietly and woke Magoosa, who had fallen asleep nearby.

Magoosa patted Victor on the back. "You see? This is what the IF needs. Mechanics who can work miracles. Engineers who have the skills."

Victor smiled. "Go to bed, Goos. It's late. We've neglected all our other repairs. Tomorrow we've got a backlog waiting for us."

But Magoosa's words stayed with him long after the boy had left and all was quiet. Was Victor right not to enlist? Did he have a duty with the Fleet?

He pulled out his wrist pad and checked his messages, pleased to see an e-mail from Mazer. He read it, surprised to hear that Mazer was being court-martialed. We're doomed, Victor thought. If the leadership of the IF are the type that would imprison their best asset, the human race didn't have a prayer.

There was an attachment. Mazer had made notes on Victor's newest design. Victor read through the notes and agreed with them all. The hook-and-release mechanism *was* too slow. He would need to rethink that. Or better yet, perhaps it was time to scrap this design and start anew.

He drew three more sketches of new designs, but by the end of the third he was fighting back sleep. He rubbed at his eyes and yawned.

"It's a lot more comfortable in the barracks," a voice said.

Victor looked up, startled. Imala was drifting up between two of the water storage tanks to his right, snaking her way into the center of the engine room.

"You've got the OE working," she said. "Nice to know we

won't die. I never doubted you." She drifted over to where he had stretched out and snuggled up next to him.

He put an arm around her and pulled her close. She was wearing soft fleece pajamas and smelled of fresh detergent. Her long, black Apache hair was braided into a ponytail that floated behind her. Victor gently lifted her chin and studied her face. Some people lost their beauty up close, where every minor imperfection became painfully obvious. But not Imala.

She had believed him about the invasion when everyone else thought him delusional. She had stood by him, fought with him, saved his life. And now she loved him. Even now, after several years together, he still couldn't wrap his head around the notion. Him. Ordinary, plain-looking him. It left him feeling inadequate sometimes, even slightly guilty, as if he were committing some great injustice by asking her to be his wife, robbing her of the actual person she deserved.

Yet he had asked her nonetheless. He couldn't imagine himself ever being happy otherwise. They had not yet set a date, but there wouldn't be much to prepare when they did. They would probably wed in the cargo bay.

"You're staring at me, Victor Delgado."

"Admiring."

"It's still staring."

She took his wrist pad and flipped through the sketches. "What's this?"

"Sketches for Mazer. Some good ideas, some bad ideas. Mostly bad ideas."

"They all look brilliant to me."

"You're biased."

"How is Mazer?"

"He's being court-martialed."

She looked at him, startled. "Why?"

Victor shrugged. "Because they're more worried about saving their careers than the human race. Because they feel threatened by people smarter than themselves. Because they despise those who have talents they don't also possess. Take your pick."

Imala sighed in exasperation. "Why is it that the people who should be in authority are usually the people who don't want it, while the people who hold authority are usually the two-faced schemers who've stepped on people's backs to get it?"

Victor was quiet a moment. "Did we make the right decision, Imala? Coming out here to reunite with my family?"

She broke away from him and studied his face. "Why do you say that? You love your family."

"Yes, but this isn't really my family anymore. Or at least it's not the family I left before the war."

"We knew that when we came, Vico. When Arjuna took in your mother and your aunts and all their children, this became a new family. It's not the one you grew up with, but it's a family all the same. They accepted us on sight even though the ship was already full, they've treated me like one of their own. If anyone should feel like an outsider here it's me. I'm not related to anyone."

"Not yet," Victor said with a smile.

"Not yet," she agreed.

Victor's smile waned. "I know you're right. But is this where we *should* be?"

"Why are you even asking this?" she said. "Is this about Copernicus? Vico, you're the one who said we weren't going to get into this war, that it was someone else's turn to fight this time."

"I know I said that. And I still believe that. But I look at Mazer and I think about the IF and all the bureaucracy and all the obstacles they're imposing on us, even before the Formics get here, and I think, how can I just float here and let all of that happen?"

"You can't fight the bureaucracy, Vico. I tried fighting it

at the Lunar Trade Department, and it got me nowhere. The IF is a thousand times bigger and a thousand times more powerful, with all of the resources of the world at its disposal. That's not a fight you can win."

"I'm not suggesting that I take on the International Fleet, Imala. I'm merely asking the question: Are we doing the most good here? You should have heard Goos today. He's dead set on enlisting. I told him to erase the idea from his mind and to leave the fighting to the soldiers, but I felt like a hypocrite saying so, as if I were trying to convince myself."

"Goos is fourteen," said Imala. "He can't enlist anyway."

Victor waved a hand. "Yes, obviously. That's not the point."

"Then what is?"

"The point is, maybe he's right. The IF needs mechanics as much as it needs pilots and soldiers and doctors."

"Your family needs a mechanic, Vico. Who would have fixed the OE if you hadn't been here? Goos? No one on this ship can do what you do."

"We don't have any more mechanics because they all enlisted with the other crewmen who've already signed up," said Victor. "Fifteen men from this crew, Imala. Do you know how I felt when they left? Did you see the look of pride in Arjuna's eyes?"

She made a face. "Is that what this is about? Earning Arjuna's respect? Having him feel *proud* of you?"

"Of course not," said Victor. "But when I think of Arjuna, I think of your father, and I imagine him—"

"My father?" said Imala, recoiling at the word. "What does he have to do with this?"

"He doesn't approve of me, Imala. He thinks I'm some ignorant rockhead who's stolen his daughter away from the comforts and safety of Earth. Me being here on this ship and not joining up is just one more reason in his mind why I'm not good enough for you. He probably thinks I'm a coward."

She laughed. It wasn't the reaction he was expecting, and it rather annoyed him. He could feel his face getting hot.

"Why is that funny?" he said.

"Because you're so bullheaded sometimes," she said. "We've talked about this. There's no way my father thinks you're a coward. You took on the whole Formic army, you went into the belly of the beast, right to the heart of the scout ship. Alone. Without any weapons. But even if you hadn't done any of that, it wouldn't matter one iota anyway because I don't care what my father thinks."

"Yes, well I do," said Victor.

"And you think enlisting is going to change his opinion of you?" said Imala. "You're not Apache, Vico. That's the issue. That's what my father cares about, me staying in the tribe, continuing the line, the traditions, the culture, having little Apache grandchildren look to him as chief. You can't alter your DNA and meet that expectation, so get over it. You are what you are."

"Fine. But I don't like that you have to choose between me and your family."

"That's what people do when they get married, Vico. They fly the coop. They leave their parents. My parents will always love me. That isn't going to change, even with you at my side. My father doesn't *know* you. With time he will, he'll see in you what I see, and he'll realize why I love you."

"But that's not what this is about," said Imala. "Or at least not completely. This is about you. You're afraid."

"Afraid?" said Victor. "Of what?"

"That we'll lose the war," said Imala, "that the Formics will win, that everything we did before to keep the world safe will be for naught and you'll have done nothing to prevent it. You felt the same way last time and it nagged at you and needled you and kept you awake at night until you were so uneasy that you threw yourself right into the middle of it. And I stood with you, even when it seemed ridiculous and insane and the most unsafe course of action possible. I went along and I supported you."

"You didn't just go along, Imala. You did as much as anyone else. We would have lost if not for you. Mazer says so, and he's right."

She was quiet a moment and then she shrugged. "All right. Then I'll enlist."

Victor blinked. For a moment he didn't know what to say. "You can't be serious."

"Why not? You said it yourself. The IF needs help in all fields. I'm sure that includes finance?"

"Finance?"

"Auditing, tracking, monitoring, what I did at the Lunar Trade Department before the war. The IF is currently moving more resources and cash into the Belt to shipbuilders than we've ever seen in the history of manufacturing. That's a massive logistical and financial undertaking. They need an army of people to manage that. The Fleet would probably take me in a hot second."

Victor stared at her. "Please tell me you're joking."

"You're needed here, Vico. You can't leave your family. I on the other hand am little more than a warm body here. Don't get me wrong, I love your family, but any of the crew can do what I do."

"That's not true," said Victor. "You're the one who's irreplaceable. You're the best negotiator on the ship. You've saved us tens of thousands of credits in supplies. You know how to work the markets. You built the economic model that will keep us afloat. You're an expert on tariffs and taxes and on building our credit. No one else on this ship knows how to do any of that."

"The model is built," said Imala. "It's all set up and will run itself. The contracts are in place. There's not much for me to do anymore. Sure I can bake bread with Ubax in the kitchen, but with the IF I could make a real contribution."

She was serious. He could see it in her expression. The idea had taken root in her mind, and she was already envisioning it playing out. He wouldn't shake her.

"You can't enlist, Imala. You'd be in danger. They'd put you in harm's way."

"Not necessarily. Auditing and finance is behind the scenes."

"Not if they put you on the supply lines," said Victor, "which is where you'd be most needed and useful. That means you'd be stationed on a ship or depot that would be a primary target."

"You're assuming Formics even know what a supply line is," said Imala, "or that they can recognize its military significance and identify which ships of ours constitute supply ships. You're the one who would be in harm's way if you enlisted. Mechanics would be needed on the front lines, right in the heat of battle as ships are damaged. If I enlist, we can still make a contribution, but in a way that will minimize risk."

*We* can make a contribution, she had said. We. He understood. She was offering to enlist so that he would feel like he was helping, giving of herself as a way of keeping him involved.

"No, Imala. You're not doing this. I'm not letting my wife go to war simply to appease the guilt I feel for not doing it myself."

She raised a finger. "First of all, I'm not your wife yet. Second, no one dictates my life but me, at least not until we're married, at which point we plot our path together. Third, I'm not being impulsive here. Losing Copernicus has bothered me, too. Ever since it happened, I've had the same nagging sense of unease that you've felt. The only difference is, I can do something about it, and you can't."

He couldn't believe they were having this conversation.

"Just like that?" he said. "You've decided to pick up and leave? How can you be so casual about this?"

"I'm not being casual," said Imala. "I'm being sensible and talking plainly. You brought it up, and the more we discuss it, the more right it feels, only not as you suggested. I wouldn't leave immediately. I can't. I'd have to find passage to a recruiting station once we reach a depot. We'll still get married obviously. But we'll do it after."

She sounded so final, so decided. How had this happened? His future had flipped on its head in an instant. And it was entirely his fault.

"I should have married you a year ago," he said. She started to interrupt, but he pushed on. "No, I should have. We wouldn't be having this conversation if I had. But I couldn't go through with it. I was too . . ."

"Uncertain?"

"Embarrassed."

She scoffed. "Of what?"

"Of me, Imala. Of this." He gestured at the room again. "I have nothing to offer you."

"What do you think I want?" she said. "My own luxury cruiser? My own crew? That's not why I came here, Vico."

"I know. But let's face it, if you marry me, you're marrying down." She started to object, but he held up a hand. "I'm not fishing for validation, Imala. I'm simply stating the truth. You gave up everything to come here—a career, your family, a life on Luna. And for what? To live in a cage in the Kuiper Belt? No wonder you want to enlist. This place has to be suffocating."

She looked offended. "Is that what you think? That I'm seizing an opportunity to run away?"

"Are you?" The words came out of him before he had even considered them, and he regretted them immediately.

She looked hurt.

"I didn't mean that," he said. He wanted to unsay the words, unsay everything, start the conversation from the beginning and take it in an entirely different direction. How had he crashed this so badly?

"I'm sorry you feel that way," she said finally.

"I don't," he said. And it was true. He knew Imala loved him.

And yet why was she so willing to go? Why had she taken to the idea so quickly? Did she want an out and not even fully realize it herself? Was her subconscious desire to get out of the relationship jumping at the opportunity? He wanted to discuss it further, but she was already moving for the exit.

"You're leaving?" he said.

"I'm tired, Vico."

He thought she would say more, but she didn't. She slid past the water tanks and disappeared.

He wanted to rush after her and apologize. She had caught him off guard. Her response had surprised him. Let's discuss this.

Yet he knew further conversations wouldn't change her. They would discuss it of course, but this new direction was locked in her mind now. It wasn't obstinacy on her part; it was recognizing a right course of action and pursuing it without deviation, putting her own emotions aside for what she had determined was a greater good. It was one of the reasons why he loved her. She was fearless, decisive, strong.

He didn't move. The bigger part of him, the wounded part, kept him rooted right where he was. She was leaving him. She claimed they would still marry, but that would only happen if we won the war and if she still loved him when it was over. Both seemed unlikely. Even if we did win, which was a high improbability, war would change her, maybe change them both.

Five minutes ago, he had held her, their future clearly defined. Now there was a wedge pounded deeply between them.

No, not a wedge, a chasm, a vast empty space of his own making.

He wouldn't try to stop her, he realized. If this was what she felt compelled to do, and if he truly loved her, he should support her, as reckless and dangerous as it seemed. Because she was right. She *had* stood by him. When no one else would give his ideas any consideration, she had helped make them a reality. How could he do any less for her?

The hatch squeaked as it opened. Victor couldn't see it from where he was positioned, but he assumed that Imala had returned.

"Vico? You in there?"

Not Imala's voice. Edimar's.

"Up beside the oxygen extractor, Edimar."

He heard her enter and move through the maze of machines until she appeared.

"What are you doing up?" he asked.

"You weren't in the barracks, so I thought you might still be here. I know why the asteroid is reflecting less light. Arjuna gave me permission to send one of our probes ahead."

She shoved her wrist pad into his hands. There was a photo onscreen, taken from the probe. At first Victor didn't realize what he was looking at. There was a large spherical object in open space, built with thin filaments in a crisscross pattern, with thin membranes between each threadlike fiber. Like a balloon keeping its shape with a spherical skeleton of string.

"What is this?" he asked.

"That's 2030CT," Edimar said. "There's a shell or a balloon or some kind of thin structure built around the entire asteroid. And I think it's filled with air. I think it's oxygenated."

Victor stared. "I don't get it. Is this some secret IF outpost?"

"No, look at it from the other side." She swiped a finger across the screen. The second photo looked identical, except now there was something protruding from the center of the shell, as if the shell had been built around it. A large, rectangular, metal structure, intricately constructed, with a round thruster on the back.

"That's a propulsion system," Victor said.

"And not one built by the IF, either," Edimar said. "That's alien tech, Vico. Formics are at that rock."

# CHAPTER 5

# Lem

Critics of the Fleet argued that since Copernicus was destroyed without warning by a close-range attack, the IF never had accurate observations of the enemy to begin with. That sentiment quickly gained popularity, and confidence in the International Fleet began to decline. Sensing a shift in public opinion, the International Fleet attempted to reassert its position of strength by submitting a nine-hundred-page document to the Hegemony entitled *Logistical Demands of a Space-Based Defense*, which requested additional troops, shipbuilders, funds, and equipment. An increase in Hegemony taxes followed, leading to an overall economic decline. In many nations whose economies were already marginal—mainly in South Asia, Southeast Europe, and sub-Saharan Africa—economic pressures led to food rationing, rioting, and revolutionary guerrilla activity.

The scarcity of goods and the diminished federal budgets led ten additional nations to sign the Population Contract by the end of the year, leaving only six noncompliant nations worldwide, and international outrage at their noncompliance seemed to be heading toward war. Everyone knew that it was insane to make war among humans while the enemy approached; but it was also unbearable to the human instinct for fairness that some nations be allowed to continue to grow their populations, using resources needed by nations that were complying with the two-child rule.

—Demosthenes, *A History of the Formic Wars,* Vol. 3

Beneath the surface of Luna, in the corporate headquarters of Juke Limited, Lem Jukes sat before his executive team, trying hard to keep his composure. "Let me stop you right there, Serge," Lem said, speaking loud enough so that his voice carried to the back of the room, where a man in his mid-thirties was giving a presentation. Serge stopped speaking midsentence and froze, his arm outstretched, pointing at a chart of data in the holofield.

Lem forced a smile. "Am I to understand you correctly, Serge, that the European Ironworkers Union is threatening to strike yet again?"

Serge remained in his frozen position. "That's correct, Mr. Jukes."

"You can put your arm down, Serge."

The man did so.

Lem sighed. What I would give for elastic arms so I could reach across this room and shake the man. Do me a favor, Serge, Lem wanted to say, grow a spine. You may only be the assistant director of operations and thus a few ladder rungs down from everyone else in this room, but right now I need you to act like the COO. Because the *real* COO, the woman who *did* have a spine and who led us well, has taken a job with my father in the Hegemony, like so many other critical players in this company, leaving me with worms and nebbishes.

But Lem said none of that aloud. Instead he smiled politely, folded his hands, and said, "Let me get this straight. The EIU, the very people to whom we just granted very generous concessions, the people who are responsible for half a dozen ulcers in this room, are making new demands?"

Serge swallowed. "That's correct, Mr. Jukes."

"Well I find that humorous, don't you, Serge? That's a real barrel of laughs to me. Because these people have squeezed and squeezed and squeezed some more. There's no more water in the stone, Serge. The well is empty. But by all means, please, for the sake of continuing the joke, tell us all what their demands are this time. Nine months of paid vacation perhaps? Free health care for their favorite countries? A servant to wipe their noses when they get the sniffles perhaps?"

A few executives snickered. The butt kissers, Lem thought. The snakes who fawned over Lem and pretended to share his interests just to remain in his good graces. Lem would have sacked them all a long time ago if they were not so good at their jobs. The other executives, the ones who could read Lem well, were smart enough to stay quiet and stare at their laps.

The conference room was centrally located at the company's corporate headquarters, a vast underground tunnel system on Luna, just outside the city of Imbrium. Lem had recently removed the large maple conference table and replaced it and its chairs with an assortment of comfortable leather club chairs. The intent was to give his executive team a more relaxed environment for these kinds of meetings, but Lem was beginning to wonder if the change had had the opposite effect. Instead of being gathered as one at a single table, now every man and woman was an island, set apart from the others and feeling vulnerable.

Serge saw that no one was rushing to his aid and referred back to his notes. "Sir, most of their demands deal with us guaranteeing work to their union members. For example, they request that at least thirty percent of our iron workforce out beyond the orbit of Mars be members of the EIU."

Lem laughed and shook his head. "Unbelievable. You realize how many of these unions there are, I'm assuming."

"Yes, sir. Quite a few."

Lem ticked the names off on his fingers. "There's the Europeans. And the Middle Eastern union. And the North African union, the US union, the Australian union, the Brazilian union, the Argentine union, the German union because even though they're in Europe they need their own union for some reason." He turned to the man to his immediate left, Norja Ramdakan, the CFO. "Who am I forgetting, Norja?"

"The Canadians."

"Ah yes. How could we possibly forget those adorable Canadians? Do you see my problem, Serge? If we concede to the Europeans and promise them thirty percent of our workforce, what's every other union going to demand?"

Serge hesitated. "Thirty percent?"

"Wrong," said Lem. "They're going to demand thirty-*five* percent or thirty-seven. Because you see the Canadians will say that they have a stronger worth ethic and that it's therefore in our best interest financially to hire more Canadians. And the North Africans will remind us of their superior production output or their exceptional safety ratings or whatever, and we'd be fools not to give them forty-three percent. Do you see where this is heading, Serge? Do you see how this could pose a problem? All those numbers add up to more than one hundred percent. And it's not fiscally responsible to hire more employees than we need. That's not smart business. Wouldn't you agree?"

Serge nodded. "Absolutely, sir."

"So what are you going to tell them?" said Lem.

"Tell them?"

"The EIU, Serge. The insatiable union bosses who are asking for a guaranteed thirty percent. What message are you going to send?"

Serge opened his mouth to speak but Lem spoke first.

"You're going to tell them no, Serge. You're going to tell them that what they're proposing is irrational and offensive to the very idea of a united global defense. Does the IF insist that thirty percent of its marines be Europeans? No. That would be asinine. That would be dimwitted military thinking. You don't hire people because they're from Europe. You hire them because they can do a job. That's what you tell them, Serge. You tell them the only number we worry about in this company is one hundred percent. One hundred percent of our employees are competent and compliant and dedicated to our cause or they are no longer our employees, regardless of what flag they wave or language they speak or team they root for at the Olympics. And if the EIU doesn't like that response, you can kindly inform them that there are plenty of ironworkers in other unions who we can pull from to meet our production needs. It's that simple. And the next time the EIU tries to strong-arm us, you deal with it. You don't bring it to this meeting."

Serge's cheeks flushed. "Of course, Mr. Jukes. My mistake." He wiped a hand through the holofield to make his presentation disappear; then he returned to his seat and began taking notes on his tablet instead of meeting anyone's eyes.

I'm turning into my father, Lem thought. I'm becoming the corporate bully. All I need is a cigar and a permanent scowl.

The mood in the room had shifted. There was an air of stiff formality now. No one was cracking jokes or making light. It was cold hard business.

"Who's next?" Lem asked.

The other executives reluctantly stood one by one and reported on the status of the projects within their departments. Lem noticed how some of them edited themselves as they went along, skipping slides and holos, or dropping whole portions of their presentation, fearful perhaps of Lem's harsh examination. I've turned them *all* into spineless worms, he realized. I nailed one of them to the wall, and now they're all cowering. Great. Now even more of them will jump ship.

He had received six resignations in the past eight weeks, all from top executives. Four of them had been employees for decades, having helped Lem's father Ukko build the company from the ground up. They were all loyal, brilliant, reliable people. Father had lured a few of them over to the Hegemony. The others had been pulled away by competitors or other corporations hoping to repeat Juke Limited's recent success.

And the company was successful. Now more than ever. In the three years since Lem had taken over as CEO, Juke Limited had grown its asteroid-mining efforts and expanded its business into advanced weaponry, avionics, nanotechnology, and a dozen other divisions, to say nothing of its shipbuilding efforts for the International Fleet, which generated more revenue than all other divisions of the company combined. Earnings were through the roof. Stockholders were riding on air. But here, among the department heads, Lem could see cracks in the ivory tower.

"Can we stop here?" Lem said suddenly.

The executive giving his presentation froze.

"Have a seat, Koshimi," Lem said.

The executive did so.

"Why isn't anyone talking about Copernicus?" Lem asked.

The executives exchanged glances.

"We built the thing," Lem said. "We designed it. We may have given control to the Hegemony, but that satellite is our baby. And now it's space dust. Why aren't we discussing this?"

For a moment no one spoke. The executives looked at one another, and then Naiyoni, who headed the avionics department, sat forward. "What's there to discuss, Lem? The teams in R&D trolled through the data. They didn't find anything. There was no evidence of any object approaching the satellite. It just winked out."

"And no one is curious as to why?" Lem asked. "A satellite we designed to see everything did not see everything. That doesn't alarm anyone?"

"I think we're all alarmed, Mr. Jukes," Serge said. "The challenge is knowing what to do about it."

Lem sat back, surprised to see Serge speak up. Maybe the man had a spine after all. Let's see. "Go on," Lem said.

Serge continued. "The first question I asked myself when I heard the news, the first question we all likely asked ourselves was: Can we get another satellite in place to fill that vacancy? Can we set up another pair of eyes and get the Formic fleet back in our sights?"

Lem waved a dismissive hand. "Impossible. For lots of reasons. Copernicus was built over a decade ago. Its tech is woefully out of date. If we were to build a replacement, we would need to redesign it. That's a year or two of development at least. Then we would have to build it and take it out there to the edge of space. Another two years. The war will be raging by then. If not over."

Serge nodded. "My conclusion as well, sir. I then wondered if we could mobilize one of the existing Parallax satellites and perhaps move it toward the fleet."

"No can do," said Lem. "They're in fixed orbits and they can't move fast enough to get into any helpful position quick enough."

"That's what the engineers told me," said Serge.

So he had asked around, Lem thought. Interesting. At least someone was looking into it.

"There's the option of building a satellite out in the Kuiper Belt," said Naiyoni. "We have some stations there. They're not equipped for a job like that, and we would still need time for development and construction. I doubt it would be useful by the time it was complete. By then the Formics would be close enough to track and detect with existing scopes."

"Why didn't we develop a backup plan?" Lem asked. "Why didn't we prepare for this?"

The executives exchanged glances. No one spoke.

"That satellite was our most crucial piece of military hardware," Lem said. "Of everything we have ever built, that was the one thing we could not afford to lose. And we did nothing to safeguard it. We left it out there totally unprotected."

After an awkward silence Naiyoni said, "Lem, Copernicus was in IF hands. We built it, yes, but it was their baby now."

Lem scoffed. "So this is the IF's fault? They carry the blame? No, people. This is our fault. We *are* the damn IF. We may not wear their blue uniforms or salute each other in the hallway, but we are their largest supplier of damn near everything. We are their brains. We are their strength. We are the weapons they wield and the ships they fly. We don't wait until they tell us what they need. We tell them what they need. We show them the weakness in their defense. We stop them from making stupid mistakes. They're not engineers. They're soldiers. And a soldier is only as effective as his equipment. The IF isn't going to win this war, people. We are. Do you think the bozos over at Gungsu Industries are going to do that? Or Symguard? Or Galaxy Defense? Those guys are scrubs. Gungsu has marines flying around in coffins, for crying out loud, breaking hulls with dinky gravity manipulators. That's not going to do squat against a Formic hull, and yet the IF is buying.

"Do you see my point here? We cannot leave the war to the IF. If they run the show, we're dead. Half of their commanders are bureaucrats. The other half are too busy fighting each other. If the human race is going to exist five years from now, it's going to be because of the people in this room. Us. The IF may take all the credit. The world may make them the heroes. But the real genius has to come from us. If we do not absolutely believe that in our core, every single one of us, then we are toast. Not just this company, but our species."

No one spoke or moved.

Lem sat back, waited. "Does no one have anything else to say?"

No one did.

"Then I guess we're adjourned here," Lem said.

Everyone but Lem and Ramdakan got up and hurried from the room like it had just been hit with an airborne virus.

"You know how to kill a meeting," Norja said. "I'll give you that."

"Everything I said was true, Norja. And you know it."

"The truthfulness of your impassioned speech is irrelevant," Norja said. "You've scared everyone out of their mind."

"Good," said Lem. "Maybe they'll take it up a notch. If we're complacent, we're sunk."

"You say that like we're plateauing, Lem, when we have seen nothing but steady growth. Our last quarter showed our highest gains yet."

"That doesn't matter, Norja. Who cares what our growth is?"

"I'll pretend the CEO of this company didn't just say that," Norja said.

"We're successful because of demand," Lem said. "We can make a ham sandwich, call it a gun, and the IF will buy it. Just look at all the trash they're buying from Gungsu, who also happens to be doing very well, I might add. Gungsu is swimming in cash. But financial success isn't going to win us this war. We can't focus solely on the bottom line, Norja."

"I'm glad to hear you say 'solely.' For a moment I thought you had erased its importance completely."

"We have to remain solvent obviously," Lem said. "We have to generate a profit. But that is a tertiary concern."

"And what are our first two concerns?"

"Killing Formics and keeping soldiers alive."

"Not running Gungsu out of business?" Norja asked.

Lem smiled. "That would be a nice bonus."

Norja sat back and frowned. "You were a little hard on Serge. The man's filling in, you know. He's doing the best he can."

"Is that compassion I hear in your voice, Norja? That's one of the signs of the apocalypse. Has the moon turned to blood already? You would think I would have noticed that, us being on the moon and all."

"Humiliating an executive is bad management, Lem. It doesn't inspire devotion. It prompts departure."

Lem sighed and reclined in his chair. "I know."

"You're going to have more people bailing on us if you're not careful. We can't afford that. The last thing we need is your father sucking away more of our MVPs. If we lose another executive, the press will make a story of it. They'll call it an exodus, a talent drain, the end of Juke Limited's heyday. And bad press—if spread around enough—can actually cause the kind of downfall they're reporting. Stocks sink. Client confidence drops. Corporate partners get gun-shy. All because the media bastards want to run a juicy story. And oh what a story it would be. The plebeians love to see the mighty stumble."

"I know," Lem said again.

"You crucified the guy, Lem. You know better than that. He's poison now. No one is going to want to work with him because they think he'll taint them. Which is only going to make it harder for him to do his job. He'll be excluded from meetings, dropped from e-mails, skipped on intel. You just dug his grave."

"You're rubbing salt in the wound at this point, Norja."

"The wounded one is Serge, Lem. This isn't how companies are run. That management style expired about a hundred years ago. That's how enemies are made."

"I'm not normally like this," Lem said. "I'm normally quite pleasant."

"Normally," agreed Norja.

"I'll need to give Serge a success," Lem said. "Then praise him profusely in the next meeting to restore him to his previous status."

"Without appearing weak," Norja said. "We need a strong CEO. Or at least the perception of one."

"A cutting insult disguised as good counsel. Glad to see that streak of compassion has passed and you're back to your old self, Norja."

Norja Ramdakan shrugged. "My soul is only visible in brief spurts, weak as it is."

"Showering Serge with praise will come off as a pathetic and obvious apology," said Lem. "Why don't *you* praise him in the next meeting, and then I'll simply agree with you?"

Ramdakan shook his head. "Oh no, you stepped in your own cow manure. No one can clean your boots but you."

"That can't be a real idiom."

Norja grunted and got to his feet. On Earth, a man of his girth would have struggled to do so. But here beneath the surface of Luna, with a fraction of Earth's gravity, Ramdakan was up with little effort. "Serge isn't chaff, Lem. He's extremely bright. You don't become the assistant director of operations if you're not ambitious, intelligent, and willing to abandon every other pursuit in your life. The man puts in eighty hours a week easy. You make him nervous."

"If my father wouldn't keep pilfering my executives and engineers, this wouldn't be a problem."

"Can you blame your father?" Norja asked. "He's the Hegemon. He needs the best people he can find, people he can trust. He built this company, so he knows how our people think, how they work with others, how they strategize. He doesn't have time to try out new blood and see if they can deliver. He needs people to hit the ground running, leading big initiatives competently from day one. If I were in his shoes, I'd steal from us too."

"You as the Hegemon," said Lem, smiling. "Now there's a thought. You would lead us all to a hedonistic ruin."

Norja smirked. "At least we would all die enjoying ourselves."

"Just don't leave, Norja. Whatever my father offers you, I'll meet it."

Norja laughed. "There was a time when you wanted to strangle me or use me like a puppet to get back at your father, if I recall. And not in the too distant past."

Lem shrugged. "You've grown on me."

"Your father can't hire me. I've got too many skeletons in my closet, most of them placed there by him. I'm what you might call a political liability."

Lem knew that Norja had been with Father from the beginning, back when the company was a single mining ship at the start of the space-mining boom. He also knew that Norja had done a lot of Father's dirty work over the years. Lem could never get rid of him for that reason alone. The man would be a danger not only to Lem and Father personally, but to the company as well.

They parted, and Lem headed back toward his office, weaving his way through the company's tunnel system. Factories, processing plants, test facilities, labs. An underground web so complex and far-reaching, that without his wrist pad to guide him, Lem could quickly get lost.

He had known about most of the company's initiatives before becoming CEO. But there were a few projects and a few tunnels that his father had kept secret even from Lem. Classified military hardware, hush-hush research and development, whole departments of people on the company payroll that Lem hadn't even known existed.

The discovery wasn't much of a surprise, though. Lem had always assumed that Father would keep a few projects close to his chest and out of the public eye.

But rather than put Lem's mind at ease, rather than give

him a calm reassurance that he now knew everything the company was engaged in, learning about the secret initiatives had only left Lem with questions. Had Father told him everything? Had he pulled back all the curtains? Or had he only shown Lem just enough to make Lem *think* he had shown him everything? That seemed more like Father's style. And if so, it meant that Father had kept a few pet projects for himself and taken them with him to the Hegemony, funding them with the vast resources that were now at his disposal thanks to the Hegemony's heavy taxation of Earth.

And even if Father hadn't taken pet projects with him, he was certainly up to something. He had siphoned off some of Lem's brightest engineers.

What are you working on, Father? What are you building?

Lem had tried answering those questions himself recently, but his searches had proven fruitless. Whatever his father was doing at the Hegemony was deeply shrouded in secrecy.

Which gave him an idea.

He spun on his heels, took a different route, and made his way to Serge's office. He knocked once and entered before waiting to be invited inside. Serge was standing at his desk, with a dozen windows of data hovering in front of him.

"Mr. Jukes?"

Lem held up a hand. "I owe you an apology. I was a bit of an ass earlier."

Serge shook his head. "No, no. All my fault, sir. I shouldn't have brought such an issue to the executive team. I should have handled it. I assure you it won't happen again."

Lem waved the apology aside. "First off, don't call me 'sir.' I'm younger than you. Call me Lem. Second, let's put the previous meeting behind us and move on. In fact, I want you to do something for me."

"Okay."

"Something secret. Only between the two of us."

"Okay."

"I want you to find out what my father is doing with all the scientists and engineers he's hired."

Serge paused. "You want me to spy on the Hegemon of Earth?"

Lem shook his head. "No, no. I want information, Serge, legally acquired. The Hegemony is taking some of the brightest minds in the world, minds that were previously working for me. That hurts our bottom line. That makes us vulnerable. I want to know why it's happening. The world has given my father a very long leash, and my father is not one to let an opportunity pass him by. I want to know what he's doing with that leash."

"You think his endeavors exceed his authority?" asked Serge.

Lem shook his head again. "No. My father may be secretive, but he's not stupid. Whatever he's doing is within the bounds of his authority as Hegemon. He wouldn't court impeachment, if that's how the world would deal with him. He values being the supreme ruler too much. But that said, there aren't many limits to his authority right now. The world's in a mad scramble to prepare for war. That lengthens my father's leash considerably. He's the kind of person who would capitalize on that."

Serge nodded. "You obviously can't ask your father directly what he's doing or you would have done so already. You wouldn't be coming to me."

"My father wouldn't tell me even if I did ask," Lem said. "He and I don't always agree. And anyway, whatever he's doing, he's keeping it quiet. When I approach him, I want to know the answers. I want to see how he responds."

"I understand."

"Good. Norja tells me you're very capable, and I believe him. That's why I'm here, asking you to do this instead of anyone else on the executive team. I want to see the greatness Norja clearly sees in you."

Serge nodded gratefully. "I appreciate the confidence, Lem. I won't disappoint you."

Lem tapped a command on his wrist pad, and Serge's holo-screen chimed with a new message. "That's the direct access to my wrist pad. Contact me when you have information. Don't send me anything. We'll meet in person."

Serge furrowed his brow. "You think someone might be monitoring our communications?"

Lem smiled. "You don't know my father."

He turned and moved for the door.

"Lem?" Serge said.

Lem turned back.

"I agree with you," Serge said. "For what it's worth. Everything you said in the meeting. About it being our duty to win the war, about us having that responsibility. I believe that completely. It's why I stayed with the company instead of joining the IF."

Lem paused, intrigued. Serge wasn't feeding him a line; Lem could spot butt-kissing a mile away. This was sincere. "You considered joining the IF?"

"I looked into it," Serge said. "After the first war, after watching all the footage coming out of China. The bodies in the streets, the burned rice fields. I think everyone considered enlisting. But I was too old, they told me. Plus I probably would've failed the physical. I don't exactly fit the soldier stereotype. The recruiters offered to give me some small administrative duties as a citizen volunteer, but I knew I wouldn't make much of an impact. My place was here, I realized. This is where I can make a significant difference."

"You made the right choice, Serge. And the people who did enlist made the right choice for them. I'm glad we have you."

"Thank you, Lem. I'll get you that information. I'm curious myself."

"Legal channels only," Lem reminded him.

He left Serge's office feeling somewhat better, but the good mood didn't last. The more he thought about it, the more unpromising it seemed. Every one of Lem's inquiries into Father's Hegemony projects had yielded nothing. Why would Serge, who had fewer contacts and less access to information, have success where Lem had failed?

And yet it didn't hurt the man to try. Hopefully. Father could be prickly about people nosing in his business.

Lem's assistants were all waiting for him when he returned to his office with matters they claimed needed his immediate attention. Lem politely told them whatever they had could wait, and he stepped into the holoroom adjacent to his office.

The room was a white, empty, circular space with floors that curved up to meet the walls—like the inside of a giant egg. A light rig loaded with holoprojectors hung from a vaulted ceiling in the center, as if the room were a theater set to stage a minimalist play. Lem removed his shoes at the entrance and moon-hopped across the glass floor to the center of the room where a pair of footprints was painted on the floor. Beneath him, below the glass surface, sat another rig of holoprojectors, all pointing upward.

Lem placed his feet on the footprints and said, "Scout ship. Exterior. Twenty kilometers out."

A column of blue light appeared in front of him, projected from the floor and ceiling, two meters square. An hourglass materialized in the column, dropping grains of sand as the system acquired the satellite images. A moment later the hourglass winked out, and a holo of the Formic scout ship appeared—a giant, red, teardrop-shaped monstrosity locked in geosynchronous orbit above Earth. The Formic ship had held that position from the moment it first arrived at the start of the first war, with the point of its bulbous shape pointing toward Earth like a spearhead.

Lem still felt a twinge of unease whenever he saw it, as if he were approaching a sleeping monster. The ship was entirely in human hands now—specifically the hands of Juke Limited, who had seized it after the war by right of salvage law.

All alien life on board had died in the final assault. But even so the sight of it always left Lem with a tingling sense of dread. It was a reminder that the enemy was coming—an enemy the human race had no chance of defeating. Sometimes it seemed to Lem that all the efforts of the Hegemon and the IF and the company were nothing but theater, a giant game of pretend: Let's all put on our smiley faces and act like we can win.

It was laughable. We are fooling ourselves. The Formics brought us to our knees with a single ship last time. Do we honestly think we can take on ten or more at a time?

Three giant rings now encircled the ship at its widest point, each rotating slightly to give the people inside the illusion of gravity. Juke Limited had built the rings to house the company's research facilities and employees who were painstakingly studying every inch of the ship. Most of the Formic tech on board had been severely damaged when Victor, Mazer, and the MOPs flooded the ship with radiation, killing everything on board. But even the broken equipment had proven to be a treasure trove of information. Nearly every major branch of science had benefitted from the discoveries made there.

Lem zoomed in on the tip of the teardrop, where the shield generators were mounted in a ringed formation. The shield generators were the company's greatest find on the ship. They hadn't sustained any damage in the fight, and Lem's people had successfully reverse-engineered them. That tech alone could keep the company afloat. Every ship being built for the IF was being equipped with Juke proprietary shield generators, which were even stronger and more resilient than the original Formic design.

But the discovery that mattered most was the one that still eluded them. The hull. How do we penetrate the hull?

He wiped a hand through the ship and it disappeared.

"Show me the main lab."

The column of blue light expanded, growing outward in the holoroom. The holofield enveloped Lem and continued to spread, stopping when it measured five meters square, with Lem at the center. Shapes composed of light flickered into existence around him. Workstations, computer terminals, various bots and lab equipment. The company had installed a holoprojector setup in the lab very much like the one here at company headquarters, albeit smaller. The holos were pixelated and monochromatic, and the time delay of the transmission made it hard to have a normal conversation. But it was good for Lem to have face time with those who were leading the work and living at the Rings.

Dr. Dublin, the chief engineer on the project, stood alone in the lab, waiting for the scheduled transmission to begin. He had not been Lem's first choice to lead the team studying the hulmat—short for "hull material," the impenetrable alien alloy that covered and protected the ship—but Dublin was capable enough. Like everything else in the lab, he appeared as a life-sized construction of light, partially fuzzy because of the transmission degradation that always happened across great distances.

"Morning, Dublin," Lem said. "What's the status?"

There was a five-second delay.

Dublin finally heard the question and winced apologetically. "Progress is slow, Lem. We've identified more weapons and chemicals that *don't* penetrate or damage the hulmat, but that's the hardly the report you want to hear." He shrugged. "Nothing we do inflicts the slightest degree of damage. We can't cut it, burn it, dent it, scratch it. We can't even chip off a tiny piece of it to put under a microscope. It's mocking us at this point."

"The gamma plasma burned through the hull," said Lem. "That's how we won the war, by using their own weapon

against them. We've established that the hull isn't indestructible."

Five-second delay.

Dublin nodded. "True. But we don't understand the gamma
plasma, either. We're not even sure what the substance was
exactly. We've been calling it gamma plasma only because
that's the name Victor gave it. Those are the closest words in
our vocabulary for what it actually represented. But it wasn't
gamma plasma technically. Nor do we know how the plasma
was laserized at the nozzles before being fired at a target."

The nozzles. There were thousands of them on the Formic
ship just beneath the hull. Each connected to a system of
pipes that carried the gamma plasma from the storage tanks.
When the ship was ready to fire, plasma was pushed through
the pipes to the nozzles, where the plasma underwent some
laserization process that concentrated the plasma into a tight
beam. The aperture on the hull would open, and the beam of
plasma would shoot outward and incinerate anything in its
path.

"I wish we hadn't released all the gamma plasma in the
war," Lem said. "We might've been able to use it as a weapon
again."

Dublin shook his head. "I don't think so. Even if there were
gamma plasma still in the tanks, I wouldn't recommend harvesting it. It was far too radioactive. Way too unpredictable. It
would cripple our electronics and communication systems.
Even if we did have a way to transport it, which we don't, we
wouldn't be able to unleash it without severely damaging our
own ships. And besides, we have no way of directing it at a
target. We don't know how the laserization process worked.
It's technically not even laserization since we're not talking
about light here. But again, 'laserization,' 'gamma plasma,'
these are the words we have to work with. Point is, gamma
plasma wouldn't have helped us. It's just as well it's all gone."

"So we've learned nothing," said Lem.

"We've learned plenty," Dublin said, "but most of what we've learned hasn't taken us any closer to a military solution, which is what we need."

"I'm sure I need not stress to you the time crunch we are under, Dublin. You heard about Copernicus. We need a solution as soon as possible. Because we'll need time after you identify this alloy to design a weapon to breach it. That weapon will need to be tested, refined, retested, refined again, mass-produced. And then we'll need to install said weapon on individual ships of the Fleet. That takes time. So you can see why I might feel a flutter of panic here. Our window of opportunity is nearly closed. Most companies would say it already has closed. But since the survival of the human race hangs in the balance, we're not going to give up just yet."

"We're doing our best, Lem. Most of my team gets less than four hours of sleep. And those are good nights. I'm already pushing them hard."

"I'm not criticizing, Dublin. You have an impossible task. I'm just sweating right now. Can I send you more people?"

"We could always use more people," Dublin said. "But I would recommend a different approach, one you're not going to like. Don't hire more people and bring them up to the ship to work in secrecy for the company. Share what we know with the world. Publish everything we've got on the hull. Open our files. Pull back the curtain and ask the whole world to help. Offer a reward to anyone who figures out how to penetrate the hull. If someone finds the answer, it will be worth whatever reward we've promised."

"If *you* can't figure it out, Dublin, I doubt the average citizen can either."

"We're not interested in the average citizen," Dublin said. "And the average citizen won't be interested in participating. This would be way over their heads. Opening the files would target the professionals in similar industries who have unique expertise. If you hire people, you're only going to bring on those who are willing and able to leave their jobs and families and fly out and live on a cramped space station. But if you open it to the world, you'll have thousands of pros or semi-pros working on this after hours. They'll likely even feel a sense of duty. People want to contribute to the war effort, Lem. This would allow them to do so."

"If I did that," Lem said, "I'd be sharing proprietary information with our competitors as well. I'd be giving Gungsu Industries the tools it needs to beat us at our own game. What if they used our intel to discover a way to breach the Formic ships and then sold that solution to the IF? We would have equipped our competitors with the very tools they needed to defeat us. That's not smart business."

"At some point we have to decide what's more important, Lem. Business? Or survival? If we were to give out the intel, and Gungsu were to find a solution, then happy day, as far as I'm concerned. We have a solution. The human race might survive after all. Would giving that victory to Gungsu chip away at our market share? No question. But when this is over, if there is no human race, it won't make much difference what market share we hold."

Lem considered for a moment. "I'll think about it."

"Think fast, Lem. Like you said, our window of opportunity is shrinking here."

Lem thanked him, gave a few encouraging words, and signed off.

The holofield winked out, and Lem stood alone in the white space once more. Three years and he was nowhere closer to finding the enemy's weakness.

I need a miracle, he thought. A show of progress, something to keep a spark of hope alive. The meeting with the executive team had yielded nothing, and Dublin had only made it worse.

He needed to see Benyawe, his chief engineer who ran his Experimental Defense Division. She hadn't attended the executive meeting. She hadn't been to a meeting in a while, now that he thought about it. He had told her that her work in the lab was more important than attending meetings, and she had taken that as an invitation to skip every one.

He took a subway car to her lab. The security sensors at the entrance scanned him, and the door opened to the common room, a space the size of a soccer pitch. Twenty glass pillars were positioned throughout the room. The pillars doubled as small conference rooms, and several groups of engineers were meeting inside them, fussing over holos or equations scribbled on the boards.

To Lem's left, behind giant hangar doors, was the workshop, where the structural engineers built, tested, and modified the specialty ships and experimental spacecrafts being pitched to the International Fleet. Most of those ships would probably never see the light of day. There were a hundred reasons to kill a project, and over the years the IF had used them all. But some of the tech would likely become a reality in some form or another.

Lem found Dr. Noloa Benyawe sitting alone in one of the pillar rooms in the back, her hands inside a holo of a Juke-designed warship. Lem tapped on the glass to get her attention, and she glanced up briefly and waved him to enter.

She was Nigerian and in her early sixties, with more gray hair than Lem remembered. Father had tried to lure her to the Hegemony more than once, but she had always come to Lem when the offers came in. Lem had done whatever was necessary to keep her. She was the one employee he could not afford to lose.

"You missed the executive meeting," he said.

She didn't look up, but continued to tap at the holo with her stylus and make quick notes. "You told me I could skip those."

"I told you the work you do here is more important than meetings. But I still occasionally like seeing your face."

She looked up at him over the rim of her bifocals. He had never seen her wear them before.

"Bad day?" she asked.

"The usual," Lem said. "We're losing executives, morale is in the toilet, and Dublin and his team have gotten nowhere with the hull."

"We've long believed the hull was indestructible," Benyawe said. "Three years of research is proving us right."

"So you don't have any ideas?" Lem said.

"On how to penetrate it? No, Lem. I don't. The hull is Dublin's project. My mind hasn't been there. I've got my own problems to worry about."

"Dublin suggests we release everything we know about the hull to the world and offer a reward to anyone who can help us crack it."

"That's a good idea," Benyawe said. "You'll get a lot of amateurs offering up terrible ideas based on bad hypotheses and half-baked science, but with a good filtering system in place, you might actually learn something helpful."

"I was hoping you could simply solve it for me. I'm feeling rather despondent at the moment."

She didn't look up at him. "I'm your chief engineer, Lem. Not your therapist. If you're looking for carefree happiness, I suggest you buy some beach property and get a mind wipe. You'll be blissfully content until the Formics come."

"You're in a sour mood today," he said.

"Ignore me. Problems with the XR-50. I'm grumpy."

The XR-50 was one of the many Juke warships currently being constructed out in the Belt.

"What problems?" Lem asked.

"Don't worry. I'm taking care of it. We're still on schedule. The crews just sent a holo with questions. We're fine."

"And *you're* handling it?" Lem asked. "Don't you have people to do that for you?"

She sat up and removed her bifocals. "Yes, I have people

to do this for me, Lem. I'm reviewing what my teams have recommended. These are structural integrity issues. I sign off on all of those."

"And that doesn't slow down the process? Having everything funneled through you, I mean. You're not micromanaging your teams are you?"

"The CEO of the company is hovering over my shoulder, questioning my operational tactics, and he's asking *me* if I micromanage."

Lem grinned. "Point taken. Whatever you're doing, I'm sure it's right." He leaned against the glass and folded his arms. "Gungsu Industries won the breach contract with their gravity disruptors."

"So I heard," said Benyawe. "A stupid decision. Mazer Rackham was one of the marines testing the tech at WAMRED. Did you know that?"

"Rackham? Really? No, I didn't know that. Who told you?"

"Victor."

"Victor Delgado?"

"We e-mail," Benyawe said. "Imala, too. They're engaged now, did you know that?"

"No, I didn't. I guess I don't get included on the buddies-from-the-past e-mail chain. Glad to hear everyone is peachy. Now I'm even more depressed."

Benyawe grinned, glanced up, and then returned to the holo. "I wouldn't worry about Gungsu Industries," she said.

"Well I am worried," said Lem. "We presented six proposals to the IF, Benyawe. Six. All of them practical. Okay, some were more practical than others, but each of them showed promise."

Benyawe wiped her hand through the holo and it disappeared. "First off, the six proposals we sent to the IF were turned down for good reasons, especially knowing now that the hulmat is stronger than we expected. The IF was right to say no. You know as well as I do that nothing we presented to them was a silver bullet."

"The piece of craptech from Gungsu Industries isn't either," said Lem. "And yet the Hegemony throws Gungsu a mountain of cash for it. You want to explain that to me?"

"You're not your father," Benyawe said.

Lem blinked, taken aback. "What's that supposed to mean?"

"It means exactly that," said Benyawe. "Your father, Ukko Jukes, the Hegemon of Earth, had a different management style when he ran this company. He was one man to the public and a very different man behind closed doors. To the public and the press he was a shrewd businessman who had flashes of brilliance and played hardball to win. Behind closed doors, visible to only a few, he was brutal and conniving and cut whole companies down at the knees. Ask your friend Norja Ramdakan. He's one of the few people who knows how your father really operates."

"You make my father sound like a gangster," Lem said.

"Gangsters are unintelligent apes," Benyawe said. "That's not your father. He was always brilliant. But he was also dangerous. If your father were running this company right now, there wouldn't be a Gungsu Industries. He would have annihilated them before they got any traction and posed any serious threat."

"Well I appreciate the criticism," Lem said. "Anything else I'm doing wrong?"

"You misunderstand me, Lem. I didn't say you were doing anything wrong. I'm merely pointing out that your father had a very different approach, and that's why Gungsu is alive and kicking, because you allowed them to exist. And since I happen to believe in the free market and its ability to drive innovation, I'm glad Gungsu exists. We wouldn't have Nan-Ooze without Gungsu. Or any of the other tech they've given to the IF. Most of it is good, practical gear. I'm glad the IF has it. Had your father run the show, we wouldn't have any of that because it never would have been developed."

Lem shook his head. "I can't understand you, Benyawe. One second it sounds like you're insulting me, the next it sounds like you're on my team."

"Of course I'm on your team, Lem. I'm still here, aren't I? My point is, a win to Gungsu shouldn't demoralize us. It should inspire us. It should kick us in the rear and drive us to make something greater. Besides, your father can't award us every big contract anyway. It would look like nepotism, for one. And it wouldn't result in the best tech. We need competition, Lem. We need someone challenging us every single day, threatening to overtake us and wipe us out."

"I don't like losing," said Lem.

"Then stop losing. You're the CEO. If you want me to make a breach weapon that's better than Gungsu's, then get your boss-man face on and tell me to. Don't mope. Lead."

Lem stood erect. "All right. Pity party's over. Gather all your little brainiacs and tell them that their workload just expanded. We need marines to get inside the Formic ships, and the hull they have to get through is indestructible. This is all hands on deck. Nights. Weekends. Whatever it takes."

Benyawe stood. "I'll call a meeting right now. Anything else I should tell them? Like, say, there's a handsome reward for the winning team?"

"They're employees, Benyawe. I pay them handsomely already."

She raised an eyebrow. "How quickly do you want results? Remember, a lot of my engineers are convinced we're going to lose. They'd rather spend weekends with loved ones with whom they believe time is short. Asking them to forfeit that might require an extra incentive."

"All right," Lem said. "Tell them I will give five hundred

thousand credits to whoever creates a weapon that the IF buys."

Benyawe smiled. "That will soften the bad news of weekends. Anything else?"

"Yes. Fire anyone who doesn't believe we can win. If they're not in this heart and soul, I don't want them. Call HR if you need more people. I don't want naysayers."

"Very well. What are *you* going to do?"

"I'm going to call the press. I'm giving the world everything we know about the hull."

# CHAPTER 6

## Wila

The Formics' biochemical process of ship deconstruction and reconstruction is perhaps the greatest evidence of their advanced bioengineering capabilities. Unlike humans, who rely on tools and machines to build and dismantle our ships, Formics relied on philotically controlled organisms specifically engineered to accomplish these tasks.

The ability of hull eaters to dismantle the hull of the Hive Queen's mothership, and of hull weavers to turn that material into a fleet of warships, while continuing to move into our solar system at a significant fraction of the speed of light, clearly illustrates the Formics' scientific superiority in biomechanics. Meanwhile, other specialized organisms were used to build propulsion drives, shields, weapons, and life support systems. Imagine Columbus in 1492 dismantling his carrack and caravels and turning them into fifty seaworthy catamarans and outrigger canoes—in midvoyage, far from land, and without losing any supplies or delaying the voyage in any way—all through the use of semi-intelligent termites and barnacles.

The Hive Queen not only contained the entirety of this technology within her mind, but also, with a bit of

help from her sister Hive Queens on other worlds, designed new ships, weapons, and structures that no
Formics had needed before. This combination of deep
and wide knowledge with astonishing creativity be-
speaks a mental superiority over individual Formic
workers that explains why she was able to dominate
them so completely that they functioned as if they
were extensions of her body, the way our hands and
feet are extensions of our own.
        —Demosthenes, *A History of the Formic Wars,* Vol. 3

Wila lifted the hem of her white mae-chee robe and hurried
toward the bridge to the old teakwood temple in downtown
Ubon Ratchathani, Thailand. It was late in the day, approaching sunset, and Wila encountered no one as she crossed the
park and made her way to the lotus pond where the temple
stood upon stilts, surrounded by water and turtles and floating lotus flowers with their giant pink petals and yellow
pointed stamens. Wila paused in the grass before crossing the
bridge and took a few deep meditative breaths. She had contained her emotions on the train ride from the university and
beaten back the tears that had welled up inside her. But now
the tears were threatening to break through, and this time in
earnest.

The dissertation committee had heard her oral defense, but
only so that they might collectively deny her her degree. They
could have easily rejected her dissertation weeks ago and
spared her the humiliation of standing before them as they
obliterated her conclusions. But no, she was to be made an
example.

Three years of research, Wila thought. Three years of
study and writing and refining her theories, and now she
would have nothing to show for it. She would never teach.

She gripped the handrail and steadied herself. No, I

will not allow my emotions to overtake me. The soul must be free of sadness and shame. It must be pure, at peace, as bright as the sun. She closed her eyes and inhaled deeply, taking in the sweet, heady fragrance of the lotus flowers standing tall in the pond below her. The plant had likely been there for over a century, Wila knew, sprouting new petals every season and surrounding the temple with its pleasant perfume. So beautiful, she thought, and yet so resilient. Am I not stronger than a flower?

She stood erect, no longer leaning on the handrail, the frustration and humiliation slowly fading. She lifted the hem of her robe once again, kicked off her sandals, and crossed the bridge barefoot. The wood was old and cool, worn smooth by the feet of thousands of monks who had walked these planks before her. Wila paused at the entrance, pressed her palms together, and gave a brief bow of respect. A small gold statue of the Buddha greeted her inside and Wila touched it gently. There was nothing in her order that required her to do so, but the coolness of the metal steeled her even further. I can be as still and strong as this statue, she thought. Unbending. Enduring. Immovable.

The sun was nearly set now, and the temple interior was growing dark. Wila busied herself lighting a few candles and then carried one with her as she moved inside toward the wihan—the great hall where monks and believers met in prayer.

Wat Thung Sri Muang was a tiny temple by Buddhist standards, no bigger than a modest home; to call the wihan a "great hall" felt like an exaggeration. Nor was the room particularly decorative. There were no golden statues of deities, demons, or mythical creatures; no ornate columns; no mosaics or pottery or framed art. There was only a single incense table—and a small, slightly wobbly one at that, built with the same ancient teakwood. A stick of incense burned for the spirits of the dead, and Wila paused to pass her hand through the thin tendril of smoke and bring the scent reverently to her face. Again, it was a gesture of her own invention, but it steadied her mind and helped prepare her for prayer.

Master Arjo was sitting in the lotus position on the cushion at the front of the room, eyes closed, facing the entrance, deep in meditation. His saffron robes were wrapped tightly around his thin and wrinkled frame, and Wila wondered how he could sit in that position for hours on end with his arthritis. Two other monks, both men, sat before him, also in prayer.

The city had risen around the temple over the centuries, crowding it with skyscrapers and commerce and the fog of pollution. Wila could hear the traffic outside and the distant wail of a siren. If she concentrated hard enough she could push the noise back in her mind until it nearly disappeared from her notice.

She found a spot on the floor in the back and began her prayer. She had many prayers memorized for the Hive Queen, but the one she recited now was her favorite. It was not a prayer *to* the Hive Queen, for Wila, like all believers of Theravada Buddhism, did not pray to any being, including the Buddha himself. Rather, it was a prayer *for* the queen, that in her current unenlightened bodhisatta state she would learn greater compassion for all sentient beings in the universe. It was a prayer for harmony and kindness, for the injured of the Formic race, that their suffering would be lifted, that their minds would be open and bright and receptive to the kindness of those not of their species.

It was a long prayer, and when Wila finally opened her eyes, she found Master Arjo sitting in front of her, eyes open staring just to the left of her head, his pupils milky white with cataracts. The other monks were nowhere to be seen.

Somehow he detected that she had finished even though Wila had not moved.

"Your prayers test my patience, Wilasanee," said Master

Arjo. "I was beginning to wonder if I should have packed myself a sandwich to tide me over until you finished."

Wila pressed her palms together and bowed low. "Master Arjo. I did not mean to make you wait."

"You went before your committee today," the old man said, "and your heart is heavy. You are sad for the outcome and sad that your prayers concerning the matter proved fruitless."

"For a man who has no eyes, Master Arjo, you see quite clearly."

Master Arjo smiled. "I have eyes, child. But I do not need them to hear the grief in your voice. You knew this committee would not accept you. There was no chance of them changing their opposition to your dissertation. And yet you went anyway."

"I allowed myself to hope," Wila said.

"You allowed yourself to be abused," Master Arjo said. "You allowed them to spit bile at you and shame you, for I imagine that's what they did."

Wila said nothing, for she did not want to speak unkindly of the committee.

"A young boy with a golden singing voice sees a ferocious tiger in a cage," Master Arjo said. "The boy thinks he can tame this tiger with a song. So he steps inside the cage and sings the tiger a melody so sweet that all the villagers nearby who hear the song weep at the beauty of it. Whereupon the tiger opens its mouth and swallows the boy whole. Now, who is to blame? The boy, for being foolish enough to face such a beast, or the tiger for doing what tigers have always done?"

"Neither," said Wila. "I blame the cage maker, for making a structure so insecure that a foolish boy could get inside."

Master Arjo smiled. "Wilasanee. Always taking the untrodden path."

"I do not walk my path alone, Master. There are many in Thailand and throughout the Buddhist world who share my belief that the Hive Queen is a bodhisatta, a creature on the path to Buddhahood."

"It is an unpopular position," Master Arjo said. "For starters, there is no evidence that the Hive Queen exists."

"We may have not seen her," said Wila. "But we have plenty of evidence to suggest that she exists. Or at least something like her. Someone was directing the Formics, Master. They moved as one in battle, responded without hesitation and without verbal communication between them. We have it all on vid. When the Formic scout ship was attacked, every Formic on Earth stopped what it was doing and raced back to the scout ship to protect it. We've noted the timestamps. Every Formic responded at the exact same instant, wherever it was in China. It was as if all of them were responding to a single impulse from a single source. That alone is evidence of a queen."

"It is evidence of something," Master Arjo said. "A mind beyond our comprehension. Perhaps it is a queen. But without physical evidence we cannot be certain. We are content to call it a queen because we associate the Formics with insect colonies on Earth. Like ants or bees or locusts. But the mind of their hive may operate differently. It might be the mind of a third species we have yet to discover, a species that controls the Formics like a farmer controls his plow horse. We simply do not know."

"I thought you believed in the queen," said Wila.

"I absolutely believe," said Master Arjo. "For the idea of a Formic queen, a creature whose mind can cross immeasurable distances and touch the mind of another sentient being instantaneously, is an appealing theological construct. It is the first true example of an omnipotent mind that I have ever witnessed. That is enlightenment. That is by definition the Buddha mind, the ability to manifest your mind in millions of forms throughout millions of universes. That is the quest of us all." He raised a withered finger. "However, why does the Buddha mind do this? For what purpose does an omnipotent mind reach across space?"

"To relieve the suffering of all sentient beings," Wila said.

"Yes, to *relieve* suffering," said Master Arjo. "This is where the idea of the Formic Queen as a bodhisatta unravels for me. The queen, if she is truly aspiring to Buddhahood, will never attain it. Her sins are too great, her bad karma too high. She did not relieve suffering on Earth, but rather created it to a degree beyond comprehension. No one invader has murdered more, burned more, broken more homes, shattered more innocence, destroyed more crops and cities and livelihoods. No being has slaughtered more innocent children. No creature has shown more disregard for order and peace and the precepts of Buddhism."

Wila said nothing. She had heard all of these arguments before. The dissertation committee had said pretty much the same thing only two hours ago—although, unlike Master Arjo, their faces were twisted with anger and contempt toward her when they had spoken. How dare she suggest that the Hive Queen's motivations were anything other than murderous.

If only Master Arjo could have been the voice of the committee, Wila thought. He would have rejected my theories with such gentleness that I would have considered the exchange a blessing. The outcome would have been the same, but at least she would have been spared all the insults and curses.

"You have grown quiet, child," said Master Arjo.

Wila smiled. She was not a child. She was eighteen now, but he would always see her as the little girl who had come to him so many years ago.

"I have offended you," said Master Arjo.

"Not at all," said Wila. "I was merely thinking how much

more I would have enjoyed my rejection had the committee employed you to deliver the news."

"I do not reject you, child. I cannot. For to reject you is to reject a piece of my own heart."

"Reject my thesis then," said Wila.

"I question your theory on theological grounds," said Master Arjo. "I cannot fathom how a creature responsible for so much death and destruction could possibly have a soul."

"Not a soul," said Wila. "A philote."

Master Arjo frowned. "I do not know the word."

"It is a new word," said Wila. "A theoretical concept. And the basis of my dissertation. The idea is that philotes are the fundamental building blocks of all matter and energy."

"A new molecular particle?"

"The true, indivisible particle that is not made up of smaller ones," Wila said. "Philotes combine to form all structures. Electrons, protons, neutrons, atoms, molecules, humans, Formics, asteroids, all things in the universe."

"How big is this particle?" Master Arjo asked.

"That is the part we do not yet understand," said Wila, "for it is believed that philotes take up no space whatsoever."

Master Arjo looked confused. "How is that possible? Everything occupies space, Wilasanee. If it has mass, even a subatomic amount of mass, it must occupy space to exist."

Wila shrugged. "That's just it. A philote has no space or dimension or inertia."

Master Arjo nearly laughed at the premise. "No inertia? Then this is not a physical thing. How can something that cannot be detected be proven to exist? It defies established laws of physics. It is no wonder that this persists as only a theory."

"Do not discount the theory completely, Master Arjo. The idea of a philote might explain many unanswered questions. Central to the idea is that each philote connects itself to the rest of the universe along a single ray, a one-dimensional line that connects it to all the other philotes in its smallest immediate structure. These strands twine together and connect to a larger structure, such as a proton. And the gathering strands twine and extend to larger and larger structures in the molecular level and beyond, until all things are connected."

"All things?" Master Arjo asked. "Both living and non-living?"

"All things," Wila repeated. "You are connected to me. And we to this temple, and the temple to the flowers of the lotus pond, and to the people of this city, and to the insects, and the birds, and the very planet itself. Consider it, Master Arjo. We have longed believed that the truly enlightened mind can, with little effort, do all that is required to benefit all beings of the universe, that it could manifest itself in millions of forms. Yet science has never answered how such a thing could be possible. In fact, science has always vehemently rejected the idea, for there has never been any basis in science for such a concept. But what if science and religion and faith entwined their fingers and worked as one? What if biochemistry and physics found place in Buddhism and vice versa? Philotical principles answer this great question of our faith. How can one mind reach out to others in the universe, crossing vast distances to communicate some message of comfort? How can the mind achieve such a seemingly impossible reach?"

"Why did this committee reject you?" Master Arjo asked. "Because of your views on the Hive Queen or your views on theoretical biochemistry?"

"Both," Wila said. "At times it was hard to tell which concept angered them most. I tried to explain that I do not condone the Hive Queen's actions. I find the devastation of the Formics as horrific as they do. I am merely trying to understand a mind that is completely alien from our own. We have imposed our morals on a creature that developed under a completely different evolutionary process. What is death to a Formic? What is a human life? Does the Hive Queen share our values of such things? And are we certain that our interpretations of her point of view are correct? That is where we fall short, I believe. We are certain we know the mind of the Hive Queen. We have defined her as a malicious and remorseless creature of pure evil. But the basis for such a reputation is our own value system. We are operating under the assumption that she sees the world as we do and chooses to act destructively. But what if the Hive Queen does not see her acts as destructive? What if she sees them as the opposite? As constructive to her own species?"

"You did your research at one of the most conservative universities in all of Thailand," said Master Arjo. "You knew your ideas would be rejected and yet you persisted."

"They are not my ideas alone," Wila said. "And I persisted because this is the path of enlightenment. Our duty is to see a creature's true nature. Not the value society places upon it, but what it truly is. That is the quest of the fully developed mind. The world may look at an acorn and see an annoying round nut that must be raked up from the yard and disposed of. It is a nuisance. But the Buddha mind must look at the acorn and see its true nature. We must see a potential oak tree."

"And that is why you think the Hive Queen may be a bodhisatta. She has the potential to achieve Buddhahood."

"It is the foundation of our belief system," Wila said. "We believe that all beings can achieve full consciousness. Perhaps it will take the Hive Queen a thousand centuries to do so, living and dying a million times. But to say that she cannot, to deny her the possibility, contradicts the very core of our faith."

Master Arjo smiled. "When monks speak with me, they come to learn wisdom. But with you I feel as if I am the student."

Wila bowed low again, appalled. "Forgive me, Master Arjo. I did not mean to give offense."

Master Arjo laughed. "No offense taken, child." He grimaced as he got to his feet with some difficulty. "But come, walk me through the garden. Give me a biochemist's perspective on the wonder of life." He held out his arm for her to take.

Wila got to her feet. "But it is dark out, Master Arjo. The sun has set."

"The world is always dark through my eyes, Wila. Isn't that what you seek? To know the world through the eyes of another? To experience their view of the universe and thereby gain compassion? How else can you know and understand *me*? Come, teach me of the flowers. Let us see the acorns for what they truly are."

Wila returned to her apartment late that evening, and for the first time in years there was no stack of books or academic papers demanding her attention. They were there on her computer terminal as always, waiting for her to read them, but they did not call to her now. She did not feel the driving sense of urgency that had carried her throughout her pursuit of her doctorate.

She would continue in her studies of course, despite the rejection. For it was her duty as a believer to expand her understanding. But that would be her only motivation. She would be doing it to grow her mind, not her income.

There were other, more liberal universities that might entertain her sympathetic views of the Hive Queen and call her progressive, but they would likely find her religious devotion off-putting if not downright disdainful. Religion had no place in academia, and especially not for a biochemist. Plus, she had no credentials. She had never been published. She had no doctorate. Who would take her seriously?

She had not shaved her head today, so she took a few minutes to do so. As always it allowed her to feel a sense of renewal. A starting from scratch. She prepared a glass of black tea with crushed tamarind and cardamom, and then settled in front of her terminal to read the news.

The lead story grabbed her immediately. Lem Jukes had released thousands of documents about the Formic hull and invited the world to help him crack it. Wila opened the files and began to browse. She had seen much of the interior of the ship already, for she had studied the vid that Victor Delgado had taken when he infiltrated the ship during the war. The vid had shown a massive garden in the center of the ship where dozens of alien life-forms were kept in a dense junglelike bio preserve. Animals and plants of every variety. The garden had served as the ship's source of oxygen, but for the scientific community it was the single greatest biological discovery in history. Or rather, it would have been if it had not been completely destroyed in the final battle when gamma radiation was released all throughout the ship.

Oh what Wila would give to have spent an hour in that garden. The smells, the soil, the plants, the creatures. So much could be learned about the Formic planet's evolutionary history. What genetic advantage had allowed the Formics to evolve as a dominant species, for example? And did the plants follow the pattern of photosynthesis? It would seem so, but how, and to what degree?

Wila had noticed in the vid—brief as it was—how the Formics had used smaller creatures to complete certain chores or operations. Had Formics evolved with these creatures or had the Formics engineered them for that specific task? The doily weapons the Formics wielded were evidence that the Formics had practiced some bioengineering. Had they engineered other, more complex organisms? And specifically, had the *Hive Queen* engineered them? And if so, could the Hive Queen communicate with an engineered species in the same way that she communicated with her own? The idea was not outside the realm of possibility. If the Hive Queen clearly understood philotic connections and how to transmit information across a philotic thread, then would she not also understand how those threads twined with an organism of her own invention?

The questions had swirled around in Wila's head for years.

Now there was this. The hull. Tech developed by the Formics. Along with years of detailed analyses from highly skilled scientists and engineers. And they were asking for help. Anyone's help.

On the surface it appeared to be a question of mechanical engineering. How do we break through this hull? What breach method or weapon do we build that's strong enough to destroy it?

But of course the real questions were metallurgical. What is this alloy? And how was it made? Those questions found their answers in chemistry. And while Wila might not be an engineer, she did know a bit about chemistry and had quite a few theories about how the Hive Queen had built her kingdom.

She downed the rest of her tea and set the glass aside, feeling a renewed sense of urgency. This was why she had studied. This was what had called her, what all of her research had prepared her for. She paused and offered a prayer: that her mind would be open, that it would see clearly and understand what others had already discovered.

Then she opened the first holo and began to read.

# CHAPTER 7

## Asteroid

To: notoccamsrazor@stayanonymous.net; lem.jukes@juke.net
From: vico.delgado@freebeltmail.net
Subject: Formics in the Kuiper Belt

Old Soldier and Lem,

Attached are images of asteroid 2030CT, a relatively
small, icy rock here in the Kuiper Belt NOWHERE near
Copernicus, which makes the following information all
the more alarming. There is a Formic vessel anchored
to the asteroid. A small miniship. By the looks of it, it
puts out very little heat, which might explain how it
was able to enter the system without being detected.

I can't say how long it's been here, but I suspect that
it arrived relatively recently. Edimar noticed a drop in the
asteroid's brightness and sent a probe ahead of us to
investigate. As the images prove, the rock is reflecting
less light because the Formics have covered it with a
membranous shell of some kind. Like a balloon or a cocoon. If we're interpreting these images correctly, the
circumference of the shell is greater than the circumference we have on record for the asteroid, meaning

that there's space between the shell and the surface of the asteroid, perhaps as much as twenty meters. I have no idea what the shell is composed of or how it was made, but I think it could be airtight. If that's true, there might be an oxygenated environment beneath the shell. The water ice on the surface of the asteroid as well as the ice in the porous rock could provide plenty of oxygen and hydrogen in gas, liquid, or solid form, depending on the temperature they maintain inside the shell.

It is quite possible that the entire surface of the asteroid has been rendered habitable and a number of Formic workers and/or soldiers might be living and working there.

We are approaching the asteroid now. I will send further information soon. Please relay this to the Hegemon and senior officers of the International Fleet immediately. We do not know if we have sufficient force and firepower to contest possession of this rock or to resist them if they decide to drive us away. We do not know if we'll be able to insert any observers—human or robotic. We have no ability to conceal our approach or disguise our intentions. Advice is urgently requested.

Vico

—Victor Delgado to Mazer Rackham and Lem Jukes,
*Mazer Rackham: Selected Correspondence,*
International Fleet Archives, CentCom, Luna

Mazer floated inside his cramped quarters on WAMRED, reviewing the images Victor had sent him, feeling more unsettled by the moment. He tapped the terminal screen and zoomed in, hoping to get a better sense of what the shell around the asteroid was composed of. No good. The image was too pixelated. He zoomed back out again. From a distance the shell looked like brown, hardened amber with a thick webbing threaded through it to give it structure. Obviously engineered. But how had the Formics built it? And why?

He tapped at the screen again and logged in to the forum. Victor was wise to send the images to Lem as well, but Mazer couldn't leave the responsibility of sharing the images solely to Lem. If Mazer could inform the IF he would.

He typed up a new post and uploaded all the images. Dozens of new threads were created in the forum every day, but as an administrator Mazer could place his post at the top and make it sticky so that everyone who logged in would see it. All he had to do now was push send.

He raised his finger but then hesitated. Vaganov had ordered him to bring all new intel and information to him directly. If Mazer posted this to the forum without first informing Vaganov, would Vaganov accuse him of violating a lawful order? Would Vaganov have an actual case against Mazer in the court-martial?

He couldn't take that risk. He would report it to Vaganov first. The colonel was a careerist. Valuable intel like this could get him noticed. He would probably trip over himself to get the images to CentCom so that he could take credit for it and bask in the commendations that would follow.

Mazer saved the post but didn't publish it. If Vaganov ignored the intel, Mazer would take matters into his own hands, and the court-martial be damned.

The door to his quarters was locked from the outside, so Mazer sent an e-mail to the colonel's aide. Simply asking to meet with Vaganov would likely be ignored, so Mazer uploaded one of the images of the asteroid and wrote that he had evidence of Formics in the system.

An MP arrived a few minutes later and ushered Mazer directly into Vaganov's office.

Vaganov waved the MP out and then pulled up the asteroid in his holofield.

"Who sent you this image?" Vaganov asked.

"Victor Delgado, sir," said Mazer. "A free miner in the Kuiper Belt."

Vaganov looked skeptical. "Victor Delgado? The free miner who warned Earth of the first invasion? Is this a joke?"

"No, sir. I assure you this is one hundred percent legitimate."

Vaganov narrowed his eyes. "Why would Victor Delgado send critical intel to you, a captain? He helped the MOPs win the war. He could send this to anyone in the IF and they would believe him."

Mazer hesitated. He had to be delicate. He had been ordered by the Strategos at the end of the war not to divulge Mazer's involvement in the final battle, which was how his friendship with Victor had developed. So he revealed what he could. "Sir, Victor Delgado and I met via holo during the first war while I was in China. He contacted the Chinese officers at Dragon's Den where I was serving and offered assistance. We have stayed in contact ever since."

Vaganov seemed impressed, but his expression still carried a hint of skepticism. "You do not strike me as a dishonest man, Mazer. A dishonest man would try to fool me into passing false information on to CentCom in an effort to humiliate and discredit me. To get revenge, so to speak. I have arranged to have you court-martialed, the circumstances of which, from your perspective, seem unfair, unjustified, or even cruel. If you were a dishonest man you might even feel justified in staging an elaborate hoax to damage my reputation. But you're not a dishonest man, are you, Mazer?"

He thinks I'm like him, Mazer realized. That's what we

do as humans; it's how we read minds. We assume that other people think like we do. So if we're nasty and suspicious and conniving we assume that everyone is as nasty and suspicious and conniving as we are.

"Sir," said Mazer, "I have nothing to gain by relaying false information. That would be career suicide."

"It would be a foolish mistake, yes."

"My only intention here is to relay critical intelligence to the senior members of the Fleet," said Mazer. "You are welcome to corroborate this however you see fit, sir. You don't need my permission to do so, of course, but I have nothing to hide. I would only encourage you to do so quickly. This is irrefutable evidence that there are Formics already in the solar system. They avoided detection. They have an agenda. They set down on that rock and built a habitat for a reason. If you examine the propulsion system, sir, you will see that it appears to be anchored to the rock. There's only one reason why they would do that. They intend to move that asteroid. And if they can move an asteroid, sir, they can put it on a collision course with Earth. They can launch it at us like a missile."

That gave Vaganov pause. He looked back to the image. "Yes. I suppose that's true."

"There are over ten billion objects in the solar system," said Mazer. "If the Formics have the capability to turn those objects into weapons, it won't matter how many soldiers or ships we assemble. An asteroid only a few kilometers in diameter would release as much energy as several million nuclear warheads detonating simultaneously. It could wipe out countries, continents. Larger asteroids would be an extinction event. The Formics could end us with a single shot, sir. We must relay this to CentCom immediately. There may be more of these occupied asteroids in the Kuiper Belt that we don't know about."

Vaganov stared at the asteroid, considering.

"And there's something else," said Mazer. "Whatever the Formics are doing at this asteroid, we need to stop them. The IF must form an assault team specializing in asteroid combat. As far as I am aware, there is no such effort currently in development within the Fleet. We never imagined we would need one. But now we do. IF marines must seize or destroy that installation and any others like it. That will take training, weapons, and tactics we have not yet developed."

Vaganov didn't respond for a moment. "This photo could be fake. There is software out there that could generate these images easily. A child could do it. I'm not passing this on to anyone until I independently verify all of this."

It's Victor on Luna all over again, thought Mazer. When Victor tried to warn the world of the first invasion no one would believe him. It was easier not to, to dismiss the intel as fake. Had Imala not come along and given him credence, we would have been wholly unprepared.

"Sir, I am not trying to deceive you," said Mazer.

"No, but someone might be trying to deceive *you*. This asteroid, 2030CT, is it remote? Would an IF ship or scope be able to corroborate what we see here?"

"It's in the Kuiper Belt, sir. Everything is remote. No IF ship or depot is close. I checked."

"And this ship—if it avoided detection, I'm not going to find a record of its approach in any of the Parallax databases either, am I?"

"Again, I doubt it," said Mazer. "The Formic ship has a very small engine. Not unlike the ship that destroyed Copernicus, which also avoided detection. Victor called them mini-ships because of their size. They likely put out a very small heat signature. We have to remember, sir, that the Parallax satellites are computers. They only detect what we tell them to detect. If this ship's heat signature was below set parameters, our satellites would dismiss it."

"Well, we have a problem, don't we?" said Vaganov. "We have potentially critical information that I can't corroborate. One image isn't enough."

"There are other images," said Mazer. "Victor sent me several. You're welcome to study those as well."

Vaganov reached into the holofield and called up an IF e-mail login screen. "Sign in to your e-mail. Show me these other images."

Mazer didn't hesitate. He had known that his e-mail account could be reviewed upon request—privacy rights in the military were different than those for civilians—so he had always erased e-mails as soon as he read them. Whatever files or designs he received from Victor were stored elsewhere in a private data bin on the nets. As were his e-mails from Kim. The only e-mail currently in his inbox was the most recent one from Victor. He stepped to the holofield, signed in, and opened the images.

"Where are the rest of your e-mails?" said Vaganov. His eyes narrowed. "You're concealing something. Who else are you communicating with? You're talking about me, aren't you?"

Mazer almost laughed. *He worries that I'm informing his superiors about his relationship with Gungsu. He thinks I'm throwing him to the wolves.* It was both pathetic and infuriating. Here Mazer was, giving him intel that could change the entire dynamic of the war, and Vaganov's primary concern was his own reputation. Mazer showed no hint of his disgust, but instead kept his face completely impassive. "I assure you, sir. I am not concealing anything."

"Then where the hell are the rest of your e-mails?"

"I erase them after I read them, sir."

"Because you don't want *me* reading them. You don't want

me discovering who you've been talking to and what you've been saying about me."

"Colonel, I assure you, you are not the subject of my e-mails."

"No. And I won't be. Your net access is revoked. You will not speak to anyone or communicate in any manner with any soldier or civilian until you are shipped off this station for your court-martial. Connection to your quarters is to be severed. Give me your wrist pad."

"Without access to the nets, Colonel, I will be unable to communicate with an attorney. With all due respect, sir, according to the Code of Military Justice you cannot violate my right to counsel."

Vaganov glared. "Your counsel can contact you once you're off my station. Now I gave you a direct order. Give me your wrist pad."

Mazer removed his wrist pad and handed it over.

"What is to be done with the information regarding the asteroid?" Mazer asked.

"I will pursue my own investigation," said Vaganov. "If this proves true, I will pass it along. You, however, will say nothing of this to anyone."

"And if you can't corroborate the information?" asked Mazer. "What you're proposing could take weeks or months."

"It's no longer your concern."

I shouldn't have come to Vaganov, Mazer realized. I should have posted the images on the forum immediately. Or figured out a way to send the images directly to the Strategos. The moment we allow the bureaucracy to impede the free sharing of information is the moment we lose this war.

Mazer reached into the holofield and signed into the forum. He had done it so many times before that his fingers were on autopilot, moving rapidly, dancing through light.

"What are you doing?" said Vaganov.

Mazer didn't stop. He found the unpublished post he had

prepared and sent it with a quick flick of his wrist, uploading it in an instant. Then he flicked and spun his wrist in the other direction to close the forum before Vaganov could delete it.

Vaganov was furious. "What did you just do?"

"I posted the information on a forum I created on the IF intranet. About two thousand junior officers throughout the Fleet visit it every day. They will see it and share it with the commanding officers. Sooner or later it will make its way to CentCom. Probably within the hour."

Vaganov's eyes darkened. "You defy me to my face?"

"You still have the images here," said Mazer. "If you send them immediately to the rear admiral, you will be the first person to do so. You might even get a commendation. If you delay, however, someone else will beat you to it. Either way, the information is shared."

Mazer waved his hand through the holofield and closed his inbox.

Colonel Vaganov straightened his jacket and smiled. "You will find, Captain Rackham, that my tolerance for insubordination is extremely low." He tapped his wrist pad. "Sergeant Nardelli. Come to my office please."

An MP arrived a moment later. Mazer didn't recognize him. He was at least a head taller than Mazer, with thick arms and a hard expression.

"Sergeant, please escort Captain Rackham back to his quarters. I want an MP guarding him at all times. His wake shift will now change to third shift. He is to have heavy work details and he is not to communicate with anyone on this station. Not in words, letters, sign language, body language, eye blinks, etcetera. Do I make myself clear?"

Nardelli nodded. "Yes, sir."

Vaganov turned back to his holotable, dismissing them. "That will be all."

Mazer felt rough hands grab him and pull him toward the door. Sergeant Nardelli wasn't the delicate type. Colonel

Vaganov had requested him by name no doubt for this very reason.

Vaganov glanced up briefly as Mazer was being escorted out. It was a look of pure indifference, as if Mazer meant nothing, *was* nothing—the way a cat might regard a mouse before pouncing and sinking teeth into flesh.

# CHAPTER 8

# NanoCloud

---

To: ukko.jukes%hegemon@heg.gov
From: sorin%ambassador@usa.gov
Subject: angry bear

---

Ukko,

A warning. I am leaving the Earth Security Summit here in Saint Petersburg, where the mood of our last session was particularly prickly, with all of the venom directed at you. Korzhakov, the Russian first deputy prime minister, who wasn't even scheduled to attend, called the Hegemony "a body of privileged autocrats who are blind to the cries of the underprivileged." He said the Hegemony taxes the nations of the New Warsaw Pact so relentlessly that families are bled dry of resources. He held up a photo of a child who froze to death in the street. The photo will trend on the nets within the hour, I'm sure.

Of course Korzhakov staged his theatrics at the end of the last session on the last day, denying anyone a chance to offer a rebuttal. I had approached Norchov, the Russian ambassador, prior to the summit to secure

Russia's support for the tax, and he assured me that Russia stood with us. Yes, yes, we must strengthen the IF, he told me. Build our defense. Russia is with you. I had forgotten the first rule of diplomacy: Russians are never more cooperative than when they are about to betray you.

The vote passed, but barely. Korzhakov concluded his diatribe by suggesting that the world needed a Hegemon who was both strong on defense and compassionate toward the free citizens of Earth. His intentions could not have been less subtle. Russia finally realized that the office of Hegemon has actual power. They want it. Watch your back.

David

—Office of the Hegemony Sealed Archives, Imbrium, Luna, 2118

Lem entered the offices of the Experimental Defense Division at Juke Limited and was surprised to find the lights still on. It was well past midnight, and yet the entire staff seemed to be on hand, as if Lem had caught them in the middle of their workday. The conference rooms were filled with engineers. Other groups were huddled at tables off to the sides, tapping away at their wrist pads and tablets and speaking in quick urgent tones. A lone engineer in need of a shave was bent forward asleep at a table, hugging his bag like a pillow. More people were asleep in hammocks in a dark corner of the room. Some looked to be in their sixties. Others looked like grad students. Lem made his way toward the back of the main hall, passing a trash receptacle overflowing with take-out boxes and stepping over a man in a sleeping bag.

He found Dr. Benyawe in the common area, where about twenty more engineers were scattered around the room, parked on sofas and loveseats, hard at work. Benyawe saw him, gave one last bit of advice to the engineer she was speaking to, and came over.

"You look nice," she said, gesturing to the formal suit Lem was wearing. "What was it? The ballet? Political fund-raiser? Midnight's a little late for that, isn't it?"

Lem was still looking around, taking it all in. "I feel like a parent who just found his teenaged son throwing a house party."

"We're a little short on space," said Benyawe. "I put a request in to one of your assistants for more square footage. This company has to have some empty offices we could use. I have people sitting on crates."

"You have people sleeping on the floor," Lem said. "How many people did you hire?"

"Close to three hundred. Most of them are on a contract basis, but a few of the really good ones are permanent."

"Three hundred?" Lem said.

Benyawe nodded. "It's a surprisingly mixed group. Our HR department has worked wonders. Your departing senior executives freed up a lot of cash."

"Cash I was supposed to use to lure and hire new senior executives," Lem said. He ran a hand through his hair to calm himself. "Where did these people come from, dare I ask? You couldn't have possibly found them all on Luna."

"Before you go nova," Benyawe said, "I'll remind you I'm doing what you requested. The only engineers on this rock already work for this company. My only option was to go planetside."

"Flying three hundred people up from Earth? Please tell me you crammed them all in a single rocket."

"It took several flights," said Benyawe. "You won't like the fuel expense. It's several times what we're paying these people. But if you want fast, miraculous results, you need new blood."

"New blood is fine. Bleeding the company dry is not."

"You're being melodramatic," Benyawe said, "and a bit obnoxious. This company employs over half a million people. Do I need to show you how much profit this department secures above the others? We're one of the smallest in terms of staff and one of the largest in terms of revenue generation. I think you can cut us a little slack."

Lem sighed. "Is this why you called me in? To show me your new recruits?"

Benyawe started walking, and Lem had to hustle to keep up. "We've actually been working on this for a while now," Benyawe said, "but it's never been developed enough to show you. I had my doubts about it as well. But we made some recent strides, so I wanted to bring you in. I thought you would've waited until morning, though. You never answered my question, by the way."

"What question?" Lem was practically speed walking to keep up with her.

"The suit. What was the event?"

"They were naming a new wing in the hospital after me," Lem said.

She looked at him. "You're kidding."

"No."

"That's a little cliché, isn't it?"

Lem frowned. "I objected to the whole thing, but the PR people insisted. Our health division donated several nanosurgical devices, and the company coughed up a lot of money for construction. Apparently if you pay for it, they name it after you."

"Ah," said Benyawe. "Tax write-offs disguised as philanthropy. It makes me feel all warm and snuggly inside."

"You know, for someone who's quick to defend herself

with claims of revenue generation, you sure have a poor grasp of how free markets work."

"I only use economics when it helps my argument. Otherwise I loathe it. I'm a scientist, remember?"

"Can you tell me why I'm here at midnight please?"

"We're calling it the NanoCloud," said Benyawe.

They were leaving the main hall and heading toward the workshop.

"NanoCloud?" Lem asked. "What is that exactly? Swarm tech?"

"Basically."

"To do what?"

"To breach hulmat on a Formic warship and get marines inside, of course. That's what you wanted, isn't it? A solution that beats out Gungsu's faulty gravity disruptor?"

"Nothing would make me happier than to cripple Gungsu," Lem said. "But let's remember that we have no idea how to penetrate the Formic hull material. If your NanoCloud is nothing more than nanobots programmed to eat through hulmat, it's not going to work."

"The Cloud doesn't eat through anything," Benyawe said. "It's designed to open the ship from the inside out."

She led him into the workshop. Crews of engineers were busy at various workstations, building or tweaking or repairing small experimental spacecraft or pieces of larger ones. Tools and worker bots and metalworking machines were everywhere, and yet everything seemed clean and well organized.

"Does everyone always stay this late?" Lem asked.

"You said to put a full-court press on this," said Benyawe. "That's what we're doing."

They weaved their way through the workstations until they reached a small observational room with a glass wall overlooking an enormous vacuum chamber. A metal structure about the size of a city bus stood in the center of the chamber, and it took Lem a moment to realize what he was looking at.

Benyawe and her team had recreated a piece of the Formic scout ship. It was as if they had used a laser to cut out a cross section of the hull about ten meters square—like cutting out a piece from the center of a cake. Every part of it looked identical to the real thing. There was the red glossy hull, with its apertures, large and small. There were the layers of pipes and shield plates beneath the hull. And there under it all, directly below the largest closed aperture, folded in on itself, was a replica of one of the Formic cannons. The cannon was unpainted, crudely sculpted, and nowhere near complete.

"We're not yet finished with the model obviously," said Benyawe, "but you can see that we built everything to scale. This is exactly as it is on the real ship. The only exception is the material used. Dublin and his team have not yet identified what the hulmat is composed of, so we built ours with steel. The metal doesn't matter for our purposes though."

She closed the door to the observation room and killed the lights. Lem stepped to the glass to get a better look. Benyawe pulled up her sleeve and tapped at her wrist pad.

"The chamber is a vacuum," she said. "It's not exactly the conditions of space, but it's close. We can't replicate battle conditions, though. So this is by no means an accurate depiction of how the NanoCloud will operate in war. This is simply to give you an idea of what we're going for."

Black smoke billowed into the chamber from a vent in the wall, like an old coal chimney puffing out soot. Only it wasn't smoke or soot, Lem realized. It was nanobots. A swarm of millions of microscopic bots, pouring into the chamber.

At first they moved like normal smoke, spreading out, dissipating, moving in what appeared to be a random pattern. But there were no air currents in the room obviously, so they had to be moving in a preprogrammed manner—spreading out to form a wall. Then, as if they had solidified into a single object with an intelligence, the cloud descended onto the hull of the ship. The NanoCloud broke as it hit the hull, but nothing bounced off. The separate pieces—or crowds of nanobots—split up and targeted different apertures, gathering at the edges or where the blades of the apertures met.

"This part takes a few minutes," Benyawe said. "Bear with me."

Lem watched the cluster of smartdust, but nothing seemed to be happening.

"Each little speck of black you see," said Benyawe, "is thousands of nanobots clustered together."

"What are they doing exactly?" Lem asked.

"They're seeping into the incredibly small gaps between the aperture blades. Widths only a few atoms wide. The blades appear airtight, and by our standards they are. But down at the atomic level, they're not. We can't see the slight divots and gaps and chasms between them, but they're there, and thousands of our nanobots are flowing through those gaps like a river, penetrating the ship at the microscopic level."

The large aperture opened, as if someone had thrown a switch, and the Formic cannon began to extend and unfold itself, reaching outward, preparing to unleash its firepower.

And then the cannon split into three pieces at the hinges and detached itself from the hull. The pieces drifted away and softly collided with the padded walls of the chamber. The aperture remained open. A gaping, inviting hole.

Benyawe turned to Lem. "The cannon, fortunately, is not made of hulmat. It's mostly iron. So we simply had to program the bots to disassemble the hinges. Another group of bots is programmed to override the mechanism that controls the aperture, which they will then keep open. Other groups descend into the smaller apertures in the immediate vicinity and turn off the nozzles that unleash gamma plasma. The hope is, once the aperture is open and the cannon removed, a team of marines in a tiny craft can pilot right to the hole and enter the ship. This will require expert piloting. They'll have to fly directly to the hole. If they deviate, even slightly, they'll expose themselves to other apertures that can unleash gamma plasma."

"Like Imala's flight in the last war," Lem said.

"That's where we got the idea actually. So the system isn't without risk. It requires the NanoCloud and trained marines to work flawlessly. But it at least gives us a tactic for hull penetration that doesn't involve us trying to damage an impenetrable alloy. We're going to lose that battle every time."

"You've programmed these bots to open this specific ship," Lem said. "But we don't know if the new enemy warships will look like this one. They may have a completely different design."

"The principle is the same," Benyawe said. "We identify the ship's access points and use the nanobots to open the hatch or aperture or whatever. Basically we find the door and we open it for our marines. It's not a perfect system yet. I recognize that. We still need to figure out how to get external scans of the ships. Probes are probably easiest. We send a few of those ahead to relay back to us detailed renderings of the skin of the ship. That will give us mathematically precise measurements to work with. We'll know exactly where the access points are located."

"What about inside?" Lem asked. "You were able to program the nanobots to disassemble the cannon because you knew exactly where it was located and what it looked like. We won't have that luxury with any new ship design. A scanner probe won't be able to see inside the Formic ships. How will we learn the ship's internal layout?"

"We send in a NanoCloud," said Benyawe. "Only its mission is to map the interior of the ship. The bots broadcast back

a three-dimensional rendering of what they find. Like inject-
ing dye into the bloodstream."

"What about a delivery system?" Lem asked. "How do you
get the cloud to the enemy hull?"

"That's what everyone is working on now. We have some
promising preliminary ideas, but they're not precise. We've
got work to do."

"Find a way," Lem said. "And hurry. Act like you're three
years behind schedule. Because you are."

"That sounds like criticism. But I know you well enough
to know you're pleased."

"It doesn't matter if I like it, Benyawe. What matters is that
the tech improves our chances of winning the war. This does.
Drastically. But I'm not foolish enough to think that the odds
just tipped in our favor. Our chances remain low. Even if every ship in the IF were to have this weapon, we would likely
still lose spectacularly. So yes, I'm more optimistic than I was
before I came in here, but we've got a long way to go."

Lem left her with the nanobots and the cross section of
the hull and made his way out of the building, hopping over
the man in the sleeping bag again, this time with a little more
spring in his step. He had given Benyawe a restrained response. His CEO face. Good job, keep it up, etcetera, etcetera.
But inside he was soaring. NanoCloud. It seemed so obvious
now it was almost a little embarrassing. They should have
had this years ago. But of course they probably did. It just
took years to create the process and hone the tech enough to
make it happen. In fact, achieving that in just three years was
nothing short of miraculous.

He left the facility and climbed back into his skimmer, secured in an underground docking station. He had taken his
wrist pad off for the hospital event and left it on the dash-
board. It was chiming quietly now, begging for his attention.
The device was a simple AI. It monitored which news stories

and electronic messages seemed to interest Lem the most, then it assigned every incoming message or holo with a priority rating. Messages deemed urgent were brought to Lem's attention immediately. Casual matters were stowed away for later.

The chime the device made now meant it had received a message from an infrequent contact the device deemed of high importance. Lem picked up the device.

The message was from Victor Delgado, which surprised him. An e-mail. With images attached. The screen on Lem's wrist pad was too small to view them properly, so he turned on the skimmer's batteries and turned on the dash's holofield. A round shape appeared in the first image, floating in space. Lem didn't know what to make of it. A small, oddly shaped ball? Or a round sack of some sort. But no, if it was coming from Victor, it had to be Formic in design. But what? A mine? A tiny probe?

He read the e-mail and finally got a sense of the scale. It was not something that would fit in his hand, he realized. It was an asteroid.

He punched in the exit code.

The docking bots lifted the skimmer to the platform, and the platform rose to the surface. Lem lifted off and flew across the pockmarked and powdery lunar landscape, heading toward the city of Imbrium—a series of massive iron domes clustered close together on the sunlit side of the moon. His father would already be asleep, but Lem would wake him. Assuming I can get through security, Lem thought. Most of the city was underground now—protected from the constant bombardment of micrometeorites and solar radiation. The original city, Old Town, still stood above the surface under the domes. After the First Formic War tourism there had come to a grinding halt. It wasn't until Father had established the headquarters of the Hegemony in Old Town that the neighborhood had found new life. Instead of tourists, however, sidewalks now filled with ambassadors, lobbyists, and defense contractors, the suits that made the world, IF, and Hegemony go 'round.

Lem flew up to the gate of North Dome and landed on the transitional pad. The bots maneuvered his skimmer through the airlock and into the oxygenated interior of the dome. Once through, Lem took off again, flying over Old Town. The city's artificial lights were turned off, and most of the borough was asleep.

The Hegemon of Earth had chosen a modest penthouse apartment for his private residence. Ukko Jukes might be one of the wealthiest men on Earth, but he understood that lavish living tended to annoy his constituency. Not that Father had to worry about voters. He had been appointed by the United Nations and ratified by votes from general assemblies throughout Earth.

A voice came over the speaker. "Skimmer 7002, you are approaching restricted airspace. Identify."

Lem rolled his eyes. "It's Lem. I'm here to see my father. You have my skimmer in your database. You know it's me." He decelerated and hovered in place a distance from the docking platform above Father's apartment.

"You know the policy, Mr. Jukes. I can't allow you to land without a signed entry pass."

"Inform my father that I have critical information regarding the Formics."

"I apologize, Mr. Jukes. The Hegemon is not taking visitors at the moment. He has already retired for the evening."

"Soldier, you're a smart individual. You would not be manning such an important post otherwise. So I'm sure I need say this only once: I have irrefutable evidence that the Formics have already infiltrated our solar system right under our noses and may be plotting an attack as we speak. If you would like to be the reason why this information is delayed to the Hegemon, Polemarch, and Strategos, then by all means, cling to your insignificant flight-control rule book. Otherwise, wake my father and let me land."

There was a long pause on the radio. "One moment, please."

Lem waited for five minutes before the uncertain voice of the soldier returned. "The Hegemon will see you, Mr. Jukes. You are clear to land."

Lem rolled his eyes again. The Hegemon will see you. Is that what you make them say, Father? As if you're some king or sultan who has granted me the great privilege of basking in your royal presence?

Lem landed the skimmer and moon-hopped up to the security entrance. The scanner lights wiped across his body, and the soldier standing guard waved him through. Father was waiting in the living room, completely dressed and very much awake.

"You're up late," Lem said, engaging his boot magnets and walking across the carpeted floor. "I guess your security detail was misinformed. You look like death, Father." It had been months since Lem had seen him last, and the months had not been kind. Father looked weary, exhausted even. His hair seemed grayer. He had lost weight. He was still Father, however. Cool, impatient, and all business.

"What do you have?" Father said.

Lem held up his wrist pad. "Any of these walls projection-ready?"

Father gestured to the wall to Lem's left.

Lem pointed his wrist pad, entered the necessary commands, and the first image appeared large on the wall. The image showed the cocoon encircling the asteroid, with the tail end of the Formic ship protruding from one side.

Father stepped close and studied it for a long moment. "Where is this?" he finally asked.

"Kuiper Belt. Asteroid 2030CT. Quite a distance from where Copernicus was located, which was my first question.

Middle of nowhere, really. Far from any military targets. There's no reason for it to be out there."

"There is a reason," Father said. "It doesn't want to be noticed. What's this material surrounding it?"

"No idea. But here, look at this second image. You can see the Formic ship anchored to the rock on the other side. It's tiny. No bigger than the craft that took out Copernicus. Which raises the question: Where did the Formics get the material to cover an entire asteroid? They couldn't have brought it with them. The ship doesn't have the cargo space. That rock has a diameter of more than a kilometer at its widest point. I haven't done the math, but I'm roughly guessing it would require over a million square meters of material to cover it. No, actually more than that because the canopy hovers away from the surface, creating a ceiling for the habitat. So that's probably twenty to thirty percent additional surface area. And the material has to be thick enough to withstand a little abuse. Micrometeorites bombarding it occasionally and whatnot. So we're talking about an incredible amount of material. Then there's this filament skeletal structure holding it all together and giving it shape. No way could the Formics have brought that with them either. They must have harvested the materials from the rock. There's no other explanation."

"Any idea how long it's been there?"

Lem shrugged. "A ship that small would have a minimal crew. Maybe half a dozen Formics at the most. And yet they built this entire canopy structure after harvesting materials. That's a lot of digging and processing and shaping and building for a group of workers that small. I'm guessing it would have taken years."

"Unless there were more Formics there initially who helped build it and who have since left, leaving only this skeleton crew behind."

"Possibly," said Lem. "But I'm guessing any movement of materials or troops would have been done with tiny ships like this one. Anything bigger and there's a good chance we would have seen it."

"Where did you get these images?" Father asked. "A Juke miner?"

"From Victor Delgado's crew, if you can believe it. Which includes Imala, Edimar, and others. Victor thinks the cocoon is a recent construction, but I don't see how."

"Are these the only images you have?"

Lem nodded.

"I'll send this to the IF immediately. They'll decide how to address it. You were right to bring it to me."

It was a dismissal.

"So that's it?" Lem asked.

"What do you want?" Father asked. "Formal recognition? A medal?"

"How about, 'Lem, how are you? How goes the company I gave you? How have you been getting along ever since I, your father, started stealing so many of your employees?' "

Father sighed. "Don't be petulant, Lem. It's unbecoming of a CEO."

"Don't you think it's a conflict of interest, Father? The Hegemony, the very organization that awards defense contracts, forms its own defense company? I'm no lawyer, but I think that may bite you in the butt someday."

"I have not formed a company, Lem. I have hired employees to help develop projects too sensitive for the open market."

"Too sensitive? I have whole departments of people with the highest level of clearance, Father. This has never been an issue before."

"Perhaps because what we're developing has never been this sensitive before. I know that must rattle your curiosity to the core, Lem, but you'll just have to trust me."

"What is it? A weapon? It can't be something to breach the Formic hulls. You gave that contract to Gungsu. Which was a blunder, by the way. Their little gravity disruptor is a joke, and you know it, Father." A thought struck him. "Unless you *are* developing a hull-breach weapon, but by not awarding the contract to somebody, you would have raised suspicion and showed your hand, so you awarded the contract to Gungsu as cover."

Though as soon as Lem had said it aloud, he realized how ridiculous the idea sounded.

Father laughed quietly. "Really, Lem. Do you honestly think I would give billions of credits to Gungsu simply to throw people off my trail? They got the contract because they presented the best product. Personally I think it's a relatively weak option considering the strength of the hull, but it was the best we saw—certainly better than anything your team developed."

"We have the solution now," Lem said. "Benyawe showed it to me only moments ago. It doesn't breach the hull. It opens the existing access points. Why create a new hole when there are already doors to get inside?"

Father hesitated. "Interesting. A nonviolent approach. How very unmilitarylike. The Strategos will hate it."

"It's not his decision, Father. It's the Hegemony's. It's yours."

"This isn't a business meeting, Lem. It's an intelligence meeting. Didn't they teach you that in business school: Never sell to someone who isn't in the mood to buy."

To Lem's surprise, an IF officer in full uniform opened a door at the back of the room and stepped out of Father's study. He was quick to close the door behind him, as if concealing something inside, and looked somewhat embarrassed. "Excuse me, Mr. Jukes. I hate to interrupt, but they're waiting."

Father glanced at Lem uneasily and then turned to the officer. "I'll be there in a moment. Thank you, Lieutenant."

The lieutenant nodded and then disappeared back inside the study.

Who did Father have waiting in his study? Lem wondered.

And why was an IF officer on hand? And in the middle of the night, no less. Whoever it was clearly had a great deal of authority to have the nerve to show impatience for the Hegemon of Earth. And if an IF officer was the liaison, it had to be someone within the IF. The lieutenant had been assigned to Father. Otherwise, if Father were meeting with anyone else, it would be a Hegemony employee on hand running the show, one of Father's people.

Yet the lieutenant had said "they" were waiting. So more than one. At least two. People of authority. People to whom this lieutenant reported.

Lem understood at once. There wasn't anyone in Father's study, not physically anyway, other than the lieutenant perhaps. Father was in direct communication with the Strategos and the Polemarch. But how was that possible? Both men were in the Asteroid Belt. Any conversation with them would take hours. The bucket brigade system that existed for communication within the Fleet was painfully slow. It consisted of a series of relay stations set up in a line stretching from Luna to the end of the Kuiper Belt. New transmissions would be sent up and down the chain, from one station to the next until the transmission reached its destination. Having a two-way conversation could take days. And yet whoever was waiting for Father in the study had grown impatient, as if they expected the dialogue to be immediate, as if they were together in the same room, facing one another.

"You've developed faster-than-light communication," Lem said. "That's your secret project, isn't it? That's what you've been developing. A way to communicate across vast distances instantaneously. Just like the Formics do."

"That would be convenient, wouldn't it?" Father said. "But no."

"You're a terrible liar, Father. The Polemarch and the Strategos are waiting for you in that room. That's why you're still up and dressed. You're coinciding with their wake schedule.

That lieutenant is some sort of communications officer. What does he do, operate the equipment? Protect it? How is this even possible?"

"Don't press this matter, Lem. And stop speculating. If such tech existed, which it doesn't, it would not be something I would discuss with you."

"I don't know why I didn't see it earlier," Lem said. "Of course this would be a military priority. How can we defeat an enemy if their communication system is so much faster and better than our own? They would have the advantage in every battle. But if *we* had the tech as well, our best commanders could be engaged in any fight anywhere at any moment." Lem laughed. "We sold you on the bucket brigade system. Juke built it and sold it to the Hegemony, and all the while you were developing your own, better system. And you laughed at my suggestion of throwing people off your trail."

"Leave this alone, Lem. You have a job to do, and I have mine."

"The Formics wiped out our communications in the last war with the gamma plasma. They crippled nearly every one of our satellites, leaving us blind and disconnected and disorganized. So of course we would need an indestructible communications grid. One apparently that doesn't use satellites at all. How does it work, Father? And how can I get one?"

"You build weapons and ships, Lem. You don't need instant communication for that. But if you go around spreading rumors of faster-than-light communication I will have you arrested and jailed, if not shot."

"That means I'm right, of course," Lem said smiling.

"No, it means that rumors of it are a treasonous offense that will end your useful life in the Hegemony. Take that how you will, but keep your mouth shut."

Lem mimed zipping his mouth closed.

"This new intelligence about the asteroid will go to the right people," Father said. "I can promise you that. And I mean what I say, Lem. Let this go. There is nothing the Hegemony won't do to protect the people of Earth."

"But why keep it a secret?" Lem asked. "Why protect it so vehemently? Why can't people know?"

"You have always suffered from a lack of vision, Lem. A narrow perspective. A view of only the here and now. Ignorance is why people can go to sleep at night." He turned and moved toward his study. "You can show yourself out."

With that, Father went through the door and was gone.

Lem stood there alone a moment longer, with even more questions than before. What vision am I not seeing, Father? What perspective is beyond my imagination?

He returned to his skimmer and lifted off into the darkness, soaring over the squat buildings of Old Town.

Instantaneous communication. It was impossible. And yet Father had figured it out, perhaps with people formerly on my payroll. He did with them what I could not.

Maybe you're right, Father. Maybe I do lack vision. But ignorance is not what lets me sleep at night. It's answers. And I will not stop looking until I have them.

# CHAPTER 9

## Council

To: vico.delgado@freebeltmail.net
From: lem.jukes@juke.net
Subject: Re: Formics at asteroid 2030CT

Vico,

I gave my father all the information on 2030CT. Uncharacteristically, he admitted that it was important AND that he had not already known about it. He assured me that he would inform the International Fleet immediately. I assume he has already told the Polemarch and Strategos.

I've looked at the charts, however. The nearest IF ship is six to eight months away from that asteroid. You could reach it within a week. I do not want to endanger your family, but time is of the essence here. The thruster the Formics have attached to the rock suggests that they intend to push it somewhere. Maybe even directly at Earth. It's not a terribly large asteroid, but it's large enough to wipe out millions of people on impact and disrupt weather for a generation. If the Formics were to target a densely populated area, they could annihilate four to five times the number of people we lost in the last war. Once that asteroid starts moving, the closer it gets to Earth, the harder it will be to redirect its course, especially if the Formics try to prevent us.

There are far too many unknowns here for us to wait for the IF to arrive and conduct a thorough investigation. Someone needs to reach that rock as soon as possible and reconnoiter. Is there anyone outside the military better qualified than you? Is it not the best of good fortune for the future of our species that it was you and your family that discovered this and are in the best position to investigate it?

I have a few Juke mining ships out in K Belt, but none of them are close enough to offer you any assistance. What I can offer I will, however. I have created an account in your name at one of my company's financial institutions. The link is below. The transfer is complete, pending your own ID check. I hope the funds will be helpful. Obviously, you can't use them until you reach a depot, after this recon is over, but it can help recoup any expense in fuel or materials, not to mention lost income because of the diversion.

My only request is that you send all data you recover to me directly. Images, vids, mineral analyses, whatever. I have attached an encryption program for this purpose. Please use it. Send the data also to the IF of course, but don't be surprised if they dither for a week, ordering you to do nothing until they reach a decision—or if some resentful and ambitious rear admiral is slow to pass it up the chain till he figures out how to use the intel to his political advantage.

Respond and let me know what you decide, though I
know you well enough to be sure that, as so many
times before, you'll take the risks and make the sacri-
fices necessary for the safety of Earth.

                                                    Lem

Victor hovered inside the small office adjacent to the helm
and watched as Arjuna reread the e-mail.

"Did you try this link?" Arjuna asked. "This account he
mentions here, is that a real thing?"

"It's real," said Victor. "There are two hundred thousand
credits there."

Arjuna's eyes widened for a moment and then he scoffed.
"Typical Lem Jukes. He thinks he can wave money under our
noses and buy us off."

"We could use the funds," said Victor. "We need to replace
the oxygen extractor."

"I thought you fixed it," said Arjuna.

"I did," said Victor. "But I used printed parts. The polymers
we have aren't nearly as durable as after-market materials.
What I've built should last for a while, but I'd sleep better
if we had a factory-assembled OE in place."

"What about Mazer Rackham?" asked Arjuna. "Still no
response from him?"

"None," said Victor, "which is strange. He's usually very
prompt with his replies, and this is obviously the most important news I've ever sent him."

Arjuna sighed and looked back at the e-mail hovering in
the holofield. "So Lem Jukes is our only way of reaching anyone of authority in the IF. He says he showed it to his father.
Any chance the Hegemon dismissed it? What if he didn't pass
it on to the Strategos and Polemarch? Should we try another
channel of communication to be sure?"

"We can send the images to a hotline the IF has set up for

reports like this, but I've heard from other free miners on the nets that the chances of anything getting passed up the chain that way are low. Lem confirms that in his e-mail. There are miles of red tape and skeptics we'd have to cut through first."

"We could send this to the press," said Arjuna. "They'd be all over it."

"And we would make the IF look like bumbling incompetents," said Victor. "The world is already losing faith in the military, Arjuna. If people found out from the press that a Formic ship had slipped into the solar system without being detected, that's another strike against the IF, another show of failure. You'd have political pandemonium on Earth. The IF is fragile right now. I get that sense from Mazer. They don't need another show of weakness to crack them any further."

"I'm worried about you, Vico. You're starting to sound like a politician."

"The International Fleet is our best chance against the Formics," said Victor. "If we can keep them strong, we should. That helps all of us."

Arjuna gestured back at the e-mail. "You're talking out of both sides of your mouth, Vico. You're saying we should rely on the IF, but you also seem to be entertaining Lem's proposal here that we go to this asteroid and investigate. We're not going to do that. I'm not putting the lives of every man, woman, and child on this ship in jeopardy for two hundred thousand credits. I say we confirm that the IF is taking this threat seriously and let them handle it."

"That's the problem," said Victor. "They *can't* handle it. There isn't anyone else out here. We're the only ship in any position to investigate what the Formics are doing there."

"The Gagak is not a military vessel, Vico. We are not weaponized for combat. We can't defend ourselves if attacked. Do you know how I have kept this family alive for years with pirates and raiders out there in the Black? By running. By never getting in a fight in the first place. If I see a threat, I run. You may call that cowardice, but I call it keeping my children alive."

"You ran because you had a salvage ship," Victor said. "Light and fast and poorly shielded. You *couldn't* defend yourself. You'd lose every time against pirates. But that's not what the Gagak is now. We've made this one of the toughest mining vessels in the K Belt. We've got more shield plates on the hull than you'll likely find on any ship in the Fleet. We're as strong as an ox."

"We're as slow as an ox, too," said Arjuna. "With all of this iron and added mass, it takes us forever to accelerate. If the Formics were to attack, we wouldn't be able to outrun them."

"I don't think they'll give chase," Victor said. "They've anchored their ship to that asteroid. If we're right about the area beneath the canopy being oxygenated, they'd create a hole in the canopy and lose their habitat by detaching their ship. I think it's far more likely that they'd let us go. Or maybe scare us off. I don't think they'll come after us if we retreat. They're at that rock for a reason. They're not going to give it up."

"You're making assumptions that could cost us our lives," Arjuna said.

"I'm giving you my best guess based on my experience with the Formics," said Victor. "These creatures are task-oriented. Once they're given a mission, they stick to it, even if doing so will kill them. I saw it time and again in the war. You saw it in the vids. If they've been given an order to take that rock somewhere, they're not going to let it go."

"What if they have gamma plasma on their ship?" Arjuna asked. "If they're armed with that, they wouldn't need to give chase. Nor would it matter how many shield plates we have. They'd slice right through us."

Victor reached into the holofield and made a few hand gestures, bringing up the most recent images of 2030CT. "Look at the photos the probe took. I can't see any weapons on that ship. All that's visible are the thrusters. So even if the ship *is* armed, the weapons are under the shell and would therefore rip the shell apart if the weapons fired. Besides, it's a tiny ship. Less than a quarter our size. I think we can rule out gamma plasma. The ship would need massive storage tanks that it obviously doesn't have. As far as I can tell, it has extremely limited cargo space. And look at the metal on the thrusters. That's not the hull material of the scout ship. That's iron. And not even particularly strong iron, either. That's crudely processed ore. It's not the pristine and indestructible hull material of the scout ship. It's vulnerable. We could take it."

"A moment ago, we were discussing reconnaissance," said Arjuna. "Now you want to orchestrate an assault?"

"No," said Victor. "I'm merely saying that based on the information we have, it's unlikely that the Formics at that asteroid are equipped with any heavy weaponry. Their ship is too small. That's why it's out here in the middle of nowhere, far from anyone who can pose a threat to it. That's why it went dark. It doesn't want to be found, and it doesn't want a fight."

"More assumptions," said Arjuna.

"Our probe has been orbiting the asteroid for several days now," said Victor, "and the Formics haven't fired a single shot. Why not? Can they not detect it? This shell or canopy or whatever it is, is it affecting their sensor tech? Do they not even know the probe is there? Or do they know it's there and choose to ignore it? Or maybe they know it's there, but they *can't* fire on it because doing so would damage the shell. We don't know, but the fact that they're not responding at all is a good sign for us. It makes me feel safer about investigating."

"I can't be any clearer," said Arjuna. "I'm not bringing this ship anywhere close to that rock. I don't care that the Formics haven't fired at the probe. I don't care that the IF isn't as close as we are. I don't care that you've constructed a logical argument about minimal risk. My only concern is this crew. We're not soldiers, Vico. We're miners, and barely miners at that."

"I'm not suggesting that we fly the ship right up to it," said Victor. "I value the safety of this family as much as you do. I'm merely suggesting that we get a little closer. We approach it from the side opposite the thrusters. Then we decelerate and hold our position, maybe a few thousand klicks out. Then I drift to it alone in a quickship and investigate."

"Quickships aren't designed to hold a pilot," said Arjuna. "They're unmanned cargo rockets. They haul mined minerals away from a dig site. Trying to pilot one would be suicide."

"I've done it before," said Victor. "I know how to build a cockpit for it large enough to carry me."

Arjuna sighed and considered for a moment. "What do you mean you'll 'investigate'?" he asked finally. "What intel are you going to gather that the probe hasn't already gleaned?"

"We don't know what that shell is composed of," said Victor. "At the very least I could take a sample of the surface."

Arjuna frowned, considering. "If you're attacked, we can't rush in there and save you. You'd be on your own."

"I realize that," said Victor, "I'm only asking that you let me modify one of the quickships and get me a little closer."

Arjuna folded his arms. "What does Imala think about this?"

Victor hesitated. "She agrees that action needs to be taken."

"But she doesn't think that action should be taken by you," said Arjuna.

"Basically," said Victor. "Although she agrees that I'm the person best qualified to do so."

Arjuna nodded then waved his hand through the holofield, closing the e-mail. "Imala told me she submitted an application to join the IF."

Victor didn't know what to say to that. He knew that Imala had gone through with it, but he didn't know she was telling people. The next time the ship docked at a depot, she would get off and find passage to the nearest recruiting station. How much time did Victor have with her before that happened? Six months? Nine?

"Your relationship with Imala is none of my business," said Arjuna. "But I heard that you two had an argument and suddenly one of you wants to singlehandedly attack a Formic outpost, and the other has signed up to join the war. If I didn't know any better, I'd say you were running from the heat and jumping into the fire."

"Imala joining up has nothing to do with me, and my wanting to investigate the asteroid has nothing to do with Imala. At least not directly. We both feel motivated to keep the other safe, I suppose, but this isn't about us. The Formics' presence here is an act of war, Arjuna. Not a war between them and the IF, but a war between them and all of us. You, me, everyone on this ship. No, we're not soldiers. But we owe it to every other human being to find out what's going on at that asteroid."

"I meant no offense, Vico. I am merely concerned for you and Imala. I would hate to think that a rift has grown between you two."

"It hasn't," said Victor, although a part of him wasn't sure if that was true. Since his discussion with Imala the other evening there was a formality between them that Victor couldn't stand. Before they had always been relaxed and playful with one other. Or it was enough simply to be in the same room together, quietly attending to their separate tasks and enjoying being close. Now there was a fog of awkwardness between them that Victor wasn't sure how to address.

"I appreciate your concern for me and Imala," said Victor, "but my concern is that asteroid. I would rather have your blessing to approach it in a quickship, but I'm going either way."

Arjuna nodded, as if he expected that. "The quickships belong to you more than they do to me. You brought them with you when you came. I can't stop you. But let me talk to the council. If they agree to take you closer to the rock, I won't veto their decision."

Victor couldn't ask for more than that. "Thank you," he said.

He left Arjuna's office and made his way out into the corridor, surprised to find Mother there waiting for him. To the crew she was Rena, Arjuna's second in command, the glue that held everyone together, the calm voice of reason, the matriarch of the ship. Her hair had grayed a lot in the last few months, and she looked more tired than usual. She slipped her arm around his and led him away.

The wall at the end of the corridor had a curved surface where a live feed of space outside was projected—a calm canvas of black, dotted with stars. It was as close to a window as you could find on the ship. Mother paused there and looked outward.

"Imala told me she enlisted," Mother said. "She seemed surprised that you hadn't told me already." She turned to Victor. "Why didn't you?"

"Because that's for her to tell you, Mother. I'm not going to talk about her decisions behind her back. If she wants people to know, she'll tell them."

"You're angry."

"Only at myself. If she leaves it will be because I didn't give her a strong reason to stay."

"If she leaves it will be because she considers it her duty, Vico. Can you fault her for that?"

"I don't fault her for anything," said Victor. "I'm the one who made the mistake here. I should have married her a year ago."

"You weren't ready then," Mother said. "I'm not sure she was either. It's different in space. You're not simply marrying an individual, you're marrying an entire family. That's a daunting commitment."

Victor faced her. "No offense, Mother, but you make it sound like people have had a choice out here when it comes to marriage. Before we joined Arjuna's crew our family practiced arranged marriages with the other families and clans. There was never any courtship, never any romance. People were simply thrown together. Marriage was a way to mix up the gene pool and discourage inbreeding."

Mother frowned. "You make it sound barbaric."

"How else would you describe it?" Victor asked. "We sent our eighteen-year-old daughters off with total strangers and hoped they would be treated fairly. That's not exactly the stuff of fairy tales."

"We knew the families, Vico. They weren't total strangers. And they wouldn't risk earning a bad reputation by mistreating a bride. That would have ended their chances for future unions. They would have been ostracized by the other clans. Brides were treated like royalty among the families. When we brought them into the family, we gave them every comfort."

"Yes, and some of them bawled their eyes out for days," Victor said.

"They always had a choice, Vico. No bride or groom was ever coerced into a marriage. They may have experienced some homesickness once their families were gone, or they may have quickly learned that marriage was not what they had expected, but everyone went into the union willingly."

"Two families come together in the middle of space for the sole purpose of marrying off their children, and you don't think the bride and groom felt coerced?"

Mother raised an eyebrow. "How did this become a conversation about free-miner marriage arrangements?"

Victor shook his head. "I wanted it to be different for me and Imala. I didn't want us to marry simply because it was socially convenient. I wanted Imala to choose me because of who I am, not because I'm the only guy available."

"She did choose you, Vico. She came with you from Luna."

"That wasn't a commitment to marry, Mother. That was a willingness to explore an idea."

"And she explored it, and she fell in love."

"I don't doubt that, Mother. I just worry it will fade. Once Imala leaves, once she gets back in the real world and we're apart, she'll realize that there are better options out there, better futures than the one I can offer her."

"You two are still engaged, Vico. She told me the wedding was still on."

"Of course she's going to say that. You're my mother. It would be painfully awkward for her to suggest otherwise. She's surrounded by my family."

"You think her insincere?"

"I think she's convinced herself for the sake of social convenience that she and I are still engaged. When she's away, when she feels a little more freedom, she might think otherwise."

"Freedom?" Mother said, chuckling. "You make it sound like she's a hostage here."

"This isn't her life, Mother. She isn't an asteroid miner."

"As of when?" said Mother. "She's been with us for over two years, Vico, and as far as I can tell, she fits right in, far more than I thought she ever would. She's one of the most productive members of the crew. Even Sabad likes her, and Sabad doesn't like anyone."

It was true. Sabad was Arjuna's youngest wife; barely twenty years old and rather difficult to tolerate for more than a few moments at a time. Victor avoided her whenever he could. She treated everyone condescendingly and with contempt, including her own husband. The one exception was Imala, who Sabad sought out and treated almost like a friend, much to everyone's astonishment.

"Imala has been happy here, Vico," Mother said. "So have you."

Victor turned to the window. "It doesn't matter. Whatever is driving her to leave is greater than whatever is compelling her to stay."

Mother put a comforting hand on his arm. When he finally turned to look at her, she smiled up at him. "You're like me," she said, "a worrier. Your father was the optimistic one, always confident that things would work out eventually, while I was pulling my hair out considering all the horrific possible outcomes."

Victor frowned. "So I'm the bad guy here?"

Mother patted his arm. "There is no villain, son. Personally I think it's best that you and Imala part for a while. It might help you determine if marriage is what both of you truly want and if you're willing to do what's necessary to make it work."

Victor smiled sadly. "You're supposed to take my side."

She laughed. "I am. I'm taking Imala's side as well. I'm also hoping that one day those two sides will be the same."

She kissed him on the cheek and returned to the helm.

He should have told her about his plans to investigate the asteroid, he realized. She would find out sooner or later, and it was best for her to hear it from him. But no, Mother wouldn't like the idea and he wasn't in the mood to defend himself again. He didn't need another objector. Not now.

He left the corridor and went straight to his workshop in the lower deck to begin building a digital model of a cockpit for a quickship. He had a rudimentary design by the time Magoosa arrived. Victor's apprentice took one look at the model and understood at once.

"If you're going to the asteroid, I want to go with you," Magoosa said. "I can help."

"I appreciate the offer," said Victor, "but I assure you that's not going to happen, Goos. Your father would never allow it. And neither would I."

Magoosa looked crestfallen. "I'm not a child, Vico. I can help."

"I know you can, Goos. Which is why I'm putting you in charge of modifying the quickship. We need to equip one with shields and batteries and some crude life support, mostly extra oxygen tanks and water. There's a quickship in the cargo bay. We'll use that one."

Magoosa seemed surprised. "You're putting *me* in charge of that?"

"Unless you don't think you can handle it?"

"Oh, I can handle it, Vico. Don't worry about that."

"Good," Victor said. "Because when it comes time for you to enlist with the IF, they're going to ask you if you've ever had any experience with combat, if you've ever had to think quickly in a moment of crisis, if you've ever been truly innovative with few resources at your disposal. Help me with this quickship and you'll be able to tell them yes."

Magoosa nodded, energized. "I am all over this, Vico. You'll find me in the cargo bay." He launched away.

Victor smiled. Then he hovered in the workshop for a moment, unsure what to do next. He needed to strategize. How was he going to approach the canopy around the asteroid? And once he reached it, how would he anchor the quickship so it didn't float away and leave him stranded. He needed Imala's brain. She was the strategist—not to mention a good sounding board for his own ideas. She could see flaws instantly and provide possible solutions in the same breath. Without her, he'd spend hours chasing a dead end.

So why didn't he go find her? Why did he hesitate?

"You're avoiding me," a voice said behind him.

Victor turned and found Imala hovering in the doorway.

"Actually I was thinking about coming to find you," he said.

"Thinking about it," she said. "That's different from doing it."

"I spoke with Arjuna," Victor said.

She launched into the room and caught a handhold near him. "And what did he say?"

"He was as resistant as you suspected, but he agreed to hold a council."

"That's good," said Imala. "I think the council will side with us."

"Us?" said Victor. "I thought you were against me going."

"I am. But I agree that someone needs to go. You've infiltrated a Formic ship before. You know how to elude them. You know how they think, or at least you understand them better than anyone else on this ship."

He nodded, grateful. And yet it pained him a little that she wasn't still arguing against the idea. Had her love for him diminished so quickly that she was willing to let him go into harm's way?

"But know this," said Imala. "You're not going without me."

He started to object, but she silenced him with a wave of her hand. "Don't argue with me because nothing you say is going to change my mind. This is a two-person job in a quickship. You can't go alone. If you were to need help, someone has to be there to offer it. We're a team, Vico. We've done this before, and if not for me, you would have died a long time ago."

He couldn't argue with that.

"Plus I'm a far better pilot than you are," said Imala.

"You've never flown a quickship before," said Victor.

"I'm a fast learner. It's not rocket science."

"Technically it is rocket science."

"You need someone helping you," said Imala. "If you go alone, a thousand things could go wrong, and you might not be in a position to do anything about it. You know I'm right."

"I don't want to put you in unnecessary danger, Imala."

"This is necessary danger, Vico. I know you're angry with me about enlisting, I know you're disappointed, but we need to put that aside right now and focus on that asteroid. I'm not letting you go alone. That's not going to happen. If you go, I'm going with you. It's not up for discussion."

Victor was going to say more, but his computer terminal chimed.

"Vico, it's Arjuna, I need you at the helm. Imala, too, if you know where she is."

Victor and Imala glanced at each other and then hurried to the helm. When they arrived, the room was quiet, and the entire crew was staring at them. Arjuna was at the holotable. Victor couldn't read his expression. Anger? Annoyance? Disappointment?

"What's wrong?" Victor asked.

"It appears your message got through to the IF after all," Arjuna said. His mouth was a tight line. His jaw was set. "We just received a transmission."

He turned to the holotable and waved his hand. The head of an IF officer appeared. Older. Crew cut. Dark complexion. Indian. It was a recorded message, sent via laserline.

"Crew of the Gagak," the holo said. "My name is Khudabadi Ketkar, the Polemarch of the International Fleet. I am responsible for building, arming, and maintaining the ships of the Fleet as well as training their flight crews. We have been informed that you have discovered an anomaly in your sector that appears to be of Formic origin. We commend you for bringing this information to the attention of the International Fleet. The defense of the human race is the duty of all men and women, soldier or civilian.

"According to the Wartime Space Commerce Act, signed by the Hegemon and ratified by a majority of the nations on Earth after the Formic invasion, the International Fleet holds the authority to commandeer any space vessel for the purpose of Earth defense when a flight-worthy vessel of the

International Fleet is not readily available. Therefore, by the authority invested in me by that law, your vessel is now under the direct command of the International Fleet."

"Is this is a joke?" Victor said.

"There's more," Arjuna said.

"We recognize that most people on your ship are civilians," the Polemarch said. "Please rest assured that the safety of your crew is our highest priority. However, under the circumstances, and considering the potential magnitude of this threat, we find it necessary for your ship to take action. We are therefore placing command of your vessel into the hands of Ensign Imala Bootstamp, who we recognize is a new recruit of the Fleet, but whose actions in the previous conflict are evidence of her abilities to follow orders and defer to command. Captain Bootstamp, when you have received this message, reply immediately so that we can relay your orders. Ketkar out."

The holo winked out, and the words END OF TRANSMISSION appeared. Imala stared at the empty holofield, mouth slightly open in shock.

Arjuna folded his arms and regarded her. "Well now, isn't this awkward."

# CHAPTER 10

# Nardelli

No punishment or penalty may be imposed upon any soldier awaiting court-martial, other than arrest or confinement. Nor shall the confinement inflict any cruel or unusual discomforts or restrict the person's access to the basic necessities of life. Minor noncorporal punishments may be imposed for infractions of discipline during confinement.

—International Fleet Uniform Code of Military Justice, Article 27

Mazer anchored his feet to the floor in the kitchen and began scrubbing inside the oven, removing all the black residue along the inner walls.

There were five such ovens in the kitchen at WAMRED, each one large enough to fit a grown man. Mazer's orders were to clean them all before the night was through. Then he was to conduct an inventory of the walk-in freezer, prep the next day's breakfast, and service the dishwashing machines. Then it was on to the latrines and showers and docking area for more mopping and scrubbing and waxing. Then laundry. Then changing air filters. Then everything else on his duty list. It was far more than he could possibly complete in a single shift, but that was Colonel Vaganov's intent: to load Mazer with too many assignments and then to dock him at the end of every shift for failing to follow orders.

The MP who stood guard was dozing off, his arms rising to his side in zero G. At first the MPs had been annoyed by their assignment to guard Mazer, but that annoyance had quickly grown to resentment, particularly since it required them to work during what was normally their sleep shift. Mazer felt sorry for them. But since he had been ordered to remain silent, he couldn't express any sympathy.

He had been isolated for over a week now, with no word on when he might be sent to Luna for his court-martial. Mazer used the time as best as he could. His earpiece contained dozens of lectures and academic studies on the Formics, and Mazer listened to them while he worked. He didn't have access to the nets, but at least he didn't feel like his time was completely wasted.

His post on the forum had been passed up the chain—or Lem had gotten word to the Hegemony. Either way, the covered asteroid was common knowledge now. Mazer had overheard the MPs talking about it. The IF was addressing the situation, though how they were doing so was unclear to everyone.

Mazer's arms and clothes were caked in black goo by the time he started on the last oven.

Nardelli, the MP who had roughly escorted Mazer from the colonel's office, arrived to relieve the MP on duty. Mazer stayed focused on his work and pretended to be disinterested, but the exchange broke routine and put him on alert. Nardelli carried himself with an air of self-importance, as if he knew he had more authority and freedom than others. He glanced at Mazer and spoke to the first MP in hushed tones.

Mazer lowered the volume on his earpiece and listened.

"The case is sealed," Nardelli said. "Nobody knows details. But I heard there was some accident during a field test and this guy abandoned his men. A marine lost his leg as a result." He gestured at Mazer. "This coward didn't even administer first aid. He was too busy trying to save himself. Also heard he leaked classified intel. Selling out soldiers to the press."

The first MP glared at Mazer. "I knew it had to be something bad. A captain getting mess duty during sleep shift. That's as low as it gets."

Nardelli glowered at Mazer. "What an emu. Has he talked at all?"

"Nope. Just scrubs away, silent as the dead."

Nardelli turned to Mazer. "Hey Rackham, you leave a man behind? Is that why the colonel busted your culo?"

Mazer didn't respond. He kept cleaning the oven.

"Don't harass him, Nardelli," said the first MP. "He's a captain."

"He won't be after his court-martial," said Nardelli. "They'll fillet him and bust him down to ensign. Colonel says so. He's nobody now. He can't touch us. Hey, Rackham, I asked you a question."

Mazer kept his eyes on his work and said nothing.

Nardelli came right up beside Mazer, his face inches from Mazer's ear. He looked even stronger and dumber up close.

"Are you ignoring me, soldier?" Nardelli said. "You think you're above us, better than us? You think your rank protects you? You must not be familiar with Article 4 of the International Fleet's Code of Military Justice. Because if you were, you'd know that when an authorized military police officer asks you a direct question, regardless of his rank or yours, you are under obligation to respond as thoroughly and as truthfully as you are able. To fail in that regard could be considered obstruction of justice, a very serious offense. You'd be looking at dishonorable discharge, forfeiture of all pay and allowances, or up to five years of confinement. Do you like confinement, Captain Rackham? Does that suit your pansy ass?"

Mazer said nothing.

"Leave him alone, Nardelli. The man can't speak. You'll get us both in trouble."

"Oh he can speak. He's just too much of a culo to respond. What's that in your ear, Rackham? Your earpiece?" He held out his hand. "Let's have it."

"Don't take his stuff," the other MP said.

Nardelli pointed a finger at the MP. "Your shift is over, Utami. Vacate. This is my prisoner now."

Utami hesitated and then left.

Nardelli turned back at Mazer and beckoned with his hand. "The earpiece, Rackham. Hand it over. You're not supposed to have any tech."

That wasn't true, but Mazer gave him the earpiece anyway.

Nardelli held it up and examined it. "You know, I lost an earpiece just like this one. In fact, I think this might be the very one I lost. How kind of you to return it to me. You don't mind if I take it back, do you, Rackham?"

Mazer kept silent.

"By all means, if you object, just say so," Nardelli said. "No? Well, that's generous of you. I could use something to play my music. What kind of music do you listen to, Captain?" He wiped the earpiece on his shirt, slid it in his ear, and tapped play. "What is this? Lectures on the Formics? Interesting. You have a little Formic fetish, do you, Rackham? A little love for the bugs? Not smart. That will reflect poorly on you in your court-martial. The judge isn't likely to take kindly to a bug lover." He tapped the earpiece again to silence it, but he kept it in his ear. Then his hand tapped his riot rod at his hip. "Give me any problems, Rackham, and I will give you bruises where no one looks. Bones and bruises. That'll be you. As purple as an eggplant." He moved away, giving Mazer his space. "Now do your list."

Mazer scrubbed at the oven and continued with his list, moving about the station, completing each task.

Nardelli scuffed his boot on the floor and left a mark. "You missed a spot over here, Rackham."

Mazer removed the scuff, but Nardelli made another one with his boot.

"You're not listening, Rackham. I said you missed a spot. Are you too stupid to see it? It's right here."

The scuff-and-clean cycle continued a few more times, until Nardelli grew bored of the game and drifted off, mumbling under his breath. Mazer was waiting for the riot rod to fall, and plotting his response if it happened. Nardelli was large, but he had the same pressure points and bones as anyone else.

But Nardelli made no move, and the rest of the shift proceeded without incident.

"Time's up, Rackham," Nardelli finally said. "Get up. Let's move."

Mazer was only halfway through his duty list, but he stored the cleaning supplies, washed up, and did as he was told.

One of Colonel Vaganov's officers was waiting outside Mazer's quarters when they returned, holding a tablet. "Did Captain Rackham finish his duties?" he asked Nardelli.

"No, sir. He did not."

"Did he ever speak to you, address you in any manner?"

"No, sir."

"Are you sure he didn't say a word? Nothing at all?"

Nardelli got the hint. "Now that I think about it, sir, he did say some rather unkind words about you and Colonel Vaganov, sir. About the Strategos as well. I don't feel comfortable repeating such language as I found it quite offensive."

The officer nodded, satisfied. "I see. I'll make a note. Now kindly escort Captain Rackham to the medical wing."

"Yes, sir."

Mazer followed without a word. The medical wing? Why?

He soon learned. A doctor put him in one of the examination rooms and told Nardelli to wait outside. The doctor conducted a thorough physical, poking and prodding and drawing blood. When he finished he asked Mazer to dress into a compression suit and run the treadmill for an hour. Mazer did so. It was exhausting, especially after ten hours of physical labor, but Mazer pushed his way through, setting a steady pace and ignoring the pain in his side. He knew the standards the IF demanded, and he watched the monitoring equipment to make sure he met them. When it was over, he legs twitched, his back ached, and his lungs felt as if they couldn't get enough air. To his surprise, the doctor then gave him a series of strength and agility tests, which Mazer had never taken in any previous physical. When it was over, his whole body was spent and covered in sweat.

The doctor flipped through the test results on his tablet. "There's no easy way to say this, Captain, so I'll get right to it. Your career as a combat soldier is essentially over. The IF has set very strict standards for physical readiness, and I'm afraid I have no choice but recommend you for light duty."

Mazer watched in stunned silence as the doctor tapped at his tablet, checking boxes that would essentially end Mazer's combat career. Any hope of getting on a warship with a decent crew vanished in an instant. He would never see action or serve alongside fellow marines. He would never again contribute in the ways that he had trained for. He'd be relegated to mindless administrative work. A desk job. All those years of pushing himself and conditioning his mind and body would be for naught.

He had been ordered not to speak, but he wouldn't remain silent now. "My results were within the acceptable range."

"You're at the lower end of the scale," the doctor said. "So technically, yes, you're still within the acceptable range. And for that you should be proud. The standard now for breach marines is extremely high. Most soldiers from Earth wouldn't make the cut. These are elite special-forces standards, the one and two percenters. The fact that you scored as high as you did at your age is impressive."

"You say that like I should be retired," Mazer said. "I'm twenty-five years old."

"It's a young man's war now, Captain. The average age for marines is twenty. You're a dinosaur by comparison."

"So you're retiring me because of my age?"

"I'm not retiring you, Captain. I'm simply recommending a different course for you. And I make that recommendation based on a number of factors. Age is one. Your endurance is another. But the primary reason is your debilitating injuries. I simply can't clear a soldier with your kinds of wounds."

Mazer's wounds. The ones he had sustained in the First Formic War.

"I've healed," said Mazer. "That was three years ago. I've passed every physical exam since then."

"And your performance has slipped every year. Only slightly perhaps, but I have the results right here in front of me."

The doctor stepped to the wall, and it lit up with data readouts and body scans. "You suffered serious abdominal trauma during the war, Captain. The wound to your stomach should have killed you, especially considering you were in a contaminated zone and hemorrhaging internally."

Mazer hardly needed reminding of that. The crash was still a vivid memory. Every so often his dreams were filled with the roar of the rotor blades and the heat of the fire and the acrid smell of charred bodies and burning plastic.

"I received lifesaving surgery in the field," Mazer said. "It's not as if my injuries went unattended."

"I wouldn't call it surgery. What you got was more of a hack job. I've read the report. A few Chinese rice farmers did a little cutting and stitching. Whatever previous experience they had wielding a knife must have come from skinning goats and peeling vegetables. I'm surprised you didn't die from infection."

"I had additional surgery after the war to correct their mistakes. I'm fine now."

The doctor pointed to a body scan. "Doctors removed another six inches of damaged tissue from your small intestines, Captain. Had I been your attending doctor at the time I probably would have recommended a medical discharge at that point." He tapped one of the charts, and it ballooned in size. "Your wounds have had an effect on your performance metrics. You used to be extraordinarily fast and flexible; it's sad to see how much function you've lost. Your knowledge, aptitude, and acuity results are off the charts, but your body is not what it used to be. What's more, I know you're in pain right now. You can put on a brave face, you can look as content as a sparrow in springtime, but I know it's an act. Your compression suit doesn't lie. You're hurting."

It was true. There was a gnawing ache in his stomach—not a stitch in his side or the discomfort of a stretched muscle, but the throbbing annoyance of his old wound. Like someone prodding him with a sharp stick. It wasn't enough to make him buckle over, and he could mostly ignore it if he focused his mind intently on a task. But it was there.

"You've performed well here at WAMRED," said the doctor. "So no one paid much attention to your medical file. Or maybe you knew someone who was willing to overlook it. Either way, I can't overlook it now." He tapped the wall, and the charts disappeared.

"Were you ordered to mark me for light duty?" Mazer asked.

The doctor looked affronted. "Absolutely not. I take offense at such a suggestion."

Mazer believed him. The man couldn't be that good of an actor. "How long have you been here at WAMRED?" Mazer asked. "I've never seen you before."

"I don't see how that makes any difference."

"It might."

The doctor folded his arms, growing impatient. "I arrived on the shuttle this morning."

"So I'm one of your first patients."

"You *are* my first patient. What are you suggesting, Captain?"

"Who scheduled my physical? I had one only five months ago. I thought these were annual checkups."

"They are. Normally. But they can be requested if a soldier's health or physical stamina is in question."

"So someone made a special request in my case?"

"I have no idea. I arrived, they gave me a schedule, you were first. I don't set the appointments."

"Interesting. On average, how many soldiers do you recommend for light duty?"

"This is beginning to feel like an interrogation," the doctor said. "We're through here."

The doctor moved for the door, but Mazer was faster. He stepped between the doctor and the exit.

"Out of my way, Captain, or I will call in the officer."

"Last question," Mazer said, "because I think you're being played here."

The doctor paused, folded his arms again, and frowned, waiting.

Mazer said, "Would you agree that other doctors within the IF are too lax when it comes to testing soldiers' physical readiness?"

The doctor sighed. "If you're asking me if I'm harder on soldiers than other doctors, Captain, the answer is, I am accurate, where other doctors are not. I am thorough. They are not. There should be no leniency in soldier readiness. Period. Any soldier who has ever sustained a life-threatening wound should be placed on light duty. That experience mars him. He is far more likely to hesitate, hold back, or buckle in the heat of battle. His fear of repeating his previous experience heightens his anxiety and diminishes his rational thinking. Physical wounds create irreparable mental wounds. I have written a paper on the subject."

"Was it published?"

"Several times."

"Did you present scientific evidence for this theory?"

"It isn't a theory. It is fact. I've been doing this for a long time, Captain. I've seen it with my own eyes."

"So you have anecdotal evidence," Mazer said. "Not statistical evidence. Your conclusions are based solely on your personal interactions with a limited number of patients who meet specific criteria. Because I could provide plenty of anecdotal evidence to counter that position. Every major engagement in the history of warfare probably has plenty of examples."

The doctor narrowed his eyes. "I do not have to justify my conclusions to you, Captain. Nor did I come here to debate soldier psychology."

"No, you came here to mark me for light duty," said Mazer. "And you made that decision the instant you saw my history. Putting me on the treadmill and through the tests was just perfunctory."

"Get out of my way, Captain."

Mazer opened the door, and the doctor launched out into the hall, where Nardelli was waiting. The doctor spun, launched again, and was gone.

Nardelli smiled sardonically at Mazer. "Good news, Rackham. I've just received orders to escort you to the dock. Your court-martial on Luna awaits."

Interesting. As soon as they build a case against me, they get right to it.

Mazer showered, changed into his uniform, packed his few belongings into a rucksack, and then followed Nardelli down the corridor. When they were alone, Nardelli stopped and faced him. "Do you have all your belongings in your rucksack there, Rackham? Every last one?" He took the earpiece out of his ear and rolled it between his fingers, giving Mazer an icy smile.

Mazer sighed inside. It was obvious that Nardelli was trying to rile him. Vaganov had probably ordered him to do so. *Get him to take a swing at you*, Vaganov might have said. *Let's add assaulting an officer to his growing list of charges.*

It was a ridiculously stupid approach, because only an idiot would fall for it. And it gave Mazer pause. Why was Vaganov so eager to discredit him? Did Vaganov's crimes go deeper than Mazer suspected?

Whatever the reason, Mazer wasn't playing.

"You can have my earpiece," said Mazer. "I don't need it anymore."

Nardelli smirked. "You're not supposed to talk, Rackham."

"I'm making an exception for you," said Mazer. "Consider it a gift, one soldier to another."

Nardelli gripped his riot rod. "You're not a soldier, Rackham. You're a traitor."

Mazer felt a little sad for the man. "I'm going to give you some unsolicited parting advice, Nardelli. Whatever Vaganov promised you, it's not worth it. His interests are terribly misplaced, and when he goes down, he's going to take you and everyone else he's enlisted to do his dirty work with him. I'm betting you already have a few strikes on your record. That's why Vaganov noticed you and made you his battering ram. But that's a doomed road, my friend. I'm not your enemy. The Formics are, and we're going to need every capable soldier when they get here. You do your family or Earth no good behind bars."

Nardelli laughed. "You're the one being court-martialed, Rackham, not me."

"That can change rather quickly," said Mazer.

Nardelli's expression hardened. "You threatening me, traitor?"

"I'm asking you to be sensible for the good of the human race. You obviously want to pick a fight. But I'm not going to take the bait. So let's just part before one of us does something he'll regret."

Nardelli grabbed Mazer by the arm and pulled him down a side corridor. "Yeah, well, my only regret is that I didn't do this a long time ago."

The space station's main cargo hold was at the end of the corridor. Nardelli dragged Mazer in, pushed him to the side, and began rolling up his sleeves. Mazer anchored himself to the floor and calmly took in his surroundings. The room was massive, at least thirty meters high, with an open space in the middle for cargo lifts to move freight around. The walls on the left and right were stacked floor to ceiling with storage bins, each bin roughly two meters cubed. The long rows and tall stacks of bins made the walls look like giant square honeycombs. Mazer stood by an empty bin on the floor level. The bins had no fronts, and only a few of them were empty. Most contained metal cargo cubes that fit snugly into each bin. Food, medical supplies, fresh water, spare parts, equipment. A short metal bar extended halfway across the front of each bin, holding each cargo cube in place. The bar was attached to the side of the bin, and when the bar was lifted, the cube was free to be extracted.

Mazer experimentally tried turning the bar nearest him and found it easy to rotate. A round button was on the side of the bin beneath the bar. Mazer pushed it, and as he had expected, the back wall of the bin slowly came outward. Had there been a cube inside, the advancing wall, and the unseen mechanism behind, would have pushed the cube free.

Nardelli assumed a fighting stance, fists up, jaw set.

"Do you really want to do this, Nardelli? This is schoolyard bully behavior. You should have outgrown this a long time ago."

Nardelli smiled. "I'm going to enjoy this."

Mazer put his hands behind his back, looking relaxed. "I'm special forces, Nardelli. They trained me how to crush a man's windpipe. It's not difficult. Normally the larynx is quite elastic. But out here in space, the thyroid cartilage and cricoid cartilage ossify. They get brittle and break easily. One hit is all it takes. All those joints and cords and sinew and cartilage will rip and pop and shatter. Pain, Nardelli. And blood. Even before it kills you, you want to die."

Nardelli raised his fists a little higher, protecting his neck. He didn't charge.

Mazer stepped to his right and turned the lever upward, freeing the cargo cube inside; then he pushed the button and continued to his right, keeping his eyes on Nardelli. The mechanism in the back came to life and pushed the cargo cube outward. Weightless, it drifted free of the bin and continued toward the bins on the opposite side.

Nardelli easily sidestepped it, letting it pass, hands still up.

"Or there's a carotid artery on either side of your neck," said Mazer. "Specifically your carotid sinus. I hit that and the baroreceptor cells get all wonky and confused and tell your brain to slow down your heart to drop your blood pressure. It happens fast. You black out. I then drive my boot into your crotch while you're asleep. If you wake up again, you'll wish you hadn't. The pain isn't pretty."

"You're trying to stall me," Nardelli said. "You're half my size. I can break you easy."

Mazer kept moving to his right. "A smaller size gives me the advantage, Nardelli. You're a big, easy, lumbering target. More mass in zero G means you need more energy to move, and when you do it's harder for you to maneuver. You don't need a PhD in physics to know that."

Mazer released another cube and kept moving to his right.

Nardelli looked like he would charge but then hesitated. The second cube passed him.

"What were Colonel Vaganov's instructions to you specifically?" Mazer asked. "To get me worked up into a frenzy? To agitate me enough so you could bust me on assault charges?"

Nardelli said nothing.

"Not a very smart plan," Mazer asked. "Fleet attorneys aren't stupid. They'll look at your record, and they'll look at mine, and who do you think they'll believe, Nardelli? You?"

Nardelli said nothing.

"Subtlety is not your strength," said Mazer. "You laid it on a little too thick. But I have to hand it to you. There were a few times when I almost gave in and broke your arms."

"So come try, Rackham."

"And how convenient that all the workers in the cargo hold are absent at just the right moment. Did Vaganov give them instructions, too?"

Nardelli said nothing.

"What you're doing here is career suicide, Nardelli," Mazer said. He kept moving to his right. He pushed another lever up, hit the button. A cargo cube scooted outward.

"Colonel Vaganov can't give you illegal orders," Mazer said. "Come with me to Luna. Talk to an attorney. You have a pretty good defense. He's a colonel. They train us to obey colonels. He put you in a difficult situation. Of course, Vaganov's probably too smart to have spoken to you directly. Your orders probably came from one of his officers. Which one was it?"

Mazer pushed up another lock bar and hit the button. The mechanism in the back whined as it turned on, and the cargo cube eased out of the bin.

Nardelli charged.

Mazer launched upward, his boot magnets already turned off, easily avoiding Nardelli's reach. Nardelli grabbed at air as Mazer tucked into a ball and got his feet pointing in the opposite direction. He landed lightly on the ceiling, but he launched again immediately, heading toward the bins on the opposite wall. He caught himself on the lip of a bin halfway between the floor and ceiling. He pulled up the lock bar, hit the button. The cargo cube drifted out, floating across the room.

Nardelli looked up at him. "That's how you fight, Rackham? Running away?"

Mazer moved to his right, pulled down another bar, hit another button. Another cargo cube drifted out.

Nardelli drew his riot rod, then launched upward directly at Mazer.

The man wasn't well trained in zero G combat, Mazer noted. He was launching all wrong. His center of mass was off, his legs weren't set, and he clearly had no plan for stopping himself other than his intended collision with Mazer.

Not smart.

Mazer moved a bar and hit a button, and Nardelli, with no way of changing his course, collided with the cargo cube as it was pushed out of the bin and into Nardelli's trajectory. There was a thud and a grunt of pain, and Mazer launched away. He released two more cubes as Nardelli drifted aimlessly, having ricocheted off the cube, arms flailing.

This is how it was in the Formic scout ship during the firefight, Mazer thought. Big chunks of debris. Obstacles obstructing our view and our flight. The Formics maneuvered around them easily, experienced in zero G, but we weren't ready for it. We hadn't trained our minds to think in a three-dimensional space. A huge oversight. That needs to be fixed.

Mazer landed on the lip of one of the bins near the ceiling and watched Nardelli struggle. There were nine cubes drifting lazily through the room at various heights, bumping into each other and forming a cluster of obstructions. Nardelli was having a hard time maneuvering around them. He jumped and landed on one, got his footing, and launched to another.

The top of his head was bleeding, and he was seething now, desperate to get to Mazer. But he was floundering too; all of his movements were uncertain and awkward, and it frustrated him all the more. He leaped to another cube, but this one must have been empty because it began to rotate when he hit it at the angle he did.

Nardelli panicked, struggling to keep his orientation with the floor. As the cube rotated one way, Nardelli countered by crawling the other way, trying to stay on what he perceived as the top of the crate, as if he feared he would fall off the cube to the floor. No Formic soldier would make such an obvious mistake.

We clearly have a lot of work to do with our soldiers.

Nardelli tried launching away from the empty cube, but its mass was not that much greater than his, and it drifted away from him with the same degree of force that he had applied. Instead of launching toward Mazer, Nardelli rotated out of control and drifted away, floundering again, flailing his arms and legs, and cursing.

He'd be that way for a minute or two, Mazer figured, which was all the time Mazer needed. He launched down to the exit, grabbed his rucksack, and headed for the hangar.

The shuttle was at the dock waiting for him. Mazer reported to the loadmaster, who scanned Mazer's ID bracelet and welcomed him aboard. Mazer stowed his rucksack and took a seat in the back. He was not the only passenger. About a dozen other soldiers were buckled in, but none of them seemed to pay him any attention, which was a relief.

Mazer watched the door, half expecting Nardelli to fight his way onto the shuttle to finish what he had started, bloody head wound and all. But several minutes passed, and no one else came on board.

Mazer lowered the terminal screen hidden in the seatback in front of him and typed up an e-mail to Kim before the shuttle decoupled and he lost the connection. He was coming home, he told her. He loved her. He was excited to see her.

He did not tell her that his military career was likely over, or that the IF was plagued with nearsighted careerists. Nor did he mention that his hope for a victory was all but extinguished. Kim didn't like depressing e-mails. And anyway, when he saw her again, he wanted to see her smiling. If they only had a little time left together, he wanted every moment to count.

# CHAPTER 11

## Shuttle

It takes a fleet to build a fleet, especially because there wasn't time to wait for mining ships in the Kuiper and Asteroid belts to bring enough raw materials to near-Earth shipyards in the months immediately following the First Formic War. Therefore every Earth-launchable shuttle became a cargo ship, lifting payloads of metal out of Earth's gravity well. Then they unloaded their cargo into space, left it in orbit, and went back down for more.

Cargo ships, tugs, yachts, lunar shuttles, and research vessels were pressed into service to pick up the orbiting cargo and carry it to the warship construction sites. The trouble was that there weren't enough of them. The cargo fleet that the IF needed was already plying routes between Mars, Luna, and the Asteroid Belt, but after seeing all the near-Earth ships commandeered for cargo service, neither the Families nor the corporations would admit that they had more than a few token ships near enough to help, while the free miners set out for deeper space.

They all understood that human survival depended on building warships to defeat the Formics, but they also knew that if the IF seized their ships, they'd never see them again. It would wipe them out, financially. They would end up stranded in some depot or station, begging for sustenance, with no hope of ever recovering from the financial loss.

Desperate for ships, the IF began planning to send expeditions to hunt down and capture the nearest cargo ships. The first Hegemon, Ukko Jukes, put a stop to that. He instead used Hegemony funds to start the Space Vessel Repurchase Program—nicknamed Repup. The Hegemon began by retroactively purchasing all the ships that had already been seized, paying a fair market price. Only then did the Corporations and Families discover that they had far more ships nearby than they had realized. The cost of purchasing the ships was greater than the Hegemony's entire budget, and the record suggests that Juke Limited guaranteed repayment to the banks that lent the money to fund Repup.

Soon there were enough vessels to clear out all the huge depots of warship parts. The original crews of these ships either continued to work them under IF officers, or they took service as shipbuilders with the various corporations contracted by the Fleet to design and build new warships. According to S. P. Mu's meticulous *Index of Cargo Crews*, more than 80 percent of these crews ended up enlisting in the IF before the end of the Second Formic War, and by all reports these space miners and transport crews became the backbone of the IF, training new recruits from Earth and Luna until they "got their space legs" and became accustomed to living and working safely in a zero G life-support environment.

The dependents of the free miners who entered the IF, along with those who refused to remain on vessels commanded by IF officers, were given passage to Luna, the only planetary surface with low-enough gravity that space-dwellers could adapt and survive. The government of Luna was ill-prepared to receive them, though the Hegemony increased Luna's food and water allotments in order to provide for the refugees. Refugee "camps"—adapted tenements and flimsy, hastily erected group shelters—were quickly established in the southern domes of Imbrium, but the delivery of food was insufficient and unreliable, while sanitation services and medical care were intermittent at best.

If not for the efforts of the Children of Earth Foundation, a nonprofit founded by Lem Jukes, which provided newly arrived free-miner families with the necessities of life and worked to incorporate them into Lunar society within months, the Repurchase Program would probably have led to mass desertions (or mutiny) by those free miners who had joined the IF and shipbuilding unions.

Instead, these new recruits were reassured that their families were well taken care of, and they stayed on the job, producing an astonishing number of warships before large combat action began in the Second Formic War. Most of them continued after the war to build warships incorporating new designs, in order to protect Earth with a shield that no future Formic weaponry could penetrate. Even if Lem Jukes had done nothing else but set in motion this vital humanitarian effort, his place as one of the architects of human survival would be secure.

—Demosthenes, *A History of the Formic Wars,* Vol. 3

Bingwen stepped down from the skimmer and onto the tarmac just as the sun was coming up over the Bay of Bengal. In the low light, the surface of the ocean was a dark sparkling amber moving gently toward the shores of Wheeler Island.

They were ten kilometers off the coast of eastern India on a small triangular shoal used exclusively by the International Fleet for discreet launches into space. The air smelled clean and briny, and Bingwen could hear off in the distance the faint call of a seabird. He had never seen the ocean before, and photos did not do it justice.

This is why the Formics so desperately want this world, he thought. There is warmth and water and life here. There is food and fuel and land and the chance not just to survive, but to flourish. Bingwen allowed the cool sea breeze to envelop him as Captain Li stepped down beside him and straightened the jacket of his new blue IF uniform.

"Savoring your last moment on terra firma?" Captain Li asked.

"Hopefully not my last," Bingwen said.

The shuttle that would take them out of Earth's atmosphere to the shuttleport in space stood on the tarmac before them. A handful of crewmen were outside it, busying themselves loading cargo and gear. The scene was a stark contrast to the highly publicized launches of the previous morning, when hundreds of Chinese soldiers sporting new IF uniforms and waving small Chinese flags had boarded shuttles and departed for Luna. They were China's first round of committed troops to the IF, and journalists from all over the world had captured the event. But here, off the mainland, isolated from everyone, there was not a single camera in sight.

"Surely we're not the only passengers," Bingwen said, as he followed Captain Li toward the shuttle.

Li laughed. "Hardly. This is an all-purpose shuttle, mostly reserved for VIPs. They can arrive minutes before liftoff. You, as a non-VIP, don't have that luxury. You're first on, last off. And since I'm forced to escort you, I must be as well. You'll stay in the back throughout the flight. Don't talk to anyone unless they address you first. Understood?"

"Yes, sir, Captain Li, sir."

The response was overly formal, but it felt natural to Bingwen's ears by now. Over the years he had learned to comply with Captain Li's particular demands for respect. To ignore them was to invite work detail or other punishments. Better to give the man what he wanted and save the objections for the battles worth fighting.

They took their seats beside each other in the back.

Li rested his elbows on the armrests, steepled his fingers in front of him, and regarded Bingwen. "Did China make the right decision?" Li asked.

It was a test. It was always a test with Li. He was obviously referring to China's decision to give up troops. And like always, there was only one correct answer in Li's mind. An answer Bingwen was expected to know and explain thoroughly.

"Without question," Bingwen said. Li had taught him not only to give direct answers, but also to give them with absolute certainty. A soldier must always exude strength. He does not waffle in his reports and replies. He responds directly, assuredly, immediately, and with confidence. If he does not know the answer, he says so without shame. Doing so may mark him as uninformed, but it will not mark him as weak.

"Which explanation do you want?" Bingwen asked. "The military reason, the economic reason, or the political reason?"

"All of the above," said Li.

Bingwen nodded. "Politically, China didn't have much choice. The media in Europe and the West were planting the idea that the loss of Copernicus was China's fault. Up until now the world has given China a free pass. We suffered the most causalities and collateral damage from the war. Our economic infrastructure was on the verge of collapse. Our centers of commerce, our biggest cities, were primary targets and left largely in ruins. Agriculturally we lost millions of hectares of crops, nearly wiping out the rice industry and ending trade agreements we had long maintained with the West. China was in an extremely precarious situation, and the world was sympathetic, allowing us to abstain from troop and other IF commitments as we went through a period of reconstruction. We took the beating for the world, so the world gave us a pass.

"But sympathy can last only so long, particularly in the face of a rising immediate global threat. So they make us the scapegoat for Copernicus and they suggest that all the trillions of credits that poured into our country to help us rebuild comes with a price. It's not a handout, they say. It's a hand up. There is an expectation there for us to step in and offer what assistance we can.

"To suggest that China is responsible for Copernicus is offensive in the extreme, but the idea seemed to be taking root in the global conscience. The world looked at us and said, you take and you take and you take, but you don't give. We could not allow that perception to persist. We would be labeled as selfish. Our ambassadors and dignitaries would be shunned. No politician would want to be seen with the Chinese. We would be excluded from summits and discussions and international efforts. And most damaging, if we didn't act, we would be susceptible to further accusations. Whenever the IF failed, the world would look at us again and say, 'See? You did this. You're not helping, and we're losing as a result.'"

"And the economic implications?" said Li.

"Very similar," said Bingwen. "By refusing to help, we invite economic alienation. Western corporations would reconsider their manufacturing efforts in China. And the threat of sanctions would send a lot of foreign companies running for the hills, making deals in less politically charged Asian nations. We have already seen much of our commerce bleed into Indonesia and Vietnam. If sanctions were imposed on China, that trickle would become a flood. We can't afford that. Literally. Even mild economic sanctions would cut us off at the knees. The Hegemon knew that. And so did Beijing. Nor can we afford losing the IF as a customer. Innovation, manufacturing, communication. Much of the nation's economic health depends on our maintaining strong relations with the IF. We are their fifth largest supplier of goods. If they took their business elsewhere, it would throw us into an immediate recession."

"If that's true," Li said, "then why didn't the Hegemon play that card before when he has asked for troops?"

"Because he didn't have to," Bingwen said. "The IF has more than enough troops and recruits already. In fact, it probably has more than it knows what to do with. It recruited heavily from corporate mining crews, it took on free-miner enlistees by the thousands, and it accepted tens of thousands of men and women serving in militaries on Earth. And the IF did this without having any place to put these people. There was no military fleet in space with empty bunks to house them all. No training facilities on Luna. No depots or stations exclusive to the IF. There was nothing. Those that could were put to work building the ships, but for the longest time, the IF had more soldiers than it had bunks. That still may be the case, but the IF certainly isn't going to say so. It's going to claim to desperately need troops."

"And the military implications?" Li asked.

"The International Fleet is not going away," Bingwen said. "If we are fortunate enough to win this war, the IF won't simply disband. The whole idea of war has changed for the human race. We can no longer afford to fight each other when there are greater enemies out among the stars. If we want to survive as a species, we must band together and maintain the Fleet, not solely for the Formic threat, but for others that might exist as well. China must have a presence and voice in that organization. The IF will hold incredible power and to deny ourselves participation is to invite our own decline. We can't allow that. We do ourselves a great disservice by standing on the sidelines. China needs to prove itself to the world again. We need war heroes. We need great military commanders who have influence in the IF and who can represent China's strength and maintain our standing in the world. The war was humiliating for China. Our position in the ranking of global powers dropped considerably. We were deemed weak. This despite the fact that no nation on Earth would have had any more success taking on the Formics than we did. Militarily, we had no choice but to commit troops."

"You make it sound so obvious," said Captain Li. "Why then did China not commit troops a long time ago? Why did the Hegemon have to force us into action?"

"Simple," said Bingwen. "Fear. The more troops we send into space the fewer troops we have defending our homeland. There persists the fear in Beijing that the Formics will break through whatever defense the IF tries to establish and that the enemy will reach the planet. And if all of our military resources are in space, the people of Earth, and particularly the people of China, would be vulnerable and exposed. China cannot withstand another land-based attack. If the Formics land in China, our nation as we know it would be wiped out. We don't have the military we did before, even by hoarding all of our troops. To give up any troops makes us even weaker and more vulnerable.

"It's easy to fault Beijing for this thinking," Bingwen continued, "but this is the culture of China. There is no nation other than China, no society and traditions worth preserving other than those found in China, no people more important than the Chinese. We have a very insular way of looking at the world. In a universe where humans are the only dominant sentient species, this perspective could be excused. But not anymore. The world is our nation now."

"You speak disrespectfully of our leaders in Beijing," said Li.

"I mean no disrespect," said Bingwen. "I'm merely trying to articulate what I think may be the ideas and perceptions that drive their decisions. But of course I cannot know for certain. I am but an ignorant child. You of course understand these matters far better than I do."

Li smiled. "Always so deferential, Bingwen. Always so polite."

"You are my elder. What can I be other than polite and deferential?"

"I sent men to kill you, and still you show me respect?"

"If you sent men to kill me, you clearly wanted me to learn something from the experience. You are a brilliant teacher, and some lessons must be learned the hard way, I suppose. Either that or I deserved to die."

Captain Li laughed. "Let's stop playing pretend for a moment, Bingwen. Do you honestly think I would want you dead, after the years of investment I have made into your training? Would I send ignorant thugs to take you down?"

"You just admitted that you had."

"I sent ignorant thugs to make an attempt on your life. That's a very different thing. And I did so because I knew you could easily best them. Why do you think you are sitting here? Because I wrote Beijing a letter of recommendation? Because I tossed your name into a hat? I am not the only commander who controls your life, Bingwen."

"So it was a test? To see what I would do to those men?"

"The men were only part of the test. My superiors also wanted to see what you did afterward. If you killed the men, there would be consequences in your unit. How would you handle that? Many in your company despised you already, which gave some of my superiors pause. A disliked commander can be effective, yes, but it is preferable if he has the loyalty and respect of his men."

"They despised me because I'm a child. You made sure

they despised me. You wouldn't allow me to keep anyone who supported me."

"Which forced you to constantly find ways to earn their respect," said Li. "Men cycle in and out constantly in war, Bingwen. Not everyone survives. When replacements and reinforcements arrive, you must earn their respect as well. You can't count on the loyalty of your original unit to carry you through."

"So I passed your test?"

"It wasn't my test. There are many people who watch you and evaluate the decisions you make, Bingwen. I'm merely their representative. But yes, you passed. Your actions were a little more theatrical than we had expected, but it got the job done. Even so, there are many who think me a great fool and fail to see the wisdom of what I'm doing."

"And what are you doing?"

"I am preserving China, Bingwen. You said so yourself. China needs heroes. China needs commanders to exude strength and wisdom."

"I'm twelve years old," said Bingwen. "I can't be a war hero. The world would think it a violation of a child's rights. I'm not a commander."

"No. But you will be someday. Years from now. When you're older. And your training from a young age, your experiences through your childhood and adolescence will make you all the more capable to lead when the time comes."

"Then why not keep me on Earth? Away from the fighting? If China hopes to use me as a tool when I am an adult, why throw me into the fray and risk my life?"

"You said so yourself," said Li. "Some lessons must be learned the hard way."

"Are there others?" Bingwen asked. "Like me? Orphaned children being thrown into war?"

Li smiled. "First off, you're not a child. And we're not

throwing you into war. You're going willingly. Second, while you are special, you are not so special that China is putting all its chips on you. There are others. Many, in fact. I can tell you that now. Some are far more capable than you. But we expect the program to experience losses. Not everyone will rise to the top. The hope is that those who excel and survive are those who have the capacity to lead in the future."

"So you're willing to kill off a few children to weed out the ones who don't measure up," said Bingwen.

"You make it sound unethical," said Li.

"Isn't it? I'm a preteen. There are international laws against this kind of thing. It's a war crime to put a weapon in my hand."

"I don't see a weapon in your hand," said Li.

"I *am* the weapon," Bingwen said. "Or at least the hope is that I will be someday."

"You're in training, Bingwen. This is a continuation of your training. There is nothing illegal about putting you in school. The state demands it, in fact."

"So this is school? Me leading a company of soldiers, that was school? That wasn't the military?"

"The respect you normally preserve in your tone is quickly eroding, soldier. I suggest you take a moment to remind yourself that you are speaking to a senior officer."

Bingwen was quiet a moment. "Yes, sir. My apologies, sir."

"It has always been school, Bingwen. From the moment Mazer Rackham saved you, to your involvement in the MOPs, to your training since the war. Those are experiences that have shaped you. Hard experiences. Painful even. But you are who you are because of them."

Other passengers began to arrive and take their seats, and Li and Bingwen fell silent. Moments before takeoff a young woman in white Buddhist robes boarded and took the seat across the aisle from Bingwen. There were no other passengers near them. Bingwen looked down the aisle and saw several commanders and dignitaries sitting in more comfortable chairs in the front. Captain Li seemed to notice also, and just before the shuttle took off, he moved seats and took an available one near the front, hobnobbing with senior brass.

The shuttle lifted straight up into the air, and the woman beside him tensed, maintaining a white-knuckle grip on her armrests. After a few minutes, the sudden shock of liftoff wore off and Bingwen felt himself calming. The woman seemed no less terrified.

"First time flying?" he asked in English.

"I flew from Thailand to get here. But other than that, yes."

"Me too," he said. "Except we flew from China."

"You're handling it much better than I am," said the woman.

"It's not so bad, really. Your body is already used to it. We'll be weightless soon, and then it's easy. Or so I'm told. I'm looking forward to it, really. You hear all about it, that constant state of free fall . . . I'm not helping, am I?"

"Just don't say 'free fall,' " the woman said. "Even though I know that's precisely what the sensation is."

He reached across the aisle. "I'm Bingwen."

She hesitated, not sure if she wanted to release her grip to take his hand. Then she finally did so. Bingwen gave it a quick shake. "Wila," she said.

"Are you headed to Luna?" Bingwen asked.

"No. To the Rings. It's a research facility that encircles the Formic scout ship."

"Are you a religious leader?" Bingwen asked. "A venerable Buddhist monk or something?"

She laughed, which relaxed her a little bit. "I'm not a monk at all, in fact. Not in our order. I'm a woman. Hence the white robes instead of the saffron ones. And no, I'm not a religious leader. Just a believer."

"So you work for Juke Limited?" Bingwen asked.

She looked at him, as if surprised that someone so young

would know that Juke ran the facility. "I'm a new hire," she said.

"Good company," said Bingwen. "Congratulations."

"We'll see. I hope I made the right choice."

"Lem Jukes has his enemies," Bingwen said, "and he can come off as narcissistic and obnoxious, but he actually has good intentions. I think you're probably in good hands."

She looked at him curiously. "You say that like you know the man."

Bingwen shrugged. "We met once. Via holo. He wouldn't remember me."

She held her gaze on him a moment, as if not sure if she believed him.

"I'm guessing you're not a factory worker," said Bingwen. "I'd say a scientist of some sort. A physicist maybe."

"Close," she said. "Biochemist. I've been studying the hull of the Formic scout ship."

Bingwen remembered then. It had been all over the press. "So you won the contest, to see who could help crack the hull conundrum?"

"It wasn't a contest, per se," said Wila. "They're just looking for new ideas and perspectives."

"And you gave them one," Bingwen said.

She shrugged. "I suppose. I don't know if I'm right, though."

"But you think you're right. And someone at Juke believes you might be right. Otherwise they wouldn't have scrambled to get you on the next shuttle out of Asia."

"And where are you headed?" she asked.

Captain Li had not given him specific instructions to keep his destination quiet, and he was curious to see how someone else would respond. It had been so long since he had spoken with anyone outside of the military, and he was certain this woman was not IF. "Immediately we're headed to Luna," he said. "Then we leave for a space station near Jupiter called Variable Gravity Acclimatization School, or VGAS.

More commonly known as Gravity Camp, or GravCamp, which is shortened to Gramp, colloquialized as Gramps. It's got all kinds of names."

"Sounds like a military facility."

"It is."

She glanced at him. He was not wearing a uniform, per Li's instructions. "Are you going to live there with your father?" she asked.

Bingwen laughed. "You mean Captain Li? He's not my father."

"Oh. I just assumed since he was sitting with you."

"No. My father was killed in the First Formic War. He was nothing like Li."

She turned her head then, regarding him intently. "I am sorry for your loss, Bingwen. I wish I could take that hurt and suffering from you."

To his great surprise, he saw in her eyes that she meant every word. If there were a way, if it could be done, she would take his sorrow and carry it for him. The sincerity in her voice, the intensity in her eyes, the gentleness in her expression so moved him that he had to swallow to fight back tears.

"That's kind of you to say," he managed. There was a moment of silence between them, then Bingwen asked. "So the hull, you figured it out?"

"No. I still have no idea how to breach it, but I floated a theory that intrigued them, I suppose."

"Which is what?" he asked.

She hesitated.

"I'm not some executive at a rival company, Wila, if that's what you're worried about."

"It's not that," she said. "This was a very public initiative. It's just . . . I think it would bore you. Most people your age aren't interested in this kind of thing."

"Believe me," Bingwen said. "I have a keen interest in all things Formic."

She looked at him strangely, as if seeing him for the first time. "Yes. I think you do." She rotated in her seat slightly to face him. "All right. When we look at the Formic scout ship from a distance, we see a perfectly smooth bulbous shape, right?"

"Right."

"The surface appears flawless. Very delicately engineered. And yet when you go inside the ship, the interior walls in the tunnels are starkly different. The metal looks poorly processed, almost like raw harvested ore. And there are imperfections in it everywhere."

"That has always bothered me," said Bingwen. "The exterior was perfect as you say, but inside, it's like an entirely different ship. Totally incongruent. Ugly metal, little regard for symmetry. The landers that set down in China were the same way. Their tops were made of that same polished hull material. But the sides of the landers seemed crude and slapped together as if the Formics had no sense of aesthetics."

"Right," said Wila. "The smaller Formic crafts were just as ugly, their metal just as crude. Nothing like the indestructible hull of the scout ship."

"It's like the hull was built by someone else entirely," said Bingwen.

Wila nodded. "Yes. You say that flippantly, but that's precisely my theory."

"That someone else built the hull? Someone other than Formics? Who?"

"Let me back up for a moment," said Wila. "We've always assumed that the hull was constructed in the same way that we construct the hulls of our ships, which is to say with plates, large sections of metal that are fastened together piece by piece like a patchwork puzzle to eventually form the shape of the ship. For big ships that's how we do it. And when we do, each of those plates must be made to mathematically precise specifications. Their measurements can't be off by a hundredth of a millimeter. Width, thickness, the curvature of their surface, it all has to be perfect. Otherwise the plate won't fuse properly with adjacent plates and you'll have a domino effect of mistakes. If plate A is imprecise, for example, then plate B is off and won't fuse properly with plate C and so on. It would be a mess. No shipbuilder would tolerate that."

"True," said Bingwen. "Shipbuilders would go nuts."

"Well, if you look at the Formic hull from a distance," said Wila, "it appears to be perfectly symmetrical. But if you get really, really close to the surface, you begin to see slight imperfections. Thousands of them, in fact. Juke Limited surveyed the surface of the ship for the first time recently with lasers for another reason entirely, but the results were surprising. The surface has slight undulations and variations all over it. It's imprecise. So they can't have used plates. Because if they had, and if the plates had all these imperfections, the plates would never align. We would see edges where plates didn't quite fit. But we don't. We only see these slight, nearly imperceptible undulations. Which leads me to only one possible conclusion. The Formic hull is a single piece of metal."

"How is that possible?" said Bingwen. "How could something that big be one piece of metal? How could a machine forge that?"

"My first guess was that it was made from a mold," said Wila. "Under high pressure. But if that were true, then we should see at least one seam, the seam of the mold. But again, we don't. And anyway, it would be incredibly difficult to generate enough heat in space to fuse that much metal together and produce that much pressure, particularly on that grand scale. The hull is enormous."

"Just because there are undulations and imperfections in the hull doesn't mean the hull is a single piece of metal," said Bingwen. "Maybe the undulations weren't made during construction. Maybe they came afterwards, formed by tiny impact craters, when the hull was struck by micrometeorites as it moved toward our solar system at a fraction of the speed of light."

Wila smiled. "Very astute. I'm impressed. I thought the same thing initially. But it doesn't add up. A, there is the ship's generated shield already protecting the hull from such collisions. B, there is the fact that nothing Juke engineers have done has made any such dent in the surface, suggesting that a micrometeorite, even one hit at high speed, wouldn't damage it either. Then there's C: The undulations aren't shaped like impact craters. And D, if these *had been* caused by impacts while moving at high speed, the damage would be congregated on the nose of the ship where the ship is most vulnerable to particles. But that's not the case. There are imperfections even in the rear of the ship. Stranger still, they go in various directions. They move around apertures and ports, for instance. They curve with the circle. No way is that impact damage."

"So these imperfections were created during construction," Bingwen said.

"I believe so, yes. They had to have been."

"But this is an engineering question," said Bingwen. "And you're a biochemist. They didn't offer you a job simply because you read their data better than they did. There's more to it than that. You think you know how the Formics did it, and you think it was biochemical."

"How much do you know about the Hive Queen theory?" asked Wila.

"Some," said Bingwen. "I know the prevailing belief is that the Formics are led by a single leader who has telepathic powers somehow. She can command her army from a safe distance, sending them messages mind to mind, and they obey her without hesitation. It all feels a little mystical to me, but it's substantiated by what we saw in the war, so I can't exactly argue against it."

She raised an eyebrow. "How old are you?"

"Old enough to read what's on the nets. You think the Hive Queen was involved in the construction of the ship somehow?"

"I think the Hive Queen dictates everything that happens in the Formics' universe. Not just with her own species, but with other species as well. We humans are a mechanical society. We build machines to accomplish tasks for us. Machines build our ships, our skimmers, our homes, our ovens. Machines are all around us. We rely on them for communication, agriculture, education, manufacturing, everything."

"The Formics have machines as well," said Bingwen.

"Some machines, yes," said Wila. "But not to the degree that we do. They are mostly a biochemical society. Consider the Formic foot soldiers that marched across China. They carried no communication devices. No radios, no transmitters. All communication was done biochemically somehow, as you said, mind to mind. Or consider their weapons. They sprayed gases. Chemical warfare. And their doily weapons are not lasers. They're living organisms. Their projectiles are organic matter. And inside the scout ship, did they have machines moving cargo around or making repairs? No, they had Formics pulling carts. An archaic system in our minds, but this is how Formics operate. Their food on their ship was a small creature that was bred and raised in their garden habitat. We call the creatures lichen eaters, because, well, that's what they did. They ate lichen. Another, larger creature in this garden habitat harvested these lichen eaters and delivered them to vats where they were melted down and turned into a slurry the Formics ate. Why did the creatures do that? Were they domesticated? Had Formics trained them to collect these lichen eaters like we might train a dog to jump through a hoop? I don't think so. There was a level of intelligence there. The harvesters had to know when to kill and bring in a lichen eater. They had to let the lichen eaters develop and mature and reach an age of ripeness, whenever that might be."

"What are you suggesting?" Bingwen asked. "That the Hive Queen dictates all that? That she sends commands to these creatures as easily as she does to her own species?"

"Why not?" said Wila. "If the Hive Queen knows how to communicate instantaneously across vast distances from her mind to the mind of one of her own, why couldn't she do so with other creatures as well? Particularly species that she has bioengineered. Take the doily again for instance. We strongly suspect that the doily is bioengineered to overexpress a peroxide polymer and thus generate the violent reaction that it does. Who could have engineered it other than the Hive Queen? And if she did, and if her communication mechanism is biochemical, then it stands to reason that she engineered it with the capacity to hear her voice. That's how it might work with all of her creations. She created them with the mechanism that allows them to communicate with her mind to mind."

"Which would explain why she can't communicate with us," said Bingwen. "Because she didn't engineer us. She didn't endow us with whatever biological mechanism is required to connect to her mind."

"Precisely," said Wila. "That's my theory anyway. But I believe that somehow we eventually will be able to communicate with her. Or at least I hope we can."

"So what does this have to do with the hull?" Bingwen asked. "You think the Hive Queen engineered an organism to make the hull?"

"I think it's certainly a possibility. We would consider the idea absurd. We would use machines. But in a society wherein organisms are engineered to perform tasks, it's not that far-fetched of a premise. And it would explain why the hull of the ship is different from the interior. This organism, whatever it is, is engineered to make this indestructible hull and nothing else."

"And it would explain the imperfections in the construction as well," said Bingwen. "This hull-building organism would make mistakes along the way, as all organisms do. It would not have the precision of a machine."

"Exactly," said Wila. "Hence the tiny imperfections."

"But you're contradicting yourself," said Bingwen. "You said the hull was a single piece of metal. How could an organism construct a single piece of metal that large? How could an organism construct *anything* made of metal, for that matter?"

Wila frowned. "I don't know. I can't prove any of this. Which is why I was surprised they offered me the job. But consider this: When we print something metal, we use lasers to melt micron layers of metal powder on top of each other on a build platform. Perhaps the Formics have engineered a creature that can do something similar. It would have to be a very small creature that adds tiny layers of dust or power to the metal, growing it centimeter by centimeter until the hull forms. How the creature would do this, however, I don't know, but I suspect it would be a biochemical process. I posited the idea to Juke, sent them my dissertation on the Hive Queen, and the next thing I know there was someone knocking on my door."

The captain's voice came over the intercom. "Good morning, everyone. We'll be going hot here in just a moment. Please make sure you remain in your seats and that your seatbelt and shoulder harness are securely fastened. Thank you."

Wila frowned and turned to Bingwen. "Going hot?"

"We fly like a plane until we reach a certain altitude and then we engage the rockets to escape Earth's gravity well. That's why we have little cargo and a small passenger cabin. Most of our weight is our huge fuel payload."

"It's probably best that I didn't know that before we set out," said Wila, pressing herself back into her seat and facing forward.

"We'll be fine. I did a thorough study of the ship's schematics yesterday. It's a well-designed spacecraft."

"You studied the schematics? How?"

"Everything is on the nets, Wila. You just have to know where to look and how to get access."

Bingwen looked down the aisle. Captain Li had been talking with several other officers. Rather than return to Bingwen's row, he remained in his seat in the front near the others and buckled in.

A minute later the engines ignited and Bingwen was thrust back into his seat as the shuttle rocketed forwarded. He saw Wila clinging to the armrests, a look of terror on her face. His heart went out to her, but fortunately the acceleration was over in a few minutes. The engines quieted, and Bingwen felt himself rise a little in his seat.

"I think we've left Earth's gravity well," Wila said, floating upward as well until her seatbelts restrained her.

Bingwen laughed, loosening his seatbelt and floating a little higher. "See? Not bad," he said.

Wila smiled. "No. I suppose it isn't. Better than the sensation of thinking we're going to plummet to Earth."

Far down the aisle, Captain Li lifted away from his seat, having made his rounds and presented himself to the other officers there. He turned and floated back down the aisle toward Bingwen.

"The colonel's returning," Bingwen said to Wila. "He won't like that we're having a conversation. Good luck."

She looked at him intently and dropped her voice. "Do you need help, Bingwen? Are you being held against your will?"

The question surprised him and he hesitated. Then he gave her a smile. "No, Wila. But thank you."

Captain Li returned and squeezed back into his seat beside Bingwen and busied himself with his wrist pad, oblivious that Bingwen had had any conversation. Bingwen kept his eyes to the front and remained silent. There were a hundred more questions he wanted to ask Wila, but the window of opportunity had closed. Was she right? Had the Formics engineered creatures to construct their ships for them? Did Juke Limited know something that validated that belief, and that's why they had hired her so quickly? Or were they casting a wide net and bringing in any theories, however odd or nonconventional they may be? And was it true that the Hive Queen had the power to communicate her will to another creature so strongly that the other creature obeyed absolutely? If so, she suddenly seemed far more frightening than Bingwen had imagined her.

And then another idea struck him. What if there is no Hive Queen? What if the Formics are no different than the lichen eaters or doilies or any of the other creatures following unseen commands? Maybe they're all slaves to another, stronger creature entirely, one that uses animal slaves to conquer worlds.

Is that what I am? Bingwen thought. An organism engineered for a purpose? I may not be bioengineered for my task, but I'm molded and shaped and refined in a similar process. Maybe humans and Formics are more alike than we care to admit.

The pilot's voice came over the speaker. "Ladies and gentlemen, just bear with us. We're having a little trouble here setting our coordinates for our shuttledock. Please be patient."

Bingwen glanced at Li who looked up from the tablet he was reading, a concerned look on his face.

"Is this bad?" Wila asked.

Bingwen glanced at Li again, as if to ask if he could answer. Li nodded his permission.

"The shuttle is guided by a computer," said Bingwen. "That computer takes us to a dock at one of the Lagrange points, where we'll get on a much bigger and roomier moonshuttle that will take us to Luna. But everything is in constant motion. So we have to coordinate our approach precisely, taking into consideration the shuttle's orbital elements and velocity, as well as the dock's orbit and velocity. If we get any of that wrong, we could miss the dock and have all kinds of problems. So when the pilot says we're having difficulty getting coordinates, he probably means this is an issue of quadration."

"Quadration?" Wila asked.

"Short for quadrangulation."

"That didn't clarify."

"On earth, you locate yourself with triangulation," said Bingwen. "It takes three reference points to get your exact location on the surface. But in three-dimensional space, it takes four points. So, quadrangulation. But it's not fun to say a lot, so pilots shorten it to 'quadration.' Or 'quadding' when they're in a hurry."

"So if we can't quad," said Wila, "what does that mean? We're stuck?"

"It means we're flying blind," said Bingwen. "The ship can't compute our necessary direction and velocity."

The captain came out of the cockpit and began speaking with one of the officers, who Bingwen had identified as the most senior member of the Fleet on board, as if looking for his counsel on how to proceed.

"Stay here," said Li. He unbuckled his harness and pulled himself forward in zero G. Bingwen strained to hear what was being said, but the group was speaking in hushed tones. After a moment, Li looked back down the aisle and waved Bingwen forward. "Bingwen, come up here."

Bingwen undid his harness and flew to the group. The men were all gathered in the aisle. A few were high-ranking

senior officers. They regarded Bingwen with a look of confu-
sion, as if they were surprised to discover a child on board.

"Explain to Bingwen what you just explained to me," Li
said to the captain.

The captain hesitated. "Why?"

"Because no one here knows how to fix the problem,
including you, and maybe he can," said Li.

"This isn't something a boy can solve," said the captain.

"Do you know this young man?" Li asked the captain,
gesturing to Bingwen.

"Well, no, but—"

"Do you know what his capabilities are?"

"This is a complex issue," said the captain.

"And this is a Chinese-engineered vessel," said Li. "And
I am a colonel of the International Fleet, giving you an order.
I don't care if you're the captain of this vessel or not. This
Chinese boy is the best-qualified person on this ship to solve
the problem. Tell him."

The captain looked miffed, but he did as he was told. "All
right. As I was saying, we have a failure in the link to the
quadrangulation system."

"Sending or receiving?" Bingwen asked.

"What does he mean by that?" one of the officers asked.
"Sending and receiving what?"

"If you make them stop to answer your stupid questions,"
said Li, "you delay them from solving the problem. Your
curiosity is less important than us getting to our destination.
So shut up."

The officer mumbled something under his breath and retreated back to his seat.

"Receiving," said the pilot. "All the transmitters seem to
be working fine."

For the quad system to work, Bingwen knew, the shuttle
needed to acquire four reference points. Any nearby object
in its correct orbital position would suffice as long as it could

ping back to the shuttle and confirm its position relative to the shuttle.

"If the problem is receiving," said Bingwen, "the issue could be the reference point. Have you tried multiple objects?"

The pilot was surprised by the question. "Um, yes. That's the first thing we did. We've tried four objects. No response from any of them."

"Then it's one of two issues," said Bingwen. "Either the transmitter is misfiring, or it's firing correctly and one of our dishes is misaligned and missing the return ping. All the avionics up in the cockpit are working?"

"They seem to be."

"Did you recalibrate each of the four stations before we took off?" Bingwen asked.

The pilot paused. "Well . . ."

"Were you *supposed* to recalibrate them?" Li asked the pilot.

The pilot looked defensive. "Look, I've got fifteen years of flight experience with this class of shuttle, and I know how to—"

"I don't care if you've been flying since the dinosaurs," said Li. He turned to Bingwen. "Was he supposed to have recalibrated before we left? Yes or no?"

"It's on the preflight checklist," said Bingwen. "So yes."

"All four of the stations were completely operative on the last flight," said the pilot.

"We're not on the last flight," said Li. "We're on this flight." He turned to Bingwen. "What do we do?"

Bingwen asked the pilot. "Which of the stations is failing? Front or rear? Left or right?"

"Rear," said he pilot. "Left side. But, look, you can only access them from outside. This shuttle isn't equipped for spacewalks."

"You can manipulate them from the inside," said Bingwen. "If you're as small as me. We just need to remove some paneling. Do you have tools? A screwdriver? Socket wrench? And we'll need the calibrator as well."

The pilot hesitated.

"Are you deaf?" said Li. "Get the boy the tools he needs."

The pilot got moving. He dug through an emergency compartment and found the equipment Bingwen needed. Then Li, the pilot, and Bingwen moved to the back left corner of the ship. Bingwen gave them directions on what to remove. A shelf, a storage compartment, the wall paneling. It all came away easily once they found the right screws. Bingwen took out a small laser and began cutting into the wall.

"What are you doing?" said the pilot, panicked. "You can't cut into that."

Colonel Li strong-armed the man when he tried to intercede. "He knows what he's doing."

"It's fine," said Bingwen, cutting a large square. "This isn't the hull. It's insulation."

He peeled the paneling away, being careful not to cut himself on the jagged edges. Then he reached in and started pulling out the insulation. "It may get a little colder in here."

The rest of the passengers had gathered, watching.

Bingwen next cut open a big conduit box, revealing several hundred different wires running parallel. He grabbed them, and pulled them out as far as he could, taking out the slack and being careful not to sever anything. He studied the wires, found the one he wanted and snipped it.

"What are you doing?" the pilot asked. "You can't cut that!"

"We need cable," said Bingwen. "This wire is for the light in the restroom. I think we can live without it."

He made another hole farther down in the conduit box, snipped the same wire, and pulled three meters of wire free. He gave one end to the pilot. "Strip the end and wire it to the calibrator. I'm going to remove the station box and check the transmitter first. You tell me if it's calibrated."

There was a headlamp in the tool kit. It was sized for an adult, so Bingwen made a knot in the headband before putting it on. Then he tucked a few tools in his pocket, tied the other end of the wire around his finger, and climbed into the hole among the insulation.

It was a tight fit. And if not for zero gravity, he would have slid down in the space between the two walls. He wiggled slowly forward, maneuvering himself to the back of the station box. The metal all around him was freezing, and he couldn't really turn his head. The back of the station box had four screws, but the screwdriver was too tall to angle it in the tight space and get the tip of it into the screw head. Bingwen took out his laser and sliced the plastic handle of the screwdriver down to a short stump.

"I smell something burning," said the pilot.

"It's me," said Bingwen. "We're fine."

He blew on the stump until it cooled and hardened, then he fit the screwdriver in and loosened the screws as far as he could before the screwdriver and screw were too tall again. Then he used his fingers.

The screws thankfully proved the hardest part. Once he pulled away the casing, it was relatively easy to reach the transmitter. He stripped the end of the cut wire he had brought using his fingernails and teeth, then connected the wire to the transmitter. "Test it now," he said.

There was a moment of silence then the pilot said. "It's fine, calibrated."

Which meant the problem was the dish. Which was both a good thing and a bad thing. Good because it was easier to repair, but bad because it was harder to access. Bingwen had to do a lot of delicate cutting with the laser, removing bits of wall here and there to make room for his arm and a thin pair of needle-nose pliers. He moved the wire to the dish, but it took him twenty minutes to secure it because he had to use the tools as an extension in the tight space. It was like trying to perform surgery with a marionette puppet.

But finally he secured it. "Try it now," he shouted.

There was a pause then the pilot said, "Calibration is off. It needs to rotate fourteen degrees."

"Tell me when to stop." Bingwen jiggled the pliers up into the narrow shaft and rotated.

"Right there," said the pilot. "That's it."

"Pass me the calibrator," said Bingwen. "We've got to maintain a constant link, and the dish can't track the reference point. I'll have to do it manually."

"Manually?" said the pilot. "How?"

"I'll monitor the calibrator and rotate the dish as we go to keep it aligned."

"We have over a day of flight time ahead of us," said the pilot. "You can't stay in the wall. You'll freeze to death."

"The heating vent runs in here between the walls," said Bingwen. "I've already cut a hole in it to circulate some air. But I'll need food and a bottle to urinate in. Not pleasant, I know. But necessary."

They gave him what he needed. Wila offered to sit by the hole he had climbed through and keep him company with conversation, for which he was grateful. He listened to her describe her upbringing in Thailand. He couldn't see her face, but the calm sweetness of her voice helped him forget the discomfort he was feeling. She was a good soul, he determined. She asked him a lot of questions, but he steered away from anything dealing with the military, as he knew Li would likely be listening. Instead he told her about his family in China before the war, and she hung on every word. When it was time to sleep, he insisted that she rest. When she refused, eager to alleviate his discomfort however she could, he told her he would be even more uncomfortable knowing he was keeping her up. After several protestations, she finally relented and got some sleep. The long hours of silence that followed were the most difficult of the trip. Every muscle in Bingwen's body ached. The stiffness in his neck was excruciating. And in the dark cold silence it was hard to think of anything else.

When they reached the dock and the shuttle was locked in, Bingwen finally crawled out. His neck was so stiff he couldn't turn it. The pilot had called ahead and a doctor was waiting to check him out. He gave Bingwen a muscle relaxer and sent him on his way. Bingwen found Wila waiting at the gate.

"Sore?" she asked.

Bingwen was slowly working the stiffness out. "Not at all. From now on I'll always insist on flying in the walls. First class doesn't come close."

She pressed her palms together and bowed. "Farewell, Bingwen. I honor the divine within you. All peace and happiness to your path."

"And to yours," he said. "Maybe our paths will cross again someday."

"I hope so," she said.

Captain Li was waiting and looking impatient. Their shuttle to Luna was ready to depart. Wila would take a different flight to the Rings. Bingwen bowed and then nodded a final farewell to Wila before launching over to Li, who grabbed the tow cable that ran along the wall and carried people still unfamiliar with zero G to their correct gate.

The moon shuttle was huge. Bingwen and Li got their own cabin with individual sleep sacks. Bingwen climbed in one and got comfortable. He was exhausted, and the muscle relaxer was making him drowsy.

"One of the men on the earth shuttle was a lieutenant colonel," said Li, smiling. "Special Warfare Command at Cent-Com. He and I had a lengthy conversation while you were in the wall. You impressed him. He very enthusiastically endorses our initiative now. Well done."

It all made sense in an instant. Bingwen felt foolish for not seeing it before. "You damaged the dish before the flight. You set the whole thing up."

Li smiled. "Get some sleep, Bingwen. You've earned it."

# CHAPTER 12

## Statistics

To: notoccamsrazor@stayanonymous.net
From: vico.delgado@freebeltmail.net
Subject: Armor

Old Soldier,

Attached is a 3D model of exoskeleton armor to go on top of my mining suit. I fear that the air beneath the canopy around the asteroid may be combustible, so I'm not going in without heavy fire protection. Lots of integrated components at the joints to allow flexibility and support. The surface of the rock is mostly ice, hence the retractable crampons in the boot soles and toes. Same with the gauntlet, which extends from the elbow to the hand. The crampons on the outside edge of the hand retract as well. I plan to print and cure the armor pieces individually here on the ship. Material is a nickel-chromium–based alloy well suited for extreme heat and pressure. When heated, it will form a thick, passivating oxide layer to protect it from further attack. Without that passivation process, and if I don't create an additional shielded coating, I'd be blown to bits and cooked alive if the air were to ignite.

As always, any notes are appreciated.

Vico

Victor was in the cargo bay, welding shielding plates to the quickship. Magoosa was perched on top of the quickship beside him, holding the next shielding plate in place with a pair of long-handled tongs. They wore their mining suits along with their welding visors, which protected them from the heat.

"Ready?" Victor asked.

"Ready," said Magoosa.

Victor slowly dragged the welding wand across the edge of the plate, melting it and pressing it down onto the plate below it, forming a seal. The metal glowed orange for a moment and then cooled, releasing thin tendrils of smoke that were mostly sucked away into the air purifier Victor had set up close by. The purifier didn't catch everything, however, and the acrid smell of hot metal left a smoky, metallic taste in Victor's mouth that made him slightly nauseous.

He finished the pass with the wand and then released the heat trigger to let it cool.

"What do you think?" he asked, leaning back to examine the work, his head and back soaked with sweat.

"Decent work," Magoosa said. "I won't fire you after all."

Victor smiled. Magoosa had done well, gathering the spare iron for the shield plates and then designing the quickship's cockpit. Originally the design had called for a single passenger, but Imala and the Polemarch had scrapped that idea. This was a two-man job. Imala was going with Victor. Polemarch's orders.

Victor stepped back and lifted his visor, getting a better

look. The quickship wasn't built as well as he would have liked, but it didn't need to be. The flight would be brief, and he could tolerate Magoosa's flaws and imperfections as long as the quickship flew straight and kept him and Imala warm and breathing.

"We're three hundred klicks out," Imala said, as she drifted into the cargo bay and came to rest beside them. "How close are you to finishing the quickship?"

"A few more plates, and we'll be done, Captain," Magoosa said.

Imala winced. "Please don't call me that."

"You're the captain," said Goos. "At least for now."

Imala looked uneasy. "Just call me Imala, all right?"

Victor slid the welding wand into its tube sheath and turned to her. "Goos is right, Imala. As much as you may dislike the formality of it all, it's important for everyone to remember that you're in charge now. You're not Imala the crewmember. You're the captain. We all have to respect that office or we'll have problems. This is a military mission now."

"Arjuna didn't make everyone call *him* captain," said Imala.

"Because his position as such was never in question," said Victor. "Nor did he answer to a higher military power."

Imala shook her head in frustration. "It's ridiculous. I'm far less qualified than Arjuna is."

"Going along with the IF is best for everyone," said Victor. "They're ordering us to do what we were intending to do anyway, which allows them to feel like they're in charge. And we get handsomely compensated. Arjuna agrees. I think he's somewhat relieved by the situation. Having the IF give you the captainship puts him in a better position with the crew. If the IF were giving *him* orders, it would weaken Arjuna's standing, especially among the men. They would see him in a servile role instead of how they have always seen him, as their absolute leader. Now he doesn't have to lose any credibility since the orders all go to you. Arjuna maintains a strong position, and if anything goes wrong he takes none of the blame."

"Great," said Imala. "So I'll take all the blame."

"Yes, but what do you care?" Victor said. "This isn't your crew. Or at least it won't be for very long. Arjuna will have command restored. That's why he refused when you insisted that he continue as captain."

After the transmission from the Polemarch, Imala had pulled Arjuna aside and privately tried to convince him to keep his post, despite the IF's orders. Arjuna had refused.

Some of the Somali men didn't like it. The idea of taking orders from a woman unsettled the patriarchal tradition. They could tolerate Rena as a second in command, but never a woman as captain. A few private words from Arjuna had shut them up, and it hadn't been a problem since.

"The IF's in a difficult position," Victor said. "They have to respond to the asteroid, but we're the only resource at their disposal. I'm sure they would prefer other circumstances as well."

Imala looked as if she might protest further, but Edimar drifted into the cargo bay, looking concerned. "I think we may have a serious problem."

She led them over to a worktable, where she anchored her tablet and extended its four antennas, creating a mini holofield. Magoosa came over to watch. Edimar used her stylus to pull up a holo of the solar system, as if viewed from deep space. She drew a small circle high above and to the left of the system. "Here's where the Formic fleet is. Roughly." She drew a small circle at the fringes of the solar system closest to the Formic fleet. "And this is where Copernicus was located."

Edimar drew a third circle in the holo, this one in the Kuiper Belt, far to the right of Copernicus, about an eighth of the way around the clock face of the ecliptic. "And this is 2030CT."

She drew a line from the Formic fleet to the asteroid.

"Assuming the Formic miniship anchored to that asteroid came directly from the enemy fleet and went straight to the asteroid, this is the path it would have taken. Now, considering the distance traveled, it had to have made that flight before Copernicus was destroyed. So the Formics came in clear view of Copernicus, but the satellite never saw them. The IF acts all surprised by this, but they shouldn't be. Copernicus was really only good for spotting the big stuff. Hundreds of smaller objects get by it all the time. Maybe thousands. I know. I've tracked a lot of objects that have come into the system that Copernicus didn't even know existed. So ever since we first discovered the shell around that asteroid, I've been asking myself, Why 2030CT? Why would the Formics pick that rock over the billions of other objects out here?" She gestured back to the line she had drawn from the fleet to the asteroid. "Look at this distance. Why would a Formic ship traverse all that space, bypassing millions of other rocks to come to 2030CT? There's nothing exceptional about that asteroid at all. Boring size, boring orbit, and by all accounts, boring composition. Prospecting probes predict iron, nickel, and some precious metals. It's just an average hunk of rock and ice. There is nothing unique about it in the slightest."

"So why do the Formics want it?" Imala asked.

"We're thinking about it wrong," Edimar said. "Because we're only considering what we know. We're looking at a tree when we should be looking at the forest. Consider the Formic miniship at 2030CT. Think about its flight here. In our minds we see it setting out from the fleet all by its lonesome to cross billions of klicks of open space to reach this seemingly insignificant asteroid. And we're asking ourselves why would the Formics give preferential attention to a nothing asteroid in a nothing sector of space way off the beaten path?

"And in those terms, a Formic ship coming here would seem odd. But what if this sector of the Kuiper Belt wasn't getting preferential attention? What if *all* sectors were getting *equal* attention? Maybe the Formics aren't solely targeting this sector. Maybe they're targeting them all."

Victor and Imala exchanged glances.

"Every mining ship has a spotter like me," said Edimar. "And we spotters have our own forums on the nets. We all look at the starcharts and make notes of new objects found and possible collision threats. We also track the movement of known pirates and keep each other informed of anomalies. All of that observational data goes into an open database we maintain. But it is by no means an exhaustive database. Movement happens all around us, and if we're not looking for it, chances are we're not going to see or notice it. There's just too much open space to view and too few of us.

"So I asked every spotter I knew to look back through their records. We all use an Eye for tracking movement, but the Eye is just a computer. It only sees what we tell it to look for, and it only alerts us when it finds an object within the parameters we've defined. Most spotters set the parameters pretty narrowly. Otherwise, we'd be getting alerts constantly, mostly for objects that pose no threat. So we tell the Eye to only alert us of objects that come within half a million klicks of us, for example, and to ignore everything else. This means every spotter is operating in a little bubble. We're not looking at the immensity of space around us and processing everything. We're only looking at the space that affects us and our family. Our immediate vicinity."

"Hence the database," said Imala. "So you can share what you're seeing."

"Right," said Edimar. "But the database isn't a thorough record because it only includes the objects within our collective set parameters. So I told all the spotters to reach back six months into their records and to search for movement under new parameters. One, did their Eye detect any objects coming in from open space above the plane of the ecliptic?

And two, could the trajectory of any of those objects intersect with an asteroid? Basically I wanted to know if other Formic ships had parked on rocks. By this morning, I had two dozen responses."

She made a gesture in the holofield and two dozen red dots appeared in the solar system. Nearly all of them were on the side of the system nearest to the approaching Formics. Most were in the Kuiper Belt, but there were several in the Asteroid Belt as well.

"Now," said Edimar, "these are only the responses I've received thus far. Most of them are from big clans with big ships that have strong Eyes and hefty laserline capabilities, meaning they can receive new posts and respond back fairly quickly. I have a few responses from small ships like us, but they're all in the Kuiper Belt and within eight months of us, so relatively close. I suspect I'll get more responses from smaller ships as time goes on. What's significant right now is how quickly the responses are coming in. A lot of ships have detected an anomaly over the past six months. And remember, these are only the anomalies that were detected. This obviously doesn't include objects that no one saw or that avoided detection."

"So these dots," said Imala, gesturing to the holofield, "while this may look like a lot, this might actually be woefully short of what's really out there."

Edimar nodded. "I ran a statistical algorithm. I had to fill in some numbers because I don't have all the variables. It's guesswork at this point. But even my conservative estimates will surprise you. Let's assume that only thirty percent of these identified anomalies are Formic ships. I think that's way low considering that all of these objects were heading for asteroids, but for the sake of argument, let's leave it there. And let's also assume that the Formics sent ships to all sectors on this side of the system. Considering the spread of known anomalies here, I don't think that's an unsubstantiated conjecture. And let's also assume that the Formics sent the same number of ships to each sector." She pointed to a cluster of asteroids in the Kuiper Belt. "Now, the highest number of anomalies was spotted here in this sector. Five. So we'll let that be the number of spotted anomalies per sector. Five. And let's also assume that the known anomalies represent only one-fifth of what's actually there. That's a big supposition I know, but considering that Copernicus didn't detect its own attacker, I don't think that number's inflated. In fact, it's probably higher. Any anomaly we spotted was probably a fortunate accident."

Imala gestured to the holofield. "So how many Formic ships are we talking about?"

Edimar waved a hand in the holofield, and their side of the solar system filled with red dots. "Well over fifteen hundred."

The others stared at the holo in disbelief, and for a moment no one spoke.

"It can't be that many," Imala said finally.

"That's not the worst of it," Edimar said. "I then went back again to the spotters and asked them to search one last time in their Eye records for any anomalies that had come in from deep space and intersected asteroids, but which had come not from above the ecliptic but from below it."

"Below the ecliptic?" Imala said. "But the fleet is up here."

"What was the result?" Victor asked.

"They gave me their numbers. I ran my algorithm. And this happened." Edimar tapped the solar system and twice as many red dots appeared. "Roughly the same number of objects came from below as from above. We're looking at three thousand Formic ships sitting on asteroids in our solar system. Right now."

There was a long silence.

"But this is guesswork," said Magoosa. "You're just making up numbers."

Victor had been so focused on the holo, and Magoosa had

been so quiet off to the side, that Victor had forgotten the boy was there. "It's not guesswork, Goos. It's statistics. One or two objects coming into the system and colliding with an asteroid would be an amazing coincidence. But dozens of objects coming into the system and colliding with asteroids is an invasion."

"But from below the ecliptic as well?" asked Imala. "You're saying their fleet is coming in from two directions?"

"Their fleet has already divided," Edimar said. "It divided a long time ago. They're coming in from above and below. I'm one hundred percent certain of this. Because remember this line?" She pointed with her stylus at the line she had drawn from the fleet to the asteroid. "We assumed that the Formic ship at 2030CT came from up here where we've always imagined the fleet to be. But the Formic ship didn't come from that direction." She erased the line. "I changed the parameters on our own Eye and did a search. The Formic ship right outside, the one parked on 2030CT, came from below the ecliptic."

# CHAPTER 13

## Luna

To: vico.delgado@freebeltmail.net
From: notoccamsrazor@stayanonymous.net
Subject: Re: Armor

---

Victor,

Your armor design is strong. But keep in mind that Formics are tunnelers. They never built any aboveground
habitats during the invasion. Instead, they dug a vast
tunnel system beneath the landers. I think this is
species-typical behavior. They're probably doing the
same on asteroids.

If I'm right, we're in trouble. A defensive position like
that is almost impossible to seize. The tunnels will be
designed for their body shape and movements, not
ours. They'll know the layout—including switchbacks,
dead ends, and traps. We won't. They also see in the
dark and share a hive mind. We don't.

Also, dust. If they're tunneling through the asteroid
inside a contained habitat, they're generating a lot of
dust that has nowhere to go. When we dig, our dust

dissipates into space, but they've sealed themselves off from space. So there may be a toxic amount of dust in the air. Breathing may be difficult. Visibility will be poor. The dust may clog our equipment, or render it useless. Impossible conditions for combat. We need to know if that's the case. Going in without knowing the environment may be suicide.

But the bigger question is: Why are they tunneling in the first place? Initially I thought they were simply turning the rock into a collision threat with Earth. Still possible. But another option is this: They've dug out and oxygenated this habitat inside an asteroid in order to breed and build their army. We don't know much about the Formic life cycle. Maybe they can achieve adulthood in a few months. And if their minds are led and guided by a Hive Queen, they might not require much training before being given a weapon and ordered into combat. Maybe she can instantly give them the skills of veteran soldiers.

I hope I'm wrong. Because if I'm not, they can replenish their forces faster than we can kill them. That gives them the victory. They'll win by attrition, wearing us down with a continual onslaught of fresh recruits that we cannot match in numbers. Game over. We lose.

One note on the armor: Tunnels will be narrow. You can't allow the armor to snag on surface walls and restrict your forward progress. Shoulders, knees, and elbows pose the most risk. You may want to round a few corners of the individual pieces to avoid snags. Also, coat all the armor in a flexible resin. No exposed

metal. It might strike rock, and you don't want sparks
in an atmosphere of pure oxygen and hydrogen!

Old Soldier

Mazer exited the lunar shuttle via the docking tube and found
a young female lieutenant waiting for him at the gate. She
came to attention and saluted. "Captain Rackham. I'm Lieutenant Prem Chamrajnagar. I'm your appointed attorney for
your court-martial."

Mazer grabbed the safety rail to steady himself. Gravity
here was only one-sixth of what it was on Earth, but it
was far more than he was used to and his legs felt heavy and
weak.

"Easy," the woman said, catching his rucksack as it slipped
off his shoulder. "You still have your space legs, sir. No rush.
They advise you take a moment before setting out. You've
been in the Black for a long time." She set the rucksack on
the ground beside him and gave him a moment.

"Thank you," Mazer said, clutching the railing and spreading his feet apart a little to widen his stance. "I never realized
I was so heavy before."

"Be glad they didn't take you straight to Earth," the lieutenant said, smiling.

Mazer regarded her. The single bar on her uniform meant
she was junior grade. Her expression was formal and military, but she wasn't exactly the seasoned attorney he was hoping for. "Don't take this the wrong way, Lieutenant, but you
look younger than I am."

"I'm twenty, sir. So, yes, I am younger. And petite. And
female. Three strikes against me, I suppose."

"That's no strikes against you," Mazer said. "I was merely
expecting someone a little older. When did you graduate from
law school?"

"Two years ago, sir. With honors."

"You don't have to keep calling me 'sir.' Mazer will suffice. Law school takes three years. How old were you when you started your undergraduate degree?"

"Fourteen, sir."

"What a fun adolescence you must have had. Keeping with the time line, I can only assume you went to junior prom while still in the womb and that elementary school happened prior to conception."

"I'm young, sir. But I'm capable."

He could see it was true. She had an air of confidence about her—a self-assuredness that didn't come off as cocky. She simply knew she could get things done because that's how she had always operated.

"If it makes you feel any better," said Chamrajnagar, "it's unlawful to assign counsel that hasn't been deemed competent by the Judge Advocate General."

"Where is that law written?" Mazer asked.

"Article 27b of the Uniform Code of Military Justice. I can recite the paragraph if you wish."

"That won't be necessary. How many times have you served as lead counsel?"

"JAG appointed you a single attorney, sir."

"How generous of him. All right, how many times have you defended someone?"

"Including your case?"

Mazer nodded.

"One."

"You're not instilling a lot of confidence here, Lieutenant. I thought you said you graduated two years ago."

"I did, sir. We shadow members of the JAG Corps for two years before we get our own cases. I've written a lot of briefs if that makes you feel any better."

"Not really."

"You can formally request another attorney, sir. I can recommend a few senior officers who may be more to your liking."

"You'd step aside that easily?"

"This is your defense, sir. Your attorney is there to advise and assist you, not to dictate. If you do not want me to assist you, then yes, it's in your best interest for me to step aside. You must trust your attorney completely. The worst attorney is the unwanted attorney. But please don't take my willingness to remove myself as a sign of disinterest. Nothing could be further from the truth. I was not assigned to your case. I volunteered."

"Why?"

"Because abuse of power like that exhibited by Colonel Vaganov will lose us this war, particularly when it jettisons good soldiers who should be leading."

"What makes you think I'm a good soldier?" Mazer asked. "Or a leader for that matter. You don't know me."

"I know you fought with the MOPs inside the Formic scout ship during the first war. I know you were instrumental in winning that war. I know you willingly agreed to avoid the spotlight so that the MOPs could take sole credit and thus prove to the world that a diverse, international military force like the MOPs is the best chance we have to defeat the Formics, thus paving the way for the formation of the International Fleet."

"Who gave you that information?" Mazer asked. "None of that is in my service records."

"There is quite a bit missing from your service records," said Chamrajnagar. "The IF has done a very good job of removing all traces of the truth. Had Colonel Vaganov taken the time to dig a little, he might have figured out who you are exactly."

"You have a very active imagination, Lieutenant."

"So you're denying you helped win the war?" Chamrajnagar asked. "You're denying you served with the MOPs? You're still protecting the Fleet?"

"Or maybe I'm denying it because it's all nonsense."

"A vigorous denial is as good as a confirmation," said Chamrajnagar.

"Did they teach you that in law school?"

She smiled.

Mazer let go of the bar. His legs still felt weak, but he was feeling steadier now. He hefted his rucksack and moved toward the end of the gate, taking slow deliberate steps. She fell into step beside him.

"We'll take a rover," she said. "It's a long walk to the front gate."

She moved ahead of him and climbed up into one of the mini rovers parked nearby, taking the wheel.

Mazer hesitated. "Those are for driving the elderly around. I can walk."

"It's a long terminal, sir. If you walk in your current state, I'll have to keep stopping to help you up off the floor." She gestured to the empty seat next to her. "Taking the rover will do us both a favor."

Mazer glanced down the terminal. It *was* a long distance. And his legs weren't up for a lengthy hike. Frowning, he tossed his rucksack in the back and climbed up next to her. She pulled away and stuck to the rover path.

"What do you know about my case?" Mazer asked.

"I know the charges that have been filed against you."

"An extensive list, I'm guessing."

"So extensive it smells rotten. Did you really strike an MP with an iron bar?"

"Is that what Nardelli is saying?"

"He got twelve stitches in his head. I've seen the photos filed with the police report. Pretty ghastly."

"He gave that wound to himself," Mazer said.

"He struck himself with an iron bar?"

"There was no bar involved. Iron or otherwise. He hurt himself attacking me. It's quite humorous in retrospect. He launched at me. I put something in his way. He wasn't wearing a helmet. End of story. I never touched him. He'll have a hard time providing any forensics."

"And let me guess," Chamrajnagar said, "if you had touched him, he would have needed a lot more than twelve stitches."

He looked at her and found her smiling. "You're mocking me," he said.

"No. It just seemed like the testosterone thing to say. But that's not who Captain Mazer Rackham is, I see."

"Disappointed?"

"Relieved actually. And I wouldn't worry about Nardelli's testimony. I've done a little digging. The man's not a credible witness. If his deposition is presented as testimony, we'll obliterate him."

"No objections here," said Mazer.

"So you're agreeing to my representing you?"

"I'm agreeing to listen and participate in this conversation. I'm stuck on this rover with you. I don't have much choice."

Chamrajnagar nodded. "Fair enough. Issue number one, the charges filed against you are rather serious. The most serious of which is leaking classified information."

Mazer chuckled. "Easily dismissed. I shared private information in an IF forum. The intel didn't belong to the IF. Nor was it classified. The IF didn't even know about it. Vaganov was just miffed he couldn't take credit for it. Which leads us to issue number two, the presiding officer at my court-martial is a personal friend of Colonel Vaganov."

Chamrajnagar glanced at him, surprised. "How did you know that?"

"Vaganov is smart," Mazer said. "He knows he doesn't have a legal leg to stand on. And yet he was completely confident that I'd be burned. So much so that he was fairly brutal with my confinement. Plus you labeled the first issue as issue number one, so I assumed there would be others. I was hoping I was wrong."

"Well, you're right. Sort of. The president of the court is Colonel Michio Soshi from Japan. He's the only officer on the panel who's from the Judge Advocate General's Corps. The other four members of the jury will be officers of senior rank. So five total. Soshi has a reputation for being merciless. His cases end in discharge far more frequently than those run by other judges. They call him the Hatchet."

"That's comforting," Mazer said. "And Vaganov and this Colonel Soshi, they're close?"

"They run in the same circles. They have connections from the past, but I wouldn't call them close personal friends. More like allies. Which hurts us because it's harder for us to prove a conflict of interest. If they had roomed together in college, we'd be in a good position. What we have instead is conjecture. So they've probably committed to protect each other, but we'll have a hard time proving it."

"Regardless," Mazer said, "due to their previous connections we should file a motion that Soshi recuse himself."

Chamrajnagar nodded. "I've already typed it up."

Mazer raised an eyebrow. "You've put a lot of time into this. When did you pick up my case?"

"As soon as we got wind of the charges. I've been working on it after hours."

"And you're doing this because you've dug up some misinformation that leads you to believe I'm a war hero?"

"No, sir. I'm doing this because I think removing you from uniform would decrease our chances with the Formics."

"Will the motion work?" Mazer asked. "Will Soshi recuse himself?"

"Probably not. He has to approve the action, and if he's doing a favor for Colonel Vaganov, Soshi will want to maintain control."

"So I'm stuck with a biased judge. What kind of judicial system is this?"

"A young one. The IF has only been around for a few years, and its member nations all have very different approaches to military justice. Russia, Indonesia, the US, Libya. Everyone had their own way of conducting military tribunals. And Russia's idea of military justice is probably a far cry from what you saw in New Zealand. Multiply that by however many member nations there are now, and you've got a rather convoluted military code of justice. It's constantly being updated. Don't expect an IF court-martial to run as smoothly as it should."

"There's something else," said Mazer. "Vaganov worked it so that a physician recommended me for light duty. I think he did it so that it could be argued that I had no business conducting the field tests in the first place."

"Did you pee in the colonel's coffee?" Chamrajnagar asked. "He really wants to see you gone."

"He's worried I'll blow the whistle on a lucrative arrangement he has with Gungsu Industries."

"Ah," Chamrajnagar said. "That does complicate things."

"Still want to take my case?"

"We'll appeal the physician's recommendation," Chamrajnagar said. "We'll get you reevaluated by another doctor, someone who will say you're perfectly fit and good to go. If we're prepared for that, we need not worry. Any other traps that I need to be made aware of? As your attorney I need to know every angle they'll use against us."

"I haven't agreed to make you my attorney yet," Mazer said.

"No, but you're warming up to me."

"What about a motion to dismiss?" Mazer asked.

"I've typed that up as well. But I doubt Soshi will drop the whole thing, especially if there are shady business deals in the background. They can't allow you to walk free. They need to silence you, which they'll do by discrediting you. Hence the court-martial. They'll make it so your voice doesn't matter and carries no weight. Which is why Vaganov is trying so desperately to gather evidence against you."

"There is no evidence against me," said Mazer. "The court can't prove criminality. I filed a formal objection before the mission. Vaganov deleted it, but I have to believe it can be recovered. Plus I have a vid of the incident. And I have at least half a dozen people who will testify on my behalf, including the officer who lost his leg. There is no case. Vaganov knew that from the beginning. He knew the court would acquit based on insufficient evidence. It has to. He's only doing this so that Soshi can end my career, which Soshi can do easily. Even if I'm acquitted, the court will file an official letter of reprimand that will forever remain on my permanent record. They will claim that my conduct, while not criminal, verged on bringing discredit to military forces, and that for the good of the service they recommend that I be removed from my current position and transferred to an area more suited for my capabilities, where my new unit commander can determine any nonjudicial punishment."

"That's certainly possible," said Chamrajnagar.

"More than possible," said Mazer. "That's how they do it. If they can't get you discharged, they damage your reputation so completely that you'll never get promoted. Then they ship you to some backwater assignment as a supply officer and leave you in total misery. That way, they still drive you out of the military, but you leave on your own accord. When your contract ends, you don't reenlist. Why would you? You've been given the worst detail, and you have no possibility of escape. You're in a hole you can't dig yourself out of. It's a slow death, but it's death all the same. They win."

"Sounds like you know the justice system as well as I do," Chamrajnagar said.

"There's nothing *just* about it, Lieutenant. We lost before we started."

They reached the end of the terminal, and Chamrajnagar pulled to the side to let them out. She and Mazer stepped down, and Mazer grabbed his rucksack. He was still a little unsteady on his feet, but better than before.

"Still want my case?" he asked.

"Absolutely, sir. Even if the outcome here seems predetermined, I want to help however I can."

Mazer nodded. "I want my wife to meet you. She's a better judge of character than I am."

"Your wife and I have already met, sir. Three times. Twice for lunch and once to shop for shoes."

He raised an eyebrow. "You and Kim shopped for shoes?"

"Mrs. Rackham has a keen sense of style, sir. I needed new shoes."

"You're aggressive," Mazer said. "I'll give you that. Is my wife the one who filled your head with stories about my involvement in the previous war?"

"No, sir. She's tight-lipped on that subject, though she did toss me a few leads to pursue."

"I see. And what does my wife think of you?"

"Her exact words were, 'If he doesn't take you on, tell him he's an idiot and that I won't ever make my cashew chicken stir-fry for him again.' "

"Then you're hired, Lieutenant. I can abide a life outside the IF, but I can't abide life without my wife's stir-fry."

Kim was waiting for him outside the security perimeter, which was as close as nonpersonnel were allowed to get to the IF docks. She was wearing her hospital scrubs and looked like she hadn't slept in twenty-four hours. Mazer dropped his rucksack and took her into his arms. She smelled the same, felt the same, embraced him the same way she always had, burying her face in his neck and squeezing him so tightly around the chest it was a little hard to get air. How could he leave her again?

She kissed him briefly and then held his face in her hands. There was a profound sadness in her eyes behind her smile. "How long do I have you?" she asked.

So she had been following the news.

"The IF will go into panic mode," Mazer said. "We're not ready for combat. Tech-wise, training-wise, fleet-wise. Our fleet isn't even built yet. Not completely. We thought we had at least two more years before war."

"And what about you?" she asked. "Where does that leave you?"

He smiled at her and brushed the hair out of her face. She was still clinging to him, as if she thought he might drift away. "Let's not talk here," he said.

"Hungry?" she asked.

"The only thing worse than shuttle food is military shuttle food. I'm famished."

They went to their favorite noodle shop in Old Town, a tiny family-run affair with only a few tables and dated decor. Kim had tended to the owners' daughter at the hospital after a skimmer accident a few years ago and saved the little girl's life. The owners, a Japanese couple, had treated Kim and Mazer like family ever since. Dakotsu, the father, threw his arms wide when Mazer and Kim entered. "Look who returns to Luna." He shuffled to them and bowed low. "Kim tells me all about your adventures, Mazer. You have been in a secret group, I hear. Very important work."

"She'll tell you anything to keep you feeding her noodles," Mazer said.

Dakotsu laughed, put an arm around Mazer, and addressed the four people eating in the restaurant. "Everyone, this is

Mazer Rackham, my friend. A captain in the International Fleet. Know that name. He will save the world some day."

The patrons glanced at Mazer and Kim with disinterest and then returned to their noodles. Dakotsu laughed and gestured for them to follow. "Come. Special seat for you. All noodles on the house."

The special seat was the table for two in the back beside the aquarium and a neon sign advertising a Chinese ale. Dakotsu wiped the table down quickly and slid napkins into the holding clips. "I'll get you the usual, yes?"

"Nothing would make us happier," Kim said. "Thank you."

The man smiled and shuffled away.

Kim reached across the table and took Mazer's hand. "You want to tell me about this court-martial?"

"Not really. It will only annoy you."

"Everything the IF does annoys me. Why should this be any different?"

The noodles were eaten and the dishes were cleared before Mazer had finished giving her all the details. She kept shaking her head as he went over the events. When he was done her mouth was a hard line.

"How comforting to know that the military is run by crooks," she said.

"There are good commanders in the IF, Kim. Problem is there aren't enough of them. There are too many like Vaganov."

"That drastically weakens our chances against the Formics."

Mazer nodded and took a sip of his tea. "That's their greatest crime."

"So what are you going to do about him?"

"About Vaganov? Nothing. The man isn't my concern."

"So you'll let him get away with what he's done to you? He'll probably be promoted to rear admiral if he isn't stopped."

"My war isn't with Vaganov," Mazer said. "It's with the Formics. And that's war enough."

Kim hesitated. "So you'll leave for the Belt."

"Unless I'm discharged. I don't have a choice, Kim."

"You don't have to give me the 'I'm a soldier' speech, Mazer. I know this is what you were made for. I knew that when we married. I accepted it then."

"That doesn't make it any easier."

"No, but I've known this day was coming, and I've had a long time to think about it. For now, I'm going to enjoy you for as long as I have you. Secretly I'll pray that you're discharged."

"They won't discharge me," said Mazer. "They don't want me free and talking to the press, kicking up secrets best kept hidden. They'll send me to some remote corner of the system where no one will pay me any mind. If you're going to say a prayer, ask that I'm exonerated and that the Formic ships all self-destruct."

"How long will the proceedings be?" she asked.

He shrugged. "Maybe a few weeks. Maybe five minutes. I'm not sure how high the situation is stacked against me."

She reached across the table and held his hand again. "Then while you're here, I want us to try again."

She meant try having a baby.

She had wanted children immediately after the wedding. If they only had five years before the Formics arrived and thus five years left of life, they deserved to have the experience of bringing a child into the world, a little wonder that was half him and half her. There were names she had safeguarded since her childhood: Gideon if it were a boy, and Margaret Elizabeth if it were a girl, after her grandmother. But after marrying Mazer she had tossed these aside in favor of Maori names: Pai Mahutanga for a girl, Pahu Rangi for a boy.

It had filled Mazer's heart to hear her say those words, to

see her embrace the culture of his upbringing and adopt it, in a loose sense, as her own. For it was a part of him, and everything that was his was to be hers also.

So they had tried.

Kim had taken the first miscarriage in stride. It was devastating, but the doctors assured them that such an outcome was common, particularly in the low gravity of Luna. And so they had shouldered the loss and pushed on. But after the third miscarriage, Kim had felt only despair. The following week, Mazer had been sent to WAMRED.

Mazer spoke gently and squeezed her hand. "Are you sure you want to do this, Kim? After everything you went through last time?"

She nodded. "I've had a year to think about this, Maze. It's what I want. I'd like to think it's what you want too."

"You know I do. It's just . . . it was so difficult before. The miscarriages. It pained me to see you go through that."

"I'm willing to take that risk."

"And the Formics?" Mazer asked.

"What about them? Why should they have any say in what our family does?"

"They're practically here, Kim. Do we really want to bring a baby into the world now when there may not be a world for it to live in soon? The Formics kill indiscriminately. They don't care if you're elderly or an infant. They'll gas you and step over your body without a second look. If the Fleet loses, that's what's coming for you and a baby. I can't stand the thought of that."

She looked hurt. "We got married to build a family, Mazer. You agreed to try before, and we knew the Formics were coming. What's different?"

"Everything, Kim. We tried having a baby before because I allowed myself to believe that what we have, our family, this between us, can't be broken. I believed that somehow the human race could win, that we could pull off a second miracle.

But I've spent a year away from you, Kim. And do you know what I did all day every day at WAMRED? I tested weapons and armor and suits and equipment and landing crafts and shuttles. And at night I studied everything I could find on the nets about the enemy, everything we've learned since they came the first time. Their tactics, their biology, the fleet that they're building. And do you know what I learned? Do you know what I gleaned from all that study and all that experience? We are probably going to lose. Earth is probably going to fall. All that equipment and weapons I tested, it's not going to be enough. I've seen the best that the human race has to offer, Kim, and it isn't enough. Half of the tech they gave us to test didn't even work right, and the half that did will be brushed aside. The Formics have been building a fleet while moving at a fraction of the speed of light, using nothing but pieces of their mothership. We can't even build a fleet while remaining stationary with all of the solar system's resources at our disposal."

She looked taken aback. "So you're saying we should give up?"

"Of course not."

"Because that sounds like surrender to me."

"It's realism, Kim. I don't like it any more than you do, but those are the facts. I am going to do everything I can; heaven knows I am going to try, but the odds are stacked so high against us that we can't sit back and pretend that all will be well if we just believe in the indomitable will of the human spirit. We are technologically inferior, fighting an enemy we do not understand."

"Which we beat before," Kim said.

He shook his head. "This war will be nothing like that. The landscape is completely different. The enemy is far more numerous. We can't concentrate our forces, because that would leave massive holes in our defenses. It's space, it's too vast. The Formics would easily scoot around us and make a beeline for Earth. We can't protect all that space. We'll try, but it will leave us vulnerable everywhere. And when the Formics decide where they want to attack, the rest of our forces won't be able to rush to the aid of those under attack because the distances between them will be too great. It would take months to reach them, by which time the Formics will have wiped out our ships and moved on to Earth."

Kim looked annoyed. "So it's hopeless then."

"I didn't say hopeless."

"You don't have to say the word, Mazer. I get the message." She shook her head, a look of disappointment on her face. "I'm sorry if you had a bad experience at WAMRED. I'm sorry if only half of the machines worked, or if the others weren't strong enough, or if your commander was a selfish idiot. And I'm sorry if some no-name doctor put some numbers together and decided you were unfit—"

"That's not what this is about, Kim."

"It's precisely what this is about, Mazer. You've given up. For whatever reason, you've decided how this is going to end. And that hurts. Because that's not the man I fell in love with. The man I married says, 'To hell with all of you. There aren't any weapons to stop the enemy? Fine, I'll make my own. You think I'm unfit? So what? I'll win the war anyway. We don't have a fleet strong enough to obliterate the Formics? No problem, I'll do it myself.'"

"I am going to try, Kim. But these are the facts. I'm not superhuman."

"You don't have to be," Kim said. "You only have to be who are you. That's all I'm asking for as well, that you be Mazer Rackham. The man I chose to be the father of my children." He started to speak but she held up a hand, silencing him. "Having a baby, building a family, that is why this marriage exists. That's what our species does. We make babies, we build families, regardless of the outside forces trying to tear us down and wipe us out."

He stared at her, saying nothing.

She grew quiet. "I want a baby, Mazer, because if I lose you, I lose us."

It was only then that he understood. She didn't want a child solely to grow their family. She wanted a child to *preserve* their family, to keep a part of him with her always. They both knew—everyone knew—that even if by some miracle the Fleet were to beat the Formics, it would not be without a cost. There would be heavy losses. Catastrophic losses, most likely. No one pretended otherwise. Yes, there were some soldiers with a blind sense of optimism, but most people who enlisted and took on the blue understood what they were getting into. They had no pretense of surviving the war. They simply wanted to go down fighting.

And yet Kim believed. The family that he and she had created would continue, with or without him.

How could he deny her that, especially when it was what he so desperately wanted as well, despite the sorrow he knew it would bring her if the Fleet failed.

"We'll try," he said.

She narrowed her eyes, a questioning look. "We'll try as in you and I will try to have a baby, or as in you and the Fleet will try to win?"

"Both," he said.

She moved around the table, took his face gently in her hands, and kissed him, a long lingering kiss that had a spark of passion in it.

When they parted, Mazer smiled at her. "Not here though. I don't want our child conceived in a noodle shop. No matter how good the ramen is."

# CHAPTER 14

# Ansible

To: imala.bootstamp%e2@ifcom.gov/fleetcom/gagak
From: ketkar%polemarch@ifcom.gov
Subject: Zip it

Perhaps we did not make ourselves clear when we commandeered your vessel, but allow me to clarify the point now. The Gagak is now the property of the International Fleet, which means the equipment ON the vessel is also IF property. Ergo, any intelligence or information of a sensitive nature that you or a member of your crew discovers while using that equipment is also property of the International Fleet.

While we appreciate your forwarding us Edimar's findings regarding the enemy fleet's movements, we do not approve of Edimar posting that intelligence in a public forum without our permission. The IF will control how intelligence is disseminated to the public, and only after we have independently verified the authenticity of that intelligence.

Now the nets are in a panic because they have learned from a pack of free-miner spotters that the enemy fleet is coming into our system from above and below the ecliptic. Do you have any idea how this erodes the people's confidence in the IF?

What's worse, you allowed Edimar to speculate in this same forum that as many as three thousand Formic miniships are already inside our solar system rooted to asteroids. Not only is this conjecture, but it's grossly exaggerated conjecture. To come up with enough material to do this the Formics would have had to completely dismantle their starship and build those three thousand miniships in flight, an obvious impossibility. Edimar is screaming fire in a crowded theater where there may be little or no fire.

Silence her. Or revoke her net access. Invoke whatever discipline you deem necessary so long as it is harsh enough to communicate the severity of this offense. Then train your crew on how to handle sensitive intelligence. See attachment. *Handbook of Military Instructions.* Section 27.3–27.7.

Ketkar

"They're calling it the ansible," Serge said. "It instantaneously transmits digital and audio communications across any distance. You could chat with someone in the Kuiper Belt just like you and I are chatting now. No lag time. No delay. Like a normal conversation. It sounds impossible, but this is legit."

Lem glanced out of the window of the empty warehouse to reassure himself that no one was outside listening to or watching this conversation. He had swept the room for any eavesdropping devices long before Serge arrived, but he couldn't shake the worry that they were not alone. Father had been so vehement the other evening about secrecy that Lem hadn't expected Serge to uncover anything. The tech was obviously well protected. Lem had only discovered it by accidentally falling into a bed of clues. Yet Serge had learned the name of the device. And maybe more.

The warehouse was on the south side of Old Town, back near the dome's inner edge in the most neglected part of the borough. Most of the buildings vacated after the war had been snatched up for government use, but the Hegemony had had little use for a dilapidated warehouse in need of serious repair, and so the building hadn't seen occupants in years. Dust was everywhere. Windows were broken. Graffiti adorned several walls. Lem felt dirty just standing here.

And yet where else could they meet? Anywhere in the company would be too risky. There were too many listening ears. In fact, Lem was regretting giving Serge the assignment in Serge's office. He hadn't thought it careless at the time, but now he wasn't so sure.

"Have you told anyone about this?" Lem asked. He had said nothing to Serge about what Lem had already learned himself.

"Not a soul," Serge said.

"Good. Keep it that way."

Lem had received a message from Serge that morning requesting a meeting, and Lem had debated whether or not to go through with it. He had half a mind to tell Serge to forget the whole thing. Father had threatened charges of treason and capital punishment. Mostly empty threats probably, but still there was an element of danger, and to keep Serge involved without telling him the risks was misleading.

Yet here Lem was, standing in a dusty dump in Old Town, curiosity getting the better of him.

"Any idea how the ansible works?" Lem asked.

"It works via paired subatomic particles," said Serge. "It's rather complicated, but basically the ansible creates a field in which particles are paired so that one particle will form and deform as the other one does. So as one changes shape, the other changes shape. That movement can be read by nearby particles, and this creates an electrical differential. And that's what's read, the electrical differential. There are still speed-of-light issues within each set—you know, receiver and sender—but it's trivial because the distance is so small. What matters is that you are sending a signal, and a subatomic particle in there is getting paired."

"I'm not following you," said Lem.

"Let me back up," said Serge. "We know the Formics communicate instantaneously across vast distances. Since the end of the war, the Hegemony has been racking their collective brain to figure out how. The belief is that the Formics use the same principle as the ansible, but they do so biochemically. So your father has been trying to pair subatomic particles. Initially what the Hegemony had was just a single pairing. It was like serial communications, sending one bit at a time, sequentially. And the fastest it could go was like three hundred baud, like the early days of modems. They had this six months after the war. But the bandwidth was incredibly low. All they could send were very short text messages as quickly as they could type them. Not massive amounts of data. Just text. And only one ansible could be paired with another ansible. It wasn't a network. So there was one ansible on Luna, and another ansible, its mate, was way out in the Belt with the Polemarch."

Serge smiled, slightly amused. "But then the Strategos wanted one. And the Hegemon wanted his own private one. And the Polemarch's admirals and commanders wanted one too. Problem was, you had to have a separate set for each pairing. Meaning you had to have a separate ansible for every person you wanted to communicate with.

"So they started dispersing them among the commanders. And they discovered that the distance between paired ansibles can go as far as necessary. It's just miraculous how far it goes. And it's instantaneous. But it only works where you have the set. So the Polemarch ended up having to carry forty sets with him, because he had twenty commanders in ships throughout the Belt and twenty bureaucrats in the Hegemony that he had to keep in contact with. So it's like he had this moving van full of sets going with him wherever he went. Very big and clunky.

"Then they discovered that they could do multiple particles. Not a single pairing, but an array of identical particles. And so they did fifty pairings at a time. Which meant they had fifty different sets all communicating with each other at three hundred baud.

"Then they jumped the speeds up to twelve hundred. They found that the particles could work at much faster rates. Or rather they figured out how to manipulate them to move faster. So they started devising better and better support structures. It's the evolution of any tech; we've seen it a thousand times. With each iteration it gets faster and faster and smaller and smaller.

"So the Hegemony is constantly updating the ansible and distributing the newer, better models. It takes time and effort and expense to distribute all that hardware to all the ships getting an upgrade throughout the system. But the Hegemony invented incredibly fast unmanned ships solely for this purpose. They're called zipships. Anyway, now, instead of a room filled with sets, the Polemarch's ansible can be carried in a suitcase."

Lem stared at Serge in disbelief. "Where did you get all this information?"

Serge laughed, pleased with himself. "A pub. I figured out where a lot of the Hegemony engineers went after hours. So I parked myself inside with a pint and listened to conversations."

"And that worked?" Lem said. "Surely they wouldn't have divulged all that in public."

"Oh no no, they didn't," Serge said. "But there was a woman there who wasn't getting a lot of attention."

"And you gave her attention."

"She was actually very sweet. But lonely. So we talked. I told her I was developing secret tech for Juke, which isn't a complete lie. And she told me she was developing secret tech for the Hegemony. Turns out we both went to Caltech. Under different circumstances I think we might have hit it off for real."

"Please tell me you didn't get her inebriated," Lem said.

Serge looked affronted. "Oh no, nothing like that. Well . . . actually that's not far from the truth, I suppose. But the drinking was her own doing. She took her wrist pad off when we started dancing, and left it at the table with her purse. All the dancing and drinking got the better of her, though, and she rushed off to the ladies' room to be sick."

Lem was suddenly angry. "So you hacked into her wrist pad? Please tell me you didn't hack into a Hegemony wrist pad."

"I know you said you do this legally, Lem. But it was just sitting there. She had received several messages throughout our conversation, so I had seen her sign in with her password over and over again. I didn't *technically* hack it. I just knew how to get inside."

Lem started pacing, furious. "Stupid, Serge. Stupid."

"Why are you getting all upset about this? I got you the information you wanted."

Lem was practically shouting. "This is not what I wanted, Serge. Far from it."

Three doors opened at once, and a SWAT team came pouring into the warehouse wearing combat gear and pointing slasers.

"HANDS IN THE AIR!"

Lem and Serge froze. Their arms went up. The SWAT

team surrounded them. The letters IF were painted on the front and back of their vests.

The lead marine was a woman. She lowered her rifle as she approached Serge.

Serge's eyes widened. "You."

Her face remained expressionless. "Me."

She grabbed his wrist and spun it behind his back. Then she grabbed the other wrist, did the same, and snapped on the hand restraints.

Serge's voice was weak and desperate. "You're arresting me?"

"No," the woman said. "Drafting you. Welcome to the International Fleet, Serge."

She grabbed his arms and roughly led him toward the exit. Serge glanced back at Lem, in a frantic plea for help. Lem didn't move. His hands were still raised. His heart was racing. The slasers were pointed at him, ready to slice him in half if he so much as twitched. Serge and the female marine exited the building. And then all at once the other marines began to back toward the exit as well, slasers still up, watching him. They moved fast, though, and in seconds Lem was alone.

"You can put your hands down now," Father said.

Lem spun. Behind him, standing in the open doorway, Father stood silhouetted against the false sunlight of Old Town.

Lem lowered his hands and Father stepped inside.

"I hope you realize how close you just came to joining the International Fleet," Father said. "If you hadn't responded the way you did at the end, getting angry, rebuking him, telling him what a mistake it was, those marines would have cuffed you too and taken you as well. Frankly, I don't think you would have lasted a week in the IF. It's just not your style."

Lem felt dizzy. "The woman. She was the one from the pub. This whole thing was a sting."

"When I said the Hegemony takes this tech seriously, Lem, I meant it. The IF takes it even more seriously."

Lem pointed to the door where Serge had exited, suddenly angry. "You can't just take someone, Father. Serge is a civilian. If he's committed a crime, he gets a trial. There's a legal process here."

"Serge *was* a civilian. He forfeited that right the moment he stole sensitive information and then shared it. And not to split hairs here, but I didn't take him. The International Fleet did. I'm just the Hegemon. I don't have any jurisdiction over what they do."

"So what, he's a soldier for the rest of his life now? He's consigned to a life of military servitude?"

"Serge will make a good soldier, I think. He considered enlisting before anyway. Did he tell you? I think he'll do fine."

Lem couldn't believe it. "Is this a joke? This isn't right, Father. The IF can't simply snatch people to silence them. They're not a military dictatorship. This is wrong."

"Sending one of your own employees out to spy on the Hegemony is wrong, Lem. *You* condemned Serge, not the IF. The ansible is the highest guarded secret of the Fleet. They will do anything and everything to protect it."

"So everything Serge told me is true?"

"Essentially."

"Then why give him the information in the first place? If the IF was conducting the sting, why give him the real intel?"

"The IF was willing to watch him. Had he left the wrist pad alone and taken the lawful route, he could have gone his merry way and no one would be the wiser. But for a crime to be committed, it needed to be real intelligence. Sharing it with you was an even greater offense. They let him do it to solidify his fate. They also wanted to bring you in as well and see how you'd react. I convinced them beforehand to wait for your response before deciding your fate. Of course this now means you know state secrets, which puts you on a watch list with the IF. Breathe the word 'ansible' in your sleep, and you'll be on a cruiser in the Belt working as a navigational grunt, wearing the blue for the rest of your days."

Lem didn't respond.

"I'm on that watch list, too, of course," Father said. "I have to keep my mouth shut as much as anyone. Which is why having you poke around is a threat to my well-being as much as it is to yours."

"So the IF *is* a military dictatorship." Lem said.

"Don't be foolish, Lem. Do you see them governing? Are they passing laws, patrolling the streets of Old Town? Their job is to protect Earth from annihilation. That is their singular mission. If people like Serge obstruct that mission, then they'll take action."

"Why go to such lengths to keep the ansible a secret? It's a communications device."

"It's the ultimate communications device, Lem. You can't hack it or tap it. It operates between paired particles. If you don't have the matching set of particles, you cannot hear the message. There are no light beams or wavelengths in the air to intercept. The message magically goes from one ansible to the mate ansible. If terrorists were to have that tech, we couldn't track their communications. They would be invisible to us. The possibility of revolution and subversion is suddenly out of control. They would always hit us unawares. So for the sheer ability of continuing to govern Earth, the Hegemony insists that this be a closely guarded secret."

"In other words, if people have ansibles you can't spy on them and record every word they say to make sure it doesn't offend your ideologies."

Father rolled his eyes. "Please, Lem. Your moral high ground is built upon a pile of pretentious naiveté. Read the news. There are people in the world who are more monstrous than the Formics. They want nothing more than to slit your throat and blow you to itty bloody bits. Why? Because you don't pray like they do, or vote like they do, or raise your children like they do. And you're going to prosecute me for keeping my eye on them? What would you prefer? That I put weapons in their hands? No. I will not let this technology loose on Earth and give our enemies the tool they need to destroy us. Despite what you may think, Lem, I actually give a damn about the people of Earth."

Lem didn't respond.

"So don't preach to me, son. Especially when you don't understand your own sermons."

Lem said nothing for a long moment. "All right. So now what?"

"Now you remain absolutely silent on the subject of the ansible and prove to the Hegemony and the International Fleet that you can be a good little obedient citizen. And I assure you someone will be listening."

"And Serge?" Lem asked. "How are you going to explain to the world his sudden disappearance?"

"We won't have to. He'll do it for us. Moved by the recent discovery of Formics in our system, he was overcome with a sense of duty and obligation to defend his friends and loved ones. He'll make a vid, give a speech, talk about enlisting. It will be very convincing. After a few takes and some coaching from the IF, he'll probably believe it himself. His dear mother will shed a few tears, she'll be so proud. The IF may even use the vid with their recruitment materials. A man touched with nobility can be an inspiring sight to see. Who knows? He might convince a few others to take the blue."

Father gave the warehouse a final disapproving look. "Don't skulk in the shadows anymore, Lem. You're a Jukes. How can the people adore us if we don't make ourselves seen?"

Father turned and moved for the exit.

Lem called after him. "Would they have arrested me, Father? Or drafted me, whatever you want to call it?"

Father turned back.

"If I weren't your son," said Lem, "if you weren't my father, would they have taken me with them?"

"You get one strike, Lem. Don't mess up again."

Then he left Lem there with the dust and graffiti.

# CHAPTER 15

## Vultures

The boom in the space economy leading up to the Second Formic War was both the cause and the result of a large increase in commercial traffic throughout the solar system. According to the Office of the Hegemony, the number of cargo ships registered in the three years immediately following the First Formic War was more than four times the number of cargo vessels in operation prior to that time. Corporations like Juke Limited, Galaxy Defense, and Lockson & Meade all built shipyards in the Belt that required a steady stream of raw materials, workers, and life-sustaining supplies, all of which had to be drawn from remote Kuiper Belt sources since anything closer in was required for building warships.

The effect was a windfall for the most remote free miners, which meant that they, too, had the money to buy long-needed or wanted equipment—up to and including new ships, so that one-ship families now had small fleets of two, three, or four ships. And of course there were the newly constructed ships of the Fleet, constantly training and running maneuvers as soon as they were built while patrols forced other vessels to detour around the war games regions, making the solar system a beehive of activity.

The rise in piracy during this era should not be surprising, considering the number of ships loaded with high-value, high-demand cargo moving back and forth between near-Earth space and the Kuiper Belt. They were ripe for the picking. Cargo vessels were generally poorly armed and ill equipped to handle an attack, and raids and seizures along the most isolated routes were common. The practice of cargo grouping became commonplace, wherein several ships would band together and fly their routes in close formation to discourage an attack, but some argued that convoys without military escort simply made for a more attractive target.

Many pirates were relatively civil in their behavior, leaving sufficient food for the attacked crew and inflicting no bodily harm. The same cannot be said for a particularly violent class of thieves and butchers known as vultures.

—Demosthenes, *A History of the Formic Wars,* Vol. 3

The mining ship was so small and pathetic and ill equipped that Khalid considered it a waste of time. He stood at the helm of his own ship, the Shimbir, staring at the image of the mining ship in the holofield, considering his options. He had traveled to this sector of the Kuiper Belt because he and his crew had heard chatter of an expensive A-class digger anchored to the asteroid here. A ship that could bring coin. A ship Khalid could strip down and sell piece by piece on the black market. A ship worth his trouble. But this ship in the holofield, this boxy, outdated, jury-rigged piece of *digada*, was about as far from an A-class digger as any ship could get.

"How far out are we?" Khalid asked.

Gut, the navigator, checked the readout. "Two hours, fifty-seven minutes."

They were practically on top of the ship. It seemed a shame to come all this way and to turn back now, empty-handed. And yet, if they attacked, they'd be taking a risk for . . . what? A few packs of noodles and some dated, worthless mining equipment? Khalid scratched at the stubble on his cheek. His crew was watching him, surrounding him at the helm, fifteen strong, armed and ready, awaiting his decision. Most of them were already high on juice, their eyes red and hungry, their faces bathed in the bluish light of the holofield. If Khalid canceled the raid now, none of them would complain. They could all see that there was little to gain here. But they would also see this whole trip as a mistake for which Khalid was solely responsible. A monumental waste of time and supplies and fuel. They may not do anything mutinous immediately, but the seed of mutiny would be planted in their hearts. Then, months from now, the whispering would start, followed by plotting, and before Khalid knew it, he would wake to find his throat slit open, filling his chambers with floating globules of blood.

No, calling off the raid was not an option. The trick was turning lead into gold, as the saying used to go—before harvested gold from asteroids became so plentiful that it devalued drastically in the market. That was what his crew lacked, Khalid knew. Wisdom. A sense of history. Intellect. They were not unintelligent, for Khalid had no tolerance for stupidity, but there was no depth to their reason, either. They were literate in the sense that they could read, but illiterate in the sense that they cared not at all for books or learning or expanding their minds. Conversations with the crew were painfully dull and uninspiring. There were exceptions, of course. Maja had a head on her shoulders, which is how she had survived among a crew of men for so long. Her dagger, the Silver Lady, had also helped in that regard.

Khalid reached into the holofield and spread his hands apart, zooming in on the pitiful ship. Now he could see detail, including the ship's name painted on its hull and the laser drill crudely mounted on its side. Magnified the ship looked even worse. Even the asteroid it was anchored to looked pitiful by association.

Khalid cursed under his breath. A month of travel for this. The fuel he had used to get here and the fuel he would expend returning to his original route would be wasted. He would find nothing inside that ship of any value. Trinkets maybe, but nothing to recoup the expense of coming here.

He turned to his crew, gesturing to the ship, appearing cheerful. "Well? There she is, in all her glory. Do we take her or not?"

A few members of the crew exchanged glances, afraid to speak first.

Ibrahim, Khalid's younger brother, scoffed. "She's barely worth the trouble, brother. Look at that drill. It's a relic. We'd get nothing for it. I wouldn't bother loading it in the bay. It's junk. And I doubt there's anything of value inside. These people are space rats. What's that language on the side? Russian? I hate Russians."

"I doubt they're Russian," said Maja. "The ship may have had a Russian crew once, but it's passed hands many times now. No telling who's inside it."

Maja was probably right, thought Khalid. There could be anyone inside. "Whoever they are," he said, "they won't put up much of a fight."

"But why go to the trouble?" said Ibrahim. "What are we going to get there? Some dirty old clothes? A few cans of meat? That's not game, brother. We're more likely to get a disease from these people than anything of value."

Some of the crewmen exchanged glances. They had seen diseases before. Fevers, blisters, viruses of the chest. They had lost a few of their own to such illnesses. Now the crew seemed wary.

Stupid, Ibrahim, thought Khalid. If you would just keep your mouth shut like I have ordered you again and again and again. Now, if I pull out, some will think me cowardly.

Maja must have sensed Khalid's frustration, for she spoke on his behalf. "You talk too much, Ibrahim. Just because you're afraid of a few decrepit old ladies, doesn't mean we should call it off."

This earned a few laughs from the men, and a glare from Ibrahim, but it had achieved what Khalid needed. "My young brother is wise to be cautious. But one man's junk is another man's treasure. The contents of that ship are worthless, true. But the ship itself might win us a fortune."

Ibrahim had the audacity to laugh at that. "I have never doubted you, brother." He pointed to the holo. "But how can you possibly turn that into a single credit?"

Khalid forced a smile, though in truth he preferred to pinch his brother's nose until it bled. "You ask good questions, little brother."

Ibrahim glared again. He hated being called that, to be disrespected in front of the men. Careful, Khalid thought, or it will be Ibrahim's knife that finds your throat. Khalid laughed and threw an arm around Ibrahim's shoulder. "You look at that ship and see a bucket of bolts. I look at that ship, and I see something much grander. Much stronger. Much more valuable. For that ship, dear brother, is not the fish, but the worm."

The men exchanged glances again, and Khalid almost rolled his eyes at their lack of vision. How could they be so simpleminded? So vacant? A plan had formed in his mind now, and no one but him had the mental capacity for it. Even Maja looked slightly confused.

Khalid turned back to his navigator. "Gut, are there any other ships nearby? I'm curious."

Gut tapped at his terminal. "There's an IF assault ship a month away."

"An IF assault ship, you say?" said Khalid, smiling now. "One of the newer models, if I'm not mistaken, am I right, Gut? The LX-40?"

Gut checked the screen again. "Looks that way."

"The LX-40," said Khalid, saying the word with a little bit of theater, as if it were a thing of wonder, as if he were not stating its name, but its value. "Now there's a prize, my brothers."

The simpletons looked at one another again. Only Ibrahim was brave enough to speak. "What are you suggesting, brother, that we take on an LX-40? That would be suicide."

Khalid smiled. Because his plan was fully formed now. A risky plan, yes. Some might even call it foolish. But it was a plan that turned lead into gold, a plan that would silence anyone who questioned him, a plan that would attach fear to his name, or respect, or awe.

"I'll explain later, my brothers. But first let us go down and take this tin can. We did not come all this way for nothing."

The men didn't object. They were curious to see what they might find.

Khalid's ship, the Shimbir, a salvage vessel painted a nonreflective black, drifted toward the asteroid on the far side, opposite the mining ship, with all of its lights extinguished. Then Khalid sent out a spy probe and waited for the crew of the mining ship to shut down the drill and kill some of their external lights, suggesting that they were preparing for sleep shift. Khalid then waited three hours to make sure the miners were asleep before beginning his attack. It was easier than Khalid thought it would be. The crew inside the mining ship were not Russians. They spoke Portuguese. Brazilians probably. There were only three of them. One of them was even missing an arm. Khalid thought them rather pathetic. Hardly worth the trouble at all.

Khalid let his men do the killing, and they were quick about it. None of them took any pleasure in it. It was one of the reasons why Khalid had selected these men and women for his crew. People who enjoyed death were unstable, dangerous, and mutinous. The best crews were hungry for spoil, not murder.

Khalid then explained his plan. He would take the tin can, fly from the asteroid, and make a distress signal. The IF would come and rescue him, Khalid would kill the crew and then seize the LX-40.

"You can't be serious," said Ibrahim. "There will be forty soldiers on that ship."

"Probably," said Khalid, shrugging, as if the number meant nothing to him.

Ibrahim laughed. "And you will take on all these soldiers yourself? Alone?"

"I am Khalid," said Khalid, as if this were answer enough.

Ibrahim waited for the joke to end. When it didn't, he said. "I do not think this wise, brother."

"You wouldn't," said Khalid. "You and Maja will share the captainship while I'm gone. You will stay on the asteroid, covered with the tarps. I will be adrift only a week away."

The tarps were massive camouflaged coverings that matched the rock and hid the ship from view.

Khalid could see doubt even in Maja's eyes, but he knew the crew would not abandon him if he put Maja and Ibrahim both in charge. Their fear of each other would keep either one from trying anything. Plus the promise of big game was too much for them to pass up.

Khalid wasted no time. He loaded food into the Brazilian tin can and flew it away from the asteroid. It was not difficult to scuttle the ship in a way that didn't threaten life support. He merely crippled the main thrusters and sent out the distress signal. A month was a long time to wait, but eventually the LX-40 came and docked with the tin can. Armed soldiers of the International Fleet boarded the ship, cautious. Khalid had had plenty of time to explore the Brazilian ship, study its documents and history, and work up his story.

The captain of the LX-40 was an American. He folded his arms and looked leery, but Khalid played the part of the coward, which he knew the captain would believe. Vultures had attacked the ship, Khalid told them. They had killed the other two members of the crew. Khalid had not fought with them. He had hidden with a stash of food in the air ducts. He had wanted to go out and help and save them, but he was weak. He had a family back in Somalia, five children. He had to survive, you see. He had to send them money. If I die, they die.

The American captain frowned, disgusted at such cowardice.

There was nothing on the ship of value, Khalid said. The vultures had taken it all and damaged the ship. When they left, Khalid had crawled out, waited a week, and called for help.

"We'll drop you off at the nearest depot," said the American captain. "And while you're on my ship, you will work for your food and abide by my rules."

Khalid bowed and almost cried he was so grateful. "Yes, sir. I will work, sir, yes. Very hard."

The American captain wrinkled his nose. "Get him cleaned up and in some different clothes. The man hasn't bathed in a month."

They led Khalid to a shower tube and gave him a blue IF jumpsuit to change into once he was done. A doctor took him to a room and poked and prodded and drew blood and listened to Khalid's heart and checked his bone density. Khalid was lithe and thin like most Somali, but toned and in peak physical condition. They fed him and gave him a bunk in a supply closet. Khalid acted submissive and grateful and apologized to everyone for the inconvenience he had caused.

The ship, he noted, was a thing of wonder. It had not been built all that long ago. The walls and floors were immaculate. The fixtures shined. Everything smelled new and unused. It was no wonder the captain had turned his nose up at Khalid. The American lived in a veritable bed of roses.

Khalid could not believe his luck. They had put him in a supply closet. There was food here. Water. Tools.

That night, during sleep shift, Khalid climbed out of the sleep sack they had given him. He cracked the door and saw that a guard was posted right outside his door. So they do not completely trust me, thought Khalid. They are not complete fools.

But the guard was nothing. A man's neck, when at rest and grabbed from behind, could be twisted and broken easily.

Khalid pulled the man's body into the supply closet and took his ID and weapon. The lights were out. The corridor was empty. Most of the crew was asleep. Khalid filled a sack with water and food and made his way to the helm. The soldier's ID card gave him access. There was only one man on duty at the holotable, his back to the door. Such carelessness, thought Khalid. Such arrogance.

Khalid shot him with the first soldier's slaser. A quick and silent kill. Then he disengaged the man's magnetic boots and pushed the corpse aside. The holotable was everything Khalid had hoped it would be, with all of its windows of data and charts and arcs and ship movements, all projected in the air above it. A treasure trove of information.

It took him a moment to find the commands he needed. He sent a laserline transmission to the station that was their destination detailing a system failure on board that the ship's mechanics were now investigating. Then he severed the laserline connection and disengaged life support. The hum of machines in the walls whined down to silence. Then alarms wailed. Lights flashed. Khalid sealed the helm doors and watched the screens on the holotable that showed him various angles of the ship's corridors. Disoriented men and women stumbled out of the barracks, roused from sleep. Most had their issued oxygen masks they had been trained to retrieve in the event of an emergency such as this one. But others were bare-faced and ill-prepared. It was easy after that. Khalid simply opened the airlocks remotely and watched as the men and women were sucked out into the blackness of space.

It was over in less than a minute. Some had fought gallantly, clinging, struggling, fighting the inevitable. But space shows no gentle hand, and soon the corridor was a vacuum.

He hadn't killed everyone, however. There were emergency doors that had engaged and sealed off areas. Other soldiers had not left the barracks and were thus stuck inside, unable to leave. He ignored the latter group. They would asphyxiate soon enough. It was the soldiers saved by the emergency doors that gave him concern. Already they were organizing and choosing a leader among them. Three of them were armed. Soldiers indeed.

Khalid watched them, wondering if any of them would be worth keeping.

But no, how could he trust them? How could he be certain they wouldn't strangle him in the night? They were blue bloods. Their hearts could not be turned. Or even if they could, it wasn't worth the risk of being wrong.

He checked his slaser, dug through his sack for the knife he had recovered from the storage room, then he left the helm and began the dirty business of finishing the job. It took him over an hour, and he did not relish the work. It was loud and messy and got his blood up. The American captain was the last one. It was only by chance that he should be the final survivor. The man wept and begged, and it was only in that death that Khalid felt any sense of satisfaction, for such a man did not deserve to wear a uniform of any sort.

He returned to the helm and settled in, opening a can of peaches from his food sack, with syrup so sweet it nearly gave him a headache. He then reengaged the laserline and sent a transmission to the IF explaining that the ship needed parts not found on board and that he, the captain, was redirecting her to another port for repairs. Then he changed course and retreated back the way they had come, back toward the asteroid.

He rendezvoused with his crew two days later. The two ships docked, and Ibrahim greeted him at the docking tube, grabbing Khalid's forearm as was the custom. "Wearing blue now, brother?"

"And a bit of red as well, I see," said Maja. She appeared beside Ibrahim and traced a finger down the line of splattered blood across Khalid's chest, now a dried rusty brown.

"You have not damaged my ship, I hope," he said to Ibrahim.

Ibrahim removed the earpiece and handed it to his captain, smiling. "No more than she already was."

Ibrahim floated down the docking tube and took in the interior of the IF ship, whistling at what he saw. "A regular pleasure cruiser, this one, brother. Fresh off the shipyard, I'd say." He inhaled deep. "Even has that new-ship smell." He knocked on a bulkhead and produced a heavy metallic clang. "Built for war. She can take a beating and then some. And faster than the sun, they say."

"Not even close to lightspeed," said Khalid, "but faster than most ships out here, yes. And shielded."

Ibrahim clapped his hands twice in celebration, laughing. "I told you you were crazy, brother. They'll send you straight to the grave, I said. No judge, no jury, just a needle in the arm and the kill juice. No way would they let you wear the blue. They can smell a vulture a million klicks away. And look at you, all gussied up like the Polemarch himself." He clapped again and looked down the corridor, rubbing his hands together like a child eager to open gifts. "Which is my room? The one nearest the kitchen, I hope. Or maybe I'll just put my hammock in there. Captain of a ship like this keeps chocolate, I bet."

"We're not taking the ship," said Khalid.

Ibrahim's smile vanished in an instant. "But—"

"The ship has a signature. They'd track us."

"Let them! Bring on the whole Fleet. We'll outrun them."

"They have ships as fast as this one," said Khalid. "And if we take her, they'll know what to look for. We wouldn't get six months out before they'd snag us. No, we strip her now, clean her to the bone and leave her to drift. Then we disappear back into the Black, and they won't have a scent to follow. We'll hole up somewhere and mount the drive and shield generator onto the Shimbir."

"But—" Ibrahim spread his arms wide, gesturing at the walls around him. "Look at this, brother. This is a palace, a palace built on heavy taxes that squeeze our country like a vise. You want to forgive this? You want to toss this aside?"

Khalid removed his IF uniform, for Maja had emerged from the docking tube with one of his own jumpsuits. He allowed her to help him into it as he spoke to Ibrahim. "You are like the little monkey who reaches through a narrow hole in the side of a box to grab a walnut. With the nut clenched in his fist, the monkey's hand is now too wide to extract it from the box. He screams and kicks and panics because he can hear the monkey hunters coming through the brush with their heavy clubs. If he would just drop the nut, he could pull his hand free and escape with ease. But the foolish monkey clings to his prize, and the monkey hunters arrive and bash his brains in. I like my brain, Ibrahim. I might even like yours if you used it every once in a while."

"Then what did we do this for?" asked Ibrahim. "You said we were taking this ship, brother."

"We're taking what's of value. The drive system, the

holotable, life support, and last of all, the shield generators. We'll mount it all on the Shimbir."

"But the Shimbir is junk compared to this."

Khalid struck him with the back of his hand. It was not as hard of a blow as it could have been, but since Ibrahim wasn't anchored, he spun away from the blow and into the far wall, bouncing off it and catching himself clumsily on a handhold. Ibrahim touched the side of his mouth, and his fingertips came back red.

"The Shimbir is your home," said Khalid. "You will give it respect. Now gather the men and empty the Shimbir's cargo bay. Dump anything we can. Make room. Then organize the men and get back in here to start stripping what we can. But carefully. Damage nothing. This haul isn't for the pawners and the scrap collectors. It's for us. Is that asking too much, little brother?"

Ibrahim wiped at his mouth again and scowled. "Of course not, brother. Anything for the wise and powerful Khalid." He launched toward the docking tube and climbed inside it, disappearing from view.

When he was gone, Maja said, "You are too hard on him. I think that unwise."

"Oh? And why is that?"

"I would much rather follow you, than him. Even little brothers have their breaking points."

Khalid buttoned up his jumpsuit, saying nothing.

Maja drew close. Her finger traced the line of his jaw. "A month is a long time to be away, Khalid. Were you lonely and cold in that tin can? Did your body hunger for warmth?"

Desire began to well up inside Khalid, but he knew better than to heed it. "It was quiet," he said, gently pushing her hand away. "I had forgotten what a rare gift silence can be."

Maja frowned at him, disappointed. Then she turned away and joined the crew in emptying the cargo bay. Khalid smiled to himself. There was power in him now, he realized. Respect. Even Maja, cold as she was, could sense it. It had filled her with desire, and Khalid had turned her away. He had actually turned a willing woman away. He almost laughed aloud at the idea. The old Khalid would have surrendered in an instant. But the new Khalid—no, the *true* Khalid—was stronger than the desperate cries of the flesh. No, nothing could weaken his will now.

Four days later, the IF ship was stripped bare of all its essentials and left adrift.

Khalid and Ibrahim retired to Khalid's quarters, where the IF holotable had been installed. Starcharts and data readouts hovered in the air above the table. A wealth of information. The entire International Fleet at Khalid's fingertips.

Ibrahim was almost giddy. "Look at this, brother. This is the mother lode. With this data, we can avoid their gunships. We can hit their supply lines at their most vulnerable points. It will be easy now."

Khalid patted his brother's cheek, as if speaking to a child. "Of course it will be easy, brother. I am Khalid."

# CHAPTER 16

## Armor

To: imala.bootstamp%e2@ifcom.gov/fleetcom/gagak
From: ketkar%polemarch@ifcom.gov
Subject: Your orders

I have been informed that Edimar Querales's findings about enemy movements may be accurate. Using intel she provided, we now suspect that there are eight motherships on approach, four above and four below the ecliptic.

We have yet to confirm how many Formic miniships have seized asteroids within the system, but we know for certain of at least one besides 2030CT. An IF probe near one of the Belt asteroids mentioned in Edimar's report returned a visual confirmation. We have since sent additional probes and manned vessels to investigate other asteroids, but no one is as close to their target as you are to 2030CT. Your orders therefore are to fly Victor Delgado to the asteroid in the modified quickship. He will then penetrate the canopy and reconnoiter, gathering intel on enemy conditions, numbers, weapons, etcetera. He will record a live feed, which your crew will relay to me immediately.

As we cannot send a civilian into a hostile environment,
Victor Delgado is conscripted into the International
Fleet effective immediately. Rank: E2. Your crew
should be prepared to fire on the asteroid using any
available weaponry, should I give the order. Make all
necessary preparations.

Ketkar

Victor crashed into the wall, shoulder first, and grunted
slightly in pain. His body bounced off and drifted back toward the center of the cargo bay, disoriented and completely
upended. As he floated he rotated his shoulder experimentally. To his relief he felt no piercing stab of pain, no grinding
of broken bone, just the slight lingering shock of impact. The
armor, it seemed, worked after all.

He brought his arms in tight to his body and tapped his
thumb throttle slightly. The tiny jets in the back of his suit
released just enough propulsion to set him upright again and
push him toward the nearest wall. Victor caught a handhold
and paused to catch his breath.

"You're not screaming in pain," said Magoosa. "That's a
good sign." He was anchored to the floor, watching Victor
from below. "But I'm not sure this is the best way to test your
armor."

"I didn't crash on purpose, Goos," said Victor. "I was actually trying to land."

"In that case I give your landing a score of zero. And that's
being generous."

"Yeah, well, I'd like to see you leap around in this thing."

"Can't," Magoosa said. "The armor's custom-fit to your
body. Though I'm beginning to think it's better suited for
breaking your bones than protecting them."

"Actually it worked pretty well," said Victor. "I probably
*would* have broken something without it."

"You wouldn't have crashed if you weren't wearing it," said Magoosa.

That was true enough, Victor thought. The exosuit of armor fit perfectly atop his mining suit, but it was taking some getting used to. It was a lot of additional mass, and launching and landing required a lot of power from Victor's legs. He had only been jumping back and forth between walls for fifteen minutes and already his quads, hamstrings, and calves were on fire.

He *was* getting better, though. His first jumps had been laughable. But now he could at least rotate and spin his body in the way he wanted to. He just wasn't rotating far enough.

He was getting into position to try another launch when Imala came in and handed him her wrist pad, looking furious.

"Our orders," she said.

He read the e-mail on screen. It informed him that he was conscripted into the International Fleet.

Victor handed the device back to her. "I suspected this."

"You did?"

"If they send a civilian into a hostile environment the IF would be held liable for whatever happens. They'd subject themselves to all kinds of civil litigation. By making me a soldier, however, it's business as usual. They can do whatever they want with me."

"You're not angry?" she asked.

"It's not something I can control, Imala. Getting angry won't help. I'm more worried about the crew. Do they know about this?"

"I came to you first. No one is going to like that you were drafted. They'll all worry that they'll be next, that the IF will pull them from their children. We should gather everyone in the helm and hear their concerns. Otherwise they'll be grumbling behind our backs."

"Can you blame them?" said Victor. "The Polemarch has as much tact as a mountain lion. He isn't exactly great with civil-

ians. He comes off as callous and indifferent and a little bull-
ish. He simply gives orders and expects them to be obeyed."

"That's how the military works, Vico. That's his world."

"I know," said Victor. "But it wouldn't hurt him to be a
little more sensitive. This ship is full of women and children.
What are you going to do?"

"I'll have Arjuna read the orders to everyone. The crew's already a little hostile toward me. I'm getting a lot of grumblings
and eye-rollings whenever I give any orders at the helm. If
Arjuna reads the orders maybe they won't grumble so loudly."

"Good idea," said Victor.

"How quickly can we go?" she asked.

"The quickship's ready. It will be a cramped flight, but we
both should fit. You're going to need armor, though. Even if
you're staying in the quickship. No one should approach the
shell unless they're fully protected. I'll need at least three
days for that. Will the IF wait that long?"

"The IF doesn't have a choice," Imala said. "If we're not
ready, we're not ready. I'm more worried about the crew. They
don't like being this close to the enemy. Everyone's feeling
very exposed and vulnerable."

"Talk to Arjuna," said Victor. "Have him read the orders
and help with crowd control."

"You're not going to try to talk me out of going along with
you?"

"I tried," Victor said. "Didn't work. Besides, I'm in the
Fleet now. I can't argue with my commanding officer."

"Technically we're the same rank."

"Yes, but you're the captain. That makes you the presiding authority." Victor smiled. "Same rank is nice, though.
Means we can still legally date."

They gathered everyone in the helm. Arjuna hadn't even finished reading the orders when the objections began.

"Conscripted?" Sabad said. "So they can take whoever they want now? We don't even get a choice? Is that how this works? First they take our ship, and now they steal our crew? Who will they take next? Arjuna? Me? Cojo?" She gestured to the infant harness wrapped around her chest, where the little Cojo was asleep, sucking on a pacifier.

"The IF isn't going to take our children," Victor said.

"Maybe not our children, but what's to stop them from taking us away *from* our children?" Julexi said.

"If they intended that, they would have done it already," Victor said. "They could have drafted every person here eighteen years old and older in one swoop. But they didn't. They conscripted only one of us, and I don't think it's a coincidence that the person they chose is one of the only single adult members of the crew. I don't have children. I'm not married. I'm the age of most enlistees. They asked me because I'm the least tied down."

"They asked you because you have experience fighting the Formics," Naishihi said. "You've done this before and successfully."

"Yes, but my point is, they asked only one of us," Victor said. "If they didn't care about our children or your responsibilities as parents, they would have conscripted a platoon of us and sent us all in there together. Strategically that would have been the better option because that would have produced far more intelligence than just a single soldier. But they didn't. Right now they need the full support of the public, and drafting parents of small children won't win them much support from Earth."

No one argued that point.

"He's right," Arjuna said. "And it doesn't do us any good to dwell on what the IF will or won't do next. We have our orders. It's what we came here to do anyway."

"We're not doing it our way, though," Julexi said. "The IF is giving the orders."

"What they've asked us to do is essentially what we always intended," said Victor. "And I think it's best if they're involved anyway. We'd be gathering the intel for them regardless."

Sabad narrowed her eyes at Victor. "You can't say 'they' like you're not part of them. You're one of them now."

"The IF is not our enemy, Sabad," Arjuna said. "There is only one enemy. The Formics. The human race needs to be cooperative or we don't stand a chance."

"We don't stand a chance anyway," Sabad said.

There were murmurs of agreement from the crowd.

"If the IF wants to cooperate," Ubax said, "they can do so without bossing us around. Subjecting ourselves to their leadership isn't the only way to cooperate."

More murmurs of agreement.

"Why should we allow them to seize our ship and tell us how to use it?" Naishihi said. "We know how to use it better than they do."

The crowd all started talking at once, all of their grievances and annoyances pouring out in a sudden flood.

Arjuna waved his arms. "Enough!"

The crowd stilled.

"We have our orders," said Arjuna. "Imala has offered to give me back the captainship many times. You all know that. I have refused. We need to work with the Fleet. Have you forgotten why they exist? Their only goal is to protect us. You may disagree with some of their decisions, you may not like how they appear to speak down to us, but we'd be fools to spurn the very people who are willing to give their lives to save our home. Now, I'll not have any more of this attitude from anyone. I've seen how you look at Imala and complain about her orders and skulk around and whisper behind her back. Before she took this position she was the most beloved person in this crew. There was not a one of you that questioned her loyalty to this family. Now you treat her like a pariah. All because she's been put in a position that she did not choose. Is that how quickly we turn our backs on one of our own? Imala has worked as hard as any member of this crew since she got here, if not harder. She has saved our skin a number of times in business negotiations and she has managed our finances in a way like I have never done. She has treated every one of you like family. And what I'm seeing right now feels like the seeds of mutiny. It stops. As of this moment it ceases completely. This is a vessel of the International Fleet. You may not like that, but that's a fact. And so we will treat our commanding officer with respect or there will be consequences. We are not going to win this war. The International Fleet is. And if they want our help, this ship is going to give it to them."

Silence. No one said a word. There were a few obstinate faces in the crowd, but not many.

Imala stepped forward. "Victor needs three days to finish preparing the equipment. Then he and I will launch. Until then we'll continue running the practice drills with the laser. If the IF commands us to go in and attack, we'll be ready. Dismissed."

The crowd dispersed and Victor launched to where Imala was anchored to the holotable.

"Thank you," Imala said to Arjuna. "You're a lot better at this than I am."

"You're doing fine," said Arjuna. "The problem is with the crew. They've never been in a situation like this before, and uncertainty leads to fear. Just keep Victor safe. We'll be ready with the laser." He gave her arm an encouraging squeeze and moved off.

Victor drifted up to Imala. "Good thing Arjuna stepped in. The pitchforks and torches were coming out."

"I don't see why the IF doesn't make him captain," said Imala. "I'm not qualified for this."

"You are actually," Victor said. "You've proven yourself in combat with the Formics. You're a skilled negotiator, and you're the best pilot I've ever seen. The IF values all of those skills."

"Yes, but I'm not a commander," Imala said. "I'm not a natural leader like Arjuna is. Which is what matters here."

"You're learning," Victor said. "Arjuna's a good teacher. Part of me wishes *he* was the Polemarch."

"*All* of me wishes he was the Polemarch." Imala said. She turned to the holotable and began typing up her response to Ketkar. "I'll tell him we need a few days of prep."

"When you're done, come down to the workshop. I need to take a mold of your body to make your armor."

She gave him a skeptical look.

"Relax," he said. "You'll be wearing a mining suit. Unfortunately." He winked and left her at the helm.

Mother was waiting for him out in the corridor. "Vico."

He grabbed a handhold and turned to her.

"So you're conscripted," she said.

"You know why they did it, Mother."

"I know why, yes, but I don't agree with Arjuna on this. I'm not going to whisper about it to anyone other than you, but I can see why the others are furious. We don't have to accept everything the IF orders us to do."

"Would you feel this way if they had conscripted someone else?" Victor asked. "Arjuna maybe? Or Naishihi?"

"You're my son. Obviously I'm going to object to you being conscripted more than someone else. But that doesn't change the fact that they're treating us like putty in their hands. We have always operated away from the world, Vico. That's why we're called *free* miners, because we're free of any nation or government or organization calling us their own. We determine who and what we are. We govern ourselves. What right does the IF have to seize this ship? Do they own all of space? Is the entire solar system and everything in it their legal property, to be picked up and seized at their whim?"

Victor opened his mouth to speak, but she cut him off.

"And don't cite some commerce act or document or constitution. Those mean nothing. They were invented by people in order to control us. Who gave them the right to draft those documents in the first place? Certainly not us. Just because they say they have power and authority over us doesn't make it true. If I type up a document stating that all Italian free miners are subject to my tax, would you honestly expect them to pay it?"

"This is different, Mother. There is a fleet of Formics coming. There may be a fleet already here. Unifying our efforts strikes me as wise."

"And when this is all over," Mother said, "when the Formics are defeated, then what? You think the IF is simply going to dissolve and voluntarily relinquish all the authority they've gathered?"

"I haven't given it much thought. We're all trying to survive at this point."

"I'll tell you what will happen," Mother said. "The IF will continue to justify its existence. It will continue to assert its authority, and it will continue to behave as if it is the ruling authority of space. And they'll do with us, the free citizens of space, as they please. At the least they will treat us with contempt, at the most they will conscript us into their organization."

"Were you this angry, Mother, before they conscripted your son?"

Mother sighed and was quiet a moment. "I lost your father, Vico. And during the last war, in the final battle, when you were in the thick of it, I was physically sick. I had no idea what was happening to you or if you were even alive. I didn't sleep. And there wasn't a soul I could talk to or turn to or find comfort in. Now the two most important people in my life are soldiers, and I have no idea what that means for their future. You're both about to face another ship of Formics, and there's nothing I can do about it."

"This is what we came here to do, Mother."

"No, we came here to put a few cameras inside. Recon is soldier's work. I don't see why we can't just send the probe inside."

"The probe wasn't made for that kind of maneuvering. It's a rocket. It's designed to cross great distances ahead of the ship and conduct reconnaissance. It's not made for wiggling through narrow, rocky, winding passageways. And anyway, it's probably too big for the tunnels. Assuming there are any."

"Then make something that *will* work, a tiny drone maybe. There's no cause to endanger yourself."

"I'll be armored, Mother. Imala will wait in the quickship. I value my life as much as you do. I won't take unnecessary risks. I'll only be gone for a few hours."

"And then what? Then you and Imala leave for the fleet?"

"I don't know. I've had about thirteen minutes to process all of this."

She took his hands and gave them a gentle squeeze, her face lined with worry.

"I'll be fine, Mother. I'll have Imala. Is there anyone else you'd rather have protecting me?"

"But recon, Vico. Tunnels."

"We're not certain there are tunnels," said Victor. "That's speculation. I'll go armed. If the air isn't combustible, I'll use my laser. In close quarters, it will do the job just fine."

"And if the air *is* combustible?"

He kissed her on the cheek. "Have faith, Mother."

"Faith is not to blindly believe, son. Faith is action. It's doing something. It's creating what we need and believing that God will be merciful enough to grant it in his time."

"And that's what we're doing. We're taking action." He

gave her hands a final squeeze and then launched down to the workshop.

Three days later Victor and Imala met in the cargo bay on the eve of their launch to try on their suits and make last-minute adjustments. First they donned their mining suits, then came the armor.

"I feel like a floating tank," Imala said.

"You look like you belong on a catwalk," Victor said. "Even combat gear looks good on you, Captain Bootstamp." He whistled.

She rolled her eyes. "Flirtatious behavior, Ensign Delgado. Need I recite IF regulations on what is and isn't appropriate communication between a commanding officer and her subordinate?"

"You can recite the whole rulebook as long as it gives me an excuse to stare at that face of yours."

"Let's focus, space born."

He nodded. "The armor isn't bulky. It only feels that way because it adds so much mass. The design is rather slim and compact."

She moved her bent arms up and down like a chicken, getting a feel for the armor. "I wish we had a few months to train in these. You should never give a soldier new equipment on the night before a mission. I haven't been to basic training, but I know at least that much. That's how mistakes are made. Mazer would not approve."

"We don't have much of a choice. Here, this is the helmet." He reached to the side and pulled the helmet off the workbench where he had anchored it. It was made of the same alloy as the armor.

"How am I supposed to see out of it?" Imala said. "It's completely solid. There's no visor."

"A solid helmet gives the best protection against heat," said

Victor. "Very small cameras are embedded in the front where the visor should be. They relay your surroundings onto your HUD inside your helmet. It's panoramic. It almost feels like you don't have a helmet on at all."

"Where did you get the cameras?"

"From the scanning equipment. Don't tell Arjuna."

He slid the helmet down over her head and sealed it to her suit. She turned her head from side to side experimentally and then faced him. Victor donned his own helmet and locked it down. His HUD and interface came to life in front of him. "Can you hear me?" he asked.

"Yes," Imala said.

"Good. First we'll try a few simple launches." He pointed across the room to where he had mounted several foam pads on the wall just below a handhold. "The pads are your target. You'll thank me for putting them up. Launching takes a little getting used to. Landing is even harder."

"You realize of course that there won't be any foam pads at the asteroid," Imala said. "It will be nothing but unforgiving ice and rock."

"I'm making it sound harder than it is," Victor said. "The trick is to put more power in your legs than you're used to. It will take a few attempts before you get the hang of it, so don't get discouraged."

Of course Imala did it perfectly on the first try. She squatted, launched, and landed softly on the foam, grabbing the handhold to catch herself with ease. She turned her helmet back to face him. "How was that?"

Victor laughed to himself. "I'd say that was beginner's luck, but I know you better than that. Can you leap back?"

She did, landing deftly beside him.

"This is supposed to be harder for you," Victor said.

"You're a good coach," Imala said, reaching up and tapping him gently on the top of his helmet.

"You're enjoying this, aren't you?"

"Immensely," she said, giving his head another condescending tap.

After ten minutes of flawlessly hopping back and forth, she moved on to full-body rotations, using a touch of propulsion from the back of her suit. She leaped, spun, landed on her feet on the opposite wall; then she used the momentum to squat again and immediately launch back. Before they finished an hour later they were both launching with confidence, hitting every target they aimed for and landing with their feet under them.

They finally removed their helmets and anchored themselves to the floor to catch their breaths.

"Don't take any risks tomorrow," Imala said. "First sign of the enemy, you're out. I'm serious, Vico. If I order you to pull back, you pull back. I want your word on that."

"I wouldn't dare disobey my commanding officer," Victor said, smiling.

She frowned. "I'm not joking, Victor. If you care about my happiness, you'll keep yourself safe."

"We're both coming back, Imala. I promise you that."

He kissed her gently on the forehead, and they parted to shower and rest for the night.

Victor slept poorly. He was ill-prepared for this and he knew it. And yet what more could he do? If he knew what was beneath the shell, he could strategize, build weapons for the situation and environment, pack gear that he knew would be useful. Here he was going in blind.

The size of the asteroid was to his advantage. The Formic miniship had obviously carried a small crew. There likely weren't that many Formics inside. And with the asteroid measuring nearly two kilometers in length, his chances of running into a Formic were small.

When he did finally succumb to sleep he found himself inside the dark narrow tunnels of the Formic scout ship. Ahead of him there was light. He knew where it would lead, and he pulled himself forward despite his rising sense of panic. No. He did not want to go this way. He did not want to see.

The wide cargo area was just as he remembered it, a space so long and expansive that the Gagak could easily fit inside it. He knew this because there were ships here of similar size, or rather pieces of ships. The Formics had destroyed every ship that had come against them, and, motivated perhaps by curiosity, they had pulled the ship wreckage inside their own ship to analyze it. The pieces all floated in the giant space like a twisted, scorched junkyard. And there in the center of the debris was the cockpit of an American fighter with the dead pilot still inside. Victor knew what was coming next. Because this was not a dream, but a memory. Two Formics pulled the canopy away from the cockpit, unhooked the pilot, and slid his body free of his harnesses. They were not gentle. They yanked away his helmet, giving little regard to the straps and harnesses that popped or came loose after repeated pulls. Next came his spacesuit and flight jacket and under garment until the man's pale, almost colorless chest was exposed.

No. Why wouldn't Victor's eyes close? Why wouldn't his feet move, his neck turn away? The Formic cut open the man's abdomen and reached up upside him, searching for something Victor knew they wouldn't find.

The next morning Victor met Magoosa and Imala in the locker room, where Magoosa helped them both into their armor. Victor tucked his helmet under his arm and faced his young apprentice. "Any last words of advice?"

"Advice? No. But I made you something."

Magoosa reached into one of the lockers and pulled out a spear, about a meter and a half long. The black shaft and leaf-blade tip were a single piece made of a hard polymer. Black grip tape had been wrapped around the shaft in two places, and an adjustable cloth strap extended from the spear's bottom to the top of the shaft just below the blade.

"You might need this in the tunnels," Magoosa said, handing it to Victor. "It straps across your back when not in use."

Victor hefted the spear and studied the blade at the tip.

"It's not incredibly sharp," Magoosa said, "but the polymer is near indestructible and it won't create a spark if you strike a rock."

"Did you design this?" Victor asked.

Magoosa looked slightly embarrassed. "No, I downloaded it from one of those groups on Earth that dress up and play fantasy quests in the woods."

Victor smiled. "Thanks, Goos."

They made their way to the airlock, where most of the crew was gathered to see them off. Mother stood by the hatch, dry-eyed and stoic, trying to be strong for him, which gave Victor a shot of courage. She gave a quizzical look when she saw the spear in his hand. Victor winked at her, opened the hatch to the airlock, and followed Imala inside.

He sealed the hatch, and then he and Imala put on their helmets and checked each other's suits to make sure they were airtight and ready. Then Victor opened the exterior hatch and carefully pulled himself outside. The quickship was anchored to the Gagak's hull beside the hatch. Victor clipped into the safety harness, passed the second harness to Imala, and then gave her enough room to follow him out. He then sealed the Gagak's hatch closed again and moved for the quickship, tapping his thumb trigger to give himself a slight burst of propulsion.

He and Imala wriggled into the cockpit. Victor secured his spear under the console and turned on the main power. The jury-rigged controls came to life, their readout screens dimmed down to low. The cockpit was extremely cramped. Victor and Imala were practically on top of each other.

"Too bad we're wearing all this armor," Victor told her. "I could get used to tight quarters with you."

"Squeezed together but forever apart," said Imala.

She had meant the separation caused by their suits, but Victor couldn't help but think it an apropos statement on their relationship as well. They had been thrown together from the beginning. She had been assigned as his caseworker on Luna when everyone thought he was out of his mind; they had flown to the Belt and back, crammed inside a tiny cargo vessel; they had squeezed in a craft even smaller than this one to fly to the Formic scout ship; they had bunked together on the freighter that had brought them out to the Kuiper Belt; they had shared a tiny barracks with twelve other adults for the past two years; and now here they were again, squeezing into a space not really big enough for the two of them. And yet there remained a distance between them.

He had forced himself to remain optimistic about the mission. But now, with Imala beside him and them both squeezed into the cockpit, ready to depart, he couldn't help but think how fragile she was, how fragile they both were.

He pushed the thought away and got back to work. He blinked a command, and his camera feed began. "Cameras are on. Arjuna, are you getting my feed?"

"Roger that. Coming through clear."

"Feed check," said Imala.

"Imala's feed is confirmed as well," said Arjuna. "But once you detach we go radio silent unless it's an emergency."

"Roger," said Victor. "We are ready to detach."

Arjuna's voice crackled over the radio. "Detaching. Be safe."

Victor felt the brief grinding of metal as the anchor clips released their grip, and then the quickship was free. Imala used the retros to steer them clear of the Gagak and orient the quickship toward 2030CT. Then she lightly engaged the thrusters. They accelerated for only a few seconds, and then

Imala killed the engines, letting inertia take over. It was best if they approached at a slow velocity without outputting any heat. There was no way of knowing what collision-avoidance system the Formics had employed, if any. It would be an anticlimactic shame for them to go to all this trouble only to be obliterated on approach.

When they were within ten kilometers Imala tapped the forward retros and slowed the quickship to a negligible speed. It took them over four hours to drift the remaining distance. As they approached, the asteroid grew larger in their view, and the sheer size of it began to sink in. It was more than twice the size of the scout ship, and even though Victor had known that all along, it was only now that he truly grasped the implausibility of the shell around the rock. No, not a shell, more like a cocoon. And certainly bigger than the rock itself. Up close it looked like a giant alien egg of dark caramel glass. It dwarfed the quickship. Victor felt like an insect approaching a boulder. How could he possibly reconnoiter something so large?

"How did they build this, Imala? Where did this material come from?"

"No one's shooting at us," said Imala. "That's all I'm worried about at the moment. Now what?"

"I'd love for us to circle this thing and see it from every angle, but that would only increase our chances of being seen. Just keep heading in, not on a collision but a flyby. I'll jump when I can, and you pull back with the quickship. You've got my camera feed. When I'm ready for extraction, I'll hold up an open hand to my face. Then I'll leap out through the canopy hole. Wait until I'm a distance away to come get me."

"I don't like you drifting through space, untethered," said Imala. "Supposing I can't find you. Or what if your tracker breaks or malfunctions? You'll drift off into oblivion."

"You'll find me," Victor said. "I'm not worried about that."

He secured a few extra canisters of oxygen to the back of

his suit, disconnected his audio cable, grabbed the spear Magoosa had made him, gave Imala a thumbs-up, and then climbed up out of the quickship, clinging to its side. He looped the spear's strap over his head and across his back, and then crawled to the front of the vehicle. He bent low, gripping the bar at the quickship's nose like a giant metal hood ornament. Ahead of him the cocoon continued to grow larger and larger in his view. He couldn't miss. If he leaped now he'd hit it certainly. And yet he hesitated. He would be flying without a tether, completely unanchored, utterly exposed. It was lunacy. Why had he thought this a good idea? He suddenly felt grateful for the armor, and yet it felt insufficient.

The quickship had far more mass than he did, but even so, the force of his leap would push the quickship off course some, and his leap would not be as strong as it would be if the quickship were anchored. He needed to leap now. The longer he delayed the closer Imala would be to the asteroid, and the harder it would be for her to maneuver safely away.

And yet he hesitated. The Formics had cut the pilot open and reached up inside him. It had happened to thousands of people all over China. The Formics had done it again and again. Reaching, searching, pulling back empty hands, covered in blood.

He should have leaped already. He was putting Imala in danger. She would collide with the cocoon. He was putting the whole crew in danger.

He jumped.

The nose of the quickship was pushed away from him, and the power of his leap was much less than he had expected. Physics was against him. He had hoped to close the distance quickly, but he was moving only slightly faster than he had been before perched on the nose of the ship. It was for the best, he realized. Too fast, and he would bounce off the cocoon. He blinked a command and brought Imala's feed up on his HUD. Could she steer safely away or had he waited too long? He couldn't tell. All he could see from her feed was the cockpit controls.

The surface of the cocoon was approaching. Victor still couldn't tell how hard the surface was, but it appeared to have some density. It wasn't buoyant like a balloon, but was it as thin as brittle glass? Would he shatter it and break through? No, it would have to have some durability or micrometeorites would rip it to shreds.

He blinked a command, and the ice crampons in the toe of his boots snapped out. He blinked another command, and the spikes in his gauntlet protruded. He had built them for ice, but they would work just as well here. He brought his arms up, pulled his boots back. The surface of the cocoon rushed up to meet him. He suddenly realized he was moving too fast after all; he'd ricochet off, he'd spin away.

He hit the surface and slammed his arms down and kicked forward with his boots, which was easy since inertia threw them forward anyway. The spikes and crampons sunk into the surface and held firm. It was hard, but pliable. Like honey left to sit out for several weeks.

He turned and looked back behind him, searching in the Black for the quickship. He felt momentarily panicked because he couldn't see it, but no, there it was, far beneath him, just a speck in a sea of black. He would have missed it completely if he'd not looked for it, which made him feel better; perhaps the Formics hadn't seen it either. And more importantly, Imala was clear.

Yet, now he was even more nervous about making the jump once he finished. If jumping to an asteroid he couldn't miss had frozen him with fear, how could he jump out into nothing?

He buried that thought and turned back to the matter in front of him. The cocoon. The IF would study every frame of this vid, and so every moment he spent here was a chance to gather and relay precious information.

He pulled one of his gauntlets free, leaving three deep impressions of the spikes in the substance. "The surface is durable," he said, giving the vid narration. "Hard, but not indestructible. Like a resin." He took a risk and turned on his helmet light, keeping it at its lowest setting. He wasn't sure if the light would be visible from the other side, but he had to take that chance so that his camera could see the surface clearly. With the light, the filaments in the resin became clearly visible, as they had for the probe, which had zoomed in and taken several shots. "The filaments are narrow, maybe half the width of my finger. They crisscross back and forth inside the resin randomly, giving the structure shape." He ran a hand across the surface. "Surprisingly smooth surface. Not tacky in the slightest, as I thought it might be. The membranes between the filaments feel less durable than the filaments do. When I apply pressure, I can feel it give a little, though I don't know that I could push through. I'm not very secure where I am right now, so I don't feel comfortable pushing any harder. The material could be semitranslucent. But I can't see—"

He stopped suddenly. "Wait a minute. The holes that I made with my gauntlet spikes just a moment ago when I landed are gone." He looked around, shining the light in a wider circle, searching for them in case he was remembering wrong he had made them. "I'm sure of it. The holes were somewhere around here, but there is no trace of them. The surface of the cocoon is completely smooth again. It can heal itself." He brought his gauntlet spikes down again and then retracted them from the cocoon, leaving fresh impressions. Then he focused on the spot and came in close with the cameras and watched as the holes filled in and were smooth again.

How? Nanotech?

He reached to the pouch at his hip and retracted a pocketknife. The blade snapped up and locked into place, and

Victor gently pushed the blade down into the resin. The blade was only a few inches long, but he felt the tip of it poke through almost immediately. The resin was less than an inch thick. He slowly sliced downward a few inches, cutting relatively easily through the resin and filaments. He pulled the blade out and pushed a button to retract the blade; then he pulled a small air gauge from the pouch and held it in his hand as he pushed it through the hole.

The gauge reading appeared a moment later on his HUD, and Victor felt his body tense. "Air inside the cocoon is roughly seventy percent hydrogen, twenty percent oxygen."

"Which means it's extremely volatile," said Imala. "You're sitting on a bomb. I'm coming to get you."

He retracted his hand with the air gauge just as the cut in the resin began to heal itself and seal up again. Once they were clear they could blow the installation. It would be easy. A single shot with a high-powered laser, and the cocoon would go up like the *Hindenburg*. But if they destroyed it, what would they learn?

"Wait, Imala."

"Wait, nothing, Vico. I am coming for you." Her voice was angry as he knew it would be.

"Let's think about this for a second," he said.

"There is nothing to think about, Vico. You can't go inside. It's combustible. One little spark, and you're toast. The whole thing would detonate. I'm coming for you." She was practically shouting.

"Think about the Formic scout ship, Imala. We blew a hole through that and filled it with radiation, killing everything inside. All the plants, the other creatures, most of the equipment and tech, we destroyed it all. We could have learned so much from that."

"We did what needed to be done to end the war, Vico. This isn't some science expedition you're on. This is your life. I am ordering you to stay outside."

"Yes, but is that what the Polemarch wants?"

"To hell with what the Polemarch wants, Vico. He doesn't care about you, about us. I do."

"Think objectively, Imala. He ordered me to do reconnaissance. If there are three thousand of these asteroids, we need to know what's going on inside them."

"There are other people who can do this, Vico. There are other asteroids that can be explored. Let the IF figure this out."

"We *are* the IF, Imala. And right now we're their only option."

He took out his blade and made another cut, long and steady and over a meter long.

Imala's voice was quiet now, almost desperate. "I'm asking you, Vico. Please. If you love me . . ."

"But that's why I have to, Imala."

He muted her volume and made a second cut at a right angle, making an L shape with the blade and creating a flap big enough for him to pull himself through. The flap pushed outward, indicating that gas was pouring out of the hole.

Moving quickly, but being careful not to generate a spark, Victor stowed the knife in his pouch, gripped the delicate edge of the resin with both hands where he had made the cut, and gingerly pulled himself headfirst into the hole. Air rushed outward, like the opened end of a deflating balloon, pushing strong and forcing him back. Victor fought against it, gripping the resin tighter, and for a terrified moment he feared that the resin would break in his hands and launch him into space away from the cocoon. But to his surprise the resin held. The material, whatever it was, proved stronger than he had expected.

He got the top half of his body inside, and then it was easy because he folded at the waist and mostly got out of the current of rushing air. He pulled his legs in and twisted his body so that he was now flush against the inner wall. He could still feel the tug of air around him, but it was not as strong as it was directly in front of the hole. Reaching up with one hand, he gripped the loose flap of resin, and pulled it down so that it was flush with the cocoon surface again. Air continued to push out, but slowly the cut in the resin began to heal itself. The gaps in the resin filled with new membranous material as if it were growing out of thin air, as if some unseen zipper was pulling it together. Victor watched it closely, trying to identify how the seemingly magical process occurred, but even up close he couldn't see how it was done. Whatever power it was, it was stronger than the rush of air, and in moments, both cuts were gone. The inner wall was a smooth flat surface again, and Victor found himself in absolute darkness.

He rotated his body and faced inward toward the surface of the asteroid. He couldn't see anything. Somewhere below was the surface, but he had no idea how far away it was. Four meters? Forty? He couldn't even make out shadows or shapes.

He unmuted his radio and heard Imala frantically calling his name.

"I'm here," he said, interrupting her. "I'm inside."

"Why weren't you answering?"

"I muted you so I could concentrate. When we get back to the Gagak you can give me a stern lecture. For now we have a job to do."

She said nothing for a moment. "I'm not getting a visual from your cam."

"Because there isn't a visual. It's completely dark. I'm going to risk a light."

Before Imala could object, he switched on two lights mounted on his wrists. The bright tight beams shined on the surface of the asteroid roughly seven meters below him. It was a rugged, iceless, porous rock with dozens of tunnel entrances all over its surface. The tunnels were not perfectly round and cylindrical—like a laser or a drill bit would dig. They were oval or misshapen slightly—as if someone without any sense of symmetry had tried to make them round but failed. Nor did the tunnels go straight down into the rock. They turned and twisted and even crossed one another randomly before disappearing into the darkness. They had the appearance of natural formations, like porous sea coral or osteoporotic bone, but that was impossible. These tunnels had been dug. Victor could not imagine how it had been done, but there was no other explanation. Stranger still, many of the tunnels were no wider than his head—far too small for even a Formic to fit into. And yet, like the others, they snaked downward in a way that no machine would ever dig.

A flicker of movement in one of the tunnels caught his attention, and Victor reflexively trained his light on the hole. The creature retreated from the beam and disappeared from view. Round and hairless, and definitely not a Formic.

# CHAPTER 17

# Defendant

**Ansible transmission between the Hegemon and Polemarch, Office of the Hegemony Sealed Archives, Imbrium, Luna, 2118**

UKKO: Every ship in this fleet is going to have interchangeable parts or it won't get built. Period. If a
part is built in Poland and shipped into space, it's
going to fit in the socket that was made in China and
shipped into space. I'm not going to allow you to
create unique ships with no interchangeable parts.
I don't care how big the ship is, or what its mission
is. We use standardized parts across the board. That
way, in battle, mechanics can repair damaged ships
from the same basic pool of supplies and return the
ship to combat as soon as possible.

KETKAR: In principle I agree with you. But there is
room for exceptions in vessels with unique purposes or—

UKKO: No. There are no exceptions. We are going to
build these ships my way. I'm not going to fund any
ships that are built of unique parts that can't be
interchanged with others. And if your design principles don't accomplish that, then you are out of a

job. I will cease working with any admiral who brings me nonsense like these specs.

KETKAR: You're not listening to reason. There are some weapons, for example, that will require an exception.

UKKO: Wrong. If a weapon can't be used on every warship, it's not getting made. It's got to be something that every ship can use. Every now and then we'll have something so big that it can only be used on a big ship, but then all the big ships have to use it. No unique anything.

KETKAR: But that's wasteful. That will lead to overproduction.

UKKO: There is no such thing as overproduction of weaponry when fighting a technologically superior enemy, since attrition will constantly deplete our stocks. No matter how much they damage a ship, we will always be able to repair it. If they destroy a valuable ship or weapon, we'll already have another just like it. Let's not forget who is the expert on manufacturing here. Your job is managing the Fleet. My job is building it.

KETKAR: This is why a civilian should not be making these decisions.

UKKO: You want to go down and ask Earth for money? No? I'm the taxing authority. I've got the money— and all the resentment over taxation. You get to be the heroes who win the war.

Mazer had to pass through three separate security checkpoints before he reached the Judge Advocate General's offices in the east wing of Central Command, three stories beneath the surface of Luna. Lieutenant Prem Chamrajnagar was waiting for him in the lobby, dressed in her white class-A uniform and sporting a single bar on her lapel. She carried a small attaché case and smiled when he approached.

"You ready?" she asked.

"Ready for it to be over," Mazer said. He also wore his class-As, and the blue wool fabric felt stiff and heavy, even in Luna's lower gravity. Kim had polished the buttons and pins on his jacket that morning despite him telling her not to bother, but now he was glad that she had. He needed to come off as the consummate soldier.

"It's just the arraignment," said Chamrajnagar. "They read the charges, we say not guilty. A few taps of the gavel, and we're done. You just have to stand there and look innocent. Keep your face expressionless. Don't smile. That makes you look unrepentant and disdainful of the whole proceedings. Only a jackass smiles in court. And jackasses go to jail."

"I don't smile much anyway. We should be fine."

"True," she said. "You generally look grumpy. Don't do that either."

"I don't look grumpy," Mazer said, a little defensively.

"Believe me, your resting face is intimidating. It's like you're considering how to break someone's fingers with a moon rock. You furrow your brow like this." She demonstrated for him.

"That's not grumpy. That's pensive. It means I'm thinking."

"Thinking about killing someone maybe," Chamrajnagar said. "Take my word for it, it's not a good courtroom face. Not when you're standing before Colonel Michio 'the Hatchet' Soshi, and not if you want to keep your job and your uniform."

Mazer nodded. "No grumpy faces, scowls, growls, or sneers at the presiding judge. I suppose I can't hit him with spitballs either. I thought you said this was going to be fun."

She handed him her tablet. "A bit of good news."

He looked at the screen. "What's this?"

"A clean bill of health courtesy of Dr. Amelie Renoir. She says you're good to go, combat ready."

"Funny. I don't remember being examined by a Dr. Renoir."

"She looked at your full medical file and the results from your last physical. That's all she needed. You're perfectly healthy."

"That was kind of her. Will this hold up in court?"

Chamrajnagar swiped the screen, and a new page appeared. "This is from Dr. Jorge Gonzalez issuing you a clean bill of health."

"I've seen a lot of doctors recently," said Mazer.

"I have five statements from five different military physicians. You're clean. We'll win that battle."

"Good. But will we win the war?"

"One day at a time. First the arraignment. And speaking of which, a warning. Lieutenant Commander Reginald Ravenshaw, the prosecuting attorney, will be there as well. Ignore him. He's a snake. He thinks he's some dynamite district attorney hotshot playing out some military courtroom drama. I don't know why JAG tolerates him, other than the fact that he wins cases and plays virtual golf with some of the judges. He's good, but he's as gentle as a heavy boulder to the head. Everyone knows he's Colonel Soshi's lapdog, too. Anyway, he'll try to intimidate you. He'll want to get into a staring contest with you. Don't. He's trying to rile you."

"Can I break *his* fingers with a moon rock?"

"After the court-martial."

"If Soshi and Vaganov are playing it safe, they're bringing in their own people to close this up," said Mazer. "Have you met with Ravenshaw?"

"This morning. He wants to cut a deal. He says he'll drop all other charges, if you'll plead guilty to espionage and agree to seven years."

Mazer laughed. "How kind of him. He was insulting your intelligence, of course."

"He was trying to intimidate me. I'm young, inexperienced. He's the schoolyard bully threatening to bloody my nose if I don't surrender my lunch money. I think he was hoping I'd counter with a softer plea out of desperation. Maybe drop espionage and assault and settle with conduct unbecoming. You wouldn't go to jail, but your life in the IF would be hell thereafter. I told him he doesn't have a case for espionage. He only sneered at me, like he knew something I didn't."

"Does he?"

She looked around, checking for listening ears. "Come with me."

He followed her to the cafeteria. It was between the hours of breakfast and lunch, and so most tables were empty. Even so, Chamrajnagar led Mazer to a table in the back, as far from the corridor as possible and well out of earshot of anyone. She sat with her back against the wall, giving her a view of the entire cafeteria. A soldier's reflex, Mazer thought. Keep your eyes on all entrances and exits. Defend your back.

Mazer took the seat opposite.

"The espionage charge is a joke," said Chamrajnagar. "Article 793 states that it's unlawful for unauthorized persons to take information of global defense and either retain it or deliver it to persons not entitled to receive it. That's not what you did. I can punch holes through their argument big enough to fly a warship through. Victor sent the information regarding the asteroid to your e-mail address. They can easily prove it was a matter of global defense, and they could argue that your sending it to other officers constitutes people not entitled to receive it. But the IF has to own the information and deem it classified first. By this logic they could arrest anyone who forwards the daily news. It's ludicrous."

"Then why hasn't the prosecutor dropped the charge? He conducted his investigation. He knows it's bogus. He'd look like an idiot in court when he presents his evidence."

"They want to scare you into a plea. That's the only explanation I can think of. They believe if they pour on the heat, you'll cave and admit to a lesser charge. I've seen their depositions and list of witnesses. They've got nothing. If this goes all the way to court-martial Ravenshaw will drop espionage before it starts. He's bluffing."

"Are you sure?"

"Mostly sure."

"What about the other charges?"

"There's the aggravated assault charge against Nardelli. Everyone knows that's bogus, too. There were no witnesses. It's your word against his. I've got three depositions from dockworkers at WAMRED who claim Nardelli ordered them to vacate the docking bay the day you were shipped out at the same hour that he staged his little attack. He threatened the dockworkers with bodily harm if they didn't comply."

"Nardelli isn't the brightest bulb," said Mazer.

"He's an idiot. And believe me, your record could not be more different than his. He has a string of offenses and second chances. How the man is even still in uniform is beyond me. My guess is Vaganov keeps him as muscle. Regardless, Nardelli won't be in the IF very much longer. He signed a deposition and perjured himself. JAG will go after him. I'll do it myself if no one else does. My point is, no jury is going to believe him over you."

"You *are* good," said Mazer. "Tracking down the dockworkers was smart. What about failure to obey a lawful order?"

She winced slightly. "This one is the trickiest of the bunch. But there's enough wiggle room in the law to get you acquitted here as well. I think. There are several counts against you. First, every time you didn't fulfill the excessive work detail Vaganov filed it as a criminal offense. That holds as much water as a sieve. No chance the jury will side with Vaganov on that. I have the work details, and they're untenable."

"So we're clear," said Mazer.

"Maybe," said Chamrajnagar. "But the jury won't like that you broke chain of command and uploaded the intel into the forum."

"I gave the intel to Vaganov," said Mazer. "That's the first thing I did. When he seemed reluctant to act, I uploaded it to the forum. We can argue that I didn't break chain of command."

"We will," said Chamrajnagar. "But the jury may think otherwise. You have to understand, these guys on the jury *are* Vaganov. They're all senior officers. They all have people under them who are smarter than they are, just like you. They see you and they see their own subordinates. That terrifies them. In their minds, you guys are their saving grace and their worst nightmare. They look to you for their best thinking, but they constantly worry that you'll take their job. That's Vaganov to the letter. And these guys will recognize him as one of their own. They won't like his methods. They'll publicly condemn his actions and his attitudes. But they can't be seen siding with you either. They can't condone someone who breaks chain of command. That sends the wrong signal to everyone beneath them."

"So how will it pan out?" Mazer asked.

She shrugged. "Honestly? Either way. We're walking a razor's edge here. But we can employ a tactic to improve our chances. A tactic you won't like."

"Namely?"

"We need to show them why your brain works the way it does. That you're special. That you're trusted by the Strategos."

"You mean use my classified service record? Show what happened in the First Formic War? My involvement?"

"Sir, you're a hero. You get things done. Vaganov was threatening to sit on the intel. What you did was in the best interest of global security. We have to make the members of the court see that. Your previous record is proof that—"

"We can't do that," Mazer said.

"Sir, this is a closed court proceeding. Anything we present as evidence can't be discussed outside the court. Soshi can put a gag order on the proceedings. Everything would be confidential."

"I don't feel comfortable doing that," Mazer said. "I made a commitment to Robinov, the Strategos. I told him I would keep my involvement quiet. He ordered me to, in fact. If I renege on that then I *am* disobeying an order. I can't break one order to excuse myself for breaking another."

Chamrajnagar sighed. "Sir, I understand your dilemma. And I respect your desire to be honorable here, but as your attorney—"

"I don't want your advice as my attorney, Prem. I want it as a friend. As a fellow officer."

She was quiet a moment. "Without the classified file, there is a very good chance that we lose on that one count and they slap you with conduct unbecoming. It's the weakest of the charges, but it's the one that might stick."

"And if it does, they'll discharge me?"

"Or tuck you away somewhere. They want you to disappear, Mazer. Soshi will impose the maximum punishment if they get a conviction. You won't see any jail time, but you won't see the inside of a warship either."

"Did you catch the news this morning, Prem?"

She nodded solemnly.

"We have confirmation now that the Formics are coming in from below and above the ecliptic," said Mazer. "We have an asteroid in the Kuiper Belt that's occupied and sealed off by Formics, possibly being prepared as a weapon. Possibly a hundred other bad outcomes. We don't have time for a lengthy trial here. We need to end this as soon as possible so I can get back in the field."

"There are only two ways to rush this," Chamrajnagar said. "We cut a deal with the prosecutor, which won't help you. Or we convince the judge and the prosecutor to drop the whole thing. Which they are obviously unwilling to do. Right now riding this thing out is your only option."

She checked the time on his wrist pad and stood, fastening the loose button on her jacket. "It's time. Show me your nongrumpy-I'm-innocent face."

Mazer frowned deeply then took his hand, palm flat, and moved it down across his face, changing his comically sad expression into an impassive one.

"You look constipated," said Chamrajnagar, "but that's as good as we're going to get. Let's go." She led him out of the cafeteria and down the hall to one of the courtrooms. The court's sergeant at arms was standing post at the door. He saluted, scanned Chamrajnagar's wrist pads, got a clearance beep, and opened the door for them.

The room was not like the historic courthouses of Earth, with heavy oak tables and an elevated wood-paneled bench for the judge. It was military. Which meant it was utilitarian, institutional, with tables exactly like every other table at CentCom. The only item of note was a large seal of the International Fleet on the wall behind the judge's seat, flanked by two identical flags of the Hegemony.

As Mazer and Chamrajnagar took their seats at the defendant's table, Ravenshaw, the prosecutor, entered. He came straight to them and set his attaché case atop their table between Mazer and Chamrajnagar, as if building a wall between them. Then he sat with his back to Mazer on the edge of the table nearest Chamrajnagar, so that he practically hovered over her. He was treating Mazer as if he were beneath his notice.

Ravenshaw grinned and made a sweeping gesture with his hand. "The courtroom, Prem. Was it everything you hoped it would be? This is your first time inside one, isn't it? Unless you count that tour you took as an elementary school student. When would that have been? Two years ago? Three?"

"You're sitting on my table, Reginald. Maybe you've forgotten that you get your own."

"Most people expect something a little more grandiose," said Ravenshaw, ignoring her comment. "Something classical, you know. High vaulted ceiling, maybe a bust of some prime minister perhaps, or some dead judge long forgotten. Or maybe a Latin motto etched in bronze somewhere. E pluribus gluteus maximus. Or whatever. Instead we get this. Disappointing, isn't it? Yes, that's the word I'd use. Disappointing. That's what this courtroom experience must be for you, Prem. Disappointing. Start to finish."

Mazer stood. "The lieutenant kindly asked you to remove yourself from the table."

Ravenshaw smiled. "Better put a leash on your client, Counsel. I've heard that these Maori boys think they're always at war." He looked at Mazer for the first time, regarding him as if he were some odd museum exhibit. "If you're going to attack, Mazer, I hope I first get to see you dance a haka. I want the dinner and a show." He frowned. "Also, I thought you'd be taller."

He slid off the desk and took his attaché case as the sergeant at arms entered, walked to the front of the room, and snapped to attention. "Ten-hut!"

Everyone was already standing, but they came to attention as the door at the back of the courtroom opened and Colonel Michio Soshi came through. He took his seat at the judge's table and struck the gavel. "Let's get started please."

Mazer watched the man. Soshi seemed focused on his tablet, bored even, another day on the clock. He didn't once look at Mazer. The sergeant at arms referred to his wrist pad. "Docket number 3627. International Fleet versus Captain Mazer Rackham. The defendant is charged with one count of espionage, one count of aggravated assault, eight counts of failure to obey a lawful order, and conduct unbecoming an officer of the Fleet."

Soshi looked to the defendant's table, his expression unchanged, as if a charge of espionage were standard fare here. "And for the defense?" Soshi said.

Prem kept her eyes forward as she spoke. "Chamrajnagar. Lieutenant. Junior Grade. Prem. Judge Advocate General's Corp. Sworn and certified in accordance with Articles 28c and 47b of the International Fleet's Uniform Code of Military Justice."

Soshi waved a hand, as if uninterested in the formalities. "Fine, fine. Does the defense wish to enter a plea?"

"Yes, sir," Chamrajnagar said. "The defendant pleads not guilty, sir."

Soshi nodded. "Enter a plea of not guilty for the defendant. We will adjourn until 0900, three weeks from today, at which time this court will reconvene for a court-martial." He struck his gavel on the table.

The sergeant at arms shouted again. "Ten-hut!"

No one had moved. Soshi got up and disappeared back into his chambers. Start to finish, the whole procedure took ninety seconds.

Ravenshaw grabbed his attaché case and grinned at Prem. "Whenever you come to your senses, Prem, and want to deal, you know where to reach me." He moved to leave but turned back. "Oh, and get used to that disappointing feeling in your gut. After this is over, you'll get it every time you step into this courtroom. Like Pavlov's dogs. Ring a ding ding." He winked. Then he pointed his finger like a gun at Mazer and fired an imaginary shot.

Prem watched him go, then she turned to Mazer. "Did they teach you how to disembowel someone with your bare hands in the special forces? I'd give anything for that skill right now."

"Too messy," said Mazer. "Especially in his case. Why wait three weeks to start the court-martial?"

"They're trying to sweat you out, I suppose. Or stall."

"We don't have three weeks, Prem. We need to end this now. Do you have lunch plans?"

"You're my only case. But remember, you don't have freedom of movement. You're confined to that office they gave you."

The International Fleet had put Mazer in a secluded office at Central Command until his court-martial. An enlisted man indicted on the same charges would likely have been thrown in the brig, but out of respect for his rank as well as his service record, Mazer had received slightly more comfortable accommodations. He was confined there during the day, and to his apartment with Kim in the evening. He wasn't allowed to go anywhere else.

"I'll go to the office," said Mazer. "After we take a detour."

He led her back through the corridors and up to the surface of Old Town, where he tapped his wrist pad and hailed a taxi.

"Am I allowed to know where we're going exactly?" Prem asked.

"What do you know about patent law?"

"Patent law?" She shrugged. "I don't know. Some. Not enough to win a case, if that's what you're asking. Intellectual property law doesn't come up very often in the military. Why?"

"Could you draw up the necessary paperwork to file for a patent?" Mazer asked.

"Maybe. I suppose. I'd have to read up on it. It would depend on where you want to file it."

The self-driving taxi arrived, and they climbed inside. Mazer ordered the taxi to take them to the offices of Gungsu Industries.

"Why are we going to Gungsu?" asked Prem.

"My men and I designed a nanoshield for marine combat. Colonel Vaganov gave it to Gungsu to develop without our consent. The soldier who deserves most of the credit is Lieutenant Mustafa Shambhani."

"The marine who lost his leg."

Mazer nodded. "He's here on Luna in recovery. Kim checked in on him. His prosthesis is working nicely, but he has a lot of hard physical therapy ahead of him. Gungsu needs to compensate him for his idea. His family could use that financial cushion."

The taxi sped down the city track, moving with traffic. "Mazer, with all due respect, I think it's noble that you want to help your friend. Really, I do. It's tragic what happened to him. But you have more pressing problems. Namely your court-martial and avoiding prison time. Flying off to Gungsu and violating your movement privileges isn't helping your case either. And I'll remind you, Gungsu is in bed with Vaganov and Judge Soshi. I wouldn't call these people allies."

"Gungsu is the root of this, Prem. They control Vaganov, Soshi, Ravenshaw. They're running this show, even if only indirectly. It all starts with them."

"So what's your plan? Threaten them with an intellectual property lawsuit? That's a bad idea. I work for JAG, Mazer. I can't sue a civilian in a military court. There's no jurisdiction. Second, you don't have much of a case anyway. Intellectual property litigation is not as cut and dry as you might suspect. For starters, we don't have a patent and have not filed one. Therefore, technically, Gungsu is not infringing on one. We can't even put them on notice since there's no proof that they got the idea from Shambhani. They could easily claim that one of their own engineers came up with the idea at an earlier date. Or—and this is more likely—they could claim that as a soldier and member of WAMRED, Shambhani created the file as an employee of the military. The file thus belongs to the military, and Vaganov, as a rep for the military, can give it to whoever he chooses. Shambhani's compensation is his salary. The military owns him. Anything he does on the job is *their* intellectual property. I'm sorry, Mazer. I hate to be the one to say so, but you have a paper-thin case. And even if your case were stronger, laws concerning damages favor the defendant in these cases."

"I realize that, Prem. Gungsu will realize that too. We're not going to sue them. Or even threaten to sue them. We will simply imply that a condition for going into business with us is that they compensate Shambhani somehow as a show of goodwill."

Prem blinked, looking confused. "I'm sorry. You said, go into business with them?"

"In a manner of speaking. And with Lem Jukes. We can't work exclusively with Gungsu. We'll work with them both."

Prem waved a hand, stopping him. "Mazer, your brain is going a hundred kilometers an hour here, and I'm at walking speed. You have a pending court-martial. We can agree on that much, correct?"

"We both know how that's going to play out, Prem. The best we can hope for at this point is an acquittal with a letter of formal reprimand and a recommendation for nonjudicial punishment. That's the result even if we win in court. Soshi won't settle for less. I'll walk away with a slap on the wrist that will haunt me for the rest of my career. I'll be passed over for promotions and opportunities. But it's inevitable. Am I wrong?"

She was quiet a moment. "You're not wrong, no. And it's not fair."

"War is never fair, Prem. And that's what this is. And like in any war, we use the weapons we have at our disposal."

"What weapons do we have exactly? I think I missed that part."

"For the past year Victor Delgado has been sending me tech ideas. Sketches mostly. I helped him identify which ideas were good and worth pursuing. Victor then developed those into highly detailed three-dimensional models with layers that could be peeled back to reveal the inner components of a complex system. Only fifteen percent of his ideas were worth pursuing, but those ideas were very good. The others were smart but impractical, usually for reasons that only an experienced soldier would recognize. Point is, the fifteen percent were all intelligent devices. Gear that could save a soldier's life and make the difference between mission success and failure."

"So we're going to sell Victor's ideas to Gungsu in exchange for compensation for Shambhani and freedom for you?"

"The money for Victor's ideas will all go to him. They're his ideas after all. My compensation will be my freedom."

"This is insane."

"Probably. But so is storming a well-defended enemy fortification. Soldiers do hard things."

"And who are we supposed to talk to at Gungsu?"

"Hea Woo Han. Director of R&D. I met her at WAMRED. Well, briefly. I think she'll remember me."

Chamrajnagar leaned back and shook her head. "You're going to get us both arrested."

"Nothing to worry about," said Mazer. "I've been arrested before. It's mostly painless."

"That's not even funny."

The taxi pulled to the curb in front of a large glass cube roughly seven meters square. A silver corporate logo of an archer drawing back his bow hung above the door along with the words GUNGSU INDUSTRIES. Mazer paid the taxi and he and Chamrajnagar stepped up onto the sidewalk.

"I'm not forcing you to come inside, Prem. Walk away now and I'll think no less of you."

She hesitated, then sighed. "Desperate times, desperate measures. Let's get this over with."

He opened the door and they stepped into the small but opulent lobby. White marble floors, decorative lighting, white leather furniture. The same archer logo glowed on the wall behind the reception desk. The Korean woman manning the desk smiled up at them, perfect white teeth, not a hair out of place, head cocked slightly to the side, the picture of hospitality. "Welcome to Gungsu. How can I help you?"

"I'm here to see Ms. Hea Woo Han. My name is Captain Mazer Rackham of the International Fleet. This is Lieutenant Prem Chamrajnagar of the Judge Advocate General's Corps. My attorney. We don't have an appointment."

The woman's hand hovered over her holospace, as if she wasn't sure who to call next. "One moment," she said smiling. She waved her fingers in a tight pattern, made the call, and spoke into her earpiece. She repeated the names, passed on the request, waited.

After a moment of listening, the receptionist frowned apologetically. "I'm sorry, sir. Ms. Woo Han's assistant says her schedule is full today. You'll need to set an appointment."

"Tell her assistant that I came all the way from WAMRED."

The receptionist hesitated then relayed the message. A moment later, she was giving Mazer and Prem each a visitor bracelet and pointing to the elevator. "Fourth level down. Someone will meet you as you leave the elevator."

"Thank you," said Mazer.

The elevator doors opened. Mazer and Prem stepped inside. The doors closed, and the elevator began to descend.

"I hope you know what you're doing," said Prem.

"I don't," said Mazer. "I'm improvising."

# CHAPTER 18

## Tunnels

**Ansible transmission between the Hegemon and
Polemarch, Office of the Hegemony Sealed Archives,
Imbrium, Luna, 2118**

UKKO: You ordered a free-miner ship carrying women
and children into a possible combat environment.
Do you have any idea how utterly asinine that was?

KETKAR: Since you have never held military command and you obviously do not grasp the immedi-
acy of our situation, I don't expect you to understand.

UKKO: Victor Delgado is a hero on Earth from the first
war. As is Imala Bootstamp. As is Edimar Querales.
Getting them slaughtered would not endear the free
citizens of Earth to our cause.

KETKAR: You and I used to be allies, if you recall.

UKKO: That was before I found out you were a political idiot.

KETKAR: This struggle transcends politics.

UKKO: Your reckless action might raise such public
outrage that the national governments demand a
complete change of the IF's high command as a
condition of continued financial support of the Hegemony. Nothing ever "transcends" politics.

Inside the Formic cocoon, Victor tapped his thumb trigger and released a few bursts of air out of his propulsion pack to push himself down toward the surface of the rock. He moved for the tunnel where he had seen the creature, a small grublike animal no bigger than his head. Slowly, hesitantly, Victor approached, worried that an arm or tentacle might shoot out of one of the smaller tunnels and pull him down. He reached back and grabbed the spear Magoosa had made him, pulling it up over his shoulder so it was free in his hands.

When he was still a meter away from the tunnel he positioned himself directly over it and shined his light inside. The creature was nowhere in sight. The tunnel wasn't completely empty however. There was a cluster of small pellets stacked neatly near the entrance.

"Are you getting this, Imala?"

"What is that?"

"It looks like worm droppings."

He got closer. The pellets were stacked on one side of the tunnel, three pellets high, held in place by a thin mucus covering that prevented them from floating off in zero G. Victor reached in and picked up one of the pellets in his gloved hand. He pinched the pellet, but it didn't give. "They're not droppings, Imala. This is hard as metal. In fact, I think it is metal."

"Metal? How?"

"I don't know, but I'm going to take a few samples." He removed a small canister from his hip pouch and filled it with several pellets. The metal looked pure and unpolluted. No trace minerals. No imperfections. The Formics were mining, he realized. They were digging through the tunnels and gathering metal. But how were they processing it? How were they purifying it? And for that matter how were they digging? There weren't any machines that he could see set up on the surface. He shined his light around him, looking in all directions across the surface, and there was nothing. No lasers, no drills, no mechanism for making the holes.

He moved to another tunnel and found the same organized pattern of pellet stacks. The stacks were each three pellets high and roughly a hundred pellets long and wide. They were stacked along one wall, every half meter or so, equidistant from each other, all covered in just enough mucus to hold them in place. Victor shined his light down into the tunnel. This one continued straight down like a well. The pellet stacks continued as far as his light would extend. He reached in and pulled the nearest stack toward him to see how easily it would be to harvest them. The pellets came off the wall with little to no effort. They scattered all around him and floated away, small groups of pellets still clinging together by the mucus.

"What does this mean, Vico?" Imala asked.

Victor moved to the next tunnel. More stacks of pellets extended downward. He lifted his head and took in his surroundings, scanning the surface of the asteroid. There were hundreds of these narrow tunnels filled with pellets. Thousands. "I don't know, Imala. The Formics are mining metal, but I can't see how or why."

He moved on, releasing gentle bursts of air to push his way forward. He stopped at another tunnel where the pellets were slightly larger and of a slightly different color.

"Looks like a different metal," Imala asked.

"That's my guess," said Victor. He got a different canister from his pouch and gathered a few more samples. A short distance later, he found stacks of a third metal, and then a fourth. He took samples of those as well and moved on. How long had the Formics been here, he wondered. There were so many tunnels. And yet the ship they had come on was small, able to hold only a few crewmembers. Five at the most. How had such a small crew completed so much excavation?

He reached a tunnel large enough for him to crawl inside, though only barely. He paused at the entrance and explored the interior with his wrist light.

"You can't go in," Imala said, as if reading his thoughts. "There's not enough room. You won't be able to turn around. And you don't know where it leads. It might narrow suddenly, and then you're stuck. We've got what we came for, Vico. Come back out, and we'll take the samples and have them tested. That's more than enough to keep the Polemarch happy."

Something sparkled in the tunnel ahead of him, reflecting his light. One of the pellet stacks on the tunnel wall five meters in. "Do you see that, Imala?"

"Leave it, Vico. Cut yourself an extraction hole through the resin, and I'll come pick you up. We were asked to reconnoiter, and we've reconnoitered."

"I want a sample of that as well, whatever it is. It might be important."

He draped the spear over his back again and pulled himself into the tunnel. It was a tight squeeze. He had a little bit of room on all sides, but not much. He kept drifting into the walls as he pulled himself forward, his feet and armor scraping on the rock. He was glad then that he had covered everything with a tough fabric as Magoosa had suggested, removing any possibility of a spark.

He reached the pellets and was surprised to see that they were transparent. He picked one up and squeezed. It cracked between his fingertips.

"It's ice, Imala. Pellets of pure ice. How? That doesn't make sense. This asteroid is supposed to be covered in ice, and yet the only ice I find is in pellets on the wall."

Movement above his head caused him to cry out and try to scramble back. He slammed back into the wall and banged around a bit until he realized he couldn't get out of such a small space quickly. He stopped and steadied himself. The movement was made by a small sluglike creature. It was right by Victor's helmet, but it ignored him completely. It didn't even seem bothered by his lights. The creature slithered across the wall, where there was a thick track of mucus that Victor hadn't noticed. It approached the stack of ice pellets, opened a hole in itself and defecated three pellets of ice covered with the same mucus substance. The ice pellets assumed their place in the perfectly organized stack, and then, without pausing in its labor, the slug moved away in the direction it had come.

Victor tracked it with his light. The slug was oblivious. It reached a hole in the wall, barely bigger than itself and wiggled inside. Victor crawled forward to investigate. The creature had stopped less than a meter in the hole, but Victor couldn't see what was beyond it. The creature was still for a minute, then two. Then, as if put in reverse, the slug wiggled its way back out and then once again toward the ice pellets. Victor shined a light into the hole and found a slab of milky ice blocking the path.

"It's eating and harvesting ice," said Imala.

"Not just harvesting it, Imala. It's cleansing the ice. It's removing all the particulates and impurities. Look how dirty the ice is in the tunnel and how pristine the pellets are in the stack. It's a water-filtration system, Imala. It's a biological water-filtration system. The slug ingests the dirty ice, cleanses it somehow, purifies it, and then deposits pure ice in the stack."

"How is that possible?" said Imala. "It can't take impurities out of the ice. Ice is a solid. It can't be strained in that state."

"That's what it's doing," said Victor. "Maybe it melts the dirty ice inside itself somehow, separates the impurities from the water, and then refreezes the water and discards the impurities."

"An animal with the ability to internally freeze a liquid?" said Imala.

And yet there was no other explanation. How else could the creatures have removed any impurities? He drew closer to the mucous track on the wall, and he could see small particles and detritus in the sticky substance. So the slug was discarding the impurities as it made its way to the stacks, spreading them out, excreting them from underneath perhaps. Victor looked around him. There seemed to be tracks of discarded particles everywhere in the tunnel, all along the walls. He just hadn't noticed them before. They were not scattered evenly across the surface, but in wide lines that twisted and turned and snaked their way down the tunnel. It was as if the slugs, over time, had created highways of discarded particles as they moved up and down the tracks, shedding impurities in the mucus as they went. And then, after a period, they had abandoned that trail and started another one, perhaps when the discarded impurities made the mucus so thick in the first trail that it had become difficult to navigate.

So the slugs had moved on to create another track, and the old mucous trail had dried up. The particles in the old trail settled against the wall with the drying mucus to form a sort of thin mortar.

Victor rubbed his finger across one of the dried mucous tracks, but far fewer particles flaked free and drifted away then he had expected. The residue was surprisingly strong.

He followed one of the mortar lines with his light. It twisted and turned in what seemed to be a random pattern, snaking down, deeper into the tunnel.

"It doesn't make sense, Imala. You see these trails of sediment the slugs leave behind? They twist every which way randomly. That doesn't sync with the ordered manner in which they operate and deposit these pellets. The pellets are stacked so evenly and yet their highways are as jagged as the cracks in the rock."

And therein was the answer, he realized. The tracks moved every which way like cracks in the rock, because they were *covering* cracks in the rock. The sediment residue felt as hard as mortar because it *was* mortar. The lines weren't random. They were intentional. The slugs were sealers. They purified ice, yes, but they had another mission as well. They patched up cracks in the rock. All of this digging, all of these tunnels so close together would naturally weaken the integrity of the asteroid. You can only drill so many holes through a rock before the rock crumbles and breaks apart. This little bug and others like him were keeping the asteroid together.

A hand grabbed Victor's ankle and yanked him back toward the tunnel entrance. He cried out, his helmet and arms banging against the wall of the tunnel.

"Vico!"

Imala's voice in his helmet. Panicked. Victor couldn't see anything. The space was too confined. Whatever had him, had him tight. Victor tried kicking with his free foot as the creature dragged him out, but as soon as he did, another hand gripped the free foot and held it firm. The tunnel walls around him were a blur, and then suddenly he was out of the tunnel, yanked free and arcing upward and around, held by his ankles as if on a pendulum, unable to stop himself.

He crashed into the surface of the asteroid on his side, hitting the rock so hard it left him momentarily dazed. His body was limp, and he began to bounce upward and away from the surface when something landed on top of him and pinned him down, strong hands clutching at rock. A Formic. With a rock in its hand. Victor tried to rotate onto his back and lift an arm to block the blow when the rock struck him in the side of the helmet. A powerful blow. With inhuman strength behind it. His face slammed into the internal wall of the helmet. His right camera feed flickered out, the external camera broken. Half of his view projected inside his helmet was gone. It was like losing an eye. Only his left view remained. He turned his head and saw the Formic bringing the rock down again. It hit Victor's helmet so hard that for a microsecond Victor was sure it had broken through. But no, the armor held.

Another blow.

And another.

He couldn't wiggle free. He couldn't protect his head. I'm going to die, he thought. It's going to beat me to death.

He could no longer hear Imala. His radio was out, busted or jostled or disconnected.

Another blow. His left camera feed flickered, threatened to go. He couldn't lose that, too. He'd be blind.

The Formic raised the rock again. Victor tapped the side of his hand, and the ice crampon that he had imbedded in the gauntlet snapped out like a blade. He swung his arm in hard and sunk the crampon into the side of the Formic just as the rock connected with his helmet again.

Several things happened at once. The Formic's tight grip on him relaxed as the creature buckled and retreated, the crampon blade coming free in a sticky muscle-tearing motion as the Formic fell away. Victor's left camera feed winked out, broken, leaving him blind. A hiss of air followed. An alarm. Victor reached up, felt his helmet. The seal at the bottom of the helmet where it locked with the shoulders was broken, bent inward from one of the blows. Air was escaping. Leaking oxygen. His helmet was broken.

A heavy blunt object struck him in the side of the helmet, knocking him away from the surface. Pain exploded from the side of his head as his head struck the interior of his helmet. His suit alarm wailed. His interface flashed a warning: OXYGEN LEAK. LIFE THREATENING. There was nothing he could do to stop it. He was drifting away blind.

The Formic collided with him in the air, setting them both spinning away violently, completely disoriented. Victor felt another blow to the head. Then another. The Formic clung to his waist, beating at his helmet. Victor had no concept of up, down, any direction at all. Another blow. The two of them struck a surface. It bowed slightly, stretched. The resin. The inner wall of the cocoon. They bounced away, spinning still. But slower now. Another blow. Victor reflexively raised his arm to shield his face then remembered the crampon in his gauntlet, the blade still extended. He lashed out and connected, a glancing blow, but he felt the blade cut in and tear. The creature stopped its assault momentarily, stunned, and then started anew. It's not going to give up, Victor realized. It's not going to let go.

It was strong, unnaturally strong for its size, pounding him like a gorilla.

Victor's alarm continued to wail. Oxygen was leaking. Another blow to his head. Another. He reached out with his other arm and wrapped it around the Formic, pulling it close to his chest in a bear hug. Then he swung the gauntlet blade out and down and buried it in the Formic's back.

The Formic went limp instantly, releasing its grip. Dead.

Victor yanked the crampon free and pushed the creature away. He was still spinning, disoriented.

His feet struck rock, and then the rest of his body followed, hitting the surface of the asteroid. He grabbed blind, scrambling for purchase. His hands gripped stone, the lip of a tunnel. It was enough to stop him. He couldn't see. His oxygen was gone. He had to anchor himself, think. He twisted his body. The tunnel was narrow. He shoved his foot into the hole just far enough to anchor himself down. The alarm in his helmet screamed in his ear.

"Cancel alarm."

The helmet went silent. The no-oxygen warning continued to flash. "Imala, are you there? Can you read me? Over?"

There was no response.

"Imala can you hear me?"

Nothing.

The Formic wasn't wearing a spacesuit. It had breathed the

oxygen in the air, yes, but the levels of hydrogen were dangerous. Victor didn't need explosive hydrogen in his lungs. Plus hydrogen could diffuse into the bloodstream and cause hydrogenation of fats and other organic molecules. Not good. He reached down and unzipped the emergency kit at his hip and pulled out the oxygen mask. The line snaked out from the kit and connected to the $O_2$ reserve in his suit. Only twenty minutes worth.

"Imala, I don't know if you can hear me, but I can't come outside. My helmet is damaged. It won't seal. I'm going to try to repair it, but I don't know if I can. Do not come for me. If I can't fix it, I'll go to the Formic ship. I'll seal myself inside. I'll wait there. Again, do not come for me."

Had she heard him? Was he getting through? Probably not. Imala would be frantic.

He pulled his helmet off, and a wave of heat and dust and smells assaulted him. Organic smells. Faint, but unpleasant, like food left out of the freezer for a few days. He put the small oxygen mask on over his head and tightened the feeble rubber straps. The oxygen regulator was a manual knob inside the kit. He gave it a quarter turn and oxygen came into the mask. It was such a small and flimsy thing, just big enough to cover his mouth and nose. His head was totally exposed, and it left him feeling vulnerable. He shined his light upward and found the dead Formic drifting through the air twenty meters away, globules of blood trailing in the air behind it.

The hive mind. What one of them sees, they all see, he reminded himself. If there were more Formics here, they would come for him. They would know he was here. He needed to move. He should have listened to Imala. He never should have come inside. And yet the IF needed to know.

The helmet. He turned it over in his hands, examining it. It had taken a beating, but it had held. Except at the bottom. The metal was creased inward from a blow right at the edge. The crease was small, but it was enough. He'd never get a true seal with the suit. He tried bending the metal back, but it was useless. The metal wouldn't budge. He had worked so hard to make the alloy strong, and now that very strength was working against him.

The ship was the only option. And even that wasn't much of an option. He wasn't even certain if he could get inside it. Or if it was oxygenated once he did. And even if he could get in the ship, there was no way for Imala to extract him. The quickship had no docking tube, no means of sealing itself to the Formic ship. Not that it mattered. He couldn't ride in the quickship. It wasn't oxygenated, and he didn't have a functioning suit. He had no way of returning to the Gagak. He was a dead man.

And yet, he had to try. What exactly, he wasn't sure. But something.

He took a moment to orient himself. Where was he in relation to where he had entered? He looked above him at the resin, trying to see if he could find the scar of his cut.

His heart sank. There was a light on the other side of the resin.

Imala. She hadn't heard him. She was coming for him.

No, Imala. Don't even try.

The light had a wide beam. That was good. It meant Imala was still in the quickship and had brought it in close. She hadn't tried leaving the quickship, which would be suicide. But she might try a spacewalk if he didn't present himself.

He had to stop her, communicate somehow what he was going to try. He bent his legs slightly and leaped upward toward the light. The resin would hold, but he worried about bouncing off. The inner wall was domed, and there was nothing to hold on to. He drew back his arm and sunk the crampon from his gauntlet into the resin as soon as he hit it. His body bounced against the resin wall, but the gauntlet held.

Imala's light had shifted while he was flying, however, so by the time he landed, the light had moved on. It hadn't seen him.

He took his own wrist light and stuck it against the resin. Did Imala know Morse code? Every free miner did, for there were moments on a ship when it was useful. So even if Imala didn't know Morse, she was broadcasting what she saw back to the Gagak, and they could translate. He began flashing with his light.

H-E-L-M-E-T-B-R-O-K-E-N. G-O-I-N-G-T-O-F-O-R-M-I-C-S-H-I-P.

He repeated it two times. Helmet broken. Going to Formic ship. Imala's wandering spotlight turned off during his first repeat. A good sign. It meant Imala had noticed his light and was paying attention. Either that or she had moved on and seen nothing.

He did the sequence once more and waited. One minute passed. No response.

Then the resin wall in front of him lit up as Imala's spotlight flashed a brief two-letter prosign sequence that meant: Understood.

Victor felt a rush of relief. She had received his message. If nothing else, she knew now not to attempt a rescue. His mistake wouldn't kill her as well.

Now he had to move. His oxygen was already a quarter gone. And the Formic ship was on the opposite side of the asteroid. He killed his lights. Formics could see in the dark, but he'd be even more conspicuous with his lights on. He tapped his propulsion trigger and moved to the right, staying flush with the resin wall as he went. He tried to slow his breathing and make his oxygen last, but he knew it probably wasn't making much difference.

The way before him was completely dark. His eyes must have adjusted by now, but he still couldn't see anything. He knew the resin wall was beside him because he ran his hand along it as he went, maintaining contact. And if his fingers began to slip away, he course-corrected quickly, tapping a burst of air to put himself back against the resin.

But he had no idea if he was going in the right direction. Generally this was the way to the ship, but sooner or later he would have to turn on his lights to find its exact position. He continued this way for a few minutes, wondering if he should turn his lights on now. Was he close? Had he passed it already? He listened for movement down on the rock, but heard nothing. The brief spurts of air from his propulsion pack seemed enormously loud to his ears. Like a trumpet declaring his position and asking to be attacked.

But maybe the Formic ship had not had a crew of five. Maybe it had only had a crew of one. Maybe he didn't have to worry about attack.

He thought he heard a soft sound below him. A rustling or scrape of rock. He paused before he tapped the trigger again, listening. Was it one of those slugs? Or something else?

A Formic collided with him and knocked him against the resin, their bodies tangled together. They didn't bounce off like they should have. Something held them against the resin. Victor lashed out with his arms, protecting his head. One strike with a rock, and it would be over. The Formic clung to him but didn't hit. It was holding him with its hind legs and reaching for the resin. Victor turned on his lights and saw to his horror that the anchor holding them to the cocoon was a sharp instrument or a knife in the Formic's hand. The creature was going to cut a hole. It was going to sacrifice itself and pull Victor out into space.

The knife pierced the resin. There was a great rushing of air. Victor threw his gauntlet crampon to the side and sunk it into the resin, anchoring himself. His body shifted, feet pulled toward the hole. It was going to suck him out, he realized. His crampon anchor wouldn't hold. He could already feel it slipping. The resin would seal shut in a moment, but the Formic would only cut it open again. He was going to die. He was going to be pulled into space without a helmet, with a Formic clinging to him, beating him, stabbing him.

The knife came down toward his head, and Victor brought his free arm up across his face just in time to block the blow. A metal shard, not a knife, was inches from his face. The Formic's wrist was pushing down on Victor's arm, trying to bury the shard into Victor's eye. The crampon was slipping. The air around him felt like a hundred hands pulling him toward the hole. The arm with the crampon was screaming for relief; it felt as if it might be pulled out of its socket. The Formic pressed down, getting closer, putting its shoulder into the downward push of the shard. The tip of the shard shifted slightly but eased closer, touching the bulbous oxygen mask, threatening to puncture it. Victor pushed outward with that arm, screaming, straining, exerting every ounce of energy he had. If he let up even slightly, the shard would end him in an instant.

The oxygen mask began to bend inward as the shard eased its way down.

Victor couldn't fight back. He couldn't knock the creature free. His blocking arm was growing weak, quivering, strained from the exertion. It would give out at any moment. His only hope was the hole and whatever magic sealed it shut.

And just as he realized this, the pull of the air began to weaken. The hole was repairing itself. The screaming vortex of air rushing around them began to die down.

The Formic realized it as well. It removed the knife from near Victor's face and turned its attention back to the wall. It was going to make another cut. The first one had not yet sealed completely, but the Formic was going to cut and widen the hole again. And if that happened, Victor would die. He didn't have the strength to hold on any longer or to fight anymore. He would be pulled out.

He was flush against the resin wall, so he couldn't see how big the hole was. Was it wide enough to pull him out? He had no way of knowing. And yet he couldn't let the Formic make the cut.

He yanked the crampon free—which barely took any effort; the blade was ready to slip free already. The pull of the air immediately yanked him toward the hole. The Formic, still clinging to him, shifted, surprised, trying to steady itself.

Victor rolled, lifting his feet, fearful that he would be sucked out feet first, and turned his back to the hole as he slid across the resin toward it, hoping and praying that the hole was too small to pull him out back first.

It was. The spear draped across his back was sucked against the hole, and for an instant he feared that the spearhead would tear through the resin.

The air continued to pull around him, but it was far less than before. His back was covering the small remaining hole like a plug on a drain. The Formic was still on him, disoriented from the movement. Victor didn't hesitate. He buried the crampon into the creature, and the Formic went still. It focused its eyes on him. The shard slipped from its hand, drifting away. The grip the Formic had on his waist loosened.

Victor pushed it away. Air continued to rush by him. He tapped his propulsion, but it wasn't strong enough to push him away from the air that held him in place. Was his back here keeping the resin from sealing? Was the spear pushing the sides apart?

He tried to roll away but couldn't. He didn't have leverage. And then the pull of air around him slowed further. And further. And stopped.

The hole had sealed beneath him.

Victor floated there, breathing heavily, heart pounding, exhausted. But alive.

His oxygen. He must have used up most of his oxygen in the fight. He needed to find the ship immediately. His wrist lights were still on, but he no longer cared. He would need them. And if the lights caused more Formics to come, so be it. He had to see. He tapped his propulsion and pushed himself away from the wall, pulling the spear free of his back. He shined his lights ahead. All he could see was more resin wall, curving around. Below him was the asteroid. He shined a light down and saw hundreds of tunnels below. And unlike before, these tunnels were teeming with grubs. He could see movement in at least ten tunnels. Small creatures moving among the pellet stacks.

He didn't stick around to investigate. Reconnaissance was over.

He continued on, moving in the direction where he thought the ship was located. But he had no way to be certain. His sense of direction was completely off. Was he going around the asteroid or over it?

He tapped his propulsion trigger, and the last hiss of air escaped from his back in a feeble double sputter. He was out of propellant. He tried the trigger again, and this time nothing. Empty. The Formic ship was nowhere in sight and he had no means of directing his movements or pushing his way forward. He drifted slowly into the curving resin wall, sliding along it, slowing.

He took a breath, and found the mask empty too. He reached into his hip pouch and gave the regulator another quarter turn. Nothing happened. He opened the regulator all the way. Nothing. He was out of oxygen as well.

A feeling of exhaustion and defeat settled over him like a physical weight. He had tried. He had fought and he had pushed and he had struggled and had persevered, but it wasn't enough. He wasn't prepared for this. He had naively come inside, and now he would die a fool. And for what? What had he gained for the good of the IF? A few samples of metal pellets that would never be analyzed? A minute of vid of a fat slug sliding through mucus. Oh yes, how monumental. How critical that intelligence must be. Congratulations, Victor, you will not have died in vain. Thanks to you the world knows precisely what a Formic slug looks like. Stop counting votes,

Nobel Prize committee, we have a late entry in the biology category and the stupidity category as well. A sure winner.

He shook his head. He had been stupid and zealous and had thrown his life away.

He reached into another of his small hip pouches and pulled out the igniter. It was a little thing, no bigger than half his thumb. He had made it before coming aboard, knowing that the air might be volatile, knowing that he might be seized by the enemy, knowing that it might be necessary. Better to blow up the whole thing than to let them cut him open and root around inside him.

It was funny really. The igniter was such a small thing, capable of causing so much destruction. He would just have to flick the switch to create the flame, and that would be it.

Would he realize what was happening in the instant before the hydrogen in the air ignited? Would he see it, hear it, feel it? Or would the explosion happen so quickly that he would be obliterated before his brain had a chance to process the event?

And what of Imala? Was she clear? Or did she have the quickship parked right next to the cocoon? If he detonated, would he inadvertently hurt her as well?

He held the igniter up to his face, examining it, considering. And that's when he saw a darker shade of black in the distance behind it. He raised his light.

It was the ship. Maybe sixty meters away, just beyond the horizon of the asteroid. The thrusters were protruding through the resin wall, and the nose of the ship was anchored to the surface via several extended legs, like a spider.

He could make it. He could get there. He didn't know if it would do him any good in the end, but he knew he could make it.

Question was how. He was in a slow drift, inching forward, sliding along the resin wall. Soon the friction would stop his forward momentum completely. Could he push off the resin to launch down to the asteroid? It was pliable, so would it just bow with the force of his launch? And would the resin hold? Or would it break and tear? And even if he could reach the asteroid below him, how would he move on the surface? And for that matter, how could he *stay* on the surface? He couldn't anchor his feet. It was solid rock. He had thought there would be ice, but the Formics had melted it all to make the atmosphere. There was nothing to cling to. So once he reached the surface, what would he do? Crawl with his hands?

He had no choice. He would have to trust the strength of the resin. And he would have to breathe the atmosphere.

He rotated his body and put his feet against the resin, squatting down. His feet were spread apart to disperse the force of the launch as much as he could, thus minimizing the likelihood of punching through the resin. He made sure he was standing on the tightest cluster of filaments and not solely on the membrane. Then he launched. It felt, for a moment as if he hadn't launched at all and that he had merely succeeded in pushing the resin away from him.

But no, there was some forward movement. Not much, but some. A negligible speed. Almost imperceptible. It would take several minutes to reach the asteroid's surface at this rate, and at any time another Formic could attack. He felt short of breath and pulled the oxygen mask down off his mouth. There was oxygen in the air, but every breath with the hydrogen felt like poison. How could he make himself go faster?

The armor. It had mass. If he shed it and pushed it away from him, it would exert on him an equal, opposite force. He unsnapped the clasps at his hip, which locked the upper, torso portion of the armor to the bottom half. Then he reached back and did the same at the small of his back. It took some wiggling, and he had to pass the spear from hand to hand, but he finally got the torso of the armor off. He would have to push it away just right, though. He would need to point his body toward the surface and align his spine with the direction of the force. If his angle was off, even by a little, the force would put him into a spin.

He draped the spear across this back again and brought his knees up close to his chest. Carefully he maneuvered the upper armor so that the chest of the armor was flat against his feet. Then he aligned his body and pushed off.

The armor shot away from him, and Victor felt himself pick up speed. Not much. But some. Enough to make him feel like the effort had been worth it. He closed the distance in a matter of seconds and came down gently onto the rock.

Without the bulky gauntlet atop his mining gloves, his fingers had greater mobility and grip strength. Even so he scrambled desperately for a moment until he grabbed something he could hold on to. His fingers found purchase on the lip of a small, narrow tunnel, and he brought his feet down and stuck the toes of his boots into two small holes. Now he was anchored on the surface. But he could no longer see the ship. He would have to climb the asteroid like ascending a cliff face. And there were just enough small holes all over the surface that it might work.

His orientation shifted in his mind. The asteroid was no longer down. The ship was up, his feet were down. He tapped the inside of his boots to make the toe crampons pop out for him to use. Then he dug in again with the toes and reached upward with a free hand and gripped the lip of another hole.

He ascended one step at a time, securing each handhold and foothold before he continued. He worried that at any moment another Formic could attack and he'd be torn away from the wall. But no Formic came.

After a minute of climbing he came to the largest tunnel entrance he had seen thus far. It was big enough for him to crawl into. He shined his light in, and the tunnel extended straight back a good distance and then turned downward. A Formic could easily fit in there.

He climbed around it and continued upward. How much hydrogen was in his lungs now? he wondered. He pushed the thought away and continued. There was nothing he could do but hurry.

After another few minutes of climbing the ship came into view. He climbed a little farther until he was certain that he could launch to it. Then he retracted the crampons in his boots, anchored his feet, bent down low, pointed his body, and launched.

He soared through the air faster than he had intended, forgetting that he had shed the mass of the upper half of his suit. Even so, he had good control. He tucked and spun as he and Imala had practiced, and he landed feet first atop the ship with a loud clang that echoed through the space. The surface of the ship was smooth, however, with nothing to hold on to, so before his momentum sent him tumbling elsewhere, he twisted and launched again immediately toward one of the spidery anchor legs. He crashed into the unforgiving metal and threw his arms around it. Pain shot through him in three places, but he clung to the metal nonetheless.

He tasted blood in his mouth and could feel more blood draining from a cut above his eye. He wiped at his brow, and sure enough his glove came back red. He shined his light on the spider leg and saw that it had six segments with internal cables and pulleys and hinges. The legs were clearly designed to fold outward and keep the ship perpendicular to the asteroid. The pulley system looked ancient, and the metal was rough and discolored.

He shined his light on the ship, searching for a hatch or door or some point of entry. But there wasn't one. The side of the ship was perfectly smooth. He shined his light at the nose of the ship and saw that the nose was blunt and flush against the surface of the asteroid. There had to be an entrance there. A door that led directly into the tunnels of the rock. But how to reach it?

He clung to the spider leg and searched with his light around the base of the ship until he found a large tunnel entrance. It extended inward for a meter and then cut to the left toward the nose of the ship. That had to be his way in. That had to lead to the nose. He began to climb around the spider leg so that he could position himself on the side of the leg closest to the tunnel. Then he would point his body and launch. But just as he was moving, a Formic crawled out of the tunnel in question and hurled itself directly at him. Victor retreated to the opposite side of the leg again, and the Formic slammed into the leg on the other side. It scrambled, trying to get its footing, reaching for him, clambering, moving around the leg, desperate to attack. Victor moved around the metal structure in the opposite direction, keeping the metal leg between them. When they had switched positions, and Victor was closest to the tunnel, he turned and launched, reaching back and pulling his spear free as he flew.

He twisted in the air and slammed his back into the asteroid right near the tunnel entrance, the wind knocked out of him, his head ramming back into the wall so hard it nearly knocked him out. He saw spots at the corner of his vision as his head rang with a dull fog of sound. But the spear was up in his hand, and its end was anchored against the wall like a pike, ready to meet the Formic that was already soaring through the air after him, arms outstretched, maw opened, ready to attack.

The Formic impaled itself on the spear point, colliding into Victor in a hairy, violent mess of flailing appendages. Victor pushed the spear away, and the creature exhaled a final raspy breath before becoming still. Victor left the spear where it was and crawled into the tunnel. And there, just as he turned the corner, was the entrance to the ship, a wide circular doorway tall enough for him to walk into standing upright. He pulled himself forward out of the tunnel and into the ship. To his right on the wall was a circular crank. He wondered if it would close the door. He turned it clockwise, and sure enough the blades of an aperture began to extend, closing the entrance.

Victor heard a noise out in the tunnel, a pattering of feet. He paused to shine his light out into the central tunnel that extended straight back into the rock for quite a distance. And there, coming toward him, racing up the tunnel, were a pair of Formics hurrying for the entrance. They were pushing off the narrow walls with their various feet, launching as much as running, soaring at him in zero G. If they got inside, he'd lose. He was unarmed and exhausted. He spun the crank as fast as it would go. The aperture blades seemed old and rusted and painfully slow. And the closer they got to closing, the harder it was to turn the crank. The blades of the aperture were almost touching when the Formics slammed into them. There was a furious scraping and pounding on the door as Victor strained and pulled and finally sealed it closed. His arms were burning from the exertion, and he felt like throwing up. A second door was behind the first, he realized. He found a second crank and turned it, and two panels came out of the floor and ceiling and met in the middle and locked.

He was inside.

He turned around and shined his light in the dark space. The ship was small. Barely ten meters long and quite narrow. The strong, putrid organic smell that he had only detected faintly outside was thick in here. Like rotted plants, mixed with feces. A single aisle extended up the middle of the ship, with oddly shaped shelves on either side. The shelves held rows of round habitats made of packed mud or stone.

For the slugs, Victor realized. The Formics had brought the creatures with them all this way. And yet he had seen more slugs in the tunnels than there were habitats to house them, suggesting that the Formics had bred more slugs upon arrival. These habitats were made just for the parents.

But why were the slugs here to begin with? What was their

purpose? What did the Formics want with pellets of metal? Why had they built this habitat around this rock? All of his struggles and fighting and nearly dying, and he still had zero answers to give the IF.

He moved up the aisle. Shining his light in each of the habitats, relieved to find them all empty.

He found another crank on the wall to his right, this one three times the size of the ones near the door. This controls the ship's spider legs, he thought. He knew it instinctively. He grabbed the crank and turned. It wouldn't budge clockwise, so he turned it the other direction, and it spun easily. Unseen gears ground and squealed, reverberating inside the ship, and Victor felt the ship shift a little. Yes, he was retracting the legs. The ship suddenly felt unsteady. He continued to spin, and the legs continued to retract and fold inward, or at least that's what Victor assumed was happening. At last there was a snapping and locking sound, and the wheel couldn't spin any farther.

All that held the ship now in place was the resin that had grown all around the thrusters creating an airtight seal. But what could Victor do now? There was no instrument panel, no flight controls. There were three cranks and rows of rock habitats. That was it. And yet somehow, the Formics had flown this craft. It had a powerful thruster. It had targeted and reached the asteroid precisely, flying billions of kilometers to get here. So where were the starcharts? Where were the nav computers? The terminals?

He hovered upright in the middle of the aisle, looking around him, desperate for a throttle or wheel or way to fire retros. There had to be retros. The ship had made a delicate landing. It had touched down on a rock hurtling through space. It had come in gently, with surgical precision. How had it done so?

He spun in the air. He could still hear the dull sound of

fists pounding on the closed doors outside, the two Formics desperate to get in.

I'm thinking like a human, he realized. I need to think like a Formic. He grabbed the lowest shelf and pulled himself down to the surface he had labeled the floor. It was dirty and sticky and smelled of grime and excrement. He grabbed at the shelf bars and positioned himself flat against the floor, staying low like a Formic would. There was a narrow empty space beneath the lowest habitat that extended the length of the shelves. A Formic could crawl in there easily, he realized. Victor couldn't fit as long as he wore his lower armor and mining suit. He was too bulky, too wide. He shed the lower half of his armor and his mining suit so that he wore only his skintight single undergarment. Now he was thin enough to crawl in under the shelf, though just barely. He pulled himself forward and found a lever and a button in front of a sliding panel. He pushed the panel up to reveal a small porthole. A Formic would crawl in this space and look out this porthole. Why? He experimentally tried the lever and heard gears beneath him. Something was moving, rotating. He pushed the button and heard a spray of propellant. The ship titled upward, pushed back.

The lever and button powered one of the retros. He pushed his body away from the wall and slid across the aisle to the other side and found an identical panel and identical lever and button. He pushed the button, and the ship lurched slightly back and up.

A crew of five Formics because it took five of them to land. He pulled himself out from under the shelf and climbed up to what he considered the ceiling and found, as he had expected, matching spaces above the habitats, just wide enough for a Formic to squeeze into.

He crawled in, pushed the button, fired a retro. The ship lurched back, and now he could feel it tearing free of the resin. He slid to the fourth retro and fired it as well, more tilting, more lurching. It was all sloppy guesswork, with the ship tipping one way and then another, but it was backing away from the asteroid.

With all of the Formics working together simultaneously, their minds linked as one, delicately navigating the spacecraft would be a simple ordeal. By himself, it was a disaster.

And yet it was working. Or so it seemed. He moved back and forth between the four retros, tapping them enough to push the ship back. The ship bucked and dipped and spun, and he tried his best to keep it moving in the right direction.

He looked out the porthole and saw that he was free. The ship was drifting away from the rock. A giant hole remained in the resin where the ship had been. The air was no doubt pouring out, turning the whole environment into a vacuum once again. The remaining Formics, the slugs, all were sucked out into space to die of asphyxiation.

He couldn't see the quickship, though he knew Imala was out there somewhere. Waiting, tracking him, following.

It was several hours before the Gagak arrived and grabbed the ship with one of its docking claws. And then another hour before a docking tube was attached to the hull of the Formic ship. A laser cut a hole through the ceiling, and someone pushed the cut piece clear.

Victor looked up to see Arjuna's concerned face looking down at him.

"He's alive," Arjuna shouted back over his shoulder.

Victor heard a chorus of cheers back in the ship.

"Are you hurt?" Arjuna asked him.

"I've got dangerous levels of hydrogen in my lungs and I may need a few stitches. Other than that I'm fine. Is Imala safe?"

"She's inside. Safe. But she's a mess, Vico. You put her through hell. Your mother, too. Rena wanted us all to charge in there and get you out. I almost had to restrain her."

"I shouldn't have gone in, not with the air as volatile as it was. That was stupid."

Arjuna sighed. "You're alive. That's what matters. And you brought back a souvenir, too." He stuck his head into the Formic miniship and made a face of disgust. "It smells like a bucket of sewage, though."

"I don't smell much better," said Vico.

"I'll bring you some sanitizer and clean clothes. We want your family to welcome you, not throw you back out into space."

## CHAPTER 19

## Soldier Brain

Formic technology is, at its root, biological. Rather than
use machines, the Hive Queen engineers and mentally
controls animals to perform certain tasks. The degree
to which she controls those animals is a subject of
much debate, but the prevailing theory is that not all
creatures are controlled at the same integrated level.
To some creatures, such as mining worms for example, the Hive Queen merely gives them an impulse to
do the thing they're genetically predisposed to do. The
worms then act autonomously, with the Hive Queen
only checking in periodically to confirm that her creatures are still following their given set of instructions.

To other, more complex organisms, such as Formic
soldiers, the Hive Queen gives more detailed instructions in the moment. Those instructions may be general or specific. Analyses of battles from both the First
and Second Formic War suggest that sometimes the
Hive Queen merely orders her troops to "attack." In
these instances, the creatures act as independent organisms, firing and jumping and fighting as autonomous
soldiers, fearless but uncreative. In other instances, it
appears as if the Hive Queen seizes full mental con-

trol, for the group ceases to act as individuals and begins to move like a single organism.
—Demosthenes, *A History of the Formic Wars,* Vol. 3

Mazer and Prem stepped off the elevator at the corporate offices of Gungsu Industries, four stories beneath the surface
of Luna. A young Korean male with styled hair and a tight
designer suit greeted them with a polite smile and a bow.
"Captain Rackham. Lieutenant Chamrajnagar. I am Ms. Woo
Han's assistant. Welcome. You will forgive us for being so
unprepared for your visit."

"You're unprepared because we didn't tell you we were
coming," said Mazer. "I hope we're not being an inconvenience."

The assistant's smile didn't waver. "Any representative of
WAMRED and the International Fleet is always welcome at
our offices. Generally we like to set such appointments well
in advance so that our schedules can be cleared to receive
you. But these are challenging times, with new threats arising
every moment, it seems. Gungsu always stands ready to assist
you. Might I inquire the nature of your visit?"

"We have a proposition for Ms. Woo Han," said Mazer.

The assistant waited for more information, and when Mazer didn't give it, he asked, "Might I share with Ms. Woo Han
any more details concerning this proposition so that she
might prepare herself to greet you?"

The assistant had clearly been sent to fish for information,
and Mazer saw barely contained panic in the man's eyes. He
clearly didn't want to return to Hea Woo Han empty-handed.

"Tell Ms. Woo Han that the International Fleet is forming
a special asteroid assault team," said Mazer, "and that we
have several tech designs we would like to present to her. The
timetable for this mission is short, and our experience with

Gungsu leads us to believe that your corporation may be the perfect partner in this endeavor."

The assistant's smile widened. "Of course." He gestured to an ornate waiting room to his right. "Won't you have a seat? I will inform Ms. Woo Han of your arrival."

"Thank you," said Mazer.

He and Prem sat as the assistant scurried away.

"An asteroid assault team?" said Prem. "That sounded official."

"That was my hope," said Mazer.

"The assistant looked like he was going to burst into tears if we didn't give him something to say to Woo Han. She must be a scary one. What do you know about her?"

"Next to nothing," said Mazer. "Except that she's Colonel Vaganov's direct link to Gungsu. Whatever deal Vaganov worked up, I think it's safe to assume that Woo Han was the one who orchestrated it all."

"Then why are we talking to her? Isn't she the enemy here?"

"She's an opportunist," said Mazer. "She makes deals. And she can probably call off the prosecution if we're right about her influence."

"You realize of course that we have no authority whatsoever to speak on behalf of the International Fleet, and that by walking into this woman's office and pretending like we do, we're inviting a real court-martial."

"I'll represent you in court if you represent me," said Mazer.

"I'm serious, Mazer. At best, I'll get disbarred. At worst we go to jail."

"I'll tell the arresting officers that you tried to talk me out of this, that you outlined all the consequences, and that you said this was a monumentally bad idea."

"It *is* a monumentally bad idea."

"My point is," said Mazer, "there's no reason why we

should both take the heat for this if it doesn't work. It's my idea. I'll go solo. You take the elevator now, and I'll meet you back at the office. If I get court-martialed, you can represent me. Could I get a two-for-one special on attorney fees?"

"You don't pay me, remember? I'm appointed."

"Even better."

Chamrajnagar considered a moment then sighed. "It's better if we both go. Alone you look like a rogue crazy man. With me—"

"I look like a rogue crazy man with a smart lawyer."

"Should we at least discuss what we're going to present to this woman before we actually do? I hate winging it."

Mazer didn't have a chance to answer because the assistant returned and beckoned them to follow. The three of them went down a corridor and into Hea Woo Han's office, a large space with a holotable on the left and a circle of contemporary armchairs on the right. Hea Woo Han stood to receive them, and she was exactly as Mazer remembered her: poised, conservatively dressed, and all business. Her face, though polite, had the bearing of someone who was completely in command.

After some bowing and formal introductions, the assistant exited and closed the doors behind him.

"Won't you have a seat," said Hea Woo Han, gesturing to the armchairs. An ornate porcelain Korean tea set sat on a small coffee table before them. Hea Woo Han lifted the teapot. "May I interest you in a cup of omija cha, a Korean herbal tea made from the berries of the schisandra? It is said to calm the spirit and refresh the heart and kidneys. Personally I just like the taste."

"Thank you," said Mazer.

Prem accepted as well, and Hea Woo Han poured and served three steaming cups.

"I remember you well, Captain Rackham," said Woo Han, taking a sip from her tea. "Our passing was brief at WAMRED, but I do not forget a face. You helped conduct tests for the gravity disruptor. If I am not mistaken, a member of your unit was injured during one of the tests. I hope he has recuperated."

"He lost the lower half of his leg and is learning to walk with a prosthesis," said Mazer.

Hea Woo Han looked genuinely surprised. "I am sorry to hear it. You will please relay my condolences to him and his family when you see him next. We at Gungsu are not indifferent to such tragedies. Many of us are veterans. Myself included. Any loss to one soldier is a loss to us all."

"You have the bearing of a soldier," said Mazer. "I'm not surprised to hear you served. What branch? ROKN?" Meaning the Republic of Korea Navy.

Hea Woo Han smiled. "What tipped you off? The way I pour tea?"

"Gungsu would want someone who has intimate knowledge of the contract-procuring process for large, self-sustaining vessels and their equipment. That's the navy."

"Yes," said Hea Woo Han. "I was an administrative contracting officer. Coming to Gungsu seemed like a natural transition."

"What was your terminal rank?" Mazer asked. "Major?"

Hea Woo Han smiled. "Not quite. I was a daewi, an equivalent to your rank of captain."

"When did you get out?" Mazer asked.

"Three years ago, when the IF formed."

"Then you should have been a major. You were the age of a major. You certainly have the presence and capabilities of a major."

Hea Woo Han bowed her head slightly. "You are kind to say so, Captain Rackham, but there are very few female majors in the Korean military. My terminal rank was quite an achievement considering the circumstances. But please, you did not come here to discuss my military service. How can we at Gungsu be of assistance?"

Mazer took a sip of his tea. It was hot and sweet and warmed his throat. "What would you say is the IF's greatest weakness at the moment, Ms. Woo Han?"

Hea Woo Han paused and considered. "An interesting question, Captain. And one with a lengthy answer. The Fleet has a number of weaknesses at present. We have too few warships, for one, and too few experienced crews to man them. We have made great strides in defense since the last war, but we must continue to innovate if we hope to defeat the enemy. Surveillance, communication, weaponry, shielding. A strong defense is rooted in advanced tech. We cannot yield in our diligent pursuit of research and development."

"Isn't that the foundational position of every defense contractor?" Mazer said. " 'The military is weak. We need to be stronger. We need more tech.' Etcetera. You'd go out of business if you said otherwise."

Hea Woo Han's expression remained flat. "Do you question my sincerity, Captain Rackham?"

"Not at all. I meant no offense. And please, call me Mazer. Prem and I aren't here as representatives of the IF. We're here representing ourselves. We can drop the formalities."

"I see. It appears I have been misinformed. I was led to believe that this was in regards to an asteroid strike team."

"It is," said Mazer. "But first, that question: the IF's greatest weakness. I would assume that you, someone intimately familiar with the intricacies of military bureaucracy, would know our real problem."

Hea Woo Han set her empty teacup down on the coffee table. "Perhaps I am not as wise as you think, Captain. You obviously have something in mind. Enlighten me."

"How many times were you passed up for promotion in the navy?" asked Mazer. "Four times? Six? Ten? You need not answer, but whatever that number, it happened not only because you were a woman in a male-dominated institution but also because you're intelligent and they were afraid of you. And yet if you had filed a discrimination complaint, which would have been well within your rights to do, you would have essentially committed career suicide. You'd have been ostracized and ignored and blacklisted. They'd have made you a supply officer up in Gangwon province, bunking with the ice fishermen."

Hea Woo Han said nothing.

"So you kept quiet," said Mazer, "and did your duty and watched less capable careerist twits get promoted again and again because they knew how to work the system. They took credit for every success and deflected blame for every failure. Bureaucrats. Men who want command but who have no idea what to do with it. Men who avoid committing their forces until they know victory is already imminent. Men who want somebody else to take the risk. Men who lose wars."

Hea Woo Han didn't reply.

"But then Gungsu comes along," continued Mazer. "A corporation that actually rewards people for being intelligent and promotes people for being effective. And they need someone exactly like you, someone whose knowledgeable of military operations, someone who can interact with officers of senior rank without seeming deferential. Someone who understands the contract procurement process and who has risen to considerable rank despite the prejudices against her. And so they made you an offer right when you realized that joining the IF would be a dead end. You weren't going to advance. Not in an environment where the bureaucracy was taken to a whole new level, with careerists from nearly every military on Earth jockeying for position and stepping on the backs of whoever got in their way. That wasn't a game you had ever played, and you certainly didn't want to play it now. So you came to Gungsu. And you love your job because you feel rewarded and validated. But you hate it as well because you have to make deals with precisely the kind of bureaucrats you despised from the beginning. Tell me if I'm getting warm here."

"You can't defeat the bureaucracy," said Hea Woo Han. "It may be our greatest weakness, but it's indestructible. It defines the IF. I can't help you."

"I think you can," said Mazer. "I think we can help each other." He unbuttoned his cufflink and rolled up his sleeve, revealing his wrist pad.

"The IF has been prepping for ship-to-ship warfare," said Mazer. "Large space battles. And we will almost certainly see those when the time comes. Yet the more critical battleground of the war may be asteroids. It's believed that Formics have already occupied thousands of asteroids in our solar system. The Formics cover these asteroids with a durable shell that holds in an atmosphere. I believe it highly likely that Formics are tunneling through these asteroids and creating habitats, possibly even mining resources. For what purpose, we don't yet know, but IF marines will need to take these asteroids. Failing to do so may cost us the war."

He extended the four small antennas on his wrist pad and turned on the holoprojector. A small holo of the spider harness Victor had created appeared in the holofield.

"This is a tunnel harness," said Mazer. "Designed by Victor Delgado, the free miner whose engineering helped win us the First Formic War. The harness was originally intended for metal tunnels inside a Formic warship, but it could work just as well in asteroid tunnels. The legs of the harness push against all sides of the tunnel to keep the marine suspended in the middle, away from tunnel walls. Or if necessary, the marine can collapse the legs on one side in an instant, allowing him to flatten himself against a tunnel wall. The legs' primary function, however, is to walk, allowing the marine to carry and aim his weapon while he advances or retreats."

"I see," said Hea Woo Han. "And what are you proposing for Gungsu?"

"An assault team will be forming and departing for the Belt to address this threat. They will need equipment on board to build prototypes of the harness. Their flight will take several months, during which time the marines will train with the harnesses and make modifications to the design as needed. If the harnesses prove effective and earn Hegemony approval, Victor Delgado and I are offering an exclusive development and production contract with Gungsu. If you're not interested, we'll take the design and others we have to Juke Limited for their consideration."

Hea Woo Han considered a moment before answering. "You realize, of course, that you're breaking chain of command. Your CO is still Colonel Vaganov. It's his prerogative to make these kind of arrangements."

Prem spoke up. "Colonel Vaganov is not the CO of Victor Delgado, whom we represent, and whose idea this is. I'd argue that we are not breaking chain of command at all. We're simply circumnavigating the bureaucracy."

Hea Woo Han pursed her lips, considering. "And what are you asking for in return?"

"Vaganov gave you an idea for a nanoshield," said Mazer. "That idea came from the soldier in my unit who lost his leg. Shambhani. We recognize that you are under no legal obligation to do so, but we would ask that Gungsu make a generous donation to Shambhani's family."

Hea Woo Han raised an eyebrow. "As long as Shambhani will agree to sign a document waiving his right to ever take legal action against us, I'm sure an arrangement can be made. Our lawyers can work up the particulars with Lieutenant Chamrajnagar here. Anything else?"

"Appropriate financial compensation to Victor Delgado and his family," said Mazer.

"Of course," said Hea Woo Han, "assuming our engineers

can evaluate the holo and agree that the tech is viable. And you, Captain Rackham? You are doing this out of the goodness of your heart? Or do you seek compensation as well?"

"You have an agreement with Colonel Vaganov," said Mazer. "I don't know what that agreement is exactly, but I would ask that you use whatever influence you have to encourage him and his associates to end my court-martial and acquit me of all charges."

"I see," said Hea Woo Han.

"They're phony charges," said Prem. "We will easily win on appeal, but the process will take months and delay the asteroid assault team."

"I am sorry, Captain Rackham," said Hea Woo Han. "But I cannot help you. You clearly think Gungsu Industries has more influence than we do. The only relationship that Gungsu has with Colonel Vaganov is a professional one. Any other type of agreement with him or any of his associates would be unethical in the extreme and threaten the flawless service record we maintain with the good men and women of the International Fleet. Nor can Gungsu intervene in a military judicial proceeding. That is the purview of the Judge Advocate General's Corps, and we would not dare to obstruct their duties. That is clearly outside the reach and responsibility of this corporation. On that point I cannot assist you whatsoever. I am afraid you have been misinformed. I'm sure you understand."

"I understand completely," said Mazer. "It was foolish of me to suggest it. If I remain in the International Fleet once the court-martial is over, perhaps we can meet once again to discuss a potential partnership." Mazer stood and extended his hand.

Hea Woo Han stood and shook his hand. "Perhaps."

"Thank you for your time," said Mazer.

They bowed, and Hea Woo Han's assistant escorted them up the elevator and out the front door of the building, where the false sunlight from the dome ceilings of Old Town shined down on the busy sidewalk.

"Well that was a waste of time," said Prem.

Mazer called up another taxi, and he and Prem climbed inside. The taxi eased into traffic.

"The conversation was being recorded," said Mazer. "Woo Han was far too adamant in her objection. The lady did protest too much. She couldn't say anything that would incriminate the company. My guess is she's on a holo with Colonel Vaganov as we speak, asking him to call off the prosecutor."

"Or maybe she was adamant because she sincerely can't help us."

"Maybe. But her eyes said otherwise."

"Ah. Her eyes. Of course. How silly of me to place greater emphasis on the words coming out of her mouth than that subtle glint in her eye that spoke volumes. Did her eyes also tell you that we've committed to an asteroid strike force that doesn't even exist? Because that was the panicked thought running through my head. You don't have the authority to form a special forces unit, Mazer. Nor do you have the freedom to participate in one, or the means to get them to the Belt. We have no money, no weapons, no soldiers, no ship, no plan. You've made a slew of promises you cannot keep, and you have zero authority to make a deal with a major contractor. Look, I applaud your ambition. I agree with you in principle, but you're a captain. You can't initiate a mission of this scale. Only colonels or officers of higher rank can propose something like this, and only after they've amassed a mountain of data on precisely what the mission is. Logistics, staff, weaponry, equipment, transportation. Plus they have a second mountain of data specifying what the enemy is and how he'll be defeated. Maps, targets, individual objectives, hazards, threats, possible countermeasures, and on and on and on. We don't have any of that. We're not even certain which asteroids may be occupied and how many of them there are. How long will it take Hea Woo Han to confirm with her IF sources that we were bluffing and that there is no asteroid strike team in motion?"

"You keep pointing out what we haven't accomplished, Prem, instead of helping me map out what we can. I want you to switch off your attorney brain and turn on your soldier brain for a moment, that part of your brain that allows you to do seemingly impossible tasks. The IF is full of smart people. We can't be the only ones who are thinking about these asteroids. We simply need to find out who those people are and join them."

"You have a chain of command, Mazer. Colonel Vaganov is still your commanding officer until you're transferred. You can't simply decide to leave and align yourself with another unit. You're not a free agent."

"Your soldier brain, Prem. That's the one you need to engage. Once we find out who is prepping for the asteroids, I'll request a transfer to that unit. Vaganov won't object. He wants me gone anyway."

"And how do we find out this information?"

"The same way all meaningful information gets passed around the military. Back channels. I'll check my forum. And I'll ask Lem Jukes. His father is the Hegemon. Maybe Ukko can connect us with these people."

The taxi dipped into the tunnel, and the vehicle's interior lights turned on as they left the domes behind them.

"We're not going back to the office, I see," said Prem. "Yet another violation of your movement restrictions. And we're going outside the city toward the offices of Lem Jukes. You do realize that you can't just drop in on the heads of corporations and expect them to entertain your visit."

"We're trying to save the world, Prem. When this is over and the Hive Queen is dead, you can give me all the lectures on etiquette you like."

# CHAPTER 20

## Interruptions

To: lem.jukes@juke.net
From: cometwatcher75@freebeltmail.net
Subject: What Victor found

Lem,

We've not met. I'm Edimar, Victor Delgado's cousin
aboard the Gagak. Victor would write you himself, but
he's been conscripted into the IF and ordered not
to share military intelligence with anyone outside the
Fleet. And apparently anything Victor finds, sees,
hears, or discovers is automatically military intelligence. Brilliant strategy, don't you think? So instead
of allowing Victor to share information that would
benefit everyone, including the free citizens of space
and Earth and Luna—which would likely lead to more
information being gathered by others—the military
genius that is the Polemarch insists that the information go only to him. That way he can share it with only
those people he chooses, which means only those
who will echo his own dimwitted opinions back at
him.

I'm considering writing the Poopmarch to remind him that this isn't a war between nations. It's a war between two species with very different evolutionary histories. We don't have to worry about secrecy and espionage and letting critical information fall into the enemy's four hands. The Formics don't speak Common—or use any language, for that matter. They don't have devices that can intercept written text and translate it into a mind-to-mind message they would understand. Nor can they disguise Formics as human beings to go undercover and spy on us. So why should we conduct ourselves in absolute secrecy when we have so much more to gain by sharing information?

And just in case our brilliant I-control-all-information-even-if-it-kills-us-all is listening in, Victor absolutely did NOT ask me to pass this information on to you. Victor is a good soldier and would never ever disobey stupid orders from stupid commanders. How did I get your e-mail address then, you ask? Victor is not my only resource. A fairy sprite gave it to me.

Now the nitty gritty. Victor found six samples of mined metals at 2030CT, all of them excreted from wormlike creatures ingesting the rock. The Formics aren't using mechanical tools to drill, they're using engineered creatures. We've thoroughly analyzed the metal samples and the results are attached. I'm also including this link that will take you to a dark site with hundreds of uploaded photos and the vid feed from Victor's helmet during the operation. The link is self-proliferating, so every time the IF tries to shut it down, it will spring up elsewhere. I assume their technicians have better tools than I do, however, so hurry and download before they annihilate it.

A certain officer in the International Fleet is also getting this information. I trust that you'll be wise and act in the best interest of the human race, passing it along to Papa Hegemon and the press. Vico tells me you are not the selfish, egotistical person you were before, and because I trust my dear cousin, I will give you the benefit of the doubt. Please prove him right.

Edimar

Lem was having lunch with a few dignitaries from Earth and Luna when his wrist pad chimed and alerted him of a message. Lem discreetly tapped it to silence it, but the chime left him uneasy. He had set the device to alert him only when a handful of people tried to reach him, and only when their message was of grave importance. And yet Lem couldn't get up and excuse himself. The men and women around the table were all VIPs—ambassadors, cabinet members, trade secretaries. It would be most discourteous for him to leave the conversation when so much of it was directed at him.

Norja Ramdakan had spent months arranging the event, which included a tour of two Juke manufacturing facilities and lunch at the company's private gourmet restaurant. Proposed legislation from the office of the Hegemony would greatly increase taxes and tariffs, and the people at the table had the power and influence to either make the legislation go away or lessen the proposed tax hikes.

"You're the son of the Hegemon," said the French ambassador. "I would think *you* have more sway over your father than we do."

The comment was said partly in jest and earned a few polite chuckles around the table.

Lem smiled good-naturedly. "My father is a very practical man, Madam Ambassador. As much as I wish he would give weight to everything I say, I assure you that's not the case. In fact, my father is so concerned about even the appearance of nepotism that we here at Juke Limited have to work ten times as hard as other defense contractors to win any bids. Isn't that right, Norja?"

Norja laughed from his seat at the opposite end of the table. "The old man gives us hell."

More polite laughter from the group.

"Even a cursory examination of how the Hegemony has allocated its funding over the last three years will substantiate that claim," said Lem. "Juke Limited has its share of contracts, true. But those are contracts we've earned. We were clearly the contender in the bidding process with the best capabilities to get the job done as thoroughly and as quickly as possible. However, if a competitor even approaches our capabilities and shows any degree of promise, my father will inevitably award the contract to them. We have lost many contracts we should have won all because my father seeks to grow other businesses and spark innovation throughout the world. And he is correct to do so. As much as it kills my finance department, he and the other members of the Hegemony are right to diversify IF clients and encourage economic growth everywhere."

Lem smiled at the ambassador. "In other words, my father doesn't really care what I think, Madam Ambassador. His primary interest is the safety of the citizens of Earth, not the financial stability of his son's company."

"A company that used to be his," said the ambassador.

"Used to be, yes," said Lem. "My father has fully divested himself of this corporation now, and those of you who know him well know I speak the truth."

There were a few subtle nods around the table.

"But I think the Hegemony is mistaken with these proposed taxes and tariffs," said Lem. "They will generate revenue for the Hegemony and thus the IF, no question, but they will also cripple innovation and discourage the free flow of ideas. Many of you may think that our interest here is purely selfish, but the companies that will be hurt the most by this are the midsized businesses that are struggling to get footing in this industry. It is a great irony to me. My father has worked tirelessly to foster growth among these companies, and now the Hegemony is making it even more difficult for them by imposing these new taxes. This is an age-old argument, ladies and gentlemen. The Hegemony has the revenue it needs. It merely has to cut frivolous spending."

"And is any of that frivolous spending going to Juke Limited?" asked Daijina, a trade secretary from the African Union. "Are you willing to concede contracts should they be deemed superfluous? I agree that the Hegemony has invested quite a bit in dead-end projects. We've lost hundreds of millions of credits in junk tech that goes nowhere. Maybe billions. And a lot of that money has gone into this company. I could cite examples."

There was a moment of awkwardness, but Lem smiled it off. "We could all cite examples, Madam Secretary. I could probably cite more than you. And I will be the first to admit that some of the innovations that we've developed here at Juke Limited have failed to measure up to their full potential. Fortunately for us, these challenging projects constitute only a small minority of Juke's total output for the International Fleet. In fact, Juke Limited has the best track record in the business. But you're right. Sometimes the final result falls short of IF expectations. Part of that is due to the mad accelerated pace that we must operate in. The enemy is approaching. We don't have the luxury of time. It has been a frantic scramble for everyone. And when time is short and expectations are high, mistakes will inevitably be made.

"But that doesn't mean we should keep paying for them. What good is it to raise taxes and tariffs if we're still wasting so much of our current spending? Norja, what's the name of that silly device they just launched at Gungsu?" Lem snapped his finger as if trying to remember.

"The gravity disruptor," said Norja.

Lem smiled. "Yes, the gravity disruptor. Here's a device that cost the IF several hundred million credits, and it won't even work against the Formic hulls. That, ladies and gentlemen, is not wise spending. That is throwing away the hard-earned income of the citizens of Earth and Luna. And who will pay for this mistake? Gungsu? No, all the other corporations who must now shoulder a heavy tax to make up for the expense."

Lem's wrist pad chimed again, and this time everyone's eyes went to the device. Lem couldn't ignore now. "Ladies and gentlemen, you will excuse me for a moment, but that sound means that this message can't wait."

He rose from the table and ignored the dirty look Norja was giving him. They had just gotten to the part they had rehearsed about Gungsu and the gravity disruptor, and Lem was walking out. Norja would give him an earful for that.

He stepped into the kitchen and checked the message. To his astonishment it was from his father. The message read, "I've just learned that all seven remaining Parallax satellites have been destroyed at the same time. We have not yet made an announcement, but I wanted you to know. Dark days ahead, son. Stay safe."

Lem stared at the words, his mind suddenly flooding with questions.

He tried calling his father but of course there was no answer. Father would be in emergency meetings with the IF. There would be chaos at CentCom.

When had it happened, Lem wondered? Did Father learn about this through his ansible? Was this happening now? Had this just occurred?

The Hegemony had not yet made an announcement. That

was smart. They were wise to be cautious. If all seven satellites were down, it meant Earth was completely blind. And not only that, but it meant that the Formics' reach already extended to every corner of the solar system. Many of the Parallax sats were positioned on the far side of the system, in the opposite direction of the Formic approach. And yet Formic probes had already reached them without detection. It meant all the arguments against Edimar's theories had gone up in smoke. Naysayers had claimed that the Formics could not possibly have infiltrated the Asteroid Belt without our knowledge. And yet here was incontrovertible proof that the Formics could go wherever they pleased, from one end of the solar system to the next.

And then there was the orchestration of it all, taking the satellites out all at once. That was no coincidence. That suggested intelligence, planning, strategic thinking. It meant the Formics were very well informed. They knew precisely where the satellites were located and how to avoid detection en route.

No, it meant more than that. Because the Formic probes that had carried out this coordinated strike must have left the motherships years ago. They must have set out long before now with an understanding of the satellites' orbits. They had to know not only how many satellites there were, but also where the satellites would be located at the exact time of attack. They had to have mapped out the future positions of their targets and set their course accordingly.

It also meant that the Formics understood that the satellites had value, even if they might not fully understand what that value was.

But then why take out the first satellite separately? Why destroy Copernicus alone? As a test? To gauge our firepower? To see how we would respond? To see how safe it would be to take out the others? That would explain why the ship that had destroyed Copernicus had put up no resistance when the

IF fighters arrived. Its mission was to destroy Copernicus and then to allow itself to be destroyed.

Did the Formics know what Copernicus was? Did they know we used them for observation, or did the Formics think them potential weapons? Threats to remove before the fighting began?

And that's what this was obviously. This was a preliminary measure. The Formics were readying the system for a full invasion.

Lem suddenly felt sick. As if a protective bubble that had given him some degree of comfort had suddenly popped, revealing a monster right in front of him.

He put on a calm face and stepped back into the restaurant. There was a lull in the conversation at the table, and Lem smiled and said, "Everyone, you will forgive me, but I need to borrow my chief financial officer for a moment."

Norja placed his napkin on the table, chuckled, and stood. "You see? This is the mad, accelerated pace Lem was referring to. We can't even pause for a good meal. Excuse me."

He followed Lem out, but the serene look on his face vanished the instant they were alone in the corridor. "I'm assuming this is a life-or-death situation, Lem, because I can't imagine anything more important than the conversation we're having in there."

"It was a message from my father."

Norja's expression changed immediately. He was suddenly on edge, which bothered Lem. It meant even Norja was surprised Father had sent Lem a message.

Lem read him the text.

Norja said nothing for a moment and began to pace.

"They destroyed the satellites all at once, Norja. They're organized. Their reach extends across the whole damn system."

"It's worse than that," said Norja. "This means we can't track any of the asteroids."

Lem hadn't thought of that. But of course that was the biggest concern. If the Formics had indeed confiscated thousands of asteroids and intended to push them somewhere in the system, how would we know if they were moving and where they were going without Parallax?

"Our only available method of observation now is the ships already in space," said Norja. "And that's not enough. That's not even close. How many ships are there in space? Roughly?"

Lem shrugged. "Between corporates, free miners, and the IF? I don't know. Two fifty? And that's probably high."

"How are two hundred and fifty ships going to track three thousand asteroids?" said Norja. "Impossible."

"We don't know that it's three thousand," said Lem. "That's just how many Edimar says there *might* be."

"The free-miner girl has been right every time about everything else. I'm not betting on her being wrong now." He shook his head. "Two hundred and fifty ships. That's nothing, Lem. And probably a quarter of those are clumped together anyway. At depots, stations, being serviced, getting supplies. Or heading in that direction. It's not like we have them all spread out over the system evenly with their Eyes trained on certain objects. We don't even know which asteroids we should be looking at. That's what Parallax was for. If an asteroid deviated from its orbit, Parallax would alert us, and we'd know the Formics were moving it. Now, we don't even have that. It's like Earth is standing in a firing range with a blindfold on."

"We have to attack their big warships," said Lem.

Norja looked at him like he had lost his senses. "The warships? We might have an army of Formic-controlled asteroids in our midst, and you want to go on a suicide mission to the warships? Each of those warships is as big as the Formic scout ship from the first war. Maybe bigger."

"Then what would you suggest, Norja? You just said we can't track every asteroid in the system and that we don't know which ones we should monitor. The warships we know about. We are one hundred percent certain they exist and they are out there. That is a target we can confront."

"Leave the ecliptic?" said Norja. "Expose ourselves?"

"It's space, Norja. The instant we leave Earth's gravity well we're exposed anyway. We won't have an asteroid to retreat to, but since the Formics have probably seized the asteroid anyway, I don't see that it makes much difference."

"This isn't a time for humor, Lem."

"Who's joking? Those warships are the only targets we can definitively identify. Is there a supreme Formic ruler? A Hive Queen? And if there is, isn't that where she would be hidden and protected?"

"They're coming at us from both sides," said Norja. "If we go after the warships, we would have to divide our fleet into two forces, and it's already paper thin to begin with."

"We can't continue to sit here and maintain a passive defense," said Lem. "We have to act. We strike them before they're prepared. They came building their fleet, right? They've been dismantling this massive mothership and building these warships, right? Well, maybe they're not finished. Maybe they're parked up there above and below the ecliptic, building their fleet as we speak, getting ready, sharpening their knives. If we strike before they're ready, we might have a chance."

"And what if these warships have indestructible hulls? We don't have a weapon for that yet. You're talking about striking them before they're ready, but we're not ready either."

"Where is Benyawe with the NanoCloud?" Lem asked.

Norja shrugged. "They've been prepping for a presentation with the Hegemony, Lem. They've been modifying a prototype. We haven't mass-produced anything. We're not ready to take this into combat. We're a year or two away from that. And even when we have mass-produced them, we still need to know the intricacies of these Formic warships so we can tell the nanomaterial where to go once they infiltrate the hull."

Lem shook his head. "That's unacceptable, Norja. You're telling me an impossible scenario. We don't have two years. The normal production schedule is out the window here. If we operate as usual on this, by the time we have our Nano-Cloud ready and loaded onto IF warships, Earth will be a charcoal briquette."

"What do you want me to do, Lem? Move the NanoCloud into production before it's been approved? Before we have funding? Do you have any idea how expensive it is to produce that material? The smaller it is, the higher the price tag, Lem."

"I'm aware of the economics, Norja."

"Then you know that if we start before we've secured funding from the Hegemony, we risk putting this company into a financial free fall. And we're not even certain the damn thing is going to work."

"I saw a demonstration, Norja. The NanoCloud works."

"You saw Benyawe wave a wand in a controlled environment. A laboratory is not a war zone, Lem. We haven't field-tested this thing."

"Then we ask Benyawe to move her team to the Formic scout ship and start conducting field tests immediately. And we get on the docket with the Hegemony to present. Or I go directly to my father on this one. Because if our fleet departs on a preemptive strike without the NanoCloud on board, we lose."

"A preemptive strike isn't going to happen, Lem. That would be the Polemarch's call. And the guy's a coward. He's like McClellan. He's way too cautious. He's not going to commit any ships until he knows the battle is in our favor."

"Which will be never," said Lem. "There will never be a scenario in this war wherein we have the advantage. He should know that."

"I know."

"Then why is Ketkar the Polemarch? If he's incompetent, what is he doing in that position?"

Norja hesitated, uneasy. "It's complicated."

"Meaning what? What do you know?"

"Look, this is not the time or place to have this conversation, okay? We have a room full of dignitaries we need to entertain."

"You think I want to sit down and finish my peas while engaging in political chitchat? I'm done with the meal, Norja. If you want to play host, fine. But I need to do something."

"There is nothing you can do right now, Lem. This is in the hands of the people at CentCom. Let the IF handle this. That's why they exist. Come back inside and pretend to be interested in these boring people. We've got twenty minutes left in this event, tops. Smile, tell a funny anecdote, be charming. That's what we need. Do that, and you *are* helping the war effort. Because if these people can help us annihilate this tax, then that's more funds for projects like the NanoCloud."

He stepped to the side and gestured for Lem to go in.

"We'll catch up later, Norja. Right now I have work to do, and it isn't here."

He turned and left. Norja didn't try to stop him. Lem took one of the company subway cars back to his office, not certain what he would do once he got there. As soon as he opened the door, one of his assistants, Xianxo, sprang to her feet. "Mr. Jukes, I've been trying to contact you for the past hour, but no messages were getting through."

"I was in a meeting. My wrist pad was off." And you're not one of the important people whose messages I really care about, he thought to himself.

"A vid message arrived for you from Captain Nikula in the Kuiper Belt. The message was marked with high importance."

"Who's Captain Nikula?" Lem asked.

"He's the captain of one of our mining ships, sir. His vessel is the Gungnir, an A-class digger. Mr. Ramdakan had ordered Captain Nikula to investigate a KBO possibly targeted by the Formics."

KBO. A Kuiper Belt object. An asteroid essentially. Norja had said that a few of our ships were close to asteroids Edimar had identified as ones the Formics might have seized.

Lem moved toward the door to this right. "Send the vid to the holo room."

"Yes, sir."

Lem stepped into the room, removed his suit coat, and hung it on a hook by the door. A large image appeared on the far wall of a middle-aged man facing camera from the helm of his ship. Captain Nikula wore a Juke flight uniform not unlike the one Lem had worn when he had captained a company vessel. Lem waved a hand, and the vid began to play.

"This is Captain Franz Nikula of the Gungnir, ship registration 450081, property of Juke Limited. We arrived at the area designated by our starmap to be the current location of 2045LJ78, a KBO measuring one kilometer in diameter with an expected surface of water ice plus ammonia and a rocky core. However, the asteroid was not there. A thorough search of the sector alerted us to a large chunk of rock not currently on the starchart. The object was several hundred thousand klicks away and measured three hundred meters in diameter. We went and investigated this object, pictured here."

The captain was replaced with vid taken from the ship's exterior cameras. It showed a disc-shaped asteroid with hundreds of small holes and tunnels all over its surface, lit by the ship's floodlights.

"We believe this smaller KBO is actually a fragment of the original asteroid 2045LJ78. You will note the holes all over the rock's surface. Initially we thought this fragment was chipped away from the asteroid as a result of a collision, but we could find no evidence in our Eye record to substantiate this idea. There was no object of considerable size coming in that could have collided with the asteroid.

"A further analysis of the sector revealed other unknown objects. When we quadrangulated their trajectories we discovered they all originated from a point along the orbit of the asteroid in question. This confirmed our suspicions that these other small objects were also fragments of 2045LJ78. The asteroid had broken apart roughly two weeks prior to our arrival and scattered its pieces in multiple directions.

"We then reexamined the records from our Eye to see if we could find when a heat signature had appeared. This would indicate when the Formic miniship had abandoned the asteroid. If we were lucky, the heat signature would also give us a trajectory of that ship, which we hoped to track.

"We did in fact find a heat signature in the record, but it was not what we had expected. There was a bright flash of heat right at the moment when the asteroid broke apart, which leads us to believe that the Formics did not *break* the asteroid but rather blew it apart with explosives.

"Also, after analyzing the original, heavily tunneled fragment of the asteroid that we recovered, we found no evidence of anything alien. No Formics, no tools, no small Formic ship. And yet something must have made those holes and dug those tunnels through the rock. They could not have occurred naturally. We will prepare a full written report and send it directly to Lem Jukes. Captain Nikula out."

The transmission ended. Lem stared at the wall, now more confused than ever. Why would the Formics mine an asteroid and then blow it to bits? To cover their tracks? To prevent humans from discovering what they were doing there?

It was all so frustrating. Just when he felt as if he were getting answers, a mountain of new uncertainties avalanched him. We're fighting an enemy we don't understand, he thought. And what was it that Sun Tzu said? One who knows the enemy and knows himself will not be endangered in a hundred engagements. But one who knows neither the enemy nor himself will invariably be defeated in every engagement. That's us, thought Lem. We don't know ourselves or the enemy. The Formics are perfectly united in a hive mind that we cannot possibly grasp, and we're a fragmented, argumentative pack of egoists with more opinions than good sense.

Lem opened his e-mail to see if Captain Nikula's written report had come through. Instead he was surprised to find one from Edimar. He opened it and read it. Victor had gone inside the shell and recovered mined pellets of pure metal. Lem reread the letter than opened the attachments. He scanned through the images and watched in horror and fascination at the grublike creatures digging through the rock in Victor's vid. Then he opened the analysis of the pellets. Victor had found iron, magnesium, aluminum, nickel, silicon, and pristine ice. There might have been other metals as well, but Victor, in his desperation to escape, had not stopped to collect more samples.

Lem went back to Edimar's e-mail. She had written that she had sent this same information to "a certain IF officer." She had not mentioned the name to protect the person's identity, but she clearly expected Lem to know who it was. It had to be Mazer Rackham. But Rackham was at WAMRED. What could he do with the information there?

The door to the holo room opened and Xianxo poked her head in. "Mr. Jukes, I'm sorry to disturb you, but there is a Captain Mazer Rackham here to see you."

Lem stared at her a moment, too surprised to speak. "Send him in," he finally managed.

Xianxo disappeared and then Mazer and a female officer entered. The woman was young and attractive, with olive skin and dark hair. Indian, maybe. Mazer looked exactly as Lem remembered him from three years ago, though now he was dressed in a rather formal-looking uniform.

"I'd offer you a seat, but there aren't any," said Lem.

Mazer spoke first. "Mr. Jukes, I'd like to present Lieutenant Prem Chamrajnagar of the Judge Advocate General's Corps."

Lem shook her hand. "An attorney. This gets more interesting by the moment."

"You should have received an e-mail from Edimar," said Mazer.

"I just finished reading it," said Lem. "So you can imagine my surprise to have you walk in right at the moment when I realized she was likely referring to you."

"I received my e-mail from her on the way over here," said Mazer.

Lem was surprised. "So it wasn't her intel that brought you here? Now I'm even more confused."

"I'm here to share information, get information, and hopefully make a deal," said Mazer.

"What kind of deal?"

Mazer extracted a small data cube from his wrist pad. "Do you have a holoprojector?"

"This entire room is a holoprojector."

Mazer handed him the data cube. "This is the exosuit Victor was wearing in his vid."

Lem slid the cube into a slot on the wall, and a holocolumn in the center of the room appeared with a 3D model of the suit lazily spinning in the air.

"The helmet obviously needs a better seal," said Mazer, "but Victor can work on that, as can your engineers. Otherwise, it's a smart design. There are other designs Victor has created as well. We need good engineers with mobile manufacturing capabilities to produce them."

"Mobile manufacturing?" Lem asked.

"So that we can make new suits and modify the design on demand as the marines move toward the asteroids. I'm putting together a proposal for a special forces strike team tasked with finding out what the Formics are doing at these asteroids and then learning how to take them out. I'm hoping Juke Limited will take part in that proposal. We already have Gungsu contributing as well."

Lem scoffed. "Gungsu? Why?"

"Short answer, some of their tech works very well," said Mazer.

"And some of it doesn't," said Lem. "Some of it is catastrophically ineffective."

"No one knows that better than me," said Mazer. "Victor is the chief engineer here. I trust his designs. Gungsu is offering expertise and manufacturing. I'm confident they can deliver. Just as I'm confident Juke can deliver. Victor had the right idea going inside the shell, but a team of trained soldiers working together has a better chance of achieving the objective."

"You said this was a proposal?" asked Lem.

Mazer and Chamrajnagar exchanged glances. "Full disclosure," said Mazer. "We're operating outside our authority here. Neither Prem nor I have the clout to put a project like this into motion. We don't have any senior-level sponsors. Nor do we have any funding. We're not even sure if the IF already has a plan in motion for the asteroids, but considering Edimar's obvious disdain for the Polemarch we're not counting on it. Basically we can't sit idle. Also, part of the reason we involved Gungsu was to end a bogus court-martial against me."

"Court-martial?" said Lem. "My interest is piqued. If the IF is court-martialing you, as clean-cut as they come, then something is rotten in the state of Denmark. But you saw Victor's vid; these asteroids are filled with hydrogen. Blowing them up will be easy. They're bombs."

"Even so," said Mazer. "We'll still need to gather intelligence on what these asteroids are being used for. Why are Formics harvesting and processing metal and ice? And where do they want to push these asteroids? Finding those answers is going to take a well-equipped insertion team. And a team is going to need suits."

Lem paused, studied the holo one more time and nodded. "Jukes will agree to produce the suits if we win Hegemony approval. I suppose you want to be paid big bucks for the design."

"Victor did the work," said Mazer. "Not me. He should get the big bucks."

"So you want nothing in return?" Lem asked.

"Talk to your father, Lem. Get the funding from the Hegemony. If there is money allotted to this, the IF will make it happen. They'll launch. I only ask that I'm on that ship when it does. Perhaps your father can put in a good word to the Strategos on my behalf."

"The Strategos knows who you are, Mazer. If it comes down to him picking people, you can bet you'll be at the top of that list."

# CHAPTER 21

## Silicon

May she see with her eyes the sorrow of destruction.
May she hear with her ears the cries of the innocent.
May she lift with her hands the load of the burdened.
May she break with her strength the weapons of war.
May she forgive with her heart the violence
    against her.
May she grasp with her mind the goodness of man.
May she find with her soul the pathway to peace.

—**Prayer for the Hive Queen, from the prayer book of**
**Wilasanee Saowaluk, Hegemony Archives, 2118**

Wila sat alone in the cafeteria in the semidarkness, eating a bowl of peach-flavored oatmeal. The food at the Rings was some of the best she had ever eaten, with dishes from all over the world and desserts so rich every bite was like a dream. But the breakfast lines didn't open for another two hours, and so she had resigned herself to one of the self-serve oatmeal packets kept in a bin near the serving lines. It was a poor substitute for the ham and cheese omelets that the kitchen staff was scheduled to serve later, but it was no worse than the food she had eaten back home.

In fact, there had been some days, working hard on her dissertation, that she had not eaten at all. Her cupboards had been bare, not because she couldn't afford to buy food but because she couldn't be bothered with such an uninspiring task as grocery shopping. Time was too precious. There was too much to write. And so rather than get dressed and go out and buy herself sustenance, she had pushed on in her pajamas and told herself she was fasting.

She smiled and shook her head at the memory; she could laugh about it now. But in truth, it had not been all that long ago. Her dissertation had consumed her life. Researching, writing, editing, cutting. And in the end all that effort had amounted to nothing.

No, that wasn't true. Her research had led to this job. It was not a job in academia like she had always hoped, but the work was important. No, more than important. It was the only work that mattered, really, and she was right at the heart of it.

She still could not believe that she was here, living in the Rings, circling the Formic scout ship. So much of her research had focused on the creatures and plant life that had thrived in the oxygen-producing garden on that ship, and now here she was, only a few meters from it.

She had not actually gone to the ship yet, but her colleagues had assured her that the opportunity would eventually come. She spent much of her spare time gazing up through the portholes in the ceiling on the top floor of the research facility, the floor that was closest to the ship. She would look up at the ship as it rushed past, as if it were spinning on its axis like a top, its red surface sometimes glinting in the sun. But of course the scout ship was motionless, locked in Earth's geosynchronous orbit, and it was Wila who was moving around it.

The size of it. That had been the most alarming thing. She had known of course precisely how big it was, but numbers on a screen could not do the real thing justice. Was she right about its construction?

"Can't sleep?"

The voice startled her. She turned and saw Dr. Dublin enter through the door behind her. He was still wearing his lab coat and the clothes he had worn yesterday. His thin hair was unkempt, his slacks wrinkled, as if he had fallen asleep in the lab again and had just now awoken to find everyone gone.

Wila smiled to herself. Dublin was an eccentric character, and yet Wila could not help but like him. She marveled at how focused he could become. Time seemed to stop in his mind whenever he stepped into the lab and began a task, as if the rest of the world had melted out of existence. It made him notoriously late for meetings—if he showed up for them at all—and it had earned him a great deal of harmless ribbing from the other researchers. Or at least they thought it was harmless. Dublin took it all in stride with a good-natured laugh, but Wila had sensed embarrassment and sorrow and maybe even a little shame in those eyes.

She had imagined him as a child among his peers at school. Awkward, quiet, isolated, bullied probably. He had made friends, no doubt, but they were probably the kind who had abandoned him as soon as their association with him had threatened their own social standing. False friends. The kind who blew about like dandelion seeds—as soon as you thought you had caught one, the slightest gust ripped it away and carried it elsewhere.

"What's on the menu there?" he asked, bending forward to examine her cup.

"Oatmeal from the bins up front," she said, pointing to where they were located.

"Hmm," he said. "I didn't know we had bins."

He shuffled off and returned a minute later with a cup of his own.

"You didn't heat it up," said Wila. "You just added water. We have mini ovens, you know."

He looked in the direction of the ovens, as if he had only remembered that they were there. Then he dismissed the idea with a wave of his hand. "Eh, it's going down the gullet whether it's warm or cold." He took a bite. "You always up this early?"

"The change in time zones," she said. "My body has not yet adjusted."

In truth, she had always been an early riser, but the change in sleep schedule here had not helped.

He gestured to the small book on the table beside her. "Your journal?"

"My prayer book," said Wila.

He looked intrigued and extended a hand. "May I?"

"By all means," she said, lifting it and giving it to him. "The more of us who reach for peace, the more likely we are to find it."

He flipped through the pages. "You wrote all these?"

The prayers were handwritten, some quickly, some stylishly, some with little doodles around their edges.

"Some of them," Wila said. "Others I found in books. Several are from Master Arjo. He is the master of a temple in Thailand I frequented since I was a child. He always prayed in solitude, but he would tell me his prayers afterward if I asked."

"You have beautiful penmanship," said Dublin. "The letters are written so small and yet so precisely that they look printed."

Wila smiled. "You are kind. Do they have prayers in your faith, Dr. Dublin?"

He chuckled. "I was raised Catholic. My mother prayed as often as she breathed. We went to Mass three times a week, she and I. I think that's what turned me off to it in the end. The relentless pursuit of it, that and the fact that my mother's prayers never seemed to do much good."

"Oh?"

"My father was still abusive and unfaithful to her, no matter how many saints my mother implored. I think she believed

God would fix the whole thing. She died before my father did, and she never left him. I find it rather depressing, to be honest."

"I am sorry for your sorrow. And for hers. In my faith we believe that those who are compassionate and kind in this life will find themselves in a better situation in their next life. By that rule, I believe your mother is happier now."

"And my father? What of him? I suppose he's a mule on a farm somewhere."

Wila blushed and lowered her gaze. "I have offended you. That was not my intent."

He chuckled, still flipping through her book. "You haven't offended me, Wila. I find your faith fascinating. But I see here that your prayers don't invoke any God or supreme being. Who do you pray to exactly?"

"To no one," said Wila. "Buddhist prayers are not addressed to any enlightened being. Not even to the Buddha. I say them to myself, to strengthen my resolve to end suffering and to see to it that all beings flourish."

Dublin closed the book and set it down. "When you say all beings, does that include the Formics? Do you pray that the Formics flourish?"

Wila hesitated. "That is a delicate question, Dr. Dublin. But a good one to propose. Buddhists have given it much consideration since the First Formic War, and I, in my time alone, have meditated a great deal on the subject as well. A Buddhist seeks enlightenment, to reach the full potential of the mind, to advance to the highest state of wisdom and compassion. This requires that we seek to alleviate all suffering around us, that we demonstrate kindness to all creatures in millions of forms throughout infinite universes, not just to the creatures that originate from our own community, but the creatures from all communities."

Dublin raised an eyebrow. "So you think we should be kind to the Formics? Even though they want to annihilate us?"

"As I said, it is a complicated question and a complicated answer," Wila said. "What is a Formic? Why did they come? Do we truly understand their mind? Is our own conscious mind fully awake on the subject? You say they want to annihilate us, but is that their goal?"

"They killed forty million people in China," Dublin said. "They murdered children and families indiscriminately. They would have kept going if we hadn't stopped them. Their intentions seem pretty obvious to me."

"Yes, to you," Wila said. "But would the Formics agree with your assessment? Would they think your interpretation of their motivations correct? I am not trying to defend their actions or condone the atrocities they committed. I only mean to propose that we do not understand the Formic mind. And until you understand the mind, you understand nothing."

Dublin frowned and scratched at the side of his mouth.

"I have upset you again," said Wila. "My apologies."

"Stop apologizing. You haven't upset me. I'm just surprised. I've never met anyone who takes the Formics' side before."

"You misunderstand me, Dr. Dublin. I do not take any creature's side. I merely seek to understand it. I cannot relieve the suffering of something I do not understand."

Dublin shrugged. "Well, no one here objects to learning more about the Formics or seeking to understand them. That's one of the purposes of this facility. But you'll be hard-pressed to find anyone else on board who wants to show the Formics any compassion."

"I recognize that my viewpoint is unique, Dr. Dublin. That is why I do not generally discuss it openly."

"I read your dissertation," said Dublin. "Or most of it anyway. There were some dry parts I skimmed over."

Wila suppressed a smile. Dublin was someone who had no clue how his candor could come off as offensive.

"You're not the only person to find fault with my dissertation," Wila said. "I was not awarded my degree."

He shrugged. "What's a piece of paper? As you said, it is the mind that matters. If you achieved greater enlightenment, who cares what the academic bozos think?"

Wila blinked, a little startled. "I have never looked at it from that perspective. Which is embarrassing since that is obviously the Buddhist perspective. Of course you are right. I see now that I allowed pride to keep me from reaching the same conclusion."

He waved her gratitude away. "Your theories on the Hive Queen. Some of them were fascinating. Some downright strange."

"They *should* seem strange. The Hive Queen is alien by definition. She evolved from a completely different protein structure. Every aspect of her life—physical, emotional, psychological, biological—should feel incongruent with our own."

"You speak as if her existence is an incontrovertible fact."

"Not at all," said Wila. "She is a theory. But we do have observational data to suggest that a being like the Hive Queen probably exists. It is a creature with mental abilities and influence unlike anything our planet has ever seen. Her mind can reach across vast distances instantaneously and command an army of Formics. And the power of that command is so strong that all Formics obey it without hesitation or resistance. The Hive Queen could be another species, certainly, but the more likely scenario is that she is an alpha of the same species. A super Formic of sorts. Nearly identical genetically to her offspring, but different enough to endow her with a heightened mental awareness and connectivity. She must be able to think for tens of thousands of her children at once. She sees what each Formic sees, and processes all that data simultaneously."

"So the Formics are her puppets."

"Puppet might be too strong of a word as that would imply absolute and total control. I think it more likely that the

Formics each have their own mental capacity. So she orders them to attack, but she doesn't dictate every swing of their weapon, or parry, or feint."

"Maybe they simply have a hive mind that self-governs," said Dr. Dublin. "Maybe their collected conscience is all there is. They are aware of each other and always act in the interest of the hive."

"Perhaps," said Wila. "But there are other signs that hint at a Hive Queen's existence. You are familiar with the disembowelment ritual that the Formics performed on slain humans?"

"I usually don't discuss it over a bowl of oatmeal, but yes. You mean when a Formic finds a human corpse, cuts open the stomach, and then reaches up inside the chest cavity."

"Any idea why they would do that?" Wila asked.

"I've heard theories," said Dublin. "None of them very convincing, truth be told. One idea is that the Formics are looking for the human heart so that they might squeeze it in a show of respect. A warrior's ritual, acknowledging the bravery of a slain enemy. Another idea is the opposite view, that they are desecrating our dead, mocking us. A third idea is that they are planting something inside the corpses, but a study of disemboweled people after the war found no evidence of that." He shrugged. "You have a theory?"

"What is the most valuable asset of any community?" Wila asked. "Particularly a warrior culture? What resource must they protect more than any other?"

Dublin shrugged. "Their food supply?"

"Their womb," said Wila. "If the women of their community cannot birth children, their culture will die out."

"You think the Formics cut people open looking for a womb? They disemboweled women as often as men. The Formics found wombs. And yet they kept looking. Rooting around inside women didn't slow their search."

"Ah. So you agree that they were searching for something," Wila said.

"It seemed that way," said Dublin. "It looked more like a search than a warrior ritual, at least."

"If the Hive Queen exists," said Wila. "And if she is the alpha of their species, the one who controls all others in her community, she is, in essence, the voice of her people. Agreed?"

Dublin nodded. "I suppose."

"And if she finds a species that is violently resistant to her wishes and is killing her offspring by the thousands, it stands to reason that she would want to communicate with that species. To demand their surrender, for example. Or to threaten them with worse destruction. Or to seek a truce. Or maybe even to send them a command like she does to her own soldiers. Wouldn't that make her life easier if she could simply send us a mental command and we would all obey it? Put down your weapons, humans. Stop this resistance. Take your own lives. Flee this land we are claiming for our own. Whatever. Many people in the war witnessed what came to be known as the 'stare.' Formics, when they cornered a human, often paused for a moment and fixed their gaze upon the individual before delivering the fatal blow. No one knows why. Personally, I believe in those instances the Hive Queen was trying to communicate with the individual. She was sending a mental command or message to the human. But of course our minds are not designed to receive it. She is screaming at us, and we are deaf to her cries."

"Possibly," agreed Dublin.

"And for the Hive Queen this would be infuriating and baffling," said Wila. "Why won't they answer? Why don't they respond? Maybe she even deems our behavior as a show of defiance. Maybe she believes we can hear her but are refusing to answer. But sooner or later she will begin to question herself. Can they hear me? Do they have the capacity to receive my commands? And so she orders her offspring to search for the Formic organ that receives the mental commands. The organ inside each one of them that enables them to receive her messages. The organ that has some biochemical process that sends messages to the Formic brain for processing. Just as our eyes take in light and send messages to our brains for processing."

"But if that's true," said Dublin, "then why do the Formics keep looking? The Formics would know after searching a single human that we don't have the organ. If they all share intelligence, then they would all have known that the organ isn't present as soon as the first Formic looked for it and failed to find it. There would be no reason to keep digging around inside other people."

Wila smiled. "Ah, but there is. If we entertain the idea that the Hive Queen is an alpha of her species, with capabilities beyond those of her children, then her anatomy would be different from that of her children. Just as the anatomy of queen bees or wasps or ants is different from their workers."

"So the Formics aren't looking for the receiver organ," said Dublin, "they're looking for the organ that can transmit. They're looking for our Hive Queen."

"That is my belief, yes," said Wila. "The Hive Queen is the queen of her hive. She is not the queen of her entire species. On her world, there are likely many Hive Queens. So she would be accustomed to communicating with alpha creatures like herself. She would negotiate with them, govern with them, perhaps even war against them. There would be communication among them. But with us, there is nothing. And the only explanation for that silence is that our Hive Queen must be dead. So she searches for that confirmation. Find me the Hive Queen, she says. She must be different from the others just as I am different from you. Find her so that I might study her and learn of her and understand this species."

Dublin sat back, his oatmeal finished. "An interesting theory. But of course it can't be proven."

"*Most* of what we assume about the Formics can't be proven," said Wila. "But that should not keep us from hypothesizing and testing what we can."

"The reason you were offered this job, Wila, was because of your theories on the hull construction and the idea that the Hive Queen uses a multitude of creatures to do her bidding and build her ships. Dr. Benyawe gave more credence to your theory than I did, but I've been on a holo with Lem Jukes for the past few hours and I think you might be on to something. Lem has gathered new intelligence on the asteroids the Formics have confiscated. I'm to call a meeting as soon as everyone is awake and get the entire staff working on this. I think involving everyone is a waste of time, though, because if anyone is going to understand this and figure it out, it's you."

He removed a data cube from his wrist pad and set it on the table in front of her. "Look over this and tell me what you think. What are we to understand from this? What are the Formics doing? What are these creatures doing? What is the Hive Queen planning?"

Dublin stood. "It's funny. As soon as the conference holo with Lem was over, I knew I needed to find you. And when I passed the cafeteria, heading toward my quarters, going a route I would not normally have taken, here you were, sitting by yourself under a single spotlight." He smiled and put his hands in the pockets of his lab coat. "I can't help but wonder if perhaps God isn't indifferent after all." He moved for the door. "I'll see you at the meeting. Get a jump on this if you can."

Wila picked up the data cube when he was gone. She should not have taken this job. They thought her more capable than she actually was. She was not an expert. She was a consumer and regurgitator of theories. Yes, she understood biochemistry, but it's not like she was the world's leading authority on the subject. And anyway, there was nothing biochemical under her microscope to explore.

She pocketed the data cube, tossed her cup in the trash, tucked her prayer book and tablet under her arm, and hurried to the top floor of the station. The porthole she frequented was in the ceiling of a small domed alcove with a wraparound padded bench and a few throw pillows. As many as eight or nine people could fit in here at once to study or meditate, but Wila had always found it unoccupied, as if it were her secret place of prayer. She slid the data cube into her tablet and went through all the videos, e-mails, reports, and data. Her heart leaped with she saw the grubs eat ice and then excrete pristine pellets of frozen water. She watched that segment again and again, marveling at how a creature could purify a substance at the molecular level and then refreeze that purified portion into a consistent stackable shape.

It was nothing short of miraculous. That such a creature existed was a marvel. That it operated in such a structured and ordered fashion left Wila nearly breathless. Had the Formics found this creature? No. Impossible. It had been engineered by the Hive Queen. Just as we would design and manufacture a machine for the task, the Hive Queen had built a biological factory.

And not only that, but here was further evidence of transspecies philotic communication. For who could doubt that the Hive Queen sent an impulse command to these creatures. Chew! Break down! Isolate elements! Freeze ice! Stack!

When Wila read the analysis of the metal pellets, however, she paused. One of the pellets was pure silicon, which was strange. Silicon was almost never found in its pure form, especially not on asteroids. It was found in various forms of silicon dioxide or silicate compounds. Stony asteroids consisted predominately of silicate minerals—olivine, pyroxene, enstatite, and hundreds of other minerals. So silicon would certainly be plentiful on an asteroid. But why would the Formics want it?

Wila set her tablet aside and lay back on the benches, staring up through the porthole at the Formic hull zipping past. Why silicon? The Formics weren't making semiconductors or integrated circuits, which is what we would use it for. We had studied their recovered vessels after the war and found no evidence of computers of any sort on board. Formic vessels were more mechanical in nature, sometimes rudimentarily so. And yet Victor's vid showed Formics harvesting a massive amount of silicon. More than any other metal, it seemed. And the Hive Queen would not harvest something she did not intend to use. The Hive Queen was many things, but wasteful wasn't one of them.

Wila considered what she knew about silicon. It was a tetravalent metalloid. Like carbon it usually formed four bonds, but unlike carbon it could take on additional electrons to form five or six bonds. The four-bond structure allowed it to combine with all sorts of elements and compounds. The most common partner was probably oxygen, forming silicon dioxide, or silica, a network solid that could form various stable crystal structures depending on the orientation of the tetrahedrons. Sand, quartz, glass, silica-based gels, ceramics, and countless others.

Silicon was also a component of some superalloys, incredibly strong metals that were resistant to thermal creep deformation, corrosion, or oxidation. Nanoparticle synthesis had allowed for the creation of a wide variety of new superalloys since the First Formic War, many of which were used by Juke Limited to build the fleet.

And of course there was biogenic silica excreted by siliceous sea sponges.

Wila paused at that thought. Sea sponges. If there was an animal on Earth that felt as alien as the Formics, it was the sea sponge. Their cells could transform into other types and migrate between the main cell layer and the mesohyl. They got their food and oxygen from the water that flowed through their central cavity, depositing nutrients along the way. And most importantly, their skeletons were often made of spicules of silicon dioxide. These tiny star-shaped spicules fused together into tightly woven structures that grew upward from the seafloor.

Wila considered this: animals that built and wove with silica.

Wila's thoughts returned to the pellets Victor had found. The purity of the silicon was very high, which was surprising. Normally such a pure state could only be achieved after repeated applications of refining technologies. And yet Victor had found no evidence of any refining process on the asteroid. No tools, no machines, just the bioengineered worms—leading Wila to assume that the silicon was formed in much the same way that the ice had been. Only instead of worms ingesting dirty ice to excrete pure ice, silicon-producing worms had ingested rock, separated the various minerals and elements in their gut, isolated the silicon, fused it together into a pellet, and then excreted the pellet into a pile. The process, if true, was even more astounding than the ice purifiers. How could a creature survive such a process? Human methods of refinement for silicon required electricity and intense heat and complex machines. But Formics were doing it with worms. A tiny, self-contained, independent, biochemical system. It was unfathomable.

Wila marveled yet again at the genius and power of the Hive Queen. Not only did the Hive Queen have a vast understanding of chemistry and molecular structures, but she also clearly understood how to manipulate those structures into desired states. And what was even more impressive was how she did it. She didn't operate out of a laboratory and rely upon highly sensitive computers that could detect and manipulate macromolecules; she built intelligent, living, breathing organisms to achieve those ends. It made Wila dizzy just to consider it. Nothing was more complex and intricate and massive in its scope than the genetic makeup of a living thing. It was miraculous to think that the Hive Queen could identify and understand macromolecules without the aid of computers, and it was even more miraculous that she could manipulate nucleic acids, proteins, and carbohydrates to achieve not just an animal, but an animal that could perform an incredibly complex chemical process. She hadn't just made a worm—which by itself was an achievement. She had made a worm that could do the impossible.

Here again was evidence that the theory of philotes might be correct, thought Wila. Somehow, down at the subatomic level, the Hive Queen was connected to her offspring. Her philotes were entwined or entangled with the philotes of her children, which is what allowed her to communicate with them instantaneously, to send them impulses and thoughts that they understood. And if that was true, if the Hive Queen had the ability to create such a connection with those she birthed, it stood to reason that she could also create that same connection with an organism she engineered. She could, in essence, build in the communication mechanism. Why not? If she knew how to create a worm that processed silicon, why couldn't she also engineer it to hear her thoughts?

Which planted another question in Wila's mind: Were the silicon-producing worms genetic derivatives of the Formics? Is that why the Hive Queen could so easily engineer them, because they were genetically similar to her own makeup? Were *all* the creatures the Hive Queen made derived from the Formic species? It was an interesting proposition, and one that Wila would have to explore at another time. Right now the focus was the silicon-producing worms.

Her mind returned to the sea sponge, which wove silicon dioxide into a structure. Was it conceivable, she thought, that the Hive Queen could engineer an organism that essentially did the same thing? A worm or creature of some sort that could ingest pure silicon and then weave it into some structure, excreting it out the back end in a continuous woven strand? Was that the reason for organizing the metals into pellets: to prepare the pellets for consumption? To make them easy for a creature to swallow them?

And then another thought hit her. If the worms had the ability to break down minerals in their gut and separate the various elements, was it also conceivable that a second creature could do the opposite? Could a second creature *ingest* silicon and other pellets of metal and combine them in the gut to form a unique compound or superalloy? If a worm could destroy and break apart, could another worm be engineered to assemble and build?

Five minutes ago she would have considered the idea ludicrous. Now the notion seemed conceivable. Maybe even likely. The Formic miniships that had reached these asteroids were tiny vessels capable of carrying only a few Formics and supplies. There was no room for drilling machines and building machines. There were the Formics and the worms. So the question that demanded an answer was: What could the Formics possibly accomplish with so little staff and supplies?

Wila felt certain she now had an answer. Or at least a possible theory. And the more she considered it, the more likely it seemed. The contents of the Formic miniship were all the supplies needed to turn an asteroid into a factory. Everything was there: raw materials, tools to harvest those raw materials, and maybe creatures that turned that raw material into something.

But if that were true, she thought, if the Formics were using those materials to build, why hadn't Victor found any construction outside the asteroid? And how could creatures build something in the vacuum of space anyway?

Because they're not building outside the asteroid, thought Wila. They're building *inside* it. The Formics were tunnelers.

They would tunnel. And those tunnels would lead somewhere. A central place. A nucleus. A core. But what would they be building? A habitat? A space station? A hatchery?

She set her tablet aside, sat in the lotus position on the bench, folded her hands in her lap, and closed her eyes, allowing herself to go into deep meditation now. Was this the way of enlightenment for the Hive Queen? Is this how she hoped to achieve the fully conscious mind and to connect herself with all creatures of the universe? By engineering them? By assembling them to her own desired specifications? By playing God?

Wila wasn't sure if she, as a Buddhist, should find the idea fascinating or revolting. On one hand it aligned with Buddhist doctrine, but on the other hand it perverted it. The fully conscious mind was omnipotent, yes, with effortless power to do whatever needed to be done to benefit all life in the universe. But what were the boundaries of this pursuit? When did the righteous quest for enlightenment cross over into something evil? The Hive Queen appeared to be connecting with all creatures in the universe, but only because she was eradicating all those who could not hear her voice. Was that her goal? Did she intend to replace all creatures with only those philotically linked with her, thus allowing her, by definition, to achieve the omnipotent mind?

It was wrong. It was fanatical. It was corrupt and twisted and profane, and Wila wanted to believe that the Hive Queen simply didn't understand, that her alien mind saw a perspective that Wila could not yet see.

And yet there was no excuse for the destruction the Hive Queen had caused. How could she get so close to enlightenment while violating its foundational principle of fostering peace, compassion, and harmony among all species? It was as if the Hive Queen found herself at two ends of the spectrum. On one end she was the greatest example of the awakened, fully conscious mind. But on the other end, she was the most dispassionate, soulless murderer ever conceived.

Wila was not sure how long she sat there and meditated. Two hours? Three? She would miss the staff meeting with Dr. Dublin, but she wanted to feel right about where her mind had taken her. She wanted to feel at peace. And so she considered her theories from every angle and possibility, taking them apart bit by bit and analyzing every piece. She replayed Victor's vids in her mind. She pictured the ice slug. Would the slug that mined silicon look the same? And what about the creatures that would use that silicon? What might they build with it? A habitat? A nursery? A throne for the queen?

And then she pictured the Hive Queen, the alpha of her species. She would be beautiful and horrible, majestic and terrifying, glorious and nightmarish. Do you hear me? Wila asked with her mind. Lady. Ruler. Queen of your kind. Can you sense my reaching? Do my philotes entwine with yours? Is there even a single thread between us? If so, feel my desire for peace.

Wila waited but heard nothing. Felt nothing.

Then she picked up her tablet, straightened her robes, and walked down the corridor toward Dr. Dublin's office, bowing courteously to everyone she passed.

# CHAPTER 22

# TAGAT

**Ansible transmission between the Hegemon and Polemarch, Office of the Hegemony Sealed Archives, Imbrium, Luna, 2118**

KETKAR: Dividing the Fleet is a mistake. Moving our ships outside the ecliptic is even more of a mistake. What you're suggesting is suicide.

UKKO: There are numerous reasons why we should strike now. We've been over this many times. I am not alone in this position. Most of the senior staff at CentCom agree with me.

KETKAR: Most of the senior staff at CentCom are bureaucratic clods. They would agree that the world is flat if they thought you were taking that position. That's all the IF is at that level. And I assure you, if we stage a preemptive strike against those warships, we will lose. We do not have the firepower or numbers to win, particularly if we divide the Fleet. We would be vaporized. And then what? The few ships left behind will ward off the entire Formic fleet?

UKKO: If you won't do this, I have an obligation to find someone who will.

KETKAR: Who? The Russians? You're going to give in
    to Russian bullying and let them dictate who leads
    this Fleet? You don't want a commander, you want
    a lapdog.
UKKO: I want a victory.

Less than a week after his arraignment, Mazer was back in
court to begin his trial. The five members of the jury were
seated to his left, eyeing him as if they already thought him
guilty. Colonel Soshi was seated beneath the seal of the International Fleet at the front of the courtroom, wearing his
judge's robes and looking irritated. "Commander Ravenshaw,
because of an apparent conflict in scheduling, we were forced
to move up this proceeding. Do you have any objections?"

Ravenshaw stood at the prosecutor's table, looking far less
contemptuous than he had a week ago. "No objections, sir."

"Very well," said Soshi. He turned to the jury platform. "I
wish to extend a special apology to the members of the jury,
who weren't given much notice of their duty in these proceedings, but who came willingly nonetheless. Thank you for your
patience, gentlemen."

Mazer thought that an amusing comment since the men
were here only because they had been ordered to attend, and
not due to any willingness on their part.

Soshi turned back to the court. "Any housekeeping items
before we begin?"

"Yes, sir," said Ravenshaw. "Permission to approach the
bench, sir."

Colonel Soshi waved Ravenshaw forward, and the two of
them had a whispered conversation. Mazer and Chamrajnagar exchanged a glance. The officers serving as the
jury looked bored.

Finally Ravenshaw retreated, and Colonel Soshi turned to
the jury again. "Gentlemen, I owe you a second apology. The

prosecutor has informed me that because of alleged threats to his witnesses, they have refused to testify and have recanted their sworn statements. The International Fleet, therefore, has no evidence to present in this case. As a result, the court has no choice but to acquit Captain Rackham of all charges." Soshi turned to Mazer, his eyes narrowing. "However, I am placing a formal letter of reprimand on your record, Captain Rackham, and inviting your commanding officer to offer whatever nonjudicial punishment he deems appropriate. You may threaten people outside this court, but I will not be intimidated by some insubordinate thug who makes a mockery of our military judicial system."

Prem was on her feet in an instant. "Sir. You are passing judgment on Captain Rackham before a jury, claiming he has threatened witnesses and committed a serious crime, which is a completely false and unfounded accusation—"

"Sit down, Lieutenant," Soshi said.

"—without one grain of evidence."

"I said sit down!"

"The prosecutor doesn't even *have* any witnesses to begin with. And never did."

Soshi banged his gavel. "You will sit down, Lieutenant, or I will find you in contempt."

Mazer put a gentle hand on Prem's, and she reluctantly sat down.

"I will also remind you, Lieutenant," Soshi said, "that I am a colonel in the International Fleet. Your outburst and flagrant disregard for authority have earned you a letter of reprimand as well. I see that you and Captain Rackham here are well suited for one another. I will take no pleasure in drafting those letters, but I consider it my duty to identify those among us who disrespect our order, obstruct our progress, and thereby threaten the safety of the free people of Earth." He picked up his tablet and read. "Let the record show that concerning the charges against Captain Mazer Rackham—

namely espionage, aggravated assault, failure to obey a lawful order, and conduct unbecoming an officer—the court finds the defendant not guilty on all counts."

He struck his gavel. "Sergeant, please escort the jury out. They are excused. Thank you for your time, gentlemen. We apologize for the inconvenience Captain Rackham and Lieutenant Chamrajnagar have caused you."

The sergeant at arms came forward and asked that everyone stand and come to attention while he led the jury out. When they had all exited, Soshi and Ravenshaw swept from the room without a word, leaving Prem and Mazer alone in the courtroom.

Prem shook her head, furious. "What a joke."

"You can get your letter expunged," said Mazer. "There's a recording of this proceeding. I'll write a letter of commendation. Not everyone at JAG can be as corrupt as Soshi."

"I'm not worried about the letter," said Prem. "I'm mad at this offensive display of human idiocy."

"It's the outcome we wanted," said Mazer. "More or less. Who cares if they made a show of it."

"I care. And they did more than make a show of it, Mazer. They implied that you had committed a crime and then basically pronounced you guilty before five senior officers. Which is deceptive and misleading and makes a mockery of the court. They didn't have any witnesses except for Nardelli, and he wasn't going to testify anyway. They knew we'd sink him on cross-examination. They could have dropped the charges at any moment. But no, they had to actually conduct a court-martial so that it stained your record. They did it out of spite. Then Sochi has the audacity to apologize for the inconvenience we caused the jury? Unbelievable."

"It's over, Prem. That's what matters."

"If these senior officers knew anything about the law, they'd know that they just witnessed a farce. Ravenshaw could've filed a continuance. He could've spoken with Soshi before the court came to session. He could've done any number of things. But does he? No. He pretends his witnesses were threatened and limps into court like a wounded animal, all so he and Soshi can burn you while they acquit you. They can't acknowledge that they're stooges and tools of higher powers, so they humiliate you in front of five senior commanders. This wasn't justice, Mazer. And this certainly isn't why I joined JAG."

"Then do something about it," said Mazer.

Prem shrugged. "How? I can't fight these people."

"You don't have to. That's not your job. A soldier's job is to learn her duty and do it as well as she is able. You want to shut these people down? Then be the best attorney you can be. Ravenshaw and Soshi will try to make your life hell, and I can't help but feel responsible for that, but any energy you exert toward them is a waste. They're not worth your time or attention. The only enemy is the Formics. Soshi and Ravenshaw are worms, and sooner or later all worms get stepped on. Ignore them."

"Aren't you angry?"

"I'm furious. But I'm still wearing my courtroom face." He pointed to his flat, emotionless expression.

She smiled, shook her head, and started packing her things. "Some lawyer I turned out to be."

"We won," said Mazer. "You're probably the only attorney at JAG with a perfect case record."

"*You* won this," she said. "And not through legal channels, through back channels."

"No soldier operates alone, Prem. *We* did this. I owe you my thanks." He extended a hand and she shook it.

"So this is good-bye then?" she asked.

"For the moment," said Mazer. "But I'm hoping you'll have dinner with me and Kim again once this is all over."

"Only if we have some of that stir-fry again. And hey, keep

your eye open for my family. I have a lot of brothers and uncles in the IF."

"I'll tell them you saved my bacon."

He saluted her, and she saluted back.

They parted and Mazer made his way to the hospital. He texted Kim when he reached the lobby, and she met him at the big fountain ten minutes later. She was nearing the end of her shift, having worked through the night in the ER, and she looked exhausted. "I wasn't expecting you for a couple hours," she said. "Are they breaking for lunch already?"

"They broke permanently," he said. "I was acquitted."

She sighed, relieved, and embraced him. When they parted he saw a hint of disappointment in her smile.

"You're not happy," he said. "You wanted me discharged."

"Is it wrong of me to want my husband safe and by my side? To have a normal job, to be out of this mess?"

"We're all in this mess, Kim. Not just the people in the IF. We simply have different responsibilities." A silence stretched between them. "How are you feeling?" he finally asked. "Any more headaches?"

Kim would always get migraines at the start of every pregnancy. A few days ago, a nagging headache had emerged, and they had both taken it as a good sign.

She shook her head. "My cycle started this morning, Mazer. I'm most definitely not pregnant."

He took Kim into his arms and held her. Not pregnant. The words rattled around inside his head, but he couldn't help but feel a small measure of relief as well. He desperately wanted a child. But the idea of Kim raising one alone while the Formics descended upon them had filled him with terror.

Why had he worked so hard to move up the date of the court-martial? Why had he rushed to put an end to it? At the time it had seemed like the logical course of action. It was the soldier in him. When there's a problem, you fix it as soon as possible. You tear down the obstacle and you advance toward your objective. But now that rationale seemed shortsighted because now he had no legitimate legal reason to stay on Luna with Kim. Their time had been so brief, and now, when she needed his support the most, he was suddenly eligible for reassignment.

"I should have let them drag it out," he said. "I should've let them stall. We could have had more time."

She ended the embrace, wiped at her eyes, and took a deep breath, doing her best to smile. "That's not in your nature, Maze. You did what needed to be done. I'm fine. Really. I'm just tired. It's been a rough night." She paused, studying his face. "When will you report to CentCom?"

Now that the trial was over, he would have to present himself at headquarters, where he would either receive orders to return to WAMRED or accept a new assignment.

"I was supposed to have gone immediately," he said. "I came here instead."

They both knew that anything could happen. His fate, the fate of their family, would be determined by the whim of someone else in uniform.

"Maybe you'll get an assignment here," she said.

"Doubtful."

"Why not? You could train soldiers. You have experience. You fought the Formics in a lot of different scenarios. Few people can say that. Maybe they'll keep you here at CentCom, teaching new recruits. Isn't that where the best soldiers go, into some teaching position?"

"Decorated officers nearing retirement get teaching positions, Kim. I'm a young, court-martialed officer with a scathing letter of reprimand. The last thing the IF wants is me corrupting young soldiers."

Kim's mouth became a hard line. "It isn't fair, Mazer. After everything you've done for them, everything you've sacrificed. If not for you, Earth might belong to the Formics right now. And they treat you like a criminal? They scorn you, when all you have ever given them is your full allegiance? Why do you tolerate these people?"

Her voice had risen, and there was a lot of foot traffic in the lobby now. A few people looked in their direction. Mazer gently took Kim's hand and led her to a door to their right. The room was a small, dimly lit chapel, with three rows of pews and an aisle down the middle. A large backlit stained-glass window adorned the front, featuring a religiously ambiguous mosaic of flowers and plant life, the colors of which dappled the walls with spots of green and yellow and red. The pews were empty.

Mazer sat in the back pew to his left, scooted in, and patted the seat next to him.

She hesitated. "People come in here to pray, you know."

"If they do, we'll pretend we're praying until they leave."

She sat beside him.

"They're going to send me away, Kim. We both know that. Probably to the Belt. Vaganov won't want me back at WAMRED. I'm a thorn in his side. I suspect he lost a lot of respect there because of how he discarded me. He won't want my face around. That would aggravate the wound."

Kim didn't look at him. "What does that mean? This asteroid-assault-team idea of yours?"

"Maybe. I don't know. I don't make the decisions."

She looked at him then. "And if you could make the decisions? What then? Would you choose to stay?"

"Of course I would stay, Kim. Do you have to ask? I can do good here. Administration isn't my strong suit, but I can do it as well as anyone else. And I'll ask for it. I'll put in a request. But it won't matter. It's not going to happen. I'm special forces. They will put me in the field. I don't get a choice in the matter. They own me."

"Which is why I hate them," she said.

"The Fleet exists because it has to, Kim. If you want to

hate someone, hate the Formics. If not for them, we'd be in New Zealand right now with three kids."

She laughed. "Three? That's ambitious, considering how long we've been married. I'd be popping them out one right after another. Breastfeeding two at once, changing eighty diapers a day."

"With the precision of a surgeon," he said.

"You'd be changing most of those diapers, you know."

"I wouldn't need to," said Mazer. "Our children will be potty trained by the time they're three months old."

"They can't even crawl at three months, Mazer. They can't reach the toilet."

"I'd build a ramp," said Mazer. "We'd run drills. I'd put them through a modified basic training, only focused on bathroom duties. And they wouldn't call it peepee and poopoo either. No silliness. We'd have military names. Like Operation Thunder Bladder. They'd rappel down from the crib, do a few combat rolls across the nursery floor, take out an enemy teddy bear or two, and then charge toward the bathroom in full camo paint."

"A baby's skin is too sensitive for camo paint," said Kim. "Other than that, it sounds like a plan."

He smiled. "Our children *will* be brilliant, though. With you as their mother, how could they not be."

She looked at his face, her expression serious. "Promise to be smart, Mazer. No heroics, okay? No unnecessary risks. Don't volunteer for anything. Don't do anything stupid."

"I'll be smart," he said. "But I have to do what I've been trained to do. That's how I'll stay alive. If I abandon that, if I put my safety above that of my unit, I put everyone at risk, including myself."

He took her hands. "And now I have a request for you. Don't stay on Luna, Kim. If they send me out, get back to Earth. Some place remote. Back to New Zealand maybe. If the Formics break through, the island will be ignored for a while. Maybe forever. Maybe they won't bother the people there at all."

She considered that and nodded. Then she laid her head on his shoulder and Mazer held her as he watched the colored light on the wall.

"How long will you be gone?" she asked. "How long is a tour?"

"No one knows. But if they send me to the Belt, I suspect I'll be there for a while."

"I'm not mad at you, Mazer. I don't want you going away thinking that's what I'm feeling right now. What I feel is love."

He smiled. "I wish there was a better word for love, Mrs. Rackham. What I feel for you, what you feel for me, love feels too small."

They sat in silence for a while, simply enjoying being together, holding each other, and then Kim's wrist pad began to vibrate. "They're calling me back downstairs."

"They won't send me out immediately," said Mazer. "I'll see you tonight."

They kissed and parted. Kim went downstairs. Mazer left the hospital and took a car across town to CentCom. In typical military fashion, the building was bland, unadorned, and dated. There were two stories here above the surface, but the majority of the building, like so many other agencies, was underground. Mazer wasn't sure how far the tunnels went, but it was said that the IF had been digging and expanding since the war.

Mazer entered and passed through security. The guard who scanned him received an alert on his tablet. "Captain Rackham, I have a message here that says you are to report to LOG 41 when you arrive."

"Thank you," said Mazer.

LOG was short for Logistics. They were the team that organized all troop and cargo movements. LOG 41 would be cubicle 41 in the department. Mazer went to the elevators and went down four levels; then he weaved through the labyrinth that was CentCom until he reached the sea of cubicles that was the logistics department. It was a busy, bustling space, with several dozen holo conversations going on at once all around him. A huge starchart on the far wall featured an overheard perspective of the solar system, with blinking dots of lights and icons, tracking the movement of ships.

Mazer proceeded down the aisles, passing soldiers at small desks, hard at work. Some wore visors with direct links to their terminals. Everyone seemed harried and on high alert, and the mood in the room was tense. Something was happening, Mazer realized. Or about to happen.

He stopped and studied the starchart. There was nothing in the ships' positions on the charts that suggested any organized movement; they were scattered dots of light on the display, without any pattern to them. But Mazer could sense from the energy in the room and the brief bits of chatter he was picking up as he moved about that everything was about to change.

We're going after the Formic warships, he realized. We're planning to divide the Fleet into two and send them above and below the ecliptic. We're taking the fight to the Formics.

If he was right it would be a massive undertaking. There were supplies to gather, weapons to modify and prepare, crews to train, assaults and tactics and battle plans to coordinate. Plus there were issues, too. For one, there was the problem of fuel. Most of the ships got their fuel from water harvested from ice off of asteroids. But there were no asteroids outside the ecliptic. Or at least not many. There were some with crazy angled orbits, and there were comets out there as well if you knew where to find them, but recovering those asteroids and comets would be a challenge. Ships would have to follow a zigzag trajectory, moving from one comet to the next to harvest ice. Otherwise, they wouldn't have the fuel necessary to get them out there and back again.

We're not ready, Mazer thought. We can't penetrate the Formic hull, and if we don't take out their ships, how can we possibly win?

He found cubicle 41 in the back corner. It was separated from the others and encased in a soundproof tube. The tube was opaque, but Mazer could see the shape of someone seated at a desk inside. He knocked, and the tube slid open, revealing a young officer at a computer terminal smiling up at him. "Captain Rackham. Won't you have a seat?" He motioned to the empty chair across from him.

Mazer stepped in and sat down. The space was cramped. He and the officer were practically touching knees under the table. The door slid closed, and immediately the noise from outside was eliminated.

"Little loud out there today," the officer said, still smiling.

"What's happening?" Mazer asked. "It looks like we're planning an offensive."

"Oh, they've been planning that for quite some time now, sir. Now they're getting the ball rolling. Please state your full name and military ID number."

"Captain Mazer no-middle-name Rackham. 7811231002."

The officer kept his eyes on the terminal screen. "Thank you, sir. One moment."

"Any chance I could request a local assignment?" Mazer asked. "One that would keep me here on Luna?" He knew it was pointless, but he had told Kim he would ask.

"Sorry, sir. Your assignment has already been issued. You're to report to Colonel Li at shuttledock fourteen."

"Shuttledock? Am I to fly out immediately?"

The officer typed at his holoscreen and then looked apologetic. "I'm sorry, sir. The only information I can access here is that Colonel Li was only recently promoted. The system doesn't tell me any more than that, including your specific assignment or your final destination. My guess is this operation is classified. Sorry I can't be more helpful. Just follow the red line on your wrist pad."

Mazer's wrist pad chimed, and the floor plan of the building appeared on the viewscreen. A red line indicated the path he should take. The tube door slid open. He was being dismissed. Mazer stepped out, and the door slid closed behind him again. He followed the red path to a subway platform, where a queue of empty subway cars waited off to the side. The front car came to life as he approached, and its door slid open. Mazer stepped to the end of the platform first and looked to his right. The tunnel seemed to go on forever in that direction, and for a moment Mazer debated whether he should get in the car or not. If they were sending him to a dock, they were shipping him out, right now. He wouldn't see Kim before this tour. He wouldn't have a proper good-bye. The subway car stood open and waiting. Mazer had not expected this. He had assumed he would have at least a day or two before the IF figured out what to do with him and arranged his passage. But here he was, with only the clothes on his back. He turned and regarded the door he had come through. He could go back out, but where would he go from there?

He hesitated a moment longer, then climbed into the first car and buckled the safety strap. The car slowly pulled onto the track and then shot away into the darkness.

Twenty minutes later the car pulled into a busy shuttle terminal. Mazer exited the car and took in his surroundings. IF work crews in safety uniforms were loading freight onto shuttles docked at the gates. Mazer counted ten gates, and all of them were occupied, which likely meant that a steady stream of cargo was moving out of here all day. As soon as one shuttle was full and departed, another empty shuttle took its place.

The work crews shouted orders, drove cargo lifts, honked

horns of warning, and moved around each other in a frenzy. Like mechanized worker bees, each doing his part in a fast-paced frenetic system.

A honk behind Mazer caused him to jump and step quickly aside. A worker driving a cargo lift loaded with freight zipped past and nodded his thanks.

"Captain Rackham."

Mazer turned. A thin Chinese officer approached from the other direction. He had colonel bars on his shoulders, and Mazer came to attention and saluted.

"I am Colonel Li. Welcome to TAGAT, short for Tactical Asteroid Guerilla Assault Team. Or TAG for short. The military has an acronym for everything, and we are no exception."

"Thank you, sir. It was kind of you to come out and greet me yourself. And I'm glad to hear the IF has a solution to the asteroid problem."

"Not a solution. An approach. And it's one you've greatly influenced. We will likely be using much of the equipment you sold to Gungsu and Juke."

So they knew about the deals, Mazer thought. He had only made them a week ago, and the IF had already seen the equipment—or the plans for it—and approved it for the field. A quick turnaround. That was optimistic.

"Whether or not our tactics will work is yet to be determined," said Li. "We're making this up as we go along, and we'll continue to develop strategies en route as we move out to the Belt. But come, if we stay out here we're likely to get run over."

Mazer followed Li through a set of double doors to their right and through a locker room no doubt used by the loading crews.

"You probably don't remember me," said Li. "But we met once. Briefly. Back at Dragon's Den, in China, the day Bingwen and the other MOPs came into the base. I was a young and cocky lieutenant trying to make a name for myself. I had a chip on my shoulder, as they say in America."

It took Mazer a moment to place him. "I remember you, yes."

Li smiled. "We had an awkward first meeting, Captain, but I'd like to think we're both a little older and wiser now. I speak Common much better than I did then, for example."

"You speak it impeccably," said Mazer.

"The language of the IF," said Li. "Learn it or perish. Had China been a little more cooperative from the beginning, perhaps we'd all be speaking Chinese."

He reached another set of double doors and pushed his way through. They entered what had once been a large concrete cargo hold, perhaps a holding area for freight being shipped out in the shuttles. Now however the room served as makeshift barracks. Bunk beds lined the walls on both sides, the bedding tight and immaculate. The floor in the center of the room was covered with foam sparring pads. A dozen young men ages twelve or thirteen were paired off on the pads, conducting hand-to-hand combat exercises, tossing each other to the floor. The boy nearest the door shouted, "Officer on deck!"

The young men immediately fell into two facing lines and came to attention, motionless. Their speed and response time was impressive.

"What do you think of our little army, Captain?" asked Li.

Mazer understood at once. "You're intending to send them into the narrow tunnels on the asteroids."

"Of course," said Li. "The tunnels are too small for grown men. Maybe not you, of course. You're rather small. But even you would have trouble with most of the tunnels we've seen. Small boys from Southeast Asia, however, will have a much easier time maneuvering in that space. Our genetics are built for this type of work. Bingwen. Front and center."

Mazer's heart leaped in his chest as one of the young men in the back ran forward, a boy Mazer hadn't yet noticed. He was older and taller and maybe even a little thinner than Mazer remembered, with his hair shaved tight to his scalp, but it was Bingwen. The boy sprinted forward without looking at Mazer and snapped to attention in front of Colonel Li, his face free of emotion. "Bingwen reporting, Colonel Li, sir."

"Do you recognize this officer, Bingwen?" Li asked, gesturing to Mazer.

Bingwen didn't turn his head or so much as glance at Mazer. "Yes sir, Colonel Li, sir. That is Captain Mazer Rackham, sir."

"You know Captain Rackham well?"

"Yes sir, Colonel Li, sir. He helped me during the First Formic War, sir."

"And Bingwen here saved my life as well," Mazer said, smiling.

"I have not given you permission to speak, Captain Rackham," said Li. "You will address a senior officer only when he poses a direct question. Otherwise you will request permission to speak when I am addressing another soldier. Do I make myself clear?"

Mazer raised an eyebrow. Was this a joke?

"Perhaps you are hard of hearing," said Colonel Li. "I asked you a direct question, Captain Rackham. Your duty is to offer a direct answer."

Mazer glanced at Bingwen. The boy hadn't so much as blinked. What hell have they put you through? Mazer wondered. He turned back to Colonel Li. "You've made yourself very clear, Colonel. May I speak with you in private please?"

Colonel Li looked annoyed. There was no hard and fast rule about honoring a fellow officer's request for private conversation, but usually officers agreed to it as a professional courtesy.

Li turned to his young army. "No one move."

He walked out of the barracks and into a small adjacent office with glass windows. Mazer followed him inside.

Li folded his arms. "Do you have a problem with how I run my army, Captain Rackham? If you have objections, let's hear them."

Mazer hesitated. He was walking on thin ice here, and he strongly suspected that whatever he said would only anger Li further. "Sir, it is my understanding that the recruitment and use of children during armed conflict is a war crime."

"You are a poor student of history," said Li. "Children have taken a direct part in war for centuries. Soldiers, spies, messengers, lookouts. Name a country, and I will cite to you the wars and rulers who have employed child soldiers. The list is long and may surprise you, and it includes those nations of the West who consider themselves above reproach, nations who scorn the rest of the world for the practice when they themselves are guilty of the act. Look at the Romans, the Crusades, the Napoleonic Wars, both world wars, the American Civil War, Africa, the Middle East; from the moment man first raised a spear to defend his campfire, we have been employing children in war."

"Yes, but that does not make the practice morally acceptable, sir. I'd like to think we're a little more civilized now than we were during the wars you mention."

Li laughed. "Civilized? When has war ever been civilized, Captain? War, by its very definition, is barbaric and horrific and the very antithesis of civility."

"All the more reason to protect children from it," said Mazer.

"You surprise me, Captain. I was told you had strategic prowess, that you had an innate ability to tackle difficult obstacles with a mind open to nonconventional tactics. I see now that such praise was mistaken."

"The additional protocol to the Geneva Conventions states that no one under the age of fifteen can be recruited or participate in armed conflict," said Mazer. "Are we ignoring the Geneva Conventions now?"

"Tell me, Captain. When they sat down around the tables in Geneva over a century ago, did they know about the Formics? Did they know that an alien race would one day seek to melt the flesh from our bones with biochemical weapons designed to destroy all biota on Earth? Did these military commanders, these wise men—who you clearly consider the only people in the history of the world capable of making moral judgments on our behalf—did they see what we would face? Did they know the threat that was coming? And perhaps more importantly, would they have made an exception to their own ethics if failing to do so meant the annihilation of our species? Because that's the question here, Captain Rackham. That's the cold hard ugly truth of the matter. If we lose, there will be no children. None. No infants, no toddlers, no preschoolers, no kids blissfully running around the playgrounds of Earth. They will each be a bloody stain and pile of bones if we don't win.

"What are you willing to do to protect them, Captain? Would you rather safeguard these twelve young men here before me? Would you rather preserve *their* lives than save the billions of people on Earth? Is that your logic? We wouldn't want Bingwen here to get nightmares and be scared, so let's step back and watch Earth burn." Li shook his head. "No. That thinking does not hold water with me, Captain. This is not a war of easy choices. We will not win by following dated rules that were created without an awareness of our unique circumstances. Do you think the Formics live by some ethical code? Do you think they will withhold any advantage because of some convention convened in their past? You served in China, Captain. You saw what these bastards do to innocent people. My people. My homeland. Are you telling me that you're not willing to do whatever is necessary to annihilate them?

"And frankly, Captain Rackham, I find your objection rather hypocritical. You were the one who first took Bingwen into conflict. Was he not your guide to the Formic lander during the First Formic War? You steered him into battle, you dragged him into war. Not once, but many times. And when you were arrested by the Chinese military, your fellow MOPs made Bingwen one of their own. This boy, this *child*, as you call him, saw more action under your direction than have most soldiers of the International Fleet. I find that far more morally reprehensible than the sins you're throwing upon me. So don't stand there and pretend to occupy some moral high ground, Captain. You are far guiltier of this *crime* than I am."

Mazer said nothing. What could he say? Li was right about Bingwen. Mazer had put him in danger. Mazer had tried desperately to remove Bingwen from conflict, but the circumstances thrust upon them had prevented that from happening.

"We're done here," said Li. He stepped out of the office, and Mazer followed.

"Tell me, Bingwen," said Li loud enough for everyone to hear. "Captain Rackham here doesn't think you're worthy to be a soldier. He thinks you're a useless child. He thinks you don't deserve to be in the IF. What do you say to that?"

"I must respectfully disagree with Captain Rackham, sir."

"You would like to show him that you're a soldier, wouldn't you, Bingwen?" Colonel Li asked.

"Yes, sir, Colonel Li, sir. I would consider it an honor, sir."

"Very well," said Li. "Then we shall grant you your request." He turned to Mazer. "Captain Rackham, you will spar with Bingwen and allow him to show you that he is worthy to be called a soldier."

Mazer hesitated. "Sir, with all due respect, I don't think that's a good idea."

"Are you questioning my authority, Captain Rackham? Are you refusing to follow a lawful, direct order? Considering your recent court-martial, one would think you would be a little more submissive to authority."

Nothing Mazer could say would change Li's mind. He would not recant his orders in front on his men and lose face. He would dig in, and Mazer would only make things worse for himself and for Bingwen. His only choice was to accept.

"You're right, Colonel," said Mazer. "I beg your pardon. A demonstration of Bingwen's prowess would certainly help me understand your perspective better."

Li smiled, victorious. And for an instant Mazer saw something else in the man's eyes as well: an eagerness to see a confrontation, a hunger for a fight.

Mazer removed his shoes and stepped out onto the mat. He was still wearing his class-As, which weren't designed for flexibility, but they would have to do. "Well, Bingwen. You've clearly been practicing a lot more than I have, but I'll warn you. I'm taller, heavier, and I won't go easy on you."

Mazer spread his feet apart, assuming a relaxed fighting position, waiting.

Bingwen turned to him and joined him on the mat, facing him, his expression still flat, as if Mazer meant nothing to him.

Then, a heartbeat later, Bingwen attacked. Mazer hopped back as Bingwen advanced with a series of kicks aimed directly at Mazer's groin. Powerful kicks, relentless. Bingwen knew he had a stronger opponent and that his only chance was to target where Mazer was the weakest. Mazer blocked a kick with his leg, then another with his hand, then he grabbed Bingwen's foot and flipped him over.

Bingwen landed hard on the mat, and Mazer saw a flicker of anger in Colonel Li's face. Mazer had to keep it going and show no mercy, he realized. He only hoped Bingwen would seize the opportunity when it came. Bingwen sprang back to his feet.

Mazer laughed. "Is that what they teach you, Bingwen? To kick a man where he's most vulnerable? Good. You're a soldier. Your job is to win, not to play fair."

The second attack came. Mazer hopped away again, moving to his left in a wide circle on the mat, acting as if he were enjoying himself. Three more kicks from Bingwen. Mazer blocked them all. "Predictable, Bingwen. You're showing me a pattern. You've got three good kicks you use too often. Everything else is weak and insubstantial. Or maybe you're going easy on me."

Two more kicks, easily blocked.

"I certainly won't go easy on you," said Mazer, stepping aside to dodge a punch. Another punch immediately followed, but he twisted again, grabbed Bingwen's wrist, pulled him off balance and landed a stunning flat-palmed blow into Bingwen's chest.

Bingwen staggered back, the wind knocked from his lungs. He clutched at his chest, but he stayed on his feet, half bent forward, desperate for air. For a moment Mazer thought he had hit him too hard.

Mazer continued to rotate around the circle until his back was to Colonel Li. "If we keep this up, I'm going to hurt you, Bingwen," said Mazer. "Better give up now and save yourself some bruises."

Bingwen's face hardened into a grimace and he assumed a new fighting stance.

"Persistent," said Mazer. "I commend you for that. Especially against a stronger opponent. But a soldier must also know when to retreat. You sure you don't want to call it? Or maybe you want to invite two of your friends to help you?"

Mazer then gave Bingwen a subtle wink, one that Colonel Li couldn't see, and he hoped Bingwen would understand its meaning.

Bingwen did, because his fastest and fiercest attack fol-

lowed. Now there was no pattern to the volley of kicks and
punches. Everything he had done before this moment had
been a feint. Now there was real power, as if Bingwen had held
himself in reserve until this moment. Mazer scrambled to his
left, dodging, deflecting, retreating. An opening came, and
Mazer took it, as any soldier would. He kicked out, but Bingwen was already dropping to the floor, anticipating the attack, and sweeping with his leg, connecting with the one
foot Mazer was standing on. Mazer didn't have to pretend to
fall. His balance was off, and he went down.

But he knew better than to lose at this moment. That would
be too obvious. He had to appear wounded and angry first.
He had to show Li a progression in his emotions for Li to
believe it. Arrogance, then surprise, then rage, then humility.
This was surprise.

Mazer cursed under his breath, then rolled away and was
back up in a crouched position, furious. Bingwen didn't pause
in the attack, as Mazer knew he wouldn't. And Bingwen
charged with an animalistic ferocity. Kick, block, kick, block,
punch, block, sweep, jump, kick, dodge, punch, block, kick—

Mazer grunted as Bingwen's foot connected with Mazer's
side. Nothing broke, but Bingwen wasn't pulling any punches.

Mazer retreated and kicked out, which Bingwen easily
dodged. Mazer gripped at his side, wincing a little, his mouth
a thin hard line. Then the fourth attack came, and Bingwen
upped his assault even further, which Mazer hadn't anticipated, and which he found pleasantly surprising. Whoever
had trained him, had trained him exceptionally well.

Mazer knocked him down, but Bingwen was right back up
again, not even pausing for breath. Again, Mazer knocked
him down. Now, Bingwen, he wanted to say. Do it now.

Mazer repeated the same move, to knock Bingwen to the
mat, but this time Bingwen anticipated the move and rolled
to the side, spinning and ramming his elbow hard into Mazer's

gut. Mazer buckled and dropped to his knees, gripping his stomach, then he lifted his head high enough to see Bingwen's foot right as it connected with the side of Mazer's face.

Mazer's head snapped to the side, and his whole body twisted and fell back to the mat. He tasted blood in his mouth. His lip was busted, his head was ringing. His jaw wasn't broken, but he'd have a facial bruise. He raised a hand meekly. "Yield."

Colonel Li came over and offered him a hand. Mazer took it and slowly got to his feet, making no effort to wipe away the blood on his lip.

Colonel Li smiled. "What do you think of our army now, Captain?"

"I'd say I almost feel sorry for the Formics." He opened his mouth, testing the flexibility of his jaw.

Colonel Li laughed. Bingwen was already standing at attention again, eyes forward like a robot.

Oh, Bingwen, Mazer thought. Is this what you've dealt with for three years? Is this what they've done to you?

"You're not going to beat anyone with fancy martial arts, though," said Mazer. "All this hand-to-combat means nothing up here. Every one of those moves is based on gravity. And the moment we leave Luna's gravity well, everything these boys know about combat and maneuvering goes out the window. Zero G is a completely different experience."

"That is why you are here, Captain," said Li. "To train them. You will ready this army for war. Our destination is GravCamp, a space station positioned at one of Jupiter's Lagrange points. There you will teach them the essentials of zero G combat."

"Who's going?" Mazer asked. "Just the group of us here?"

"TAG also includes four special forces units," said Li. "Adults. Seasoned soldiers. They'll be joining us on the flight. We'll also have a workshop and representatives from Juke Limited and Gungsu to help prepare and repair equipment.

It's going to be tight quarters. We leave at 0700. Bingwen, please show Captain Rackham to his bunk."

"Yes, sir, Colonel Li, sir."

"What about my belongings?" Mazer asked. "I wasn't aware that I'd be leaving so soon. I haven't packed anything."

Li smiled. "This is the military, Captain. We always provide."

Mazer didn't object. He couldn't.

"Follow me please, sir," said Bingwen.

Bingwen led them to the far corner of the room to one of the bunks. A toiletry set and a uniform Mazer's size were waiting for him. Now that they were out of earshot, Mazer said. "I hope I didn't hit you too hard in the chest."

"It was perfect," Bingwen said. "Sorry about your lip."

"It was perfect," said Mazer. "You really rang my bell. How long has Li been your CO?"

"Since the moment I left you."

Mazer's heart broke then. "I'm sorry, Bingwen. I should have been there for you. I had no idea."

Bingwen shrugged. "Our e-mails were screened. I couldn't tell you how things really were. How's Kim?"

"She'll be thrilled to know I've seen you and she'll be irate to know you're here."

"She can't know I'm here," said Bingwen. "This whole operation is top secret. They'll censor every message you send her. Have you seen Victor's vids of the tunnels?"

"Many times," said Mazer.

"What do you think is inside?"

"I have a few theories. But if I have a say in the matter, you won't be the one who finds out."

Bingwen shook his head. "You don't understand Li. We're his ticket, Mazer. He's invested everything into this program. He has to validate it. He has to prove to CentCom that he was right all along. I assure you I'm going in."

"You're not going in alone, Bing. I promise you that."

"You can't defy him, Mazer. He'll destroy you. What you saw today, that was his pleasant side."

"I'm sorry, Bingwen. I feel like this is my fault. I told you about the school. I encouraged you to go. I thought it would provide opportunities, a future, safety. I had no idea it would be this."

"My situation isn't your fault, Mazer. I've learned a lot. Li, as difficult and coarse as he is, has taught me more than you know. He has tried relentlessly to make me the kind of soldier he wants me to be, but so far I've been carefully resistant. He believes we should think and act like him to be effective, which is to say without compassion and mercy."

"He's wrong, Bingwen. He couldn't be more wrong. We're not barbarians. We're soldiers. There's a difference."

"You don't have to tell me, Mazer. I learned that from you long before Li came along."

Mazer smiled. "It's good to see you again, Bing. I can't believe how big you are."

Bingwen smiled. "Remember when I asked you to come with me to the school? I wanted you to teach there. Guess I got my wish after all."

"Wipe that grin off your face, soldier. Tomorrow your *real* school begins."

# CHAPTER 23

## Tubes

To: imala.bootstamp%e2@ifcom.gov/fleetcom/gagak
From: shongwe%rear.admiral@ifcom.gov/kuiperbelt
Subject: New orders

Captain Bootstamp,

Your orders are to fly the Gagak immediately to the co-ordinates indicated in the attached file, where you will receive further instructions. The IF is taking steps to remove your family from danger. Please reassure them that their safety is our primary concern.

Sincerely,
Rear Admiral Shongwe

Victor hovered at the holotable at the helm, reading over the message a second time. He chuckled to himself and turned to Imala, Mother, and Arjuna. "Our safety is their primary concern? As of when? Does anyone else find that painfully amusing?"

"Notice who wrote the orders," said Imala. "Or rather, who didn't write them. Ketkar the Polemarch resigned, or was forced to. This guy, Shongwe, is one of the territory commanders out here in the Kuiper Belt. I think this is a shift not only in command, but also in policy. I suspect the Polemarch took heat for putting us in jeopardy."

"If it's a change in policy, it's a minor one," said Mother. "They're still giving us orders as if the ship is their own. Nor did they return the captainship to Arjuna. They haven't cut us loose yet. So they're pretending to distance themselves from the Polemarch's policies without really abandoning them."

"I'm not sad to see the Polemarch go," said Arjuna. "I didn't like the man."

"I'm not shedding any tears either," said Mother.

"So where are they sending us?" Victor asked. "What's at these coordinates?"

"An IF outpost," said Mother. "Four months away. What's interesting, though, is its position." She waved her hand through the holofield and brought up the starchart. "We're not going inward. We're going outward, deeper into the Kuiper Belt, which doesn't make any sense to me. If they're taking steps to remove us from danger, you would think that would mean sending us inward toward the Belt or one of the stations at Jupiter."

"Why send us to an outpost?" Victor asked. "If they want to remove us from danger, why not simply leave us alone? Stop sending us on missions."

"They clearly have something else in mind for us," said Mother. "It says we'll receive further instructions at the outpost."

"I don't like it," Arjuna said. "They say they have plans, but they don't reveal what those are. The only reason they would withhold information is if they knew we would find it disagreeable."

"We should go back in that asteroid and see where those tunnels lead," said Victor. "That's more important than us going to an outpost."

Imala shook her head. "Nobody is going back to that asteroid. Even if the IF were to give us that order, we're not doing it. We held a council. We decided. We do nothing to endanger this family again."

"There is no danger," said Victor. "Or there shouldn't be. The hole I made with the ship was too large to repair. The atmosphere was sucked out. Any living creature inside died of asphyxiation. The tunnels are a vacuum now. We should be free to explore."

"There weren't any tunnels big enough for you, Vico," said Arjuna. "Even the one you squeezed into eventually splintered into smaller tunnels. It only went so deep."

"We didn't explore the whole asteroid," said Victor. "We might find a way in."

"That's not an option," said Imala. "We've moved on. It's out of our hands now."

Victor didn't argue the point further. Imala was still angry with him for going inside the cocoon, and he would only aggravate the tension between them if he didn't let it go. "So what should we do?" he asked. "Go or ignore the orders?"

"We can't ignore them," said Mother. "You and Imala are members of the Fleet. If we disobey, there could be repercussions for the both of you. Nobody wants that. And technically the ship is still in IF hands. If we bolt, we could all be in trouble. It might be a weak legal case against us, but we shouldn't take that chance. Our best bet is to believe that the IF has our well-being in mind. And anyway, we need supplies."

The others exchanged looks. "No objection from me," said Imala. "I agree with Rena."

Arjuna frowned. "Rena's right. We don't have a choice. I don't like being in that position, but that's the position we're in."

"Will you please take the captainship now?" Imala asked Arjuna. "With the Polemarch gone, I think we can get away with making a change here. It's best for the crew. They will feel much more at ease about this uncertain move if you're leading."

"No, they won't," said Arjuna. "You may not want to admit it, Imala, but you're a good captain. No, let me finish. You're a peacemaker, which is what this crew needs right now. Anyone can stand up here and relay orders. But it takes someone with your gift for negotiation to keep everyone feeling at ease and valued. That's crucial right now. Besides, I don't think we should do anything to disrupt what the IF has ordered. Once we reach the outpost, we can make the case for a change, but I suspect that will happen organically anyway. You and Victor are in the IF now. They'll likely send you elsewhere."

"You're both excellent captains," said Mother. "But what the family needs right now is consistency and unity. If we give the captainship back to Arjuna some people will see it as a division among us. That leads to whisperings and mistrust and people taking sides. We should avoid that. Imala, you should remain as captain. Everyone supports you at the moment. And you never make a decision without consulting with Arjuna anyway. I know you don't like the position, but I think it's best if everyone stays where they are for now."

"I agree," said Victor.

Imala considered for a moment then nodded. "All right. Let's gather the crew and read them the orders. I'd appreciate each of you sharing your thoughts during the council before we take a vote."

They gathered the crew. There were a few people who thought they should break all ties with the IF and ignore the orders, but the vast majority listened to wisdom, and in the end the vote was in favor of heading for the outpost. A few hours later, once all arrangements had been made, they accelerated toward the coordinates.

When they finally reached a cruising speed, and it was safe

to get up and move around again, Victor headed for the cargo bay where the Formic miniship was now anchored to the floor. He had hit the miniship with short-wavelength ultraviolet radiation a few days ago while it was still outside to kill off any microorganisms or bacteria clinging to its surface. Then he had sliced off the thrusters, left them adrift, and brought the small remaining piece, the cabin, into the cargo bay. Victor and Magoosa had gone over it with other chemical disinfectants since then, and now the whole room smelled like scented cleaner. Victor had received his fair share of complaints from the crew—the smell was so strong—but he thought it important that the IF get their hands on the ship.

He floated into the Formic cabin and imagined the five Formics inside it, tending to the mining slugs, piloting the ship, going about their day, doing their duty. How long had they lived in this cramped environment? A year? Two? The worms must have provided some food, otherwise where were the rooms to hold all the food storage? There was the issue of fuel, but Victor had concluded that they had landed on comets on their way in and mined any ice they found.

"Knock knock."

He turned and saw Imala hovering in the doorway of the miniship. He had apologized a dozen times to her since the incident with the asteroid, but still there was an uneasiness between them that Victor didn't know how to reconcile.

"Is this where you come to meditate now?" Imala asked.

"You could call it that," said Victor, "although I don't know what good it does. It's all speculation now. What I can't figure out is how they could travel so far and carry so little. There is barely room in here for a crew, much less for supplies. There was the big tank I cut away with the thrusters, but that must have carried fuel."

"The crew didn't have a wardrobe," said Imala. "They fly in the buff. That's one less thing to pack."

"Good point," said Victor. "Of course that means they're nudists, which makes them even creepier."

Imala smiled and pulled herself into the miniship. She paused at one of the worm habitats and looked inside. "What's that?" she asked, pointing to a short, cylindrical tube floating in the habitat.

"Goos and I found it in here," said Victor. "I think the mining worms used these." He picked it up and rotated it in his hand. "It's about the size of a worm. And the holes on the two ends are big enough for a worm to crawl in one end and out the other."

"Yes, but why would the worm need it?" asked Imala. "It's in a controlled environment. It doesn't have to protect itself from predators."

"Maybe the worm grows in here from a larvae stage. Maybe it can't move along the surface of rock until its skin has callused and hardened enough for it to crawl. So the shell is a little incubator, maybe. That's one theory anyway. Another possibility is that these are like spacesuits. You see this residue here at the two ends. I saw the ice worm excrete something similar. A thick mucous substance. It's possible that the worm crawls in, covers the holes on both ends with the mucous membrane and seals itself inside. If it has water in its gut, maybe it could provide itself with its own supply of oxygen. So it's a self contained habitat."

"Yes, but what could it do sealed in a tube?" asked Imala. "It can't work or chew through rock."

"Maybe the mucus is thick and malleable," said Victor. "So thick, in fact, that it could attach to the rock and create an airtight seal. Much like our own docking tubes. Then the mouth of the worm could extend and begin chewing through rock without exposing itself to the vacuum of space. It could excrete pellets out the other end the same way, through a mucous membrane. That way, a worm could start digging into rock as soon as the Formics land, even before the big cocoon has been woven."

"Woven?" Imala asked.

"I've been e-mailing back and forth with someone on Lem Jukes's staff he put me in contact with. A biochemist named Wila. She was desperate for a sample of the cocoon shell. I found a small piece of it stuck to the miniship from where I ripped it away from the cocoon. It wasn't much, but it was enough. I put the piece into the scanner bed and sent Wila the data."

"And?"

"The cocoon is made of microstructures of silicon. The skeletal material is a silicate. The membranes are silicone. With other trace minerals woven in. The structures look alive, but the chemistry to support life just isn't there."

"That explains why you found such massive amounts of silicon," said Imala. "But how could the shell heal itself so quickly if it wasn't organic?"

"Wila thinks another creature was healing it."

"What creature? You were there, Vico. You didn't see any creatures."

"Wila thinks maybe they were too small to be seen. Like nanomaterial. Microcreatures that are embedded in the resin material, or which are anchored inside along the inner wall. Millions of them. They'd have to be anaerobic because they'd have to be able to survive in a vacuum. And they'd have to be anchored securely to the resin so they don't get sucked out into space whenever there's a hole. But somehow these microscopic bugs are sealing up the holes. Think of honeycomb. Bees build these incredibly symmetrical hexagonal cell structures using nothing but nectar from flowers, which the bees ingest, partially digest, and then regurgitate. Maybe these microcreatures do the same."

"Wait, are you saying honey is essentially bee vomit?"

"Essentially. The point is, the activity we're seeing from these Formic creatures appears completely alien to us, and it is. But we can also see echoes of this behavior in some organisms on Earth. An asteroid has far more material in volume and in variety than a flower does. Maybe these cocoon weavers use a mix of silicates and oxygen extracted from the rock to build the cocoon. Maybe the cocoon's amber color comes from gold woven into its structure. Or maybe the framework is organic, and the microbugs simply weave around the framework. We don't know exactly how it's done, but Wila says there's a pattern in the resin. It looks random to us, and from a macro view it is random. But on the micro scale, a dot of resin is actually thousands of individual strands of compounds woven and entwined together. That's the word Wila uses. Entwined. She calls it the pattern of philotic construction. The creatures don't assemble, they weave and entwine. They spin and crisscross and fly in and out of each other, trailing microscopic strands of resin behind them. To us it looks as if the resin is growing out of thin air, but the cocoon weavers are actually ingesting the resin that's there, and then weaving as they excrete it out the back, stitching up the hole in a matter of seconds. That's the theory anyway. We've never seen these creatures. So we have no way of knowing if Wila is right."

Imala took the tube and turned it over, examining it. "Why are the Formics doing this, Vico?"

"That's why I wanted to keep exploring the asteroid. I think the answer is there somewhere."

Imala shook her head. "I couldn't let you do that. When you went in last time, when you were attacked, I thought I had lost you. I thought the one person I cared about was gone. And it was my fault."

"It wasn't your fault, Imala. It was mine. I'm the one who went inside. That was my choice, and it was the wrong one. I put you and everyone else on this ship in danger. And for what? To find some rock-digging worms? What good did that do us? I thought I could learn something of value, something that would help us win the war, and I was wrong. I'm sorry."

"You've apologized twenty times already, Vico. Let's move on."

"I can't. If the cocoon had blown, it could've harmed you as well. It makes me sick to think about it."

"I'm alive, Vico. You're alive. We've extracted the hydrogen from your lungs. All is well."

"Is it?" Victor asked. "Because ever since I've been back, I've felt a distance between us. Like I've broken something. Like whatever we felt for each other before has dissolved into something else. Everything is formal between us now. I see you, and it's awkward. I'm not sure if I should embrace you or shake your hand. It's driving me insane. This isn't how two people who are engaged to be married should act. Am I wrong?"

She hesitated. "You're not wrong, no."

"I feel like I've lost the one thing I care about, and I don't know what to do about it. The noble thing, I know, is to end the engagement. To let you free of this. To remove that burden from you. I feel like the only reason we're still engaged is because you're too kind to simply tell me it's over. You don't want to hurt me, and so you've let it continue. I love you for that, Imala. Your compassion is one of the reasons why I was drawn to you in the first place. But you can't marry me out of compassion. No one can sustain a marriage with that. I guess I'm saying this can't continue, Imala. The way we're existing right now, I can't keep this up. I would rather be your dear friend and see you happy than be your fiancé and see you unhappy. I want to be the source of joy in your life, not the source of whatever it is you're feeling right now. Regret, disappointment, sympathy. I don't know what it is, but I know that's not a marriage. If ending this is what you want, that's okay."

"So you want this to be over?" she asked.

"I want you to be happy, Imala. I want you to feel certain about the man you marry. I don't want there to be a shred of doubt in your mind about that. And I want the awkwardness between us to end. I want us to be what we were before. Comfortable with each other. This limbo phase we're in right now is killing me. If we have to end the engagement and redefine what we are to each other for you to be happy, then yes that's what I want to do."

"Do you still love me, Vico?"

The question surprised him. How could she doubt that?

"Is that what you think?" he asked. "That my feelings for you have changed at all?"

"Have they?"

"Imala, you are the smartest, wisest, kindest, most levelheaded person I know. Everything you do, everything you say, is right. It's precisely what must be done and what must be said. I usually don't realize it until after you've acted and spoken, because what *I* want to say and do is different sometimes. But my ideas are always less right than yours. Always. I value your judgment more than anyone's, your friendship more than anyone's, your counsel more than anyone's. I look forward to talking to you, being with you, watching you from afar every chance I get. There is a sense of wonder about you that I have never seen in anyone. I dream about you constantly. I've thought about us being intimate a thousand times. Yes, I'll admit it. I tell myself I need to have good Catholic chivalrous thoughts, gentlemanly thoughts, but I fail in that regard every single time. I want to eat my meals with you, brush my teeth with you, fold laundry with you. And if that isn't love, then I don't know what is. But I would be miserable, Imala, utterly completely miserable if we were together and I knew you didn't feel the same way."

She put the tube back in the habitat and was quiet a moment. "I do feel the same way, Vico. But sometimes I want to wring your neck. You going in that cocoon, that terrified me more than anything I've ever experienced. And the fact that you went in despite me begging you not to, that hurt."

"Imala—"

"No, let me finish. Because I need to say this. It hurt. It made me feel like you didn't value what I wanted, what I considered important. I know you needed to do it, but I felt betrayed. I know that's silly and selfish of me. But it's true. That's what I felt. Betrayed."

"I was wrong, Imala."

"No, you weren't wrong, Vico. It needed to be done. There are bigger things at stake here than you or me or anyone on this ship. And I didn't have that perspective. I'm not sure if I do even now, but it's the right one to have. So you're wrong about me being always right. I'm not. But that's not what I learned from the experience. What I learned was that I saw a life without you in it, and it terrified me. It made me realize that that's not a life I wanted. I've been standoffish ever since because I've had to figure things out on my own. I've had to acknowledge that I may lose you in this war. And if that happens without me ever being your wife, I think it would be the greatest regret of my life."

"What are you saying?"

"I'm saying I think we should get married. As soon as possible. We have four months until we reach that outpost, and when we get there, I suspect they'll send me one way and you another. When we part, I want it to be as husband and wife. Not as friends who mutually love each other, not as a betrothed couple who may or may not be wed someday. But as one."

He stared at her. "Are you serious?"

"Do I sound insincere?"

"You never sound insincere. I just . . . this isn't what I expected. Thirty seconds ago I thought we were breaking up. Now we're getting married. Are you sure? You had reservations before. And all I've done since then is reinforce those reservations. I don't want us to get married because it's the practical thing to do, or because the IF has set a time line for our travel. I want us to get married because it's what we both want to do. This war is going to end someday, and when it does, you'd be stuck with me. Is that what you want?"

She smiled. "Yes. It's what I want."

He laughed and embraced her and it didn't feel uncomfortable in the slightest.

They held the service a week later at the helm because there was no room in the cargo bay. Mother sewed Imala a dress, sacrificing a lot of other garments for the fabric. In the end, the dress had about five different shades of white, but it looked more like a unique fashion choice than one made out of necessity. Victor owned no suit, but the men on the ship had scrounged together their best garments and offered up what they had. A pant here. A vest there. A pair of polished boots from this person. A white shirt from that person.

Victor paused outside in the corridor before the ceremony and looked at himself in the steel reflection in the wall. "How do I look, Goos?"

Magoosa regarded him with a discerning eye. "Older. I've never seen you comb your hair before."

Victor's hair was slicked to one side. "I comb my hair, Goos."

"No you don't. You've usually got it pulled back in a band or something until you get annoyed with the length and shave it all off."

"Imala won't let me cut it."

"You see?" said Magoosa. "That's why I'll never marry. I refuse to let a woman control me."

Victor laughed. "Imala doesn't control me, Goos."

"That's what they lead you to believe. They seduce you with their female wiles, and the next thing you know, you're wrapped around their fingers."

"Thanks for the expert advice, Romeo. I'll keep my guard up. Speaking of wrapping around fingers, do you have the rings?"

Magoosa held them up. Victor had designed them himself. The bands were iron, platinum, and gold braided together. All metals the family had extracted from asteroids.

"Good. Thanks for being my best man. I appreciate it."

Magoosa stood a little taller, smiling.

"Vico?"

Victor turned and found Edimar behind him, looking somewhat distraught.

"I know this isn't a good time," said Edimar, "but we have a situation here."

"What situation?" Victor asked.

"The asteroids. The ones the Formics have occupied. They're moving. Well, a few of them are moving. The ones we know about and are tracking are moving. There are about eight of them. The Formic miniships have turned on their thrusters and pushed the rocks out of their orbits."

"Pushing them where?" Victor asked.

Edimar shook her head. "Hard to say this early. But they're all moving inward. And these are only the ones we know about. There are likely thousands of others. They could be moving as well. I don't know."

Victor considered for a moment. "Come with me," he said.

She and Magoosa followed him to the single women's quarters where Imala was getting ready. Victor knocked and Sabad cracked the door open.

"You can't come in here, Vico," Sabad said. "Imala isn't ready yet."

"This is kind of an emergency," Victor said.

"It's all right, Sabad," Imala said, opening the door wide. Victor stared at her in wonder. Her hair was up and laced with flowers from the ship's garden. The white dress fit her perfectly; the bottom hem had ornate strings tied to her feet to keep it from billowing up in zero gravity.

"It's bad luck for the groom to see you before the ceremony," said Sabad. "Disease, misfortunate, death. You bring this upon yourself and your children."

"I appreciate the concern," said Imala. She turned back to Victor. "What's the emergency?"

Edimar told her.

"Are any of these asteroids close to us?" Imala asked.

"No," said Edimar. "Not even remotely."

"Does the IF know?" Imala asked.

"Doubtful," said Edimar. "This information is being passed around fellow spotters on the nets. They don't have the kind of access to the IF that we do."

"Put everything you have on the ship's public server," said Imala. "I'll go to the holotable and forward it to the IF. Victor will forward it to Lem Jukes and Mazer."

"You can't do this now," said Sabad. "Everyone is waiting in the helm. We are ready to begin."

"They can wait a little longer for the sake of the world," said Imala. "Edimar, please let Arjuna know what's happening and that Victor and I will need a minute at the holotable before we begin."

Edimar nodded and launched in the direction of the helm.

"You're supposed to be married in front of the holotable," said Sabad. "What are you going to do? Send e-mails in front of everyone before you wed?"

"Unorthodox but it's necessary," said Imala. "We can't sit on this information."

"It's also good luck," said Victor, smiling. "Sending e-mails to the IF counters any bad luck we've earned earlier. So we'd balance the scales."

Sabad scowled at him. "Why someone so beautiful and smart as Imala would settle for someone like you is a mystery."

"I couldn't agree more," said Victor.

Sabad huffed and flew off to the helm. Magoosa and the others followed, leaving Victor and Imala alone.

"You don't want to get on Sabad's bad side," said Imala.

"I've been there for years," said Victor. "You look lovely."

"You don't look so bad yourself. You've combed your hair for once."

"I'm taking this wedding fairly seriously. Did you know they make deodorant for men?"

"I'm glad you can joke right now. If the asteroids are moving, should the IF destroy them or see where they're going?"

"If there are thousands of them," said Victor, "the IF can't destroy them all anyway. There are too many to reach and target."

Imala took his hands and looked him in the eye. "Everything is going to change once we reach the outpost, isn't it?"

"It already has." He gently squeezed her hands. "And now that we're getting married, I can let you in on a little secret. I was going to tell you after the ceremony because I didn't want it to influence your decision. But this is close enough."

She looked wary. "If you tell me you're already married, I'll knee you where it hurts."

"We're very wealthy. Mazer sold some of my designs to Juke Limited and Gungsu. I've been negotiating through a broker. The deals are finally done."

Imala raised an eyebrow. "How wealthy are we?"

"When this is over, we'll get our own ship and have a dozen children."

"A dozen is a little ambitious, space born."

"Eleven then," said Victor, smiling. He offered her his arm. "Shall we go awkwardly send some e-mails in front of our wedding guests and then get married?"

She slid her arm into his. "I thought you'd never ask."

# CHAPTER 24

## Training

**Ansible transmission between the Hegemon and
Polemarch Averbach, Office of the Hegemony Sealed
Archives, Imbrium, Luna, 2118**

UKKO: Any leads?

AVERBACH: The LX-40 responded to a distress sig-
    nal from a mining ship registered to a Brazilian free
    miner. We don't think it was the Brazilian, though.
    We pulled his registration photo. He's in his fifties
    and has one arm. Our perp took down a ship of
    forty-two trained marines. It was someone else.

UKKO: A crewmember?

AVERBACH: Maybe. But we don't have a manifest.
    Records are sloppy out there. A lot of harvested
    minerals are sold under the table. Crew get paid the
    same way. Could be anybody.

UKKO: This is getting a lot of bad press. It's hurting us.

AVERBACH: When I can afford to make this a priority
    I will. For the time being, we have a war to win.

Mazer checked the time on his wrist pad, worried that he was
going to miss his shuttle. He had been standing in line for

almost two hours to make a holocall to Kim, and there were still five people in front of him. The spaceport had three holobooths, but of course two of them were out of order. Mazer had come early that morning, skipping breakfast, with hours to spare before his shuttle departed, thinking that would give him more than enough time, but every other soldier leaving Luna that day had apparently had the same idea. The line when he had arrived had stretched all the way down the corridor and out the double doors to the loading docks.

He wasn't going to make it, he told himself. He would have to step out of line right before it was his turn, and Kim would be a nervous wreck for weeks until he could get a message to her.

For a brief moment he considered pulling rank. He was a captain. The men in front of him were all enlisted men. But no, they loved their families as much as he did. He checked his watch again. He needed to step out of line—but just as he prepared to do so, the loudspeaker made the final boarding call for a shuttle that wasn't his, and everyone in front of him cursed and ran for the loading docks.

The holobooth opened, and Mazer quickly squeezed inside and shut the door. The computer informed him that he had five minutes to make his call. Mazer leaned his face into the holofield and entered the connection data. Kim answered after the first tone. He had hoped to see her face, but it was only her voice—she wasn't at a holofield.

"It's me," said Mazer.

"Where are you?" She sounded half panicked and half relieved.

"Spaceport on Luna outside Imbrium. My shuttle leaves in a few minutes. They're putting me on a cargo ship to a training facility near Jupiter. They only gave me five minutes for this call." There was a timer in the upper right corner of the holofield counting down the seconds.

"Jupiter." She said the word like it was a life sentence.

"It could have been much farther," said Mazer.

"Is that all you're allowed to tell me?"

"I can't say much. But I can say that something big is about to happen. The IF is taking a huge risk. I suspect an announcement will be made soon."

"We're going to attack the Formic warships above and below the ecliptic," said Kim. "That's it, isn't it? The media is already speculating."

"This call is probably monitored," said Mazer. "Just know that I'm not going with them. I probably have the safest commission in the Fleet."

She was quiet a moment, and when she spoke again there was emotion in her voice. "Thank God. When you didn't come home last night, and what they're saying on the news . . . I thought . . . I didn't know what to think. How did you even end up there? One minute we're making dinner plans, the next minute you're gone."

He told her what he could. "I'm sorry," he said finally. "I would've called sooner if they had let me."

Her voice sounded composed again. "I don't blame you, Maze. I blame the soulless idiot bastards who run the IF and who give so little consideration to families and spouses. I hope this call *is* being monitored and they take note of who said it."

Mazer smiled. "You wouldn't be the first."

"What about the asteroids?" she asked. "They're moving now. What's being done? Will you be a part of that?"

"I can't say," he said. Which was as much of a confirmation. "But I can say that there are nearly one hundred special-ops marines assigned to my ship. Kaufman and Rimas, who were part of my breach team at WAMRED, are two of them. Along with a lot of other people from WAMRED I know. Which makes me think that even if the court-martial hadn't happened, I'd probably be where I am right now anyway." He checked the time. "This call is going to shut off in two minutes. I wish I could see your face."

"It's best you can't. I was called in to the hospital in the middle of the night. I look terrible."

"Not possible," he said.

She was quiet a moment. "Come back to me, Mazer Rackham."

"I will," he said. "And we'll make some chubby little fat-cheeked babies that look like me and look like you. And they'll cry in the night and spit up on our clothes and pee on everything and it will be exhausting and wonderful."

"I'm okay," she said. "I want you to know that. I'm going to be fine. I'll go to New Zealand. Or to the US to stay with my parents. I haven't decided. But I'll be fine."

"We only have forty seconds left," he said.

"Sing to me," she said.

She meant a Maori song, one from his childhood, a myth song, or a warrior song, or a hunting song. Mazer knew many. He had learned them all from his mother before cancer took her at a young age. Kim couldn't understand the words, and Mazer wasn't a particularly good singer, but he could carry a tune, and the melodies always calmed Kim. He imagined her standing there in the emergency room at Imbrium Memorial with her earbud in and her hand cupped over it to block out the ambient noise. People moved around her: doctors, nurses, patients, children, men, women. All safe for the moment because Kim Rackham would care for them and show them kindness.

He sang to her a song of healing. A song sung over the wounds of an injured warrior. A song that would call upon the mauri—or life force—of all living things around her to gather and join their strength with hers. He sang softly, not because he worried that he would be overheard outside the booth, but because it was a song of respect, honoring the warrior who had sacrificed so much.

The seconds ticked away too quickly. Mazer only got one stanza out before he stopped. "Right now, right in this moment, I love you more than I ever have," he said.

"Obviously," she said.

He smiled. That had always been her response when he told her he loved her.

"I love you, too, Mazer. Every moment, every day."

Then the seconds reached zero, and the holo disconnected.

The cold finality of it angered him. He had given the IF so much, and their gift to him in return was a few minutes of audio with his wife. How generous.

He pushed the thought away. Resentment toward the Fleet wouldn't accomplish anything.

He left the booth and hurried to his shuttle. The other soldiers had already boarded and were strapped in. Bingwen and the young cadets were seated near the back. Mazer found a seat up front, and the shuttle took off moments later. The flight was a short one. The shuttle docked with a cargo ship waiting just outside Luna's gravity well. Mazer and the others drifted through the docking tube and retrieved their rucksacks. A soldier scanned Mazer's wrist pad and gave him his cabin assignment. The room was as small as a closet. Mazer dropped his rucksack and pulled up the schematics of the ship. If he was going to be training the cadets, they would need a large open space to work in and he would need to claim that now.

There were nine cargo bays on the ship, but according to the ship's computer the bays were already 70 percent full. The rest of the ship was cramped quarters and small offices. There was a small exercise facility, but it was clearly designed for a few people at a time, and the hundred marines on board would occupy it nonstop. How was he supposed to provide any training without any space to do so?

There was a knock at the cabin door. Mazer opened it and was shocked to find Colonel Vaganov smiling back at him.

Except the rank insignia on Colonel Vaganov's uniform wasn't that of a colonel. It was a rear admiral's.

"I told the ship to alert me when you arrived," said Vaganov. "Walk with me."

He was wearing magnetic greaves and turned from the door, not giving Mazer the opportunity to object. Mazer switched on his own greaves and followed. When initiated, the greaves pulled your feet to the floor to simulate gravity. Vaganov and Mazer moved down the corridor and stopped at a small alcove nearby with a projected view of space.

"I suppose you're surprised to see me," said Vaganov.

Horrified was more like it, but Mazer kept his face a picture of calm. "I assumed you were still director of WAMRED, sir."

Vaganov waved a dismissive hand. "A dead-end commission. A good place to be during peacetime, perhaps, but a forgotten corner of the world during war. When they started taking my best soldiers away from me and bringing in scrubs, I told the Polemarch and the Strategos that I might better serve the IF as the commander of a warship. No one remembers the clerks, after all. And that's what I was becoming at WAMRED. A glorified clerk. My battle cruiser is being built in the Belt. It's quite the ship. They even promoted me. But don't worry, I'm not in your chain of command. Colonel Li reports to Rear Admiral Zembassi. I'm just here for the ride."

Mazer said nothing.

"I suspect you despise me for what happened to you," Vaganov said. "The court-martial, attorneys, accusations. All of that. An ugly affair."

"It *was* ugly, yes," said Mazer.

"You broke chain of command, Mazer. You forwarded sensitive information to an online forum of junior officers who had no business seeing it. But I suppose I should thank you for that. You left me no choice but to forward the information to my superiors, which earned me a few points with

CentCom and largely led to my promotion." He smiled. "I know, I misjudged you. I thought you were trying to ruin me, and you were actually trying to help me."

"You're mistaken, sir. I wasn't trying to help you. I was trying to help the human race."

Vaganov smiled. "You can't fault me for being skeptical, though. I've been duped and slighted before, you see. It makes a man cautious."

Mazer said nothing.

"After you left, I did a bit of digging on you, Mazer. Connections with the right people can give a man access to certain classified information. And what did I find? Mazer Rackham served with the Mobile Operations Police and played a critical role in the Formics' defeat in the last war. You never told me that. Our relationship might have been different had you been more open with me."

Mazer said nothing.

Vaganov laughed. "Even now, your lips are sealed. I find that admirable. Loose lips sink ships. Or in our case, blow them up in space."

Mazer only stared at him.

"Your new CO," said Vaganov, "this Chinese colonel. Li. What do you think of him?"

"I think he is my commanding officer and that I owe him my service and respect," said Mazer.

Vaganov laughed again. "I can never tell when you're joking and when you're serious, Mazer. I find that endearing about you. If you ask me, Colonel Li is a dangerous man. The only reason he's here and holds his rank is because the Chinese wouldn't agree to give us any troops unless we agreed to maintain a certain number of senior Chinese officers in the Fleet. Li was on that list from the beginning. If it were up to me the man wouldn't wear a uniform."

"If it were up to you, I wouldn't wear a uniform, either," said Mazer. "Guess that makes me a dangerous man as well."

Vaganov chuckled. "You're hardly dangerous, Mazer. You're an idealist. When reality finally takes root in your head and your perspective matures, when you've seen as much as I have, then you'll be dangerous. For now, you're simply a soldier doing his job. Which is why I'm here, to give you fair warning. One officer to another. Li has no future in the IF, not beyond the second war anyway. Careers like his implode sooner or later. Particularly considering this ridiculous tactic he's pursuing, the training of preteens for space combat." Vaganov laughed. "He can't expect anyone to take him seriously."

"Someone is," said Mazer. "Or they wouldn't have given his cadets any room aboard this ship."

"I know why they're here," said Vaganov. "Only small people can fit in the tunnels of these asteroids, and the children of Southeast Asia are as small as they come. Have they been trained in tunnel warfare?"

"Not in zero G," said Mazer. "That's my job."

"I see. Well, you're one of the best commanders I know. These boys are in good hands. But I must say having you play babysitter is an insult to a man of your capabilities and rank. You were made to lead soldiers, Mazer, not preschoolers. It's an offense. You must be furious. I won't stand for it. I'm going to help you."

"How?" said Mazer.

"I have a good relationship with the Polemarch and Strategos, as well as with a number of the rear admirals of the Fleet. I could put in a good word and maybe even arrange for a transfer for you onto a warship. Not with some lifeless assignment in navigation or logistics, but combat. The work you were made for."

"And what would you expect in return?" Mazer asked.

"We're not making a back-alley deal here, Mazer. We're simply two fellow officers helping one another."

"Of course. And how would I help you exactly?"

"Information. I want to keep my eye on Colonel Li and his superior, this Rear Admiral Zembassi. You'll be in their inner circle. Zembassi is not a man to be trusted. He led a coup in Liberia before the first war. Did you know that? It was all in the name of democracy, but he's nothing more than an opportunist disguised as a man of the people. A power-grabbing bureaucrat. Men like him should not be leading."

"So you want me to spy on him for you?"

"The IF is littered with bad apples, Mazer. If we don't watch them closely, they'll lead us to ruin."

The irony of that statement almost made Mazer laugh. "I'm sorry, sir. I can't help you. I've been trained not to break chain of command." He saluted and walked away.

"I did not dismiss you, Mazer," Vaganov called.

Mazer turned and stood at attention, eyes forward, waiting to be dismissed. Vaganov merely walked away in the opposite direction without another word. When he was out of sight, Mazer went looking for Li. He found him in the docking bay, overseeing the arrival of the cadets' equipment.

"I spoke with several of the marines last night," Mazer said. "Most of the men on board have never been trained for zero G combat."

"Which is why we're taking them to GravCamp," said Li.

"Yes," said Mazer, "but I highly suspect that we will intercept asteroids along the way, sir. If we do, someone will have to infiltrate the tunnels. The men aren't ready for that. Navigating tunnels in zero G requires an enormous amount of training. I propose we begin that training now, here, on the ship. We could start as soon as we reach a cruising speed. All we would need is space to practice in."

"I doubt you'll find a room big enough," said Li. "We're nearly full of cargo."

"This ship has nine cargo bays," said Mazer. "We might be able to squeeze the contents of one bay into the cracks and spaces of the other eight."

"If I can get approval," said Li. "What do you have in mind?"

"We need to re-create the tunnels of an asteroid. We can't enter that environment unless we've mastered how to move and execute specific tactics. We'll also need access to the ship's machine shop and at least two dedicated machinists."

"Why? For gear? We have suits and equipment already."

"This is new gear," said Mazer. "Lem Jukes and Gungsu are both working with Victor Delgado as we speak to perfect his designs. So we'll need to maintain contact with all those parties as they shape and develop the tech. And our machinists here will need to be ready to develop every iteration of the prototype."

"If there is proposed tech," said Li, "doesn't that go to WAMRED for testing? There's a process for this, Mazer."

"A painfully slow and inefficient process," said Mazer. "I know. I saw it firsthand. If we give this gear to WAMRED, it will get mired in the bureaucracy. We only need a few units of highly specialized gear. Some for the marines, and some for the cadets. If it proves effective here on the ship during training, that will serve as well as any field test they'd conduct at WAMRED. Plus we must consider the sensitive nature of what we're doing here. If word were to get out that WAMRED is testing child-sized exosuits, the press would beat the IF with a club."

"Good point. Two machinists, you say?"

"As many as you can afford," said Mazer. "At least two. Three or four would be better. And an engineer."

"I'll speak to Rear Admiral Zembassi and see if we can't bring up some more people from Luna. He won't like that. It would delay our launch."

"Once we leave, there's no turning back. If we don't take it with us, we won't have it."

"Anything else?" asked Li.

"Asteroid tunnels won't be our only war zone," said Mazer.

"Victor Delgado fought Formics above the surface of the asteroid as well. I propose we also begin training the men for zero G combat in wide open spaces. Launching, landing, handling a weapon. Those are different skill sets than navigating a tunnel. Flying in a wide open space is a disorientating experience. You have to be willing to abandon your current orientation. It takes a great deal of practice and coordination."

"You're already taking over one of the cargo bays for tunnel simulations," said Li. "There isn't any room for more zero G training. We do one or the other. Not both."

"Perhaps we don't have to do it inside the ship," said Mazer.

"You certainly can't do it outside."

"Why not?" said Mazer. "Once the ship stops accelerating and we're moving at a constant speed, it would be safe for us to build. The structure wouldn't be a solid-walled cube, but a grid cube, like a cage. That way any man drifting away would come up against the lightweight grid and be contained within that space. We could practice in flight and run tactics and maneuvers."

"Build a giant cube outside the ship? You can't be serious."

"There would be no acceleration, so the position of the soldiers would be relative to the grid and would remain constant, except for whatever motion they create with their arms and legs. It's not as reckless as it sounds. This flight will last at least seven months, sir. Are we going to let all that time pass without conducting any physical training, particularly training that we may need to have before we reach our destination?"

"And the materials for this supposed training cage, where will those come from?"

"We gather scrap from Luna now. Then we use our engineers and machinists and volunteers to build it after we've launched and reached a cruising speed."

Li considered the idea. "Four machinists won't be enough."

"Not if we want to build it well," said Mazer. "For that, we'd need at least a dozen."

"You're delaying our launch even further," said Li.

"Time we can make up easily if we accelerate a little faster. We adhere the scrap to the ship's exterior, and we're on our way, ready to assemble later."

"And who's going to design this training cage?"

"Victor Delgado," said Mazer. "With my assistance. And yours, if you want to participate. Once it's built, the men could conduct mock skirmishes inside it."

"Using what weapons?" Li asked.

"Practice weapons," said Mazer. "Slasers with low-powered lasers that can't do any harm. And tight-fitting suits that won't snag on obstacles and hinder movement."

"What about cosmic radiation?" Li asked.

"I defer to Victor and the engineers," said Mazer. "We already have such protection in our EVA suits. It might be a simple matter of adapting the design and tech."

"You have this already figured out, I see," said Li.

"The Formics know how to maneuver in zero G, sir. We don't. That puts us at a crippling disadvantage."

Li was quiet a moment. "I'm beginning to wonder if bringing you aboard was a good idea. New ideas make the rear admiral nervous."

"Old ideas don't win wars," said Mazer.

Li sighed. "Anything else?"

"A minor request," said Mazer. "Let's not refer to it as the training cage. 'Training' sounds laborious and regimented. Soldiers groan at the word. These men joined the IF to fight, sir. Let's call it the Battle Room."

# CHAPTER 25

# Unraveling

To: vico.delgado@freebeltmail.net
From: lem.jukes@juke.net
Subject: Wars and weddings

Vico,

I'll pretend I got a wedding announcement. May you have many children as handsome as me.

I have passed the information you sent on to Father. He has no doubt relayed it to the new Polemarch and Strategos. I'll return the favor by giving you some intel of my own. The Polemarch has divided the Fleet into three divisions. Two of them will attack the Formic warships above and below the ecliptic. The third and largest division will stay behind to protect Earth and address the Formic-occupied asteroids. It will be a year before the departing IF ships join up outside the ecliptic and continue toward their respective targets. And then another six months before they reach warships. I still haven't decided if the whole operation is brilliant or ill conceived.

There is one bit of good news: the asteroids explode easily. One of our Juke ships fired on one and the hydrogen-oxygen atmosphere detonated immediately. To our astonishment, however, the shell that covered the asteroid began to grow back only a few days later. Considering the speed of growth, it should cover the asteroid again in two weeks. I'm not sure what to make of this. Wila believes the cocoon weavers must be incredibly resilient and reproduce exceptionally fast.

You should also know that the number of Fleet ships assigned to take out these asteroids is woefully insufficient. We were poorly defended before. Now it's even worse.

Stay safe,
Lem

Lem climbed into his private shuttle and buckled in to one of the posh leather seats in the main cabin. Benyawe was the only other passenger, already sitting in the adjacent seat, strapped in and ready to go. The pilot lifted off, and they left Luna's gravity well behind them. Lem arranged the locking blankets around his legs and torso to keep himself snug in zero G; then he reached to his right to the bar and made himself a drink with a light sedative.

"You didn't have to come," said Benyawe. "It's not like you don't have a thousand other problems to deal with."

"Figuring out a way to breach the Formic hull has always been my number-one priority," said Lem. "That and finding the best cupcakes on Luna. Incidentally there's a new bakery in Old Town that makes red velvet cake like a cloud. When we win this war, I'll take you. I'll even pay."

"I've cut sugar from my diet."

"Ah, so you're into self-torture now," said Lem. "Me too. I've picked up flogging. The scars get itchy, but the flesh-tearing is fun." He paused. "Come on, you're not even smiling."

"Because your jokes aren't funny."

"Honest friends are the truest sort. Here. I've made you a drink. It will help you sleep."

"No. But thank you."

"It's a long flight, Benyawe. And you look frazzled. I doubt you've slept in days. You might as well get some rest now, while we can get it."

They were headed toward the Rings. Benyawe and Wila had worked for over a month now on a new version of the NanoCloud, and they were finally ready for a field test.

"Never tell a woman she looks frazzled," said Benyawe.

"Your eyes are bloodshot, hairs are out of place, you look barely conscious. What would you call that?"

"Wearied," said Benyawe, trying to brush her hair with her hand.

He offered her the sealed cup. "Here. Just hold this. In case you change your mind."

Benyawe hesitated, then took the cup. She stared at it for a moment. "What if it doesn't work?" she asked. "The Nano-Cloud, I mean. We've modified it completely. It's nothing like what you saw last time. Its entire function is different."

"You're not allowed to doubt," said Lem. "That's my job. I'm the skeptic. You're playing the part of the wise and seasoned optimist."

"Never call a woman seasoned either. That's the same as calling her old."

"You're in your sixties, Benyawe. You're stunning for a woman in her sixties, but you're seasoned. Get over it. And relax, this new NanoCloud is going to work."

"You made sure it was loaded?"

"I checked the cargo hold myself. We've got five giant

crates filled with millions of inactive nanobots. As long as they don't come alive and disassemble the crates and the shuttle, we should be fine. That was a joke, by the way. They won't come alive, will they?"

"We're fine," said Benyawe.

"That's the spirit. You sound like the seasoned optimist already. Though you may want to work on your delivery. I'm not feeling your performance."

"Everything is riding on this, Lem. It's not like we have a lot of time here."

It was true. The two divisions of the Fleet had already left for the Formic warships above and below the ecliptic. The Fleet ships hadn't gone very far, of course. They were massive and slow to accelerate. Smaller, faster, cargo-carrying quickships loaded with supplies could still catch up with them and deliver those supplies, if needed. But that window of opportunity was closing fast. Soon the Fleet ships would be too fast to catch.

"We've armed the Fleet with the original NanoCloud," said Lem. "They have the gravity disruptors from Gungsu. It's not like we've left them defenseless. If we can get them something better, great. If not, they still have a pretty good chance. But if it will make you feel any better, we can pretend that I'm the doubter, and you're trying to reassure me. Walk me through it."

"I did. You got a glazed look in your eyes last time."

"It was two in the morning. That doesn't count. Come on. I haven't taken my sedative yet. Try again. If I start to fall asleep, break into song or do jazz hands."

"All right," she said.

Lem immediately threw his head back into the headrest and snored loudly. He opened one eye a moment later and peeked at her. "Finally. A smile from the iron-hearted Noloa Benyawe. So you're not soulless after all."

"You're trying to put me in a good mood, Lem. It isn't working. It's only annoying."

"And yet you're still smiling. Come on. NanoCloud 2.0. Let's hear it. I'll punch holes in it if I can."

"Actually it's more like NanoCloud version 7.0. But that's irrelevant. Picture in your mind a rope. A big thick climbing rope."

"A rope. Thick. Got it." He threw his head back and started snoring again.

"Are we playing a game or can we act like adults?"

"Sorry. I couldn't resist. I'm listening. This is important. Go on."

She glared for a moment then continued. "This thick rope. It's woven with twine, which is woven of thread, which is woven of tiny fibers, which is woven of nanofibers, which is woven of molecules. So everything is woven on top of each other. It's weave, weave, weave, weave. Over and over and over again. And the more woven it is, the stronger it is. Hundreds of woven layers, back and forth, in and out."

"Makes sense," said Lem.

"Wila believes that all Formic-made structures are built that way. Formic microcreatures weave. That's their pattern. At the molecular level, inside the guts of these microcreatures, they take the trace minerals and elements mined from the rock, and they weave these molecular structures together, building microscopic threads like DNA. Consider what Victor found on that asteroid. Some of those minerals are essential elements for DNA molecules. I say iron, and you think building material for colossal ships, right? Or zinc, or magnesium. But these are essential elements of DNA as well. It's possible that these microcreatures aren't using the iron like we would, on a macro scale. Maybe they're building proteinlike structures on a micro scale."

"All right."

"And if that's true," said Benyawe, "then the solution to this impenetrable Formic hull is not a big macro weapon that tries to punch through, like the gravity disruptor. The solution is a microweapon like an enzyme, a catalyst that undoes what the microcreatures have built. A nanobot weapon that can go in there at the rate of millions of transactions per second and unwind what the microcreatures have built. So it doesn't break the rope, it unwinds it. First it unwinds the twine, then the thread, then the fibers, then the molecules. And on and on. It just follows the thread, unwinding as it goes. A chemical reaction. Destructive metabolism."

"So instead of programming the nanobots to sneak into the ship and open the door or hatch or whatever from the inside, we're programming the nanobots to simply find the hull and make it magically disappear," Lem said.

"It's not magic," said Benyawe. "It's chemistry. Your body does the same thing every time you swallow a piece of red velvet cake. It breaks down the sugars and carbohydrates. The problem is, we don't know the chemical structure of the hull exactly. The hulls were built near the Formic planet. We have no way of knowing what elements and minerals they used when they wove the structure together. So we're guessing. And we're basing that guess on the metals and minerals Victor found on the asteroid. We're essentially saying, the Formics clearly value these minerals. Is it conceivable that they used the same minerals to build their hulls? Could it be possible that they choose to harvest these specific elements and minerals because this is what they use on their home world?"

"That's not too big of a leap," said Lem.

"It's a huge leap," said Benyawe. "It's a gargantuan leap."

"We're doing the best we can with the information we have," said Lem.

"Which isn't much," said Benyawe. "But we suspect that one of the main elements is silicon. The Formics used it to build the cocoon shell, maybe they also use it to weave their hulls. So the NanoCloud has been designed to act like an enzyme and find and remove silicon. We've essentially turned each nanobot into a motor protein that functions like a helicase, except instead of separating nucleic acid strands by breaking hydrogen bonds, we're breaking silicon bonds. Unwinding and unwinding, again and again and again."

"Are my eyes glazed over yet?" said Lem. "You had me at red velvet cake, but you lost me at hydrogen-bonding mumbo jumbo."

"Should I break into song?"

"You should drink your sedative and close your eyes and stop worrying."

"We're guessing, Lem. I worry because this tech is a shot in the dark."

"I trust your guesses more than anyone's facts. Do you think Wila is right?"

Benyawe hesitated. "I think she *could* be right."

"That's good enough for me." He raised his cup to her. "To a good night's sleep, with dreams free of Formics and plenty of cake."

"I'll drink to that."

They tapped cups and drank.


Lem's shuttle approached the Formic scout ship a day and a half later. The massive red teardrop-shaped ship looked like a child's discarded top, with three giant white rings slowly spinning around it. Lem's shuttle approached the ship and made its way toward the gaping hole on the far side. The hole had been made by a massive burst of gamma radiation during the First Formic War. Lem remembered the moment vividly. "If we could make our own gamma-radiation weapon, this would be so much easier," he said. He and Benyawe were floating at two of the shuttle's portholes, watching the Formic ship as they approached.

"Gamma radiation would fry our electronics," said Benyawe. "Plus we have nothing to store it in, or any way to fire it."

"That's what Dublin told me," said Lem, "but a man can dream."

Benyawe craned her neck to see more of the hull. The ship was so close, it consumed their view. "It's so big."

"I had forgotten you haven't been here before," said Lem. "I want to vomit whenever I look at the thing."

The shuttle circled the ship until the massive hole came into view, with its jagged edges and uninviting darkness inside. The pilot flipped on the searchlights and carefully navigated the shuttle through the tight space. The interior of the Formic ship had not been constructed with the hull material, and the human crews had had no trouble disassembling most of the interior walls. Gutted and stripped of its various decks and passageways, the ship was little more than a shell at this point. The inner wall of a giant metal teardrop. Lem felt as if he were a spelunker drifting into a massive underground cavern as tall as a skyscraper and wide as a stadium.

"Much of this space is where the original garden was housed," said Lem. "We cleared out the surrounding area and made the space even bigger to make plenty of room for the habitat."

He pointed to a man-made structure that the company had built. It was a single-story facility with opaque glass walls. Another shuttle was docked on its roof.

The pilot brought Lem's shuttle down beside it, and soon Lem was opening the hatch in the floor and pulling himself down into the habitat. Dr. Dublin and a few other scientists were anchored to the floor inside the airlock, waiting to receive him. Wila was beside Dublin, her head shaven, her expression kindly, dressed in a tight white jumpsuit covered with a series of white robes and a pair of moccasins. Lem had seen pictures, but he thought her even more striking in person.

"Welcome to the Garden," said Dr. Dublin. "Lem, I'd like to present Wila Saowaluk."

Wila bowed. "It is an honor, Mr. Jukes."

"The honor is mine," said Lem. "But Mr. Jukes is my father, the Hegemon. I'm Lem."

"Of course," she said, bowing again.

Lem felt a tug of disappointment. The idea of religion had always struck him as somewhat silly, and he failed to see how any self-respecting scientist could ever call herself a theist. And yet here was a believer. And a very devout one at that. Someone who seemed perfectly content with one foot in science and another one in . . . in what exactly? Did Buddhists believe in a heaven? No, they believed in a form of rebirth. Your next life was determined by how well you performed in this one. Which means I'd probably be a dung beetle next, thought Lem.

Benyawe drifted through the hatch. Wila welcomed her with an embrace. More introductions followed. There were other chemists and physicists and metallurgists and xenobiologists present. Fifteen in all. Lem had seen their names and photos before, but he had never met any of them in person.

"It will take a few minutes for the technicians to unload the cargo and prepare the sling for the test," said Dublin. "I suggest we retire to the main conference room where we have some refreshments waiting."

The conference room was all glass, including the ceiling, affording them a view of the interior of the Garden. A large circular light, like a giant sun, shined down from the inner wall high above them, bathing the entire space in a warm brilliant light. Before the war, this space had been teeming with plants and small alien woodland creatures. Now it was nothing but ugly metal, completely devoid of life. Lem watched as Wila went alone to the far side of the room and faced outward, as if taking in some beautiful vista. Several of the scientists tried to strike up a conversation with Lem as he made himself two drinks, but he politely excused himself and joined Wila at the glass.

"Enjoying the view?" he asked, offering her a juice. "Nothing like a breathtaking vista of metal walls."

She smiled and accepted the drink. "There is not much to see now, I agree. But I cannot help but imagine the giant alien trees that once stood here. Their limbs grew straight out and upward, their vines and branches slowly growing for decades across this room until they reached and entwined with vines growing from the opposite side, creating a dense, green canopy like a living web of leaves. I would very much have liked to have seen that."

"If I had not seen the vids Victor took," said Lem, "I don't think I could have imagined it. I'm so used to a forest with a horizon line. It would be difficult to imagine this one, with everything rooted to the inside of a giant ball growing inward. It boggles the mind that something of that scale could exist."

"It was a beautiful example of different species coexisting," Wila said. "Everything here worked harmoniously together. There was no enmity, no hatred, no greed. There was suffering, yes, for there is always a measure of that in death, but there was compassion also, in how the trees linked and embraced one other, in how branches gave their fruit, in how the dead were placed at the base of trees to act as fertilizer."

"An Eden," Lem said. Then realizing that she might not know the term, he asked, "Or is that strictly a Judeo-Christian myth?"

"There is no Adam or Eve in our text," said Wila, "but there is the idea of a beautiful idyllic Earth flourishing naturally before becoming corrupted by the greed and conflicts of man."

"Ah yes, those pesky greedy men," said Lem. "I suppose I'm one of them since this former Eden is now corporate property, and all the biota in it was vaporized."

Wila blushed and quickly bowed. "I meant no offense, Lem. The events that occurred here were wholly necessary."

Lem laughed softly. "Don't apologize. I was joking. But now you've piqued my curiosity. You say the events here were necessary? You don't morally object to us fighting the Formics? I thought all Buddhists were pacifists."

"That is a common misconception. While it is true that Buddhists historically prefer a path of nonviolence, we readily admit that killing is sometimes justified. There are many stories in Buddhism mythology that illustrate this principle. The man who kills the robber who is prepared to murder the man's family, for example. This act of defense, though violent, prevented the suffering of his wife and children. So it counters the negative karma generated by taking the robber's life. It is a matter of karmic balance, you see? So it is with the Formics. Our defense is designed to prevent the pain and suffering of billions of our own species. My preference would be for the Formics to retreat and live in peace in their own system, and to allow us to live in peace in ours. But I do not think that likely."

"We'll never live in peace again," said Lem, "even if the Formics do leave. We would always wonder if they were returning. That fear would never fade. If we ever want real peace, we have to find their home world and wipe them out completely."

Wila appeared startled by the prospect. "But that act, an act of aggression, that would make *us* the monsters."

"It would make us the survivors," said Lem, "which is always better than being the corpses."

"We're ready to begin, everyone," said Dublin. "The technicians and equipment are in place. If we could all gather up here at the front, please."

Everyone wore magnetic greaves on the shins anchoring them to the floor, so the group stiltedly walked to the designated spot and formed into a semicircle facing Dublin. Behind him, past the glass wall, was the massive curving inner wall of the Garden.

"The inner wall of this vessel, the wall you see behind me, is made of hulmat. One layer of impenetrable metal separates us from space. We have stripped away any interior pipes or internal walls to access the bare hulmat. And the interior of the Garden is already a vacuum, so if we penetrate that wall, it will be a cause for celebration, not alarm." He pointed above him. The sling mechanism was mounted on the roof, ready to fire, visible through the glass. "The sling has been loaded with a black membranous balloon filled with several million nanobots. We'll launch that balloon at the hulmat. As the balloon approaches its target, I will activate the nanobots remotely. They will eat through the balloon and spread out in a wide NanoCloud. That cloud will descend upon the hulmat, and the nanobots will immediately begin to unwind the threads, with several million transactions occurring every second. For a ship in battle, a breach in the hull would obviously be catastrophic as it would result in a loss of atmosphere and a quick death to the crew. IF marines could then enter the ship and seize the vessel if necessary. Unless there are questions, let's begin."

"I have a question," Benyawe said. "This building is mostly glass. I don't know what the precise chemical composition of this particular glass is, but most glass is essentially silicon dioxide. We're about to unleash a million nanobots that generate a violent enzymatic reaction to all things silicon. If a few of those bots were to fall on this building, they would eat right through it. And it's a vacuum beyond these walls. That would end very poorly for all of us."

Dublin smiled. "Very observant, Dr. Benyawe. And you're right. As a precaution we will all move into the annex." He gestured to a door to his right. "That room is completely devoid of glass, and it has direct access to the shuttles should we need it. The test will be projected on the interior walls."

The annex doors opened, and everyone filed inside. The room felt cramped compared to the glass ceilings of the conference room. Dublin tapped at his wrist pad, and several data screens appeared on the wall. A wide shot of the Garden. One of the sling. Another zoomed-in shot of the wall.

"Any other questions?" Dublin asked.

"Fire it," said Lem.

Dublin tapped at his wrist pad, and the sling fired. Everyone watched as a black ball shot from the sling and flew across the vast space toward the hulmat. Dublin waited a moment and then tapped at his wrist pad again. Lem expected the balloon to burst open and for the NanoCloud to disperse, but nothing happened.

"Hm?" said Dublin. He tapped at his wrist pad again.

The black ball drew closer to the wall.

"The cloud needs time to disperse," said Benyawe.

"I'm trying," said Dublin. "The bots don't seem to be responding." He tapped again at his wrist pad. Nothing.

The black ball struck the far wall and bounced off, ricocheting back into the Garden, drifting lazily. Lem could almost hear the disappointment in the room.

"I don't understand," said Dublin. "They should break the membrane easily."

"Could there be interference in the room?" asked Lem. "Residual radiation from the First Formic War that's disrupting the signal? Maybe you didn't even turn the bots on."

"The Garden has been tested for radiation," said Dublin. "There is some residual radiation present, yes, but only a minute amount. Not enough for us to be alarmed about being in here, and certainly not enough to cause interference. We send signals from this facility all the time."

"What's the balloon made of?" Benyawe asked. "What material did you use?"

"Silicone rubber," one of the chemists said. "If the nanobots are silicon-removing enzymes, we thought that a natural choice. They could break through silicone easily."

"You didn't test it beforehand?" Lem said, his voice rising.

The chemist—Lem couldn't remember his name—recoiled a little. "We didn't have the nanobots, Mr. Jukes. You only brought them today. This is the first time we've had a chance to test them with the silicone."

Lem sighed and rubbed at his eyes. All this effort, all this work and money and time and sleepless nights.

"Could it be that the signal is not getting through the silicone rubber?" Benyawe asked. "Maybe the carrier mechanism is acting as a barrier. The nanobots are extremely sensitive. They're not like giant dishes or receiver towers. They're the size of molecules. They could easily miss the message."

"Launch them again," said Lem. "But lose the rubber ball."

"But . . . we don't have a mechanism for throwing them that way," said Dublin.

"Then put them in a bucket and toss them out like bathwater," said Lem. "I don't care. We can work on a different launch mechanism later. What matters now is the bots."

Dublin blushed. "Of course. Give us a moment."

Dublin and most of the scientists scurried away, leaving only Benyawe and Wila and Lem behind. Wila looked at the floor, embarrassed.

"I'm throwing off my karmic balance, aren't I?" Lem said. "I'm earning strikes against me for losing my patience. If I died right now, what would I be next? A snake? A rat?"

"I am not a judge of character, Lem," said Wila. "And certainly not a judge of you."

"I'll be a judge," said Benyawe. She turned to Lem. "You're being a bit of an ass, yes, but for once I happen to agree with that behavior. And if I had to guess, I'd say you'd come back as a shrew, maybe. Or a mole."

"You flatter me," said Lem, and he was pleased to see Wila smiling along with him.

A short time later Dublin and the others returned. "We're doing what you suggest, Lem. We're going to use manpower. The technicians are taking up one of the shuttles."

And just as he said the words, the shuttle came into view on screen. Lem and the others watched as the shuttle approached the far wall. It fired retros when it was about thirty meters away and hovered there. A moment later, one of the technicians floated out of the airlock in a spacesuit, carrying a large chest.

"Tell him to turn on the NanoCloud before he throws it," said Lem.

Dublin spoke into his wrist pad and relayed the message.

"Most of you here don't believe in God, I suspect," Lem said, addressing the group. He turned to Wila. "But you're a person of faith, Wila. What prayer would you offer?"

Wila hesitated. "A prayer that would keep us believing in ourselves even if this does not work. A prayer of hope."

"Good enough for me," said Lem. He turned to Dublin and nodded, giving the order.

They all watched as the technician opened the chest, activated the bots, and slung them forward at the far wall.

The cloud dispersed, growing wider and wider like a net, thinning out so much that they began to disappear from view. And then, right before the cloud would have struck the wall, the bots did disappear, like water thrown outside in zero temperatures that freezes and vanishes as it strikes the air.

"What happened?" Lem asked. The hulmat was unchanged.

"They're widely dispersed," said Benyawe. "They're there. We just can't see them. Give them a minute to take root before they begin."

They waited. Nothing happened.

"Are we certain he turned them on?" Lem asked.

"Just wait," said Benyawe.

"Something should have happened by now," said Dublin.

Lem felt the pit of his stomach tying into a knot. Failure. And not just here. But for the ships of the Fleet as well. *We were going to lose. We would fire on the Formics and unleash* everything we had, and it would not so much as scratch the surface of their warships. The images of the first war flashed through his mind, wave after wave of mining ships and corporate ships and military vessels attacking this Formic scout ship and being annihilated, brushed aside like pesky mosquitos, barely worth the enemy's notice.

"Maybe the inner side of the hulmat is different," said Dublin.

"Or maybe there is no silicon in the alloy at all," said Lem.

He glanced at Wila. She was not staring at the screen like the others. Her eyes were closed, her feet off the ground, her magnets turned off, her arms drifting weightless by her side.

Don't waste your time, Lem wanted to say. I was wrong. Prayers aren't going to save us.

The technician began to shout over the radio. The signal crackled in and out.

"What did he say?" Lem asked.

"He said it was working," said Dublin.

"I don't see anything," said one of the scientists.

"Looks solid to me."

"Is he sure?"

"Everyone shut up," said Lem. "Dublin, have him zoom in with his visor, and send us his helmet feed, let us see what he's seeing."

But it wasn't necessary. Because before Dublin could relay the order, the hulmat began to show dots of black. Tiny at first, but then they grew. Wider. And wider. Like it was dissolving at a hundred places at once.

Everyone was shouting and cheering. One of the men began to cry, embracing a colleague. Lem heard the noise like a sound happening to someone else, a muffled commotion happening far away. It felt as if a vise that had been gripping his heart without him even noticing it had suddenly released its hold on him. He could see space beyond the wall. Beautiful glorious never-ending space. With stars and worlds and galaxies. He watched the hole grow larger, then he turned his head and regarded Wila.

Her eyes were still closed. Her body had not moved. But as he watched, the corners of her mouth curled up into a smile.

# CHAPTER 26

# Profiteers

---

**Ansible transmission between CentCom and IF supply ship Bajovník, Kuiper Belt, 2118**

---

BAJOVNÍK: Hello, bastards. Can you hear me?

CENTCOM: Captain Merryweather?

BAJOVNÍK: An instant response. How fascinating. Is this the CentCom on Luna?

CENTCOM: Who is this?

BAJOVNÍK: How's the weather there on Luna? Raining again?

CENTCOM: Please state your name and rank.

BAJOVNÍK: Last name Mellow. First name Marsha. Get it? Marshmallow! Oh I kill me.

CENTCOM: Put Captain Merryweather on.

BAJOVNÍK: I'm afraid Captain Merryweather can't answer right now on account of a fresh hole in his head.

CENTCOM: Am I speaking with a soldier of the Fleet? Have you harmed Captain Merryweather?

BAJOVNÍK: You're asking a lot of questions. How about a question from me? How much wood could a woodchuck chuck if a woodchuck could chuck wood?

Khalid laughed to himself and turned away from the device. Instantaneous communication. A marvel. And now it was his. He surveyed the helm of the IF supply ship he and his crew had just raided. The room was a mess. Three corpses floated in the space, their blue IF uniforms now heavily stained with blood. The monitors and equipment at the helm were all new and flashy, but Khalid's crew had not been careful with their aim during the firefight. There was little that could be stripped at this point and recovered. They would have to do a better job of that next time.

And yes, there would be a next time. The stolen holotable had given him good intel. The shipping lines, the position of the supply ship, everything had proven accurate. A part of him had worried that it was a trap. He had taken the information too easily. But no, the IF was as stupid and incompetent as he had suspected. And now it was all at his fingertips.

Only two of the IF crew remained alive. One of them stood stoically nearby, unflinching. Maja had a gun on the man to keep him from trying anything. Someone had broken his nose, but to the man's credit, he defiantly ignored the pain.

Khalid gestured to the instant communicator. "What is this device called?"

"Do you want the Formics to win?" the man with the broken nose said. "We are trying to protect the human race from—"

Khalid shot the man and turned to the other officer. No, the second one was not an officer. He was a boy. Barely eighteen. An ensign, shaking he was so frightened.

"My patience is a little thin today," said Khalid. "What is that device called?"

"The ansible," the boy said.

"The ansible," said Khalid, testing the word. "What language is that?"

"I . . . don't know."

"Doesn't matter. It connects with Luna instantly?"

"Yes."

"And I can send a message to anyone with it?"

"No," said the boy. "It only connects with other, paired ansibles. It's not like the nets. The IF is building a bigger network, but it's not ready yet."

"So who else can I send a message to?" asked Khalid.

"Other ships of our supply line. Other commanders. There are a total of twelve contacts in this network. Plus CentCom."

"All blue bloods? Soldiers like you, I mean? IF ships?"

"Yes, sir."

"That's not very helpful," said Khalid. "And rather disappointing. Can the IF track it?"

The boy furrowed his brow. "The ansible? No. We use other equipment for tracking. The ansible is only for communication."

"If you're lying to me, my friend over there will cut out your intestines and choke you with them." Khalid gestured to Cleeg, the largest member of Khalid's crew. All muscle and dirty clothes and ugly complexion. In truth, Cleeg wasn't much of a fighter, but he looked like he could be.

"I'm not lying," said the boy.

"Where are the transmitters?" Khalid asked.

"There aren't any," said the boy. "That's it. It's just the ansible."

Ibrahim drew his knife. He had gathered in close with the rest of the crew, surrounding the boy. "Lie to my brother one more time."

"I swear to you," the boy said. "That's it. There are no transmitters. There's only the ansible."

"There's no time lag, Ibrahim," said Khalid. "This is new tech. Put the knife away."

Ibrahim sheathed his knife.

"What's your name?" Khalid asked the boy.

"Ensign Rynsburger."

"Your first name."

"Gustaaf."

"Well, Gustaaf, this is where you agree to help me. You do want to help me, don't you?"

Gustaaf's eyes shifted back and forth to the members of Khalid's crew, who were hovering around him now, looking menacing. Maja had blood on her face, but it obviously wasn't her own. Khalid rolled his eyes. They were all being a little theatrical.

"Look at me, Gustaaf," said Khalid. "Not them. I'm the one you want to help. This ansible, can it be moved?"

"Yes. I know how. I help with the upgrades."

"It gets upgrades?"

"Every four or five months. It's always getting smaller and smaller."

"Good," said Khalid, "because you're going to put it on my ship for me. Maja, Cleeg, watch him while he works. He'll be very careful with the ansible, won't you, Gustaaf?"

The boy nodded, cowering a little from Maja.

"The rest of you come with me," said Khalid. He led them to the cargo bays. The ship was packed with supplies. Food, tools, raw materials, weapons. It was intended for a large shipyard in the Kuiper Belt, and it was more wealth than Khalid had ever seen in his life. The crewmembers whooped and hollered and flew off through the cargo bay like children given free rein in a candy store.

Ibrahim hung back at the entrance with Khalid. "What are we going to do with all of this?" said Ibrahim. "We can't take this with us. It won't fit on our ship. And we can't fly anywhere with this ship, either. It's slow. The IF would track us and catch us."

"We load what we can into our ship and we run," said Khalid. "Food and other essentials. It seems a shame, though, doesn't it? All this wealth, and we can only take a tiny piece of it."

Ibrahim frowned, looking troubled.

"Speak your mind, brother," said Khalid.

"What that officer said back there," said Ibrahim. "We don't want the Formics to win, do we?"

"Do you think we're the only profiteers in this war, brother? Contractors steal and swindle along every step of the process. There's corruption from the top to the bottom. All we are is a bit more friction. Lem Jukes has made billions of credits off this war. We work harder than he does. Why shouldn't we get ours?"

Ibrahim nodded, but he still looked unconvinced. "Perhaps. It's just . . . we didn't use to be this hard, brother. You used to hate the killing."

"I still do," said Khalid. "I despise it. But this is war. This is the world the Formics and the IF have created. We can let them brush us aside, or we can live like we deserve."

"Then what will you do with that ensign once he's moved the ansible? Kill him?"

"No, Ibrahim. You'll do it. Because you know I'm right."

# CHAPTER 27

# Deception

To: notoccamsrazor@stayanonymous.net
From: vico.delgado@freebeltmail.net
Subject: Boots and Battle Room

Mazer,

There are two attachments. One is for the Battle Room. A simple construction. I've probably erred on the side of durability. Outer-space cage fighting will soon become a popular sport. Wish I had thought of it.

Second attachment is my redesign for the Stability Boots—which Magoosa has taken to calling Stab-Boots or Stabs. As you'll see from the 3D model, the boot is equipped with a triangle of rods that extend outward and anchor to the tunnel wall. So each boot triangulates. You set the anchors by flexing your toes, and withdraw the rods by relaxing your toes. This gives you greater control inside the Formic tunnels and allows you to stabilize yourself in an instant.

Magoosa climbed into our heating ducts with a proto-type. It was a major workout for his toes, but the boots worked well.

This design obviously replaces the spider harness that would have gone around a soldier's waist. The mechanics of that are just too complex. There are far too many ways a marine could get tangled up in the extending rods. And the last thing we want to do is obstruct a marine's movements. Applying the same principle of the anchor rods to the feet works much better. Let me know your thoughts. We've come a long way since I suggested a tunnel cart. I wince at the idea now.

Vico

Bingwen pushed himself deeper into the practice tunnel, holding up his slaser and listening for the enemy. The barrel of the weapon poked through the nanoshield that hovered in the air in front of him like a pane of flexible glass. The shield moved forward as he did, expanding and contracting at the edges to conform with the ever-changing shape of the tunnel. The metal exosuit was a tight fit, but Bingwen didn't find it restrictive. The helmet had no visor, which had taken some getting used to, but the built-in cameras worked well, affording Bingwen a wide panorama, even in the near total darkness of the tunnel.

The cargo bay was full of mock tunnels like this one—with twists, switchbacks, forks, and dead ends. Mazer and the engineers had used metal cargo crates stacked close together to create the tunnels, and they were always moving the crates around to make new and more complex tunnel scenarios. Hardened foam had been sprayed onto the cargo crates, creating random shapes and textures that resembled the tunnel walls of an asteroid. Excess clumps of foam created realistically narrow passages and gaps. Because of his smaller size, Bingwen navigated the narrow tunnels better than most cadets during the training exercises. But today the odds were stacked against him. Every cadet in the squadron was hunting him.

Bingwen had thought that his experience with the Formic tunnels in China would prepare him for this, but he could not have been more wrong. Moving through cramped spaces in zero G was much harder. Yes, it was easier to push his body along in zero G, but with gravity he had always been in control. Here, any quick movement could send him into a spin or destabilize him. To say nothing of the need to maintain his orientation. On Earth, down was obvious. Here inside the tunnels it was much easier to get lost.

Bingwen stepped forward with his StabBoots, flexing and unflexing his toes to extend and retract the anchor rods. The muscles of his feet and toes were well developed now, and moving with the boots was second nature.

He paused, listening. Had he heard a sound ahead of him? A rustling perhaps, like the sound of fabric brushing against the tunnel wall? Four cadets were hunting him, playing the Formics. Bingwen wasn't sure where they were located, but the external mike on his helmet was sensitive.

He waited until he heard the sound again. There. Yes, definitely ahead of him.

Or was it behind him?

Sound echoed so easily inside the tunnel that it was hard to pinpoint where it came from.

Bingwen waited a minute. Then two. Nothing. Had it been a distant echo?

He advanced a step. The nanoshield advanced as well. After months of practice with the shield, it still felt strange to have hundreds of thousands of nanobots so close to his head, responding instantaneously to his movements, like an extension of his own body. It was the one piece of gear he would never get used to. Nanobots could disassemble hulmat, the hardest substance ever discovered. Bingwen shuddered to think what the bots could do to his face.

He heard a sound again. Louder this time. Close. But not the brush of fabric. This was a foot pushing off the metal floor, like a scratch of rough sandpaper. Was the Formic just ahead around the corner?

He looked behind him. Nothing.

He normally had a second nanoshield guarding him from the rear, but for today's exercise Mazer had allotted him only one.

The Formics were closing in. He could feel them, like a noose slowly tightening. He heard the scraping sound again and this time there was no question as to where it had come from.

"Rear," he said.

The nanoshield in front of him collapsed into a tight haze then flew down the length of his body past his feet, where it formed into a flat shield again, protecting him from the rear.

"You're dead," said a voice in front of him.

Bingwen looked up to see Chati pointing a finger at him, a wide grin on his face.

"A doily just blew you to itty bitty bits, Bingwen," Chati said. Then he cupped his hand to his mouth. "Bingwen soup in Tunnel Four. Bingwen soup in Tunnel Four. All you can eat. Crackers not included."

Below him, past Bingwen's feet, Nak, another cadet pretending to be a Formic, appeared. "Suckered you, Bing."

Bingwen laughed along with them, but inside he was groaning. He hated losing.

They wiggled their way out of the tunnels and met at the entrance to hold a debriefing.

"Good work," said Mazer. "Bingwen, don't look so glum. You had one shield. Anyone here in those circumstances would have had the same outcome."

"Bing hates losing," said Chati, smiling.

"I hope so," said Mazer. "I hope he hates it so badly he doesn't sleep at night. Because in close-quarter fighting, you only lose once. After that you're dead. Bingwen, moving your shield to your feet in response to an approaching threat was the right move. Anything you could have done differently?"

"I should have advanced and checked the tunnel ahead first. It bent to the right just half a meter in front of me. Had I checked I could have wasted Chati."

"Possibly," said Mazer. "These are split-second decisions. But securing the area before dropping a defense is a good idea. Anyone else? Chati, what could you have done differently?"

"I should have brought a bowl for the free Bingwen soup," said Chati, which earned a round of laughter.

Mazer's face was impassive. "I know you're having fun, Chati, but I have seen a doily obliterate a friend. There is nothing amusing about that in the slightest."

Chati blushed. "Yes, sir. My apologies."

They debated how to use the nanoshield when only one of a soldier's two shields was operative. When they had finished Mazer said, "Tomorrow we rotate the tunnels. New missions, new assignments. Right now, last thing of the day, we're heading to the Battle Room."

There was a clamor of excitement.

"To observe," said Mazer.

The cadets groaned. The marines on board were constantly training in the Battle Room outside the ship, and the cadets rarely got a chance to run maneuvers. Bingwen didn't mind observing. Sometimes he learned more about strategy by watching the whole battlefield at once, than by being in the middle of the fighting with a myopic view of what was going on around him.

The cadets gathered in the observation room and watched as Red Army battled Green Army. Mazer had helped to organize the teams and designate captains when the Battle Room was first completed. Someone had started a scoring system, and individual soldier and team scores were posted periodically in the exercise room.

When the battle ended, Mazer reviewed with the cadets what they had observed. What worked? What didn't? Why? What would you do differently?

"Why a cube for the Battle Room?" he asked them. "Why not a sphere?"

"We don't think in spheres," said Bingwen. "We're planet-based. Yes, the Earth is a sphere, but we still think north, south, east, west. Left, right, up, down. We need opposites like that. We need to have the ability to say, go left, go right, go north, go south in order to use the human brain the way it's been programmed to work. It's hard to do that in a sphere because there is no plane of reference. Plus a sphere is simply harder to construct. A cube, with its straight lines, is much easier to build."

Mazer's wrist pad began to vibrate. He read the message, then addressed the group. "That's all for today. Dismissed. Bingwen, could you stay after please?"

When Mazer and Bingwen were alone, Mazer said, "We're wanted in Rear Admiral Zembassi's office."

Bingwen understood at once. Months ago Li had appointed Bingwen as commander of the cadets. Now that the ship was in the Belt, they were close enough to approach an asteroid.

"You think we're getting orders to attack an asteroid?" said Bingwen.

"That's my guess," said Mazer. "Are you ready for this?"

"You can answer that better than I can."

"You've seen more combat than most men on this ship," said Mazer. "You've been ready for a while. It's the other cadets I worry about."

They reported to Zembassi's office. Colonel Li and a few other senior officers had already gathered. Zembassi waved his hand in the holofield and brought up a starchart of the Belt with thousands of dots of light. He made another hand movement, and hundreds of the dots turned from white to red.

"The red dots represent the asteroids we believe the Formics have seized," said Zembassi. "We initially feared that these rocks might be missiles intended for Earth, but we have yet to identify a single asteroid on a trajectory to Earth. In fact, they seem to be going in every direction *but* toward Earth."

The red dots on the screen began to move in random directions.

"The trajectories make no sense," said Zembassi. "There's no order. Some asteroids have coalesced into groups of four or five. Others have moved out of the ecliptic, only to change course and come back down again. Others are moving away from Earth. It's random."

"Why would the Formics send asteroids away from Earth?" said Li. "That's what I don't understand."

"They're feints," said Bingwen.

The men all turned to him as if they had forgotten a twelve-year-old boy was present.

"There *is* a pattern to these movements," said Bingwen. "It's the same pattern the Formics have used from the beginning. A pattern of deception. First with Copernicus. Then with the other Parallax satellites. And now these asteroids. Everything they've done has been subterfuge. They seized these asteroids using miniships that we didn't even know were in our system. That took planning, logistics, and solid intelligence on where our ships were located so that the miniships could avoid them. Even more impressive is that the Formics also had intelligence on what these asteroids are composed of. Think about it. Every seized asteroid is a known water-ice asteroid with high concentrations of silicon and other useful metals. These aren't random rocks. These are specified targets because of their chemical composition. Note also that only one Formic miniship went to each asteroid. So no redundancies. This is an enemy that is extremely organized and extremely well informed. Nothing they do is random. If their actions appear random, it's simply another form of deception."

"He's right," said Mazer. "We can't determine the intentions of these asteroids based on their current movements. The Formics know we can see them. They're going to be even more deceptive than normal."

"So we can infer nothing?" said Li.

"We can infer a few things," said Bingwen. "We may not be right, but we can guess with confidence."

"Give us an example," said Li.

"These asteroids are easy to blow up," said Bingwen. "Their atmosphere is volatile. So they're vulnerable. The Hive Queen knows that. She also knows we'll figure that out. So she seizes a lot more asteroids than she actually needs because she expects us to take out a large number of them. Maybe she only needs thirty percent of these rocks. Or five percent. We don't know. But it's safe to assume that a lot of these rocks are expected casualties. The seeming random flight of these asteroids reinforces that idea, because hey, if you don't technically need them in the end, why not use them to confuse the enemy?"

"That doesn't tell us anything useful," said Zembassi.

"It tells us the Hive Queen has a unique purpose in mind for at least some of these asteroids," said Bingwen. "And it puts the extinction-weapon theory into serious doubt. Because if she were sincerely trying to annihilate Earth with asteroids, she would have simply done so. This is far more asteroids than we can stop. The Hive Queen knows that. But does she send the asteroids to Earth? No. She doesn't even put a single one on a trajectory to Earth because she doesn't want to take that risk. She won't even try to deceive us on that because it endangers her prize."

"This is still only speculation," said Zembassi.

"Of course," said Bingwen. "We can't know anything definitive until we identify which asteroids matter."

"Which is impossible," said one of the senior officers.

"Not impossible," said Mazer. "But like Bingwen said, we can guess with confidence. So let's guess. First we have the ones that are moving away from the center of the ecliptic, away from Earth. Let's assume that Bingwen is right and that these are feints. We ignore these." He looked at Zembassi. "How do we make those go away in the program?"

Zembassi entered the command, and a portion of the asteroids that were red turned white again.

"We can also dismiss those asteroids that went out of the ecliptic and came back down again," said Zembassi. "Those are obviously feints as well."

"Maybe not," said Mazer. "Those might be the important ones. Think of the logic. The Formics send them so we'll assume they're not important, so we'll dismiss them as non-threatening. Then they bring them back in when they think we're not looking."

"Sounds deceptive to me," said Li.

"But the Formics will use deception on top of deception," said Bingwen. "Let's hold that thought and consider the last group. Asteroids that are coalescing into a group. Of these asteroids, the most valuable asteroid is the one that has to travel the least distance because it will be exposed to the enemy for the least amount of time. The Hive Queen would make the other asteroids come to it. To protect it."

"Now we're anthropomorphizing a rock," said Zembassi. "An asteroid can't protect anything. It's a rock."

"For the sake of our argument," said Bingwen.

"Yes, but the entire argument is based on the assumption

that some asteroids are more valuable than others," said Zembassi. "We don't know if that's true."

"That's warfare," said Bingwen. "Picking the targets that matter the most and not wasting time on targets that inflict little damage to the enemy. And even if we're wrong, if the asteroids are all equal, we will have lost nothing by taking out one we think might be more valuable than the others."

"Except the time it takes to reach it," said Li.

"Consider that last group again," said Bingwen. "Again, all we're doing is guessing with confidence. Right? Looking for a pattern within the deception."

"Go on," said Zembassi.

"Let's assume we're right about the last group," said Bingwen. "That the one asteroid in the group that travels the least distance to reach the group is the most valuable. And let's also assume that Mazer is right, that the asteroids that go in and out of the ecliptic might also be valuable. How many of the asteroids meet both of those requirements, I wonder. In other words, how many asteroids went out of the ecliptic and returned to join a group and were also the asteroid in that group that traveled the least distance to join it?"

"Deception on top of deception," said Li.

"I'm completely confused," said Zembassi.

Bingwen stepped to the starchart. "May I?"

"Be my guest," said Zembassi, stepping away from the holotable.

Bingwen reached into the holofield and started entering code. "We first have to assume that every asteroid is on its ultimate trajectory," said Bingwen. "That may not be true, but we can only work with the data we have. So first we need to speed up time here and see if there are any more groups that will eventually form in the future based on these trajectories."

The red dots in the starchart began to move faster.

"Then we set the parameters we outlined and see if any asteroids meet them," said Bingwen.

The dots all disappeared except for twelve red dots.

"Twelve," said Li. "What does that mean?"

"It may mean nothing," said Zembassi. "We're playing guessing games here."

"It may mean a lot," said Mazer. "Which of those asteroids is nearest to us?"

"Castalia," said Bingwen. "A peanut-shaped asteroid."

"How long would it take us to reach it?" asked Li.

"Those aren't our orders," said Zembassi. "I called you here because our orders are to go to an asteroid already near our trajectory."

"An asteroid that may not be worth investigating," said Mazer.

"Just as Castalia may not be worth investigating," said Zembassi. "We're grasping at straws."

"We can reach it in under two months," said Bingwen. "It's remarkably close, all things considered."

Everyone turned to Zembassi, looking for an answer. He sighed and considered. "I called you here to give you orders, not to have you alter my orders. We could be chasing a ghost."

"Or hitting a high-priority target," said Mazer.

"And what am I supposed to tell the Strategos and the Polemarch? That a thirteen-year-old boy played an elaborate guessing game and chose Castalia?"

"If they knew *which* thirteen-year-old they might not disagree with the idea," said Li.

"Actually, I'm only twelve," said Bingwen. "And it wasn't my suggestion. We all reached this conclusion together. Could it be totally wrong? Absolutely. We might be way off. But there are plenty of IF ships out there heading toward random asteroids to investigate them. We'd be the only one testing a theory."

Zembassi said nothing.

"Would you like to consult with Rear Admiral Vaganov?" Bingwen asked. "I noticed he's not present here."

"He's not present because this is not his command," said Zembassi. "It's mine. He is a passenger on this vessel. Nothing more."

"I'm glad to hear you say that," said Bingwen. "Because Vaganov would bury the idea. He wouldn't even bring it to the Strategos and the Polemarch for fear that it might tarnish his reputation. Too risky. He's more concerned about doing what's right for him than in doing what's right."

Zembassi turned to Li. "If I didn't know any better, I'd say this boy was trying to manipulate me."

"If you know that I'm doing it," said Bingwen, "and if what I say is true, it's not manipulation. I'm only giving voice to what you're already thinking. I'm twelve. I can get away with a little petulance. Also, if we deviate in our course, we'd delay getting Vaganov to his destination. I suspect he wouldn't be too pleased with that."

"That may be the best argument for going that I've heard yet," said Zembassi. He scratched his chin, considered a moment, then turned to his assistant. "Lieutenant, open an ansible transmission with the Polemarch. If all of you will excuse me, I have a call to make. Bingwen, you stay. I can't explain this nearly as well as you can."

# CHAPTER 28

# Observer Ship

**Ansible transmission received at Turris Outpost, Kuiper Belt, 2118**

STRATEGOS: You are a go. Godspeed. Don't come back until the Wicked Witch is dead.

Imala stood anchored to the floor at the docking hatch, watching the Gagak approach the IF outpost. After four months of travel she was eager to stretch her legs a little and take a break from the cramped confines of the ship. Her hope was that the space station would have one of those new zero G showers, with hot water floating inside a tube. Or maybe a large cafeteria with a variety of foods to choose from. After three weeks of rationed black beans and rice she was ready for a change.

But one look at the outpost told her she was in for a disappointment. The outpost was no bigger than the ship, and maybe even slightly smaller. If it was comfort she wanted, she wouldn't find it here.

"You notice anything strange about this space station?" Victor said. He was anchored to the floor beside her, looking out the porthole.

"Other than its size, you mean?" said Imala.

"It doesn't have any transmitters," said Victor. "No dishes, no receivers, no antennas. It's just a box."

Imala hadn't noticed that, but he was right. How did the station send and receive transmissions, especially this far out? "You would think their transmitters would be bigger than normal," she said.

"You would think," Victor agreed.

"What do we know about this place?" Imala asked.

"Next to nothing. It's not even on our starcharts. Had the IF not sent us the coordinates, we never would have known it existed."

Imala didn't like that. They were going into this blind, without any idea of what the IF had in mind. The transmission they had received had promised that by coming here the IF could help keep the family safe. Imala had assumed that that meant the station would be a hub of sorts, with lots of ship traffic coming and going. Perhaps the station would provide an escort for them as they headed back toward Luna. Or perhaps the IF would offload the family onto a large transport with other miners seeking refuge. Or . . . something. But this, how was this tiny box of a station going to keep them safe? There were no ships docked here. And no ships in the vicinity heading this way either. This wasn't a hub; it was a dead end.

"I'm starting to get an odd feeling about this," said Victor.

"You and me both," said Imala.

The Gagak rotated and finished its approach, then docking tubes from the outpost extended and locked into place. There was a buzzer and then the all-clear light came on. Imala opened the hatch, and a young officer in an IF uniform greeted them with a salute.

"Captain Bootstamp, Ensign Delgado, I am Captain Mangold. Welcome to Turris."

He was American, probably in his mid-thirties, young to be running an outpost.

"Thank you," Imala asked. "How does this work exactly? Do I invite you aboard our ship, or do we board you?"

"I would be honored to meet with you both in the captain's office aboard the station. There is much we need to discuss."

"If we're discussing the welfare of my crew," said Imala, "I would appreciate it if two of my advisers could join us. Arjuna, the former captain of this vessel and patriarch of the Somalis on board, and Rena Delgado, our second in command."

"I would be honored to receive all of you," said Mangold. "The office is not very large, I'm afraid. It will be crowded with five people, but we can manage."

Victor retrieved Rena and Arjuna, and the five of them made their way through the docking tube and onto the station. To Imala's surprise there were not many IF crewmembers here. She counted only three as she followed Mangold to his office. Each of them was very young, barely old enough to enlist.

The interior of the station was a sight to behold. Everything was new and immaculate, as if the station had only been built recently and equipped with the latest tech. It made the Gagak look like a dinosaur.

"We noticed that there aren't any laserline transmitters or receivers on the station's exterior," said Imala. "How do you communicate with the IF?"

"A good question," said Mangold. "We'll get to that momentarily." He opened the door to his office and motioned them inside.

The five of them filed in and gathered around the holotable, anchoring their feet to the floor. Mangold positioned himself at the head of the table and smiled pleasantly. "Before we begin, there is a bit of business to take care of. The International Fleet is prepared to buy your ship."

A document appeared in the air above the holotable in front of Arjuna.

"This contract outlines the particulars of our offer," said Mangold. "Essentially the International Fleet will purchase the Gagak for sixty thousand credits plus we will provide safe passage for you and your crew to an IF station in the Asteroid Belt."

"The Gagak isn't for sale," said Arjuna. "And especially not for a mere sixty thousand credits. She's worth three or four times that, easy."

"Giving your family safe passage to the Belt aboard an IF transport is a huge expense," said Mangold. "You must take that into consideration as well."

"We can fly to the Belt ourselves," said Arjuna. "What is this? We were told that by coming here the IF would protect our family."

"That is precisely what I am attempting to do," said Mangold. "But the human race is at war. My first responsibility is the preservation of our species. For that, the IF needs your ship."

"It's not for sale," said Arjuna. "And you owe us four months of fuel and supplies for bringing us here under false pretenses."

"I encourage you to read the contract," said Mangold. "I think you'll find it very generous. If you refuse to sell us the ship, we will exercise our right to seize it."

Arjuna was furious. "You little bastard. You commandeer our ship, you send us on a military mission, you endanger our families, and now after all of that, you have the gall to threaten to seize my ship? What gives you the right to—"

"The Hegemon," said Mangold. "The supreme ruler of Earth. Appointed by the United Nations and ratified by every voting government on Earth. *He* gives me the right. As does the Polemarch and the Strategos. I assure you, sir, I am acting within my authority."

"Let's calm down for a minute," said Imala. "We're all a little wound up here, and that's not going to help." She turned to Mangold. "What you're offering, Captain, is not what we were led to believe. From our perspective this whole affair seems rather deceptive. The Gagak is our home. What could the IF want with it that it can't get from some other ship of the Fleet?"

"There's something out in deep space," said Victor.

Everyone turned to him.

"That's it, isn't it?" said Victor. "There's no other explanation here. You need to investigate something out in deep space, and we're the closest ship. Every other vessel of the IF has been mobilized in the assault on the warships or in destroying seized asteroids. So they've all gone inward. Now there aren't any IF warships even remotely close to this sector. That's why you had us come out here, toward the fringe of the solar system instead of having us head inward, because you intend to take the ship out into space."

Mangold didn't respond.

"Is that true?" Imala asked him.

"I am not at liberty to say," said Mangold, "not until I know I have your full cooperation."

"That's all the confirmation we need," said Rena. "What is out there exactly?"

"I am not at liberty to say," said Mangold.

"Well you *don't* have our full cooperation," said Arjuna. "You don't have even part of it. Come on, everyone. This conversation is over." He unhooked his feet from the floor and moved for the door.

"And where will you go?" said Mangold. "You need fuel. And you probably need supplies as well. Food almost certainly, but other supplies, too. Clothing, medical supplies. We are prepared to provide you with all of these things if you cooperate. You can't leave. Not without our help."

It was true. The ship was nearly empty of everything. They had fuel in the reserve tanks, but it wasn't enough to accelerate them fast enough to reach a destination before they ran out of food. They either restocked here or they died out in the Black.

"So that's how this works?" said Rena. "You essentially hijack us and our ship and force us to comply?"

"There is a third option," said Mangold. "You can keep ownership of your vessel if you relinquish temporary control of it to me and my crew. I will take Captain Bootstamp with me since she is familiar with the ship. The rest of you will remain here, where you will be recovered in five months' time by an IF transport and carried to the Belt. I think that's the best offer I can give you."

Arjuna scoffed. "So you'll take my ship and *not* pay me? How incredibly generous of you."

"You're welcome to join us," said Captain Mangold. "In fact, I would prefer to have you. You would need to enlist with the International Fleet and operate under my authority, but I would be delighted to have your assistance."

"How kind of you to let me be a passenger on my own ship," said Arjuna.

"What about me?" said Rena. "Would you take me?"

Arjuna and Victor turned to her, surprised.

"And before any of you say I'm too old to join the IF," said Rena, "you should know that I'm the best navigator you've got. Every crewmember I've seen on this outpost barely looks old enough to vote. I'm certainly more experienced and qualified to fly the Gagak than they are."

"You don't even know what this mission is," said Arjuna.

"I don't need to," said Rena. "If I can help in any way to win this war, I will. And frankly, I'm really the only person on board who is in any position to help. I don't have young children in the family. I don't have another obligation. I've been a tagalong since Arjuna took me in. I can help, if you'll have me."

"You're not too old," said Mangold. "I would consider it an honor to have your assistance."

"Well, I'm obviously not letting my wife or my mother out of my sight," said Victor. "If they're going, so am I."

"I'm afraid that's not possible," said Mangold. "I have orders to send you elsewhere."

Imala's heart broke at the words. So she and Victor *were* being separated.

"But there aren't any ships here," Rena said. "How is he supposed to go elsewhere?"

"We'll send him on a high-velocity interplanetary craft," said Mangold. "An HVIC. Or as they're called in the IF, zipships. They're small, one-man vessels that move at an incredible speed. We'll launch Victor in one of those."

"*Launch* him?" said Imala. "He's flown like that before in a quickship, which sounds like the same thing. It nearly killed him."

"We're familiar with Victor's quickship flight before the First Formic War," said Mangold. "The vessel he built is what inspired engineers to construct something similar. But I assure you, the zipships are much safer. We've learned a lot in the intervening years, and Victor's ship was slapped together with the few materials he had available at the time. Our design is equipped with the latest life support. It won't be pleasant by any means, but it won't kill him either."

"How reassuring," said Imala.

"Where am I going exactly?" Victor asked.

"You're to rendezvous with the Fleet heading toward the Formic warships above the ecliptic," said Mangold. "You'll reach our ships before they attack and serve as a mechanic and engineer during the assault. The Polemarch requested you for his ship personally."

There was a silence in the room. Imala fought back a rising sense of panic. For Victor to be sent to the Fleet attacking the warships felt like a death sentence.

"And if he refuses?" said Imala.

"He would be court-martialed for dereliction of duty and placed under arrest," said Mangold.

Imala scoffed. "Ah. There's justice. So you conscript him without his consent and then you arrest him if he doesn't obey your will? Doesn't that strike you as egregiously unfair?"

Victor put his hand atop hers. "It's all right, Imala."

"No it isn't. You didn't sign up for this, Vico. There is nothing right about it."

"I'm needed, Imala. I can help. You and Mother are right. All of us have a responsibility here. This is bigger than us."

She had spoken those same words to him when she had joined, but now, when they were directed back to her, she hated their logic. She knew it was true. She knew he could help, maybe even save the Fleet. But that didn't make it any easier to let him go. They were one now. A family. And now the IF was tearing them apart.

She turned to Mangold and gathered herself. "There is a fourth option here that perhaps you haven't considered."

Mangold raised an eyebrow. "I'm listening."

"You threaten to seize our ship, but we both know that's an empty threat. Seize us, and every mining vessel in space would know about it. The IF has been losing public confidence. You don't need a media frenzy labeling you as bullies. Your recklessness with our family threatened the lives of young children. I doubt that story will play in your favor on the nets. So let's stop pretending that you can muscle us into a decision here."

Mangold was quiet a moment. "What is your offer?"

"You said the transport wouldn't be here for five months," said Imala. "Those of us going with you obviously won't be back by then or you would have said so. Meaning wherever we're going isn't close."

"No," said Mangold. "It isn't. It's possible that you won't see your family for two to three years, or perhaps even longer."

Three years, thought Imala. It felt like a lifetime. But of course it would be that long. Victor's flight on the zipship would probably take at least a year one way, depending on how fast the zipship flew. And she would be going in the opposite direction. Three years was probably a generous estimate.

"Arjuna is a father to four children under the age of six," said Imala. "He is the patriarch of this ship. The crew look to him as their leader. Without him and Rena, there would be a vacuum of leadership within the family. I propose therefore that Arjuna stays behind with his family and that the IF offers to rent the Gagak from him for one hundred thousand credits a year."

"One hundred thousand?" said Mangold. "To rent? Per year? That's ridiculous."

"It's a small price to pay to preserve the human race," said Imala. "And I'm not done. You will return the ship in perfect working condition to Arjuna and his family at the conclusion of the mission within four years' time or you will pay him the full price of the ship, which is now four hundred thousand credits."

Mangold balked. "Even he didn't say it was worth that much!"

"I'm still not finished," said Imala. "The IF will stick to this schedule or you will pay an additional fifteen thousand credits for every thirty days that you are late to deliver the ship, the appropriate payment, or reach a mutually agreed upon new contract no less than the amounts we settle on today. This, of course, is in addition to the IF providing passage to Arjuna and his family to the Belt as aforementioned."

"Now you're just taking advantage of the situation," said Mangold.

"And you aren't?" said Imala.

Mangold sighed. "I'm not at liberty to approve an offer like that."

"Then we will wait for you to send a transmission to whoever is authorized to approve it. Otherwise no deal."

"I'll remind you that you're an officer of the International Fleet," said Mangold. "You're supposed to be on my side."

"I am on your side," said Imala. "I am only helping you with the negotiations. The IF's original offer was offensively low and getting you nowhere, particularly considering the unique nature of this ship, which Victor rebuilt from the inside out and made near indestructible. The money isn't yours, Captain Mangold. And last time I checked the International Fleet had a very healthy war chest."

Mangold sighed again and then turned to Arjuna. "The ship is registered in your name. Do you agree to these terms?"

Arjuna hesitated.

"It's the best offer you're going to get," said Rena.

"It's not the money," said Arjuna, "it's leaving the ship."

"Imala and I will make sure it gets back to you," said Rena. "Your place is with your family. If we lose this war, they'll want you by their side."

Arjuna turned to Mangold. "And you'll keep me and my family here until the transport arrives? We'll be cared for? Fed? We have children on board."

"There aren't many comforts here on the station," said Mangold. "And it will be crowded. But the few IF crew that stay behind will feed and provide for your family until the transport arrives, at which point your family will be taken to the Belt."

Arjuna considered a moment then nodded. "Then I agree."

Mangold took a moment to read his wrist pad. Then he typed something into it, and the contract that was in front of Arjuna disappeared, replaced with a new one. "The ship's computers have revised the contract based on our conversation. It includes the offer to rent the ship as proposed."

A different document appeared in front of Rena.

"For Rena, this is our standard enlistment agreement," said Mangold. "If everyone signs, we can proceed." He turned to

Victor and Imala. "You two need not sign anything. As members of the IF, you're already under orders."

"I thought you said you couldn't approve my offer," said Imala.

"I didn't," said Mangold. "The ship's computer did. It's aware of IF assets, and I assure you this is a legally binding agreement."

That struck Imala as odd. She had known of algorithms on Luna that could predict the likelihood of financial deals being approved by two parties, such as in the case of mergers and acquisitions, but she had never heard of a computer that could approve an offer. It was more likely that someone of a higher authority was listening in on their conversation and had just given Mangold the green light. But if so, who was listening? Someone else here at the station? It had to be. Sending a laserline transmission to Luna and Earth and then awaiting a response would take hours.

Rena and Arjuna read their documents and signed.

"Good," said Captain Mangold. The documents disappeared. "Now, as this is a highly classified mission, I must ask that Arjuna and Ensign Delgado excuse us so that I may speak with Rena and Captain Bootstamp in private."

"They'll just tell us later," said Arjuna.

"No," said Mangold. "They won't. Doing so would be an act of treason. I hope everyone here understands that."

"So I can't know where you're sending my wife?" said Victor.

"I don't make the rules," said Captain Mangold.

"It's all right," said Imala. "We'll meet you back on the ship."

Reluctantly Victor and Arjuna unanchored themselves and drifted outside. When they were gone, Mangold said, "There is a small Formic ship out in deep space. It detached itself from the Formic fleet some time ago, but it has kept its distance ever since. While the warships came in close and positioned themselves above and below the ecliptic, this ship hung back from an elevated position. We're calling it an observer ship because we think that is its purpose, to observe the proceedings of the coming war from a safe distance. We have no way of knowing for certain, but we believe that this ship may be carrying the Hive Queen."

Rena and Imala exchanged glances.

"And what is our mission?" Rena asked. "To attack this ship? The Gagak isn't a warship."

"It's equipped with the latest Juke mining lasers," said Mangold. "And as you said, it's heavily shielded and near indestructible. We've reviewed the schematics. The Gagak is as durable as they come. It's the primary reason why we chose it."

"It's not designed for interstellar flight," said Imala. "How far out is this observer ship?"

"We believe we can reach it within a year," said Mangold. "Assuming we can make a few modifications to your ship first. We have the equipment here already. It should only take a few weeks to prepare."

"So our mission is to assassinate the Hive Queen?" said Rena. "Imala and I aren't trained combatants. So I'm assuming your crew is prepared to carry out that mission."

"My crew are young, but they are all uniquely trained for this, yes. They'll do the fighting. Your job is to get them there."

"If it's an observer ship," said Imala, "won't the Formics see us coming? What's to keep them from firing on the Gagak or simply running away? Or is that the point? Are we the guinea pigs here? The expendable soldiers sent into battle to make the enemy reveal his weapons capabilities? That way, the IF will then know what it's up against and can prepare the real team?"

"That's not the case," said Mangold. "I promise you. We're it. This mission is ours and no one else's. I didn't come out here to die for the sake of revealing enemy intelligence. Nor would the IF ask that of you. I came out here to kill the Hive Queen. She is more than the general of their army. She is their mind, their heart, their will. Her soldiers rely upon her guidance and instruction. If we can sever that communication, we could destabilize their entire army."

"Or you might just infuriate them," said Rena. "Kill their queen and they might fight all the more savagely out of vengeance."

"Perhaps," said Mangold. "But they won't be organized. They'll scatter and fragment and fight without order. We could defeat them. Their Hive Mind is their greatest strength. It allows them to share information instantaneously and respond as a single organism. If we can stop that, we might actually have a chance in this war."

"But the Hive Queen is only a theory," said Rena.

"True," said Mangold. "But the evidence that she exists is greater than the evidence that she doesn't. And if you were the Hive Queen, set to battle an alien species, where would you be? With your forces in the thick of battle, or tucked away at a safe distance to watch the action unfold? And even if we're wrong, even if the Hive Queen isn't there, the Formics put that observer ship out there for a reason. And whatever their purpose, we want to thwart it."

They discussed the particulars, going over the modifications that needed to be made to the ship, but Imala was only half listening. Her mind kept returning to Victor. All those years they had been together and only a few months as husband and wife.

That night, zipped up together in their sleep sack, as she held him close, she wondered why they had waited so long to marry. Their need for each other was so glaringly obvious now. Why had they delayed? Because love wasn't instant, she reminded herself. Love had come gradually, moment by moment. She had always enjoyed his company, she had always wanted to be near him. But not as his spouse, not as the woman that would bear his children and commit her life to his. He was a friend. No, he was more than that. He had always been more than that. And maybe that was the problem. Their relationship had been so close for so long that its ascension to something greater, to love, had been so short of a climb that she hadn't realized it had happened. But she did love him. There was no question. It was not what she had always expected love to be; those perceptions seemed silly and juvenile now. It was simply joy. Joy to be with him, to see him, to hear his voice. A coming home.

And now she was losing it all. Maybe for three years. Maybe forever.

They launched him the following morning. The zipship was about as tall as a bookcase and as deep as a dining room table. Mangold gave Victor a booklet entitled *Getting Unzipped* with instructions on exercises he would need to perform and medicines he would need to take once he arrived at his destination. Victor's body would be a wreck, but he would live.

It took the technicians over an hour to hook Vico up to his IV and all the electrodes that would occasionally activate his muscles to prevent them from atrophying. A crowd of technicians surrounded him the whole time, and so Imala didn't even have a private moment with him before they put him to sleep. They covered his face with the oxygen mask and then sealed him in the gel.

It felt like a burial. Like she was watching them lay her dead husband into the ground.

She stood at the porthole and watched him rocket away, never taking her eyes off the dot of light that was his ship. She was still there much later, long after the dot had disappeared, lost among a canopy of stars.

# CHAPTER 29

# Castalia

No one was looking at Eros. Perhaps that was the IF's
greatest mistake.
—Demosthenes, *A History of the Formic Wars*, Vol. 3

Mazer pushed off the caged wall of the Battle Room and flew
to the other side, spinning as he went so that he landed feet
first. He bent his knees at the moment of impact and grabbed
the bars of the grid wall to anchor himself. It was early, and
he was alone. But it felt good to be flying again. The Battle
Room had been closed for two months now, and it was liber-
ating to stretch his legs and get his blood up for a change.

When the ship had altered its course for the asteroid Castalia, everyone on board had had to strap themselves into their
flight hammocks. No one could get up and move around as
the ship decelerated from its old course, reoriented itself, and
then accelerated again on a new trajectory. It was madden-
ing. The men were all special forces, trained to move, to
march, to infiltrate, to attack. Lying in a hammock for weeks
on end doing nothing was the ultimate test of patience and
perseverance, especially with the Battle Room so close by,
calling to them.

Mazer had known that the men would like the game. As

soldiers they all had an innate love for combat. Conducting mock battles that stretched them to their limits and that taught them new and useful tactics was what each of them lived for. But Mazer had not expected them to become so devoted to the game. It was more than a means of exercise, more than an escape from the tedium of spaceflight. It was what they lived for. It had become the beating heart of their culture. Teams made uniforms, flags, war cries, chants. The trophies they made and awarded were silly homemade trinkets, but the men displayed them like priceless statues.

The corridors of the ship were filled with harmless trash-talking and the clapping and hooting that followed any victory. Sleep schedules had been altered so that more teams could get practice time. Mealtimes were changed to accommodate battles or special training sessions. Everything revolved around the Battle Room.

And now that the ship had arrived at Castalia, now that they had finished their deceleration and were ready to begin their attack, Mazer could rush outside and enjoy a moment alone before the mission began.

He looked to his left, out into space. Castalia was a hundred klicks out. The ship was tracking alongside it. The attack would begin within a few hours.

Rear Admiral Zembassi had given Colonel Li the assignment of planning the mission, but Li had relied on Mazer and Bingwen for the particulars. It hadn't been difficult. Blow the atmosphere. Send in a team of marines to confirm that the Formics and other creatures were fried to space dust, then bring in Bingwen and the other cadets to explore the tunnels and gather what additional clues they could.

Mazer did two more launches, then went back inside to get ready for the mission.

Li was at the hatch, waiting for him. "The rear admiral wants you in his office immediately."

"Something wrong?" Mazer asked.

"Everything. Vaganov is trying to sandbag the entire operation."

They hustled to Zembassi's office and found Vaganov and Zembassi giving each other the silent treatment. The tension in the room was palpable. Zembassi looked furious. Vaganov smiled pleasantly.

"You asked to see me, sir?" Mazer said.

"We have a problem, Captain," said Zembassi. "Rear Admiral Vaganov here has taken it upon himself to change our orders and turn this mission into a bureaucratic mess."

"You're overreacting, Fareed," said Vaganov. "I merely pointed out to a few colleagues that your team had failed to consider a few critical details."

"What exactly did we forget, sir?" asked Mazer.

Vaganov winced, as if he were embarrassed for Mazer for even asking. "If you had been more thorough in planning this mission, Mazer, you wouldn't have to ask that question."

"Stop toying with him and get to the damn point," said Zembassi.

"The creatures, Mazer," said Vaganov. "The creatures are the clues. The mining slugs, the grubs, the bugs, all of the little alien creepy-crawly things inside that rock. They will tell us more about the Formics' intentions than an empty hole in a rock ever would, which is all your cadets are likely to find if you blow the asteroid. These creatures have DNA, Mazer—or whatever it is their protein structure is composed of. And a study of their DNA might give us the definitive answers we seek. The prevailing belief on Earth is that they were engineered by the Hive Queen herself. If we can capture them and dissect them and do whatever it is that scientists do, we might legitimately learn what the Hive Queen has in mind. At the very least, we'll learn more about how she communicates with creatures mind to mind. Perhaps that will give us the information we need to cut off that communication line."

"We considered what you're proposing, sir," said Mazer. "But there is an obvious danger to the idea. The atmosphere—"

"—is composed of volatile gas," interrupted Vaganov. "Yes, yes. But that doesn't change the fact that by blowing up the asteroid, you might be incinerating critical intelligence. What if there is a computer at the heart of that asteroid with all of their sensitive information? Are we going to blow it up without even trying to seize it?"

"The Formics don't use computers, sir," said Mazer.

"Not that we know of," said Vaganov. "Just because we haven't seen one doesn't mean they don't exist. And even if there is no computer, there could be something else of military value. Some device, some weapon, something we can use against them. Are we going to simply destroy it without checking first?"

"We considered this," said Mazer. "We debated it at length. But in the end, sending marines and cadets into an area that is essentially a massive bomb set to explode seemed like a bad idea for multiple reasons. First, there is the possibility that a marine will create a spark and detonate the atmosphere."

"Victor Delgado didn't," said Vaganov.

"Victor Delgado was extremely lucky," said Mazer. "With more marines in that environment, the chances of a spark increase dramatically."

"We send our soldiers into dangerous places," said Vaganov. "That's what we do for a living. We take risks."

"There are other reasons as well," said Mazer. "If the Formics do indeed have a hive mind, then it's likely that the Hive Queen knows that Victor Delgado infiltrated one of her asteroids and stole a miniship. So she knows her asteroids are vulnerable. And if there is something of value inside Castalia, as you suggest, then the Hive Queen will do anything to keep us from acquiring it, including blowing up the asteroid herself. Remember, she cares little for her individual workers. She would willingly sacrifice a few to prevent humans from acquiring whatever would give us an advantage. All she would have to do is send a mental command to any of the Formics at Castalia to create a spark. The Formics would obey her without hesitation."

"If that's true," said Vaganov, "then why didn't the Hive Queen detonate the atmosphere and kill Victor?"

"She probably thought her Formics could handle one intruder," said Mazer. "And when Victor lost his helmet, she knew he couldn't escape. I doubt she'll make the same mistake twice. Now that she knows we have an interest in her equipment and operations, she'll be especially cautious."

"This is all speculation," said Vaganov. "And it doesn't matter anyway. Your orders have changed. You are not to blow up the asteroid. You are to recover samples of the creatures, and then you are to send in the cadets to infiltrate the tunnels and reconnoiter."

Mazer blinked. "Sir, with all due respect, sending the cadets into a volatile atmosphere is a bad idea."

"You've been training these cadets for tunnel warfare for months," said Vaganov. "What did you think we were going to do with them?"

"They can move through tunnels, yes," said Mazer. "But it would be much safer to send them in once the atmosphere is destroyed and the area is secure."

"Your personal attachment to Bingwen is clouding your judgment, Mazer. We have much to gain from what I'm proposing. I spoke with Rear Admiral Cormack and Admiral Denashi, who made my case to the Polemarch, who made my case to the Hegemon. This is a done deal."

"In other words," said Zembassi, "he used the ansible on this ship to send his own private messages. He went behind my back and usurped my authority and created a situation that endangers my men."

"I did what you should have done, Fareed," said Vaganov. "I thought about the big picture here."

Mazer looked to Zembassi. "The Hegemon agreed to this?"

"Vaganov got an army of people involved. Xenobiologists, contacts at CentCom. He made them all believe that there might be a valuable acquisition to be made here. Considering that I had already told the Polemarch and the Strategos that this asteroid might be special based on Bingwen's logic, it wasn't a difficult argument for Vaganov to make."

"I am not the villain here," said Vaganov. "I am merely correcting a strategic error on your part."

"You're advancing your own career is what you're doing," said Zembassi.

"You're mistaken," said Vaganov. "I am taking a huge risk here. If something were to happen to your men in an explosion, the blame will fall upon me."

Mazer almost laughed out loud at that. Of course Vaganov wouldn't take the blame. Vaganov would do everything in his power to avoid that. He'd pass the blame to Mazer. Or to Colonel Li. Or to the marines conducting the op. He'd run for the hills and point an accusatory finger at everyone else. That's how people like Vaganov survived. And if we *do* find something, thought Mazer, which we expected to anyway, Vaganov will push everyone else aside and take every ounce of credit.

But Mazer kept his face impassive and simply said, "And what will we say to the world if Bingwen and the cadets are killed? How will we justify putting children in such an egregiously dangerous combat situation?"

"The Hegemon was very clear about that," said Vaganov. "As far as the world is concerned, this cadet program does not exist. There is no program. If there are casualties, there is to be no record of them whatsoever."

"So we'll send them into harm's way and then we'll pretend they didn't exist?" said Mazer. "How noble of us. What honor."

Vaganov's face darkened. "The cadets are the only people small enough to navigate those tunnels. We don't have a choice. Or perhaps you would like the Formics to slaughter that wife of yours once they win this war."

It took all of Mazer's self-control not to bury his fist in the man's face at that moment.

"You're out of line, Vaganov," said Zembassi.

"I am the only man speaking sense here," said Vaganov. "These cadets are orphans. They're collateral damage of the first war. They have no connections. Do you think that's a coincidence? Why do you think they were chosen for this program? Besides, what are you worried about? Mazer trained these cadets. If he trained them correctly, they'll be fine." He moved for the door. "Now if you'll excuse me, you have a mission to plan. I wouldn't want to get in the way of that."

Vaganov gave a little bow and then exited.

"I propose we send that bastard into Castalia and then we detonate the whole thing," said Zembassi.

Li was standing off to the side. He had stayed quiet for the whole conversation, but he spoke up now. "Mazer has trained the cadets well. They'll execute whatever mission we give them."

"We can't send anyone in there unless they're doubly protected," said Mazer. "Especially the cadets."

"You all have exosuits," said Li. "Victor designed them to take the heat."

"Yes," said Mazer, "but it's not like we have a lot of definitive data on whether the suits are strong enough to protect us. If you fill a balloon with hydrogen and oxygen and blow it up, the ignition temperature is around 580°C. Which is hot. Steel can go soft at 538°C. And there's a lot more air inside that cocoon than inside a balloon. It will get a lot hotter as the air molecules strike one another and push outward at the moment of detonation."

"The suit is a nickel-chromium alloy," said Li. "What are their melting points?"

"Far higher," said Mazer. "Nickel is nearly 1,500°C. Chromium is over 1,900°C. So more than three times that of steel. Victor's alloy is probably even stronger. But even so, it might get very hot inside the suit."

"Maybe not," said Zembassi. "The explosion would be a flash, not a continuous application of heat. It would disappear instantly in the vacuum of space. I worry more about the amount of energy released. You would be hit with the rapidly expanding gas and debris of the explosion."

"We need additional shielding," said Mazer. "Just to be safe. My suggestion: We gather all the nanoshields on board and we put them all together to create a single bubble around a marine or a cadet. Or better yet, we make a smaller bubble with multiple layers of nanoshield. So one nanoshield atop the other. As many as we can make."

"We only have so many shields," said Li.

"You want a small team anyway," said Mazer. "Should the Formics detonate the cocoon while we're inside it, the blast would likely blow the marines away from the asteroid in multiple directions. Those marines would have to be recovered by the ship's small landing craft before the marines disappear into oblivion. The more marines you have to recover, the more likely you are to lose some. I'd suggest sending in no more than three. Me, Kaufman, and Rimas. I worked with them both on WAMRED. We've run hundreds of field tests together. We're a very good team. We'll go in, draw out the Formics, kill them, secure the area, and then bring in a cadet to check the tunnels and gather samples of the worms."

"A cadet?" said Zembassi. "As in just one?"

"We minimize the risk of casualties and the risk of detonation," said Mazer. "The more cadets we send in there, the higher the risk of someone creating a spark."

"It should be Bingwen," said Li.

"I was going to suggest Chati," said Mazer. "He's smaller than Bingwen."

"Bingwen is a better soldier," said Li, "and you know it.

He has more combat experience from the first war than most men on this ship."

"I agree," said Zembassi. "No one thinks faster. And no one is better trained. Besides, he's only slightly bigger than Chati. He'll navigate the tunnels as well as any of them. I know you and Bingwen are close, Mazer. But he's our man. And that's an order."

He's not a man, Mazer wanted to say. He's a boy.

But he knew they were right. If anyone could do this safely, it was Bingwen.

"You said the marines would be slung away from the ship if there's an explosion," said Li. "So why not attach each of you to a long tether? That way you wouldn't have to be recovered."

"A blast would inflict a tremendous amount of G-forces on our bodies," said Mazer. "If we were attached to a tether, we would stop instantly once the line grew taut. The sudden force of that stop might kill us. Bones might puncture critical organs. A gradual deceleration would be preferable. So the landing craft reaches us, grabs us, slows us down. That is, assuming we survive the explosion."

"I like the idea of using the nanoshields to create a protective bubble," said Zembassi.

"Two bubbles," said Mazer. "One inside the other for additional protection. We'd need the engineers to reprogram the nanobots to do that."

"Can the bots take that level of abuse if there's an explosion?" said Li. "They're microscopic. Wouldn't they be incinerated?"

"Let's ask the engineers," said Mazer. "We'll let them do the math."

Two days later they were gathered in the cargo bay ready to launch. Mazer, Kaufman, Rimas, and Bingwen were all in their exosuits. They had not yet donned their helmets, and they quickly reviewed the mission objectives one last time. Mazer created a holo of the asteroid in the air with his wrist pad.

"Castalia is shaped like a peanut," said Mazer. "Like two small asteroids smooshed together. We're going in here, near where the two bulbous parts meet. The Formic miniships have a crew of five. So we kill five Formics, collect some slugs, then bring in Bingwen once the area is secure."

"Secure except for that fact that it could explode at any moment," said Rimas.

"Except for that," said Mazer.

Three small landing crafts were beside them, ready to go, each with an expert pilot at the controls.

"If any one of us is thrown out into space," said Mazer, "the landing crafts will recover us."

"They better," said Kaufman. "We're having ravioli in the mess hall tonight. I don't want to miss that."

They grabbed their gear and began loading it into the first landing craft.

Vaganov arrived just before they were ready to launch. He approached Mazer and spoke softly. "Stay safe, Mazer. I'll be all broken up inside if something were to happen to you." Vaganov smiled then launched away.

Mazer watched him go, saying nothing. Then he secured his helmet, ran a quick suit check, and climbed into the landing craft next to Bingwen.

The flight to Castalia was a short one. The pilot carrying the marines brought the landing craft within fifty meters of the cocoon. Mazer opened the airlock and let himself out. A giant spool of rope was mounted on the landing craft's hull. Mazer took the end of the rope in one hand and unzipped the pack on his chest. The nanobots flew out of the pack and encircled him in two bubbles, forming a hazy, opaque cloud of protection.

Mazer launched to the cocoon. The nanoshields moved with him. The reel of rope unspooled behind him. He cleared the distance and landed delicately on the cocoon surface, anchoring himself with the toe rods of his StabBoots. The plan was for him to anchor the rope to the asteroid's surface, allowing Kaufman and Rimas to zip-line in as safely and quickly as possible.

Mazer took his knife from his pouch but hesitated. Would the Hive Queen know he was here as soon as he started cutting? Would she detonate everything instantly? His whole body was tense, like he was lying face down on a giant atom bomb.

He gingerly pushed the blade in through the resin and waited. The cocoon didn't detonate. There was no fireball, no silent explosion.

Mazer sliced downward, making a long vertical cut in the cocoon. The incision parted as air rushed outward. Mazer cut again, this time horizontally, making an X. The sudden rush of air pushed the four loose flaps of cocoon skin outward.

"Pyramid," said Mazer.

The nanobots formed into a tall pyramid in front of him, with their point forward, so that they directed much of the air away from him. He still felt pushed back, but it was easier to get inside. Once his whole body was in and clear of the gale he said, "Bubble."

The nanobots encircled him again. Mazer hit his thumb trigger, and his propulsion pushed him down to the surface.

"Lights. Vision."

The nanobots near his helmet lights brought the edge of the bubble in close so that his light protruded through their shield. The same occurred around the cameras on his helmet. The bubble was now a misshapen multi-bulbous shape that allowed him to see clearly. His spotlight fell upon the surface of the rock, and Mazer saw hundreds of tunnels, just as he had seen in Victor's vid. His boots touched the surface, and his Nan-Ooze soles clung to the tiny cracks in the rock. The end of the rope had an anchoring mechanism with triangulating spikes. Mazer shoved the mechanism into one of the small holes, and the rope anchored.

"Rope set."

Moments later Kaufman came flying down the zip line, pushed by his propulsion. Rimas followed, pausing at the cocoon to pull in the loose flaps and help the hole seal itself. He landed moments later, surrounded in a hazy cloud of nanobots.

Mazer drew his crossbow—an elaborate carbon-titanium weapon that the engineers on the ship had made. They had tested their crossbows repeatedly to ensure that the firing mechanism didn't create a spark and ignite the air. But even so, the weapon still felt dangerous in Mazer's hands. It carried twenty bolts, had a self-cocking mechanism, and fired at one hundred meters per second. Mazer brought it up and set the stock against his shoulder.

"Weapon."

His nanoshield bent inward again, allowing the tip of the crossbow to poke through the shield. Kaufman and Rimas were armed as well, and the three of them split up, moving outward from the rope as a center point.

Mazer walked along the surface, pausing to look down the larger tunnels he came to, fearful that an attack might come from below. There were hundreds of small tunnels like the ones he had seen in Victor's vid, just big enough to house a mining worm. Mazer shined his light down into those as well, but he saw no signs of life.

"Anyone see any worms?" Mazer asked.

"I got nothing," said Kaufman. "Just empty holes."

"Same here," said Rimas. "The tunnel walls are all lined with mucous, but I don't see any pellets of metal. It's like the worms did their digging, and the metal was all collected."

Mazer was thinking the same. Worms had obviously harvested here, but their metal had been taken elsewhere.

"Maybe the worms mine the asteroid in stages," said Kaufman. "So they mine one section, pick it clean, then the Formics move them to another side of the rock."

"That's not a bad approach, actually," said Rimas. "Attacking the asteroid all at once might quickly weaken it structurally. Doing it bit by bit would preserve the integrity of the rock."

"Let's move to another location," said Mazer. "There's nothing here. Stay sharp."

They moved to the far side of the asteroid and patrolled there as well, finding nothing. Eventually they stopped walking on the surface and just used their propulsion to view the surface from the air. That proved just as fruitless.

Mazer called Zembassi. The colonel's face appeared on Mazer's HUD. "There are no creatures near the surface, sir. We've circled the whole rock. The worms couldn't have gone anywhere, so they've obviously burrowed deeper into the rock. No sign of Formics."

"Bring Bingwen in," said Zembassi.

"Sir, the area is not secure."

"We have our orders, Mazer. I don't like it any more than you do."

Zembassi's image disappeared.

Mazer met back with Rimas and Kaufman at the rope.

"Kaufman, you're the biggest," said Mazer. "So you're out. Head back to the landing craft and help Bingwen inside the cocoon. Give him your nanoshields, and all the spare canisters of $O_2$ and propulsion he can carry. Then return to the craft and wait. Rimas and I will go in with Bingwen. I'll take point. Rimas will take rear. We'll stick to the larger tunnels and see how far we go."

"We won't go very far judging by what I've seen so far,"

said Rimas. "The tunnels narrow pretty quickly. We can't go as far as Bingwen can. We're twice his size."

"Let's do our best," said Mazer. "I don't like the idea of Bingwen going in alone."

Kaufman took off, and five minutes later Bingwen came down the rope. He handed Mazer and Rimas their spare air and propulsion canisters and Mazer and Rimas switched them out.

"Ready?" Mazer asked.

"Let's not keep Kaufman from his ravioli," said Bingwen.

They found a tunnel nearby that was one of the larger ones they had seen. "I go first," said Mazer. "All of my nanoshields will be in front. Rimas, your shields cover our rear. Bingwen, your shields should cover any side tunnels we hit along the way. That way we are boxed in and shielded at all times. Understood?"

"All this for some stupid worms," said Rimas.

"Let's move," said Mazer.

He crawled in first, activating his StabBoots to stabilize himself in the tunnel. He took slow deliberate steps, the rods triangulating in and out, in and out. Bingwen and Rimas stayed a short distance behind, spacing themselves apart to give them each the room they needed. Mazer felt as if he were ascending some giant twisting chimney. At first the tunnel was fairly spacious, but the farther they ascended, the narrower the tunnel became.

"It's getting a little tight in here, Mazer," said Rimas. "You and I can't go much farther."

He was right. Ten meters later the tunnel narrowed. Mazer had gone as far as he could go.

"We'll try another tunnel," said Mazer.

"It's all right," said Bingwen. "I'll be fine."

"There are hundreds of tunnels to explore," said Mazer. "We'll find one that fits all of us."

"No," said Bingwen, "we won't. These are made for Formics, Mazer, not human adults. Besides, we don't have time to explore for something we're not likely to find. We have limited oxygen, and it will take a lot longer to get out of the tunnel moving backwards than it does to go forward. You need to let me go ahead alone. Just loan me your weapon."

Mazer knew he was right. But there was so much uncertainty, so much that could go wrong. What if Bingwen got stuck or injured? He suddenly wished he had brought in an entire team of cadets.

Bingwen held out his hand for the crossbow. "I'll meet you back outside at the landing craft. You can monitor my every move."

Mazer put the safety on and gave him the weapon. "You know how to fire that?"

"I'm going to take a wild guess and say point the bolt at the bad guy and pull the trigger."

"Be sure you're anchored before you fire," said Mazer. "Otherwise—"

"I've got it," said Bingwen. "I'll be fine."

"Watch your oxygen," said Mazer. "Be sure to give yourself more than twice as much $O_2$ as you think you might need to get back."

"I was listening during all your training sessions, Mazer. I took good mental notes. I've got this."

Mazer hesitated. Then he scooted downward and let Bingwen take the lead.

Bingwen waited until Mazer and Rimas had backed out of the tunnel before he pushed on. He easily moved through the spot that had blocked Mazer, and then he turned off all of his lights. He would use dark vision from here on out. No need to fill the tunnel with light and tell the Formics he was coming.

The tunnel remained narrow, but as he advanced it didn't get worse. Bingwen actually preferred this width. The Stab-Boot rods didn't have to reach out so far to triangulate, and Bingwen felt steadier as a result. His two nanoshields were positioned in the front and rear, moving with him, boxing him in.

He went about fifty yards, and then the tunnel ended at a much larger tunnel that ran perpendicular. Bingwen poked his head out of the smaller tunnel and looked right and left. The way was dark in either direction.

"What have you found?" Mazer asked over the radio.

It felt good to hear Mazer's voice. It steeled Bingwen's courage a little.

"Looks like a main thoroughfare," said Bingwen. "It's much wider here. I'd say you could fit five or six Formics abreast in here shoulder to shoulder. And the tunnel is taller, too. I can almost stand up in here."

"You're in the middle of the peanut shape, right where the two bulbous ends of the asteroid meet," said Mazer.

"Then we can infer a lot from this tunnel," said Bingwen. "It likely means the Formics have two important sites down here. One is at the center of the bigger half of the peanut, and the other is at the center of the smaller half. This tunnel connects the two, and the Formics expect a lot of traffic between them. I'm not sure what to make of that. If there are only five Formics on this rock, why would they feel the need to make such a wide tunnel?"

"Any signs of movement?" asked Mazer.

"Nothing. It's like everyone skipped town. I'm going to the left. That's the bigger half of the peanut."

"Be careful," said Mazer. "If you sense movement, duck back into one of the smaller tunnels, feet first, weapon out."

Bingwen pulled himself out of the narrow tunnel and into the thoroughfare.

"Bubble."

His nanoshields came and encircled him. His Nan-Ooze soles adhered to the floor. He had to stoop a little, but he could nearly stand upright. He moved down the thoroughfare, taking cautious steps, looking for any signs of movement, the crossbow up to his shoulder, ready to fire. It was designed for someone twice his size, and it felt bulky and awkward in his hands, but he felt better having it.

He paused and looked back over his shoulder every so often to ensure that no one was behind him. He was using the lights on his wrists to guide, with the luminance at the lowest setting. The light didn't reach far, and the near total darkness left Bingwen feeling vulnerable. But he resisted the temptation to turn on his high beams.

The thoroughfare ended a hundred meters later, opening up into a wide, dark cavern. Bingwen felt as if he were standing at the edge of a cliff overlooking a massive underground chamber. He couldn't see far into the cavern however, for a dark metal wall stood ten meters inside the cave, blocking his view and extending in every direction. Bingwen flipped on his helmet lights. The metal was flat and smooth, with a closed aperture in the center.

"What are we looking at, Bingwen?"

"It's hulmat," said Bingwen. "It's the indestructible hull of a warship. These asteroids aren't missiles, Mazer. They're factories. The Formics are building a ship inside each one."

"How is that possible?"

"This was their strategy all along," said Bingwen. "Not to *bring* their fleet here, but to *build* it here right under our noses. That's why the warships above and below the ecliptic haven't attacked yet. They don't have to. The fleet is already here. All they needed were a few Formics and a few creatures, and the asteroids provided everything else. Don't you see? The worms mined and processed the metal, some other creatures used that metal to build the hull of a ship. We never saw any construction outside the asteroid because it was all happening in here, at the asteroid's core, where we couldn't see it."

"And when they're done building the ship," said Mazer, "the Formics climb inside, and they detonate the atmosphere inside the asteroid. That's how the ship gets out. One of Lem Jukes's mining ships in the Kuiper Belt found an asteroid broken to pieces. That's what the Formics do. They blow the ship free once it's ready."

"You're right," said Bingwen. "It would be easy to do. They could use the worms to dig perforations in the rock above the warship and in the shape of the warship. So when the explosion happens, the surface of the asteroid above the warship pops off like the shell of an egg. It doesn't even have to be a big explosion. They could build the ship right near the surface of the rock. And when the ship is ready, boom!, the warship is free."

"There's a problem with this theory," said Mazer. "You need more than five Formics to fly that ship, and only five Formics arrived here."

He was right, Bingwen realized. A ship this size would require a crew of dozens. Maybe as many as a hundred.

"The asteroid isn't solely a ship factory," said Mazer. "It's also a Formic factory."

Of course, thought Bingwen. The Hive Queen wasn't solely building her fleet. She was also building her army. That's why the thoroughfare was so wide: so that the crowd of Formics birthed here had plenty of room as they made their way to the ship.

"I guess we now know what's at the other end of this thoroughfare," said Bingwen.

"Listen to me, Bingwen," said Mazer. "You need to get out now. We've learned all we're going to learn. We have vids of everything. Find a tunnel and come back to the landing craft."

"We haven't learned everything," said Bingwen. "We don't

yet know if we're right. If there is in fact a nursery on this rock, we need to confirm that, and more importantly we need to find out what happens there. Are Formics hatched from an egg? Do they crawl from a womb? Are they grown in vitro? What's their life cycle? If we understand that, if we can learn how they're grown, maybe we can discover some contraceptive or method to retard their growth. We could prevent them from ever gaining any reinforcements."

"Bingwen—"

"You know I'm right, Mazer. Whatever we discover at the end of this tunnel could determine whether or not we win this war."

"You're not prepared for that kind of recon," said Mazer.

"I have a helmet cam," said Bingwen. "I don't have to understand what I see. I just have to record it. People much smarter than me will analyze the recording and tell us what we've learned."

"You can't go in alone," said Mazer.

"There isn't time to equip more cadets and get them in here. I don't have enough oxygen to wait for them."

A new voice sounded in Bingwen's ear. "This is Rear Admiral Zembassi. Bingwen, you are ordered to proceed."

"Yes, sir."

Bingwen switched off his helmet lights, muted his radio, and headed back down the thoroughfare the way he had come, his nanoshield bubbles surrounding him, his wrist lights giving him just enough light to see.

He passed the spot where he had entered the tunnel and then went another one hundred meters until he reached a second cavern. The space was wide, but the ceiling was only two meters above him. Bingwen swept the room with his lights and found trails of glistening mucus all along the floor and ceiling. The mucous trails weren't random, however. They all seemed to point in the same direction: toward a passageway on the far side of the room.

Bingwen's light found a single grub on the wall, inching toward the passageway ahead, like a latecomer to a party.

Bingwen killed his lights and cautiously advanced, the crossbow up to his shoulder, moving toward the passageway. He reached the hole just after the grub did and found that it wasn't the entrance to a passage but rather the entrance to a third cavern.

The Formics were all there. Maybe sixty of them, all surrounding an elevated platform in the center of the chamber. Flat bioluminescent creatures that Bingwen recognized as doilies lay around the edges of the platform, shining a dull light on the stone altar that stood in the center of the platform. And there atop the altar, held in place with thin filaments, was a pod about the size of a small pumpkin.

No. Not a pod, Bingwen realized. A cocoon.

The Formics were fixated on it, worshipping it, oblivious to Bingwen.

A throne room, Bingwen realized. A queen.

The cocoon on the altar twitched. Only slightly, but the movement sent a ripple of silent excitement through the Formics.

The cocoon twitched again.

Then the filaments that surrounded the cocoon—like the strands of a spider web—began to stretch, as if something were trying to push its way out. Then another push from inside. And another. Then Bingwen heard a soft ripping sound as the filaments of the cocoon broke. And then slowly, purposefully, majestically, she rose up out of her cocoon. Her wings spread, their damp thin membranes glistening in the light from the doilies, shimmering with a dozen different colors. She stood erect upon the altar, her head held high, presenting herself, baring her glory and splendor.

And then she saw Bingwen.

Her head snapped in his direction. And a heartbeat later, every Formic in the room turned to him as well, their eyes now as fixed on him as they had been on the Hive Queen. The mass of them attacked at once, rushing toward him, arms out, maws open. They did not stumble over each other as any pack of humans so tightly compressed together would have. But they moved like a single organism, fluidly, precisely, coming at him like a wave.

Bingwen ignored them. He was going to die anyway.

He steadied the crossbow and squeezed the trigger. The recoil was much harder than he had expected, but his feet were anchored well.

The bolt buried itself in the queen's eye, and her head snapped back, skewered through.

The organized wave of Formics broke, like puppets whose strings had been suddenly cut. Rather than fall upon Bingwen with the feral ferocity they had possessed moments ago, they crashed into him and his nanobots like dead weight, limp and lifeless.

Bingwen was thrown backward into the cavern, arms flailing. He slammed into the far wall, sinking a little into the mucous there. For a brief moment, he allowed himself to believe that he would live. Killing the queen killed her workers.

But no. As he watched, the inactive Formics regained their faculties. They rose, collected themselves, and charged again. But this time they were not as organized, not as unified. They were not one organism now, Bingwen realized. There was some order, yes, but there was also autonomy. Fewer strings to hold them now.

It didn't matter. The crossbow was no longer in his hands. He quickly scanned the room, but he didn't see it. His back was stuck to the mucous, but only tenuously. He pushed off the wall easily. Not to flee, because they would be on him in seconds, and he could never outrun them in the tunnels. He merely wanted to steady himself and free his hands.

"Wall. Front."

The nanoshield around him formed a wall in front of him, and the first wave of Formics hit it, pushing it inward. The wall could not hold them off, Bingwen knew. It would struggle and persist but it would break at any second. There were too many Formics filled with too much rage. Their faces didn't express emotion, but the ferocity with which they came at him was all the evidence he needed. They would pound at him with stones, break open his suit, rip him from it piece by piece.

He only needed another second though. The igniter was already pulled from his pouch and in his hand. He hoped Mazer wouldn't be disappointed.

Then he dropped his nanoshield and made a spark.

# CHAPTER 30

## Children

To: mazer.rackham%captain@ifcom.gov
From: imala.bootstamp%e2@ifcom.gov/fleetcom/gagak
Subject: Deliver a message
___

Dear Mazer,

I am writing in the hope that you can relay a message to Victor for me. He is heading toward a ship of the Fleet above the ecliptic called the Vandalorum. I do not have the ability or permission to contact that ship directly. Victor is in a zipship and therefore unreachable. My hope is that Victor will find my message waiting for him when he arrives.

I cannot tell you where I am, but I can say that I am on a ship whose course is set and whose intentions are secret. We are accelerating. I spend my days strapped in an elaborate harness. I feel like I'm being squeezed like a lemon. It is more G-force than I have ever experienced. Nothing about it is pleasant.

At first I thought my sickness was from the flight, but my urine is constantly analyzed, and the ship has confirmed that I am pregnant. I don't know what effect the acceleration will have on the baby, but I fear the worst. Please let Victor know that I am going to try to figure out a way to minimize the threat to our child. I don't know how exactly. But I can't just sit here and do nothing. There may be ramifications if I alter the ship's acceleration schedule, but a mother must do what is necessary.

Tell Victor this: If our child lives, she will be at least three or four years old when she meets her father. I will teach her who you are and give her every reason to love you and look forward to the day you can hold her in your own arms. It might be a boy, of course. But when I sleep I dream of a girl who has your eyes. Come back to me when you can, space born. Your space-born child and I will be waiting.

Love,
Imala

"It was not the Hive Queen," said Mazer. "We're certain of that."

He was standing in Rear Admiral Zembassi's office, where images from Bingwen's helmet cam hovered above the holotable.

"How can we be sure?" said Zembassi.

"Several reasons," said Mazer. "First there is the matter of her just being born. She could not have been controlling the Formic army for all these years from a cocoon. Her growth was recent. Perhaps she was laid by the real Hive Queen some time ago and placed in the miniship and brought to Castalia to mature. Our belief is that she was to be placed inside the ship and given charge of some of the Formic army."

"So we didn't kill the president, but maybe we killed a general?"

"A baby general," said Mazer. "A daughter of the Hive Queen. We sent the vid to CentCom and several xenobiologists studied it and pointed out that this creature has not yet fully developed." Mazer zoomed in on one of the images and circled parts with his stylus. "You can see here that the base of the wings is thick and well pronounced, more so than you might expect for wings as small as these, suggesting that she has a lot of growing to do. There is also the fact that her wings are not yet large enough to carry her body weight. Plus there's the issue of her enlarged feet, which suggest that they are built for a creature of a much taller stature."

"Maybe," said Zembassi, "but she's the first one we've seen of her kind. How do we know that's not exactly how they're supposed to look as adults?"

"We don't," said Mazer. "Not definitively. But the height of the ceiling in the hatchery is another clue. It's a very tall room, and the Formics are not ones to waste space. The belief is that the daughter would mature there until ready to enter into her ship, at which point she would crawl forward down the long tunnel on her stomach and climb into her vessel. We had originally thought that the tunnel was wide to accommodate multiple Formics moving abreast through the tunnel, but now we suspect that it was designed specifically to accommodate a large adult Hive Queen."

"And there was nothing recoverable at the scene?"

"No," said Mazer. "The blast incinerated everything."

"What about the Formics?" asked Zembassi. "They went from well organized to dead to alive again to stupid."

"The behavior of the Formics is perhaps the best evidence we have that the creature killed by Bingwen was not the Hive Queen we have come to fear. If you watch the vid enough, you see that the Formics react when she does. She sees Bingwen, and his presence is communicated to every Formic there. Then they fight as one, clearly under her direction, a suspicion that's made incontrovertible once Bingwen kills her. When the headshot occurs, the Formics lose all sense of awareness. They go stupid, as you say. Lifeless. They are reanimated a moment later when the *real* Hive Queen steps in and takes control of them. But what's interesting is the difference in the Formics' behavior. They were slower and less organized when they were under the real Hive Queen's spell. But when they were under her daughter's control, they were tightly controlled and fast. This leads us to believe that the Hive Queen's proximity to her subjects directly affects the degree of her control over them. Or perhaps it's not a matter of proximity, but a matter of number. This Hive Queen daughter was likely only directing these sixty or so Formics. And with that few, her control was absolute. But the real Hive Queen has tens of thousands under her control. Maybe hundreds of thousands. And therefore, her command of them is weaker because it's spread among so many organisms."

"So what does this tell us about the war?" asked Zembassi.

"It tells us that the Hive Queen is very smart indeed. She can control her entire army, which we have always known. But she can also make her soldiers better organized and faster to respond if she places groups of them under the control of her daughters. And by relinquishing control of some of her soldiers, the Hive Queen will also have greater control and influence over the smaller number of soldiers she now directly controls. In essence it is a way to turn her highly effective soldiers into super soldiers. Their individual abilities may be only marginally improved, but collectively, they can be far more effective and lethal."

"So now we have multiple Hive Queens that we have to kill?"

"I wouldn't call these daughters Hive Queens," said Mazer. "They have not yet matured to adulthood. They are more likely Hive Queens in training. But there is good news from this. We know now that by killing a daughter, we render her workers momentarily stupid. That might prove critical in the fight ahead. If we can kill the Hive Queen, the Formics might weaken and destabilize, giving us the perfect opportunity to strike hard and inflict massive casualties."

"And what about the ship?" asked Zembassi. "The one they built. Any news there?"

"The ship broke free of the asteroid as a result of the explosion, as you know," said Mazer. "But it's just drifting out there. It appears to be unmanned. All of the Formics had gathered for the birth of the Hive Queen's daughter. The ship appears complete, but we can't get inside it. It's sealed shut, and we don't have any of Lem Jukes's special hulmat-destroying nanobots to penetrate it. CentCom is considering putting a hulmat weapon on a zipship and sending it to us so we can get inside the ship and explore its interior."

"What about the Fleet heading for the warships above and below the ecliptic? I think we should ask CentCom to return some of those ships. We need to destroy as many of these asteroids as we can before the entire Formic fleet is hatched."

"I agree, sir," said Mazer. "The more immediate threat is here."

Zembassi waved his hand through the holo and made the images disappear. "There is more bad news you should be made aware of, and I wanted to tell you in person. Vaganov has been promoted to vice admiral. He will be my commanding officer."

"I am sorry, sir."

"He wasted no time taking credit for our victory," said Zembassi. "To hear him tell it, he shot the Hive Queen daughter himself. Our lives are about to become a living hell."

They commiserated a moment longer and then Mazer went to find Bingwen. The boy's survival had been a miracle. His suit had saved him, but the force of the blast had knocked him unconscious. Mazer had rushed in through the hole the blast had made above the Formic warship. And then he had flown down the wide tunnel to reach the hatchery, not sure what he would find when he got there. The blast had destroyed Bingwen's helmet cams, but the exosuit was still intact and operative.

Mazer had found Bingwen's body limp and nonresponsive, but the suit was still delivering oxygen. The temperature inside was normal. Mazer had frantically tapped at the cracked readout screen beneath a flap on the suit until it had indicated that yes, there was still a heartbeat. Yes, there was life.

Kaufman and Rimas had arrived then, and the three of them had rushed Bingwen back to the ship.

Now Mazer stood anchored to the floor of the observation deck of the Battle Room, watching as several of the Battle Room teams presented Bingwen with one of their ridiculous homemade trophies. Mazer couldn't see what it was exactly at this distance, but it looked like a statuette of the Hive Queen's daughter made of bolts and scrap metal and wire. Bingwen held it up, and the marines pumped their fists.

"He'll be insufferable now," said a voice.

Mazer turned to see Colonel Li.

"You must be proud of him," said Mazer.

"Hardly. He nearly blew himself to bits. He's no good to us dead."

No good to *you*, you mean, Mazer thought.

"He respects you more than you know," said Li.

"We've been through some harrowing experiences together," said Mazer. "Far too much for a kid his age."

"You still see him as a child then?" said Li.

"You don't?"

"What is a child but an adult with less experience. Bingwen has had the experience. I think that makes him more of an adult than most people."

Mazer nodded. "Maybe you're right."

"Not all children are our future, Captain Rackham. Some of them are our present."

He moved on without saying another word.

On the screen, the marines in the Battle Room had formed a line and were each presenting themselves to Bingwen to give him a formal salute. It was a long procession and would take a while.

Mazer paused to tap at his wrist pad and check his e-mails. There was one from Imala. He read it quickly, eager for an update. Pregnant. And with the baby at risk. Where was she? What mission had they given her?

He would get word to the Vandalorum. The message would be waiting. Victor's suit had saved Bingwen. It was the least Mazer could do.

Imala. Pregnant.

Mazer's mind went to Kim then. She was in New Zealand now. Not pregnant. Not growing a child. Which meant she would feel alone. I am coming, Kim. No alien army or jack-ass vice admiral or Hive Queen or Hive Queen's daughter is going to stop me. We will have our little Pai Mahutanga and our little Pahu Rangi and maybe a few others besides. And I will sing to you a calming song every time you ask.

# ACKNOWLEDGMENTS

First and foremost, we would like to thank the army of talented people at Tor who made this book possible, particularly our editor, Beth Meacham, whose support never wavered and whose counsel was always wise. Thanks also goes to Professor Ryan Julian at the University of California, Riverside, for helping us solve a particularly difficult chemistry conundrum. Many thanks goes to Emily Rankin for her careful reading of the manuscript and for suggesting refinements that greatly improved the novel. We owe a great debt of gratitude also to Cyndie Swindlehurst for catching errors you will thankfully never see. Thanks also to the retired and active military officers and specialists who allowed us to interview them for this novel, namely Andy Johnson, Ben Shaha, Tracy Mann, and my dad and hero, David Johnston. Jeanine Plummer gets our thanks as well, for opening her home and allowing some of the book to be written there.

Of course, none of this would be possible if not for our loving wives, Kristine Card and Lauren Johnston. They are our first readers and our wisest counselors. Without their support, faith, and encouragement this book would not exist. Family, dear reader. That is the engine and fuel of life. And oh what a ride.